The Be
Afghanistan

A Novel

by

Martin Krewson

PUBLISHED BY
BRIGHTON PUBLISHING LLC
501 W. RAY ROAD
SUITE 4
CHANDLER, AZ 85225

The Bee Flies Over Afghanistan

A Novel
by
Martin Krewson

PUBLISHED BY
BRIGHTON PUBLISHING LLC
501 W. RAY ROAD
SUITE 4
CHANDLER, AZ 85225

COPYRIGHT © 2012

ISBN 13: 978-1-621830-53-5
ISBN 10: 1-621-83053-2

PRINTED IN THE UNITED STATES OF AMERICA

First Edition

COVER DESIGN: TOM RODRIGUEZ
COVER ARTWORK: MARTIN KREWSON

~ Acknowledgements ~

I would like to render my heartfelt thanks to the numerous family, friends, and customers who read, critiqued, and encouraged this endeavor. Also, Don McGuire and the editorial staff of Brighton Publishing. Last, but not least, my loving wife, whose spelling and typing skills far surpass my own. Without all of you, it would only be a story untold.

Martin Krewson

5/17/17

— Dedication —

In Loving Memory of Martin W. Krewson, Sr.
Oct. 28, 1911 - Jan. 26, 2012

— Foreword —

The action in this book takes place in the late 1920s, using the historical spellings of place names and historical figures of that era.

— Chapter One —

A s Buzz tossed his duffel bag on the seat across from the one he had chosen, the train's whistle gave two short, high-pitched blasts. It lurched forward, pitching Buzz into his seat and raising a large, choking cloud of dust. He looked around the car that would be his domain for the next eighteen hours.

The train, which traveled from the seaport of Karachi to Peshawar, had probably been the gem of the rails fifty or sixty years ago when it was new, with its velvet seats, gold inlay, and teak framing. Now the seat had only a trace of faded glory and greeted any sudden movement with dust from the past. The carved teakwood bore the marks of carelessly tossed baggage and the initials of dozens of thoughtless, bored passengers of bygone years.

Across the aisle were two gentlemen in European dress, setting up a chess set. Two seats up the aisle was a large man with a small fez perched atop his rather plump head, arranging his plethora of packages tied with fuzzy-looking string, as though he were preparing for an expedition. Behind him was a compartment labeled with a sign in four different languages—none of which happened to be English. Buzz figured that must be the rest room. Toward the rear of the car were two older ladies wearing European clothing and the matching "we are better than thou" attitude.

After completing his survey, Buzz settled down for a long, boring, uneventful ride. Putting his feet up on the seat across from his, he tried to view the passing countryside, but the blackness of early morning and the dim lights in the car made it impossible. All he could see was his reflection, and that of the aging compartment behind him. It was starting to rain, and the drops on the windows reflected the lights of the train car as they raced to and fro, gathering the black soot of coal dust previously deposited, and forming large, dark rivulets as they merged. They looked like little black bugs skittering over the dirty windows until they were blown away by the winds of the train's passing speed.

Leaning back cautiously in his seat, so to avoid a dust storm, Buzz thought of the past few years. His father had been murdered, and he had been quickly hustled into military service when he was sixteen. He thought of learning to fly a Sopwith Camel over France. After the war, he'd stayed in Paris, joined a circus, and became a stunt pilot—until the circus burned three weeks ago. His clothing still seemed to reek of smoke. *Damn*, he mused. *Here I am, almost twenty-seven, and all I have to show for it is a patched-up canvas traveling bag, a change of clothes, a couple of Webley pistols, and two strangely shaped gold crosses.* Not much to show for the eleven years since the Great War ended in 1918.

Maybe the new job that Jack Perry, the circus owner, had set up for him would prove to be something worthwhile. All Buzz knew about it was that a friend of Jack's in Afghanistan, a Mr. Harry Whitecliff, needed a pilot who could repair planes as well as fly them, and was willing to pay Buzz's traveling expenses. If he didn't like the job, Whitecliff had agreed to compensate him for his time and pay his fare back home to New Mexico, in the good old U. S. of A. *Heck, what can I lose?* he thought. *Maybe when I get back to Paris, Jack will have the circus back up and running.*

"Sir, is this seat taken?"

Startled from his reverie, Buzz looked up at the window and saw the reflection of the interior of the coach behind him. It hadn't changed, except for the appearance of a young girl standing beside his seat, who seemed to have little black bugs racing crazily across her. He turned to face her. She was much more attractive without the reflected bugs.

"I said, 'Sir is this seat taken?'"

Buzz, his mind still muddled by his thoughts of the moment before, looked up inquiringly at the young lady who was again asking the question she had posed. She was probably about twenty years old, a little over five feet tall, slender, and pleasantly proportioned. Her dark, almost coal-black hair was held back with a red velvet ribbon, and she wore a gray traveling suit with a tight-waisted skirt, topped by a wide black patent-leather belt encircling her slim waist. Her bolero-type jacket seemed to have some difficulty in confining her outstanding features. A gold watch hung on a chain around her slim neck, nearly hidden by the ruffles of her blouse. Its reading was several hours off, indicating that she was not a stickler for details. Her face bore the expression of a schoolgirl who'd answered a question the rest of the class had missed.

"Oh! No, it isn't! Here, let me move my bag," Buzz stammered as he quickly dumped the bag on the floor with a resounding thud, and attempted futilely to clean the seat. The resulting cloud of dust made him sneeze.

"God bless you," she said demurely, but with the hint of a giggle.

"Thank you," replied Buzz matter-of-factly.

She sat down in a ladylike manner, considering the never-ending bouncing and jolting motion of the train.

Buzz noticed the book she laid on the seat beside her small handbag—*Poems of the Great Masters*. A bulge in the middle betrayed a dime novel tucked inside. *Adventures of ...*was all he could read; the rest was obscured by the first tome.

"Are you traveling far?" she asked shyly.

"I'm going to a little town near Peshawar. The conductor said he would let me know when to get off."

"Oh, good. This is my first trip to Afghanistan. I'm going to Peshawar with my aunt and uncle. They come here every year to do missionary work or something like that. My father thought the trip would be good for me. Do you come here often? What kind of work do you do? I noticed your clothes. Are you an engineer, or maybe an archeology professor? Oh! I'm sorry to ask so many questions, but all I've met so far on this long trip is stuffy old people. You're not stuffy, I hope? It's nice to meet someone my own age. I'm twenty-two. How old are you? Are you married or something like that? Oh, I shouldn't have asked that! Do you smell smoke? I smell smoke. I hope the train isn't on fire!"

"Well," Buzz said, grinning, "I'll answer your questions as best I can. Yes, this is my first trip to Afghanistan. The jodhpurs, boots and leather jacket I'm wearing are the apparel of a pilot, which I am. I'm not stuffy; at least I don't think I am. I'm twenty-seven, and I'm not married. Finally—no, the train isn't on fire. I was in a fire, and my clothes still smell of it."

"Oh, I'm so sorry! I didn't mean to babble on like that! I've been at a fine girls' school with strict rules on how a proper lady should behave." She emphasized her description by pointing her nose in the air.

"Do you like fast cars and wild parties?" Buzz asked.

"I like fast horses and adventure! You said you were a pilot. Did you fly in the war?"

"I learned to fly in the war, but I wasn't a pilot. I was in armament; I worked on the guns and such. My father and I had a gunsmith shop in New Mexico, so when I joined the army, I was assigned to the Army Air Service. In trade for special work on their guns, the pilots taught me to fly. After the war, I stayed in Paris and landed a job with a circus, and did a show flying a Sopwith Pup. I was with the circus until it burned three weeks ago."

"Tell me about it, please?" The look in her eyes was that of a little girl asking for the last piece of her favorite kind of pie.

"First, I have some questions of my own. Why did you choose this seat? And where are your aunt and uncle?"

"Well, the two empty seats behind you—the ones across from the two women—well, they would have given me the cold shoulder because I'm a girl alone, so I surely must be a 'Hussy.' And the other was with a gentleman who has a hungry look in his eyes—and I don't mean for food! The fat man across the aisle in front of you probably has a large, drippy sandwich of God only knows what, and would insist on sharing it with me. My aunt and uncle are in their compartment three cars up. I picked this seat because you look interesting. Now, tell me about the circus. Oh! My name is Kimberly Smith. My friends call me Kim. What's yours?"

"My name is Mark Kramer. My friends call me 'Buzz.'"

"Buzz? How did you get that name?"

"At the end of my act, I would buzz the crowds with my plane."

"Oh, I see. Now will you tell me about the circus, Mr. Kramer?"

"I'd be more comfortable if you'd call me Buzz."

"I will, if you will call me Kim. Now tell me about your life with the circus."

"Well, Kim, I signed up with the Jack Perry Circus as a roustabout—that's the guy who takes care of the tents, feeds the animals, and does anything else that's needed to be done. After about six months Jack found out I was a pilot, so he bought the plane, and promoted me to

4

the rank of a performer. Together we worked out a flying routine that came to be one of the top billings.

"But in Jack's circus, you did more than just one thing. He's quite a showman. He'd have me made up as a Western frontier man, doing trick shooting with rifles and pistols, and bill me as 'Buffalo Bob,' the old buffalo hunter from Montana, U. S. A. Flamme Blanc—that's my horse, who's all white and can go like the wind—and I would come into the ring with me dressed like an old man in rags, and Flamme Blanc looking dirty and limping. Jack announced us, chanted a 'magic spell of yesteryear,' and under cover of a cloud of smoke I'd drop the old cloak and the dirt cover on the horse, and we'd come charging out of the smoke as a young man on this fabulous white charger. The crowds loved it!"

"Did you do other things?"

"Sure. Sometimes I did trick riding in the horse act, or assisted with the high-wire act. One time, when Spengoli the knife thrower was sick, I had to do his act. I don't know who was more scared—me or his assistant."

"Did you make a lot of friends?"

"Yeah, I did. And two very special ones—Boris and Calliope Bob."

"Calliope Bob! How did he get that name?"

"Well, Bob was more or less the handyman of the circus; he could build or fix anything. He thought we should have a calliope, so he built one out of an old steam crane. That's how he got his nickname. And Boris did the horse act. God, he's good with horses! He even taught Flamme Blanc to limp on command. In one act, which was a battle re-enactment, the horses would lie still as the dead; when it was over, they would rise with their riders as if they were coming back to life. I think Boris was an officer in the Czar's army, because once he slipped and mentioned that he had taught the Czar's children to ride. I have the feeling that he had to leave Russia after the revolution; the way he rides and handles a saber, I think he must have been with the Cossacks. He spent many hours teaching me the art of the blade."

"It sounds as if the circus is a harbor for many ships with a past," Kim said thoughtfully. "The three of you must have had some wild times in Paris—wine, women, and song, as the saying goes."

"No, not really. We were saving our money to buy a ranch, so we spent most of our time at the Paris Opera House."

"Whew! That's not cheap!"

"There's a story about that, too," Buzz replied, chuckling. "One night, Boris decided he wanted to see Ravel's 'Bolero,' and asked me if I would go. I agreed, and then we asked Bob to go, too. He was reluctant at first, but finally gave in. Boris had tails, and I was able to borrow some from one of the other performers. Bob said he would dig something up out of his trunk. Since no one had ever seen Bob wearing anything other than overalls, we all wondered what that 'something' would be. When we were ready to leave, Bob showed up clad in the finest tails, opera cape, and top hat that money could buy.

"When we arrived, we found the performance had been sold out. Boris was devastated—he had really been looking forward to the show, and then to come so close, and not be able to attend really was a big disappointment. Bob told us to wait outside. He went into the manager's office, and after about twenty minutes, came back with tickets in hand. That's when we learned that he had been a concert harpist before the war, but a bullet to his right hand ended that part of his life. He knew the manager very well; afterwards, we were invited to dine with the cast. And it turned out that Boris knew the choreographer—Nijenska, too, and she invited us to another party later that night. It seems we made an impression with our various backgrounds, and were wined and dined with the finest on a shoe string. And Bob must have realized how much he missed the camaraderie of his fellow musicians. When we were invited to those parties, he began to live again."

"That's really something! Occasionally, someone you think you know really well has much more to them than that which meets the eye. Buzz, while you've been talking, I couldn't help noticing the gold cross you're wearing around your neck. It's so unusual—I've never seen anything quite like it," Kim remarked.

"Oh, this." Buzz reached up to stroke the heavy gold pendant. "I'm told there were only three made. My father and I were each given one by my grandmother; I don't know where the third one is. My father said I should give it to someone special someday, but that's another story."

"I hope I hear it someday," Kim replied softly. "What was your act like?"

Before Buzz answered, he glanced at the little fat man across the aisle. He'd tucked a large white napkin with a red zigzag border under one of his many chins—it looked as if there must be at least three—and was in the process of carefully unwrapping a sandwich as though it was a priceless Ming Dynasty vase. When he placed this masterful creation into his cavernous opening and bit down, juices spurted in all directions, and cascaded down his chins onto the fortuitously tucked napkin. *Kim seems to be a good judge of people*, Buzz thought, laughing inwardly.

Buzz turned away to focus on the much more pleasant sight of Kim seated directly across from him, and responded to her question. "When I first started flying for the circus, it was just loop-the-loops and barrel rolls. Then Bob fixed up a device that trailed smoke behind the plane, so I could do some skywriting. For the finale, I would fly low over the crowd—hence my nickname.

"Two years ago, Jack bought an old German Fokker DR I triplane. When I first saw it being unloaded, I said to Boris, 'My God, is that von Richthofen's plane?' Well, Jack heard me, and that's the way it was billed on the marquee. 'See von Richthofen's Tri-plane Fly Again!' Jack even hired a German pilot, who we called Fritz, who'd flown one during the war. He could speak a little English, but no French.

"Well, Fritz, Bob, and I rebuilt the engine, patched up the bullet holes, replaced all the guy wires, and painted it a bright red. We even put von Richthofen's markings on it, and I altered the guns on both planes to fire blanks. For about a year, Fritz and I would dogfight and, at the end, I'd shoot him down. To make it look like he'd really been shot down, Fritz would turn on a smoker and leave a trail behind him, as if he were on fire. He would circle the crowd a few times, fly down behind a little hill, and land out of sight of the crowd. As soon as his plane dropped behind the hill, Bob set off an explosion with a lot of flash and smoke, so it looked like the plane had really crashed and blown up. The crowd loved it!

"After a year or so of me shooting Fritz down five days a week and twice on Sundays, (we were closed on Mondays) Jack decided we needed something new. Fritz suggested that he shoot me down for a change. We didn't think that would go over too well with the French, but Jack liked the idea,—with some changes, though. I was to rise like the phoenix and down Fritz. Well, Boris and Bob and I worked all night on the idea; we placed a row of gas jets on the trailing edge of the wings and smokers on the leading edges. It really did look like the phoenix rising

7

out of the ashes! Boy, the crowd loved it! Especially when I buzzed over them in a victory roll. In fact, Boris even had a bee painted on the side of the fuselage."

"It sounds as though you, Boris, and Bob were very close," Kim remarked quietly.

"We were called the 'Three Musketeers' by everyone in the circus group. We even toasted each other with 'all for one, one for all.' But that's enough about me. Tell me more about yourself."

"Well, let me think." Kim hesitated for a few moments, gathering her thoughts. "I grew up in a little town at the southern tip of Florida called Flamingo, between the gulf and the mangrove swamps. I loved to ride my pony on the beach. Daddy had some kind of boating business; he and Uncle George would take their boats out at night and not return until the next morning. I never saw any fish, because they'd take them to market before they came home. And they would never take me with them—they said it was too dangerous or something to that effect. It must have been, too, because one time Daddy came home all bloody and had to see a doctor. Uncle George said he had been caught by a hook or something like that.

"Then, one day, Daddy announced all out of the blue that he and Uncle George had bought a small shipping line in Le Havre, France, at a real bargain. So we packed up, lock, stock and barrel, so to speak, and moved to France. I used to wonder who got the real bargain, Daddy and Uncle George, or the seller.

The company, which Daddy called Smith & Smith Import and Export, consisted of a small dock with a crane, a warehouse with a leaky roof, and a tiny office with broken windows. The ships were practically derelict; I called them the *Titanic* and the *Lusitania*. The *Titanic* was listing against the dock and, by the look of the rust on her hull, an ice cube would have been enough to punch a hole in her. The *Lusitania* was still afloat, but the decks looked as if she had been torpedoed —maybe two or three times. There were crates, ropes, and cables strewn all over the deck. The doors of the cabins were swinging open and closed with any motion of the water. I could easily imagine, on a moonlit night at eight bells, the captain and crew of the *Flying Dutchman* floating eerily in and out of the open portholes.

"With mom, Aunt Jane, and me working in the office and parts of the warehouse, and Daddy and Uncle George and their crew of dockhands, it took more than six months to get the dock facilities shipshape, and another month to get the *Lusitania* sea-worthy. A year later, the *Titanic* was sailing. So, you see, I wasn't born with a silver spoon in my mouth, but my mother made sure that I went to all those fine girls' schools so I would know how to use that silver spoon!"

Buzz was trying to picture Kim in faded blue dungarees and a man's plaid shirt, tied at the waist with her shining dark hair tied back in a ponytail and maybe a sooty smudge on the tip of her pert little nose, scrubbing floors. Then he noticed Kim's feet were occupying very little space on the floor due to the position of his canvas bag under her seat. He hurriedly transferred it under his own area with a thud. "Sorry," he apologized.

"That's all right. You wouldn't by any chance happen to have a gun in your bag, would you?" Kim asked with raised eyebrows.

"Two, to be exact. Why?"

"I was just wondering. Automatics?"

"No. British Webley .455 Caliber," Buzz answered matter-of-factly.

"I thought everyone used automatics nowadays!" she exclaimed with mock surprise.

"Automatics are fine guns, but I prefer a revolver. With a revolver, I can reload nearly as fast as an automatic—not quite as fast, but almost. I don't have to worry about jams or a bad magazine, and I can shoot more accurately." Buzz spoke authoritatively.

"I can shoot," Kim said rather smugly. "In fact, I often used to outshoot some of the men who practiced at Daddy's range. Does that surprise you, a girl shooting a gun well?"

"Not really. My mother was a very good shot. I once saw her shoot two men on horseback at a full gallop at a range of at least a hundred yards."

"Oh, I could never shoot a man!" Kim's eyes were wide.

"That's what mother used to say, but the men she shot were part of a raiding party from Mexico, across the border.— It was the Peralto brothers and their band of banditos. They were after my father's guns from his shop. Mother said that she didn't shoot men, she just shot some rabid animals."

"Your mother sounds like an interesting person. Is she still in New Mexico?"

Buzz gazed out the dirty windows of the train, oblivious to the countryside gliding by. With a trace of moisture in his eyes, he answered, "No. My mother passed on some years back, when I was about fourteen. The doctors said it was the fever."

"And your father?" Kim asked sympathetically.

"Dad was killed two years later," Buzz said shortly, a look of steel in his eyes.

"How, may I ask? I don't mean to intrude, but...." Kim's own eyes were tearing.

"That's a story for another time. You said you like to ride. Fox hunts, shows?" Buzz said in an attempt to change the subject.

"That's what mother wants me to do," Kim answered, following his lead. "But what I like most is to ride through the surf, or on the beach, or to zigzag through the woods as fast as Midnight wants to go. (Midnight is the name of my horse—that's because he's as black as coal.) When I was a little girl, I used to daydream of being captured by bandits while riding my Arabian stallion—I've always wanted an Arabian horse—and out of the mist would come a knight, all in white, riding a huge white charger, to rescue me. Or something like that. I guess all little girls have a dream something like that."

"I guess little boys dream of being the white knight," Buzz chuckled.

As Buzz leaned forward to push the troublesome canvas bag further back under his seat, his cross and chain again caught Kim's attention.

"That is so beautiful! May I?" Without waiting for his reply, Kim gently cradled the piece in her hand. The cross was about one by two inches and weighed about an ounce. The strange, runic markings on it did not appear to be religious symbols. When Buzz looked down at the cross in her small, soft hand, it seemed to have an ethereal beauty he had never before noticed.

"I've never seen anything like this," Kim remarked.

"I'm told that there were only three of them made. Dad and I each had one. When he died, he gave his to me to be given to someone special someday."

"Didn't you say they were originally from your grandmother? Where did she get them?" Kim's curiosity was obviously piqued.

"They were given to my grandmother by her great-grandfather, with a story of a fabulous Spanish treasure. If all three crosses are fitted together like a puzzle, they're supposed to show the location of the treasure, but the third cross is lost. That's something I'd really rather not go into right now," Buzz answered rather stiffly.

"Well, Mr. Mysterious, will you at least tell me about the circus fire, or is that something else you'd rather not speak of at this time?" Kim replied huffily, her inquisitiveness thwarted.

"No! No! I'm sorry! I didn't mean to be rude. It's just that it's a rather long, involved story, and... Yes, I'll tell you about the fire. If I bore you, just stop me."

"Oh, please! Continue!" Kim begged, sitting on the edge of her seat, and leaning forward.

— Chapter Two —

THE FIRE

"Well, it was on a Monday morning, and the circus was closed that day, so I was to meet Boris and Bob for breakfast."

As Buzz began, the reality of the train and its environs faded. And as though it was a film unreeling in her mind, Kim pictured the tale that he told.

"Come on, Buzz, we're going to miss breakfast!" Boris called, who was running to catch up with his friends.

"Sorry I'm late. I went back to my tent to get my flight jacket. It's a bit chilly," Buzz apologized.

"Yeah, the wind must be at least twenty miles an hour, maybe gusting up to forty," Bob commented.

"I'm glad we're not flying today. It's bad enough doing some of those stunts on a calm day," Buzz noted.

"Well, I for one would ... damn! Look at the smoke coming from the grab joint!" Boris interjected.

"What's a grab joint?" Kim interrupted.

"It's circus lingo for a restaurant—a place to eat while sitting down. A grab stand is a place where one eats while standing," Buzz explained.

"Oh! Well, please go on," Kim urged.

"Well, Boris pointed to a large cloud of smoke coming from the vicinity of the grab joint. Then Bob noticed there was smoke pouring out of the prop tent, too. That's when we heard someone yell, 'Hey, Rube!'"

"Who's Rube?" Kim asked, obviously puzzled.

"A Rube isn't a who, it's a what."

"A what?"

"Actually, it's a call for help. It means 'Drop whatever you're doing, and come running, ready for trouble.'"

"Oh! More circus lingo."

"Yeah, more circus lingo," Buzz replied, and then continued.

"When we reached the source, of the 'Hey, Rube,' we could see flames engulfing the front opening of the tent where a few minutes before, people had been enjoying their breakfast. Now they were fighting for their lives. I could see the thick canvas sides of the tent bulging where the terrified occupants were trying to claw their way out. I'll never forget those screams.

"Boris drew his dagger from his belt—thank God he carries it; in fact, I've never seen him without it—and began to slash openings in the tent. Smoke billowed out, and people pushed and shoved their way through, some carrying the bodies of their friends. It was like potatoes pouring out of a bag. As soon as some people got their breath, they went back into the blazing tent to help more out, while others formed a bucket brigade. The wind was fanning the flames up to twenty feet or more in the air, which was creating more wind, like a tornado overhead.

"Then the oil from the cook stoves ignited and exploded, sending a cloud of black smoke and sparks even higher than before. I could see the fire was out of control, so I grabbed Bob and Boris and told them we needed to move the powder wagon out of the way. If the fire reached that wagon, with all the black powder and the fireworks that Bob used for the shows, it would have blown us off the face of the earth.

"The smoke, with the smell of the paraffin that was used to water-proof the canvas, was blotting out the sun, giving it the effect of a summer night full of fireflies. When we reached the powder wagon, the heat was already blistering the paint.

"Boris ran to get a team of horses, while Bob and I pushed a flatbed work-wagon between the powder wagon and the fire. We tipped it over onto its side to make a sort of a berm to block off some of the heat. When we saw Boris with the horses, Bob and I ran to help him hitch them to the wagon. Then, suddenly, there was a huge explosion that sent a shower of sparks and burning debris down on us. The horses broke away from Boris and ran off for God only knows where. I can't say I blamed them.

13

"Boris grabbed the wagon tongue; Bob and I grabbed the spokes of the front wheels and rocked it back-and-forth three times and then shoved forward with all our might. It moved—slowly at first—but it was moving. Boris yelled, 'If we can push it another hundred feet, it's downhill to the elephant pond!'

"Bob shouted, 'I don't think we should take any smoke breaks along the way.'

"I looked behind me, and I could see flames crawling up the back half of the wagon. Those hundred feet seemed more like a mile. The wheels were beginning to move easier, and then they were finally rolling on their own. Boris climbed up on the seat, still holding on to the tongue, and rode the burning wagon down the hill, steering with the tongue toward the deepest part of the pond where the elephants had wallowed in the mud. What a sight! Boris standing in the blazing powder wagon, racing against time downhill toward the elephant pond, one hand steering, and the other waving in the air like he was leading the Cossacks in a glorious charge!

"The wagon entered the pond with a huge splash, and floated away from the bank, and slowly sank, although three feet or so of the back end was still above water and still burning. When Bob and I reached the pond, Boris was kneeling atop the burning wagon, splashing water on to the fire as fast as he could. I'm sure he fully expected to find himself trying to put out a much bigger fire in a much lower place. Bob and I used buckets we found on the bank to toss more water on the flames until the last ember died. Standing on top of the wagon, pointing toward the gigantic cloud of smoke, Boris yelled, 'The big top! We need to drop the big top! If the big tent burns in this wind, it'll send burning debris for miles!'"

"What's the big top?" Kim interrupted, wide-eyed.

"That's the tent where the circus acts are performed," Buzz explained.

"Oh! How big is it?" she asked.

"The big tent was 138 feet high in the center, 210 feet wide and 335 feet long. In the center were three 148-foot center poles with a large iron ring around each one. The canvas was laced to these by support ropes, and then they were hoisted almost to the top by ropes and pulleys and tied off at the base of the poles. It's really a magnificent sight to see the roustabouts and elephants pulling the ropes, slowly raising the mountains of canvas.

"We planned to cut the ropes holding the center rings, dropping the whole tent to the ground where, hopefully it could be soaked with hoses. On the way there, we stopped at one of the small emergency fire sheds scattered around the grounds containing buckets of sand, a water pumper on wheels, and four fire axes. We each grabbed an axe. When we entered the tent, I ran for the center pole, and Boris and Bob ran for the other two.

"There were four ropes an inch in diameter, which tied off at a bracket about three feet from the bottom of the pole. It took several whacks to cut through each rope with those damn, dull axes. When I got the last rope severed, it snapped like a ringmaster's whip and shot upward. I could hear the ropes screaming through the pulleys at the top, and the iron rings banging and scraping on their plunge downward. I ran for my life, because I knew I could easily be crushed or suffocated by the tons of canvas.

"When I had fifty more feet to go, I could feel the pressure of the canvas collapsing like a deflating balloon. The roar of the air escaping from any opening it could find, and the screeching and clamoring of the canvas rope and the poles sounded like a dying animal. Ten feet from the exit, I tripped over a coil of rope and fell flat on my face. My mouth was full of old sawdust and trampled, dirty popcorn; I could see the canvas closing the exit like a curtain at the end of the play. I just hoped it wouldn't be the final act for me.

"It was then that I suddenly realized I still had that ax clutched in my hand. I propped it up like a tent pole and made an air pocket as the canvas closed down on me. I could hear Boris and Bob yelling like a couple of madmen."

"Can you tell me what Boris and Bob are like?" Kim interrupted excitedly. "I mean, what do they look like? Then I'll be able to picture the scene better."

"Well, let's see," Buzz said thoughtfully, rubbing his chin. "Boris is a little over six feet tall and broad-shouldered, weighs about 190. He has black hair, graying sideburns, a large mustache, and a short Van Dyke beard. His eyes are steel gray, and dance with mischief except when he's in deep thought or angry—then they burn right through you. He has high cheek bones and a small scar across his right cheek. His complexion is ruddy and weathered from the harsh Russian winters. His voice is soft and deep, but can be loud and commanding, when necessary. His hands are big and strong, but gentle. I've seen him free a butterfly from a spider's web without breaking the strands. When he has his shirt off, his chest looks like a road map because of the scars. Bob and I figure they're probably from saber cuts. He usually wears a cap, pulled down toward the right eye. He dresses in the usual garb of a Russian from the steppes—white shirt, red sash, black pants tucked into highly polished black riding boots. And, as I think I mentioned before, he always carries a dagger in his sash—always."

"What did he do before the circus?"

"He would never say. Bob and I think he might have been an officer of high rank in the Czar's Army. In fact, we figure he must have been very close to the Czar and Czarina. By the way he speaks of his 'family,' he seems to be actually referring to the Royal Family of Russia. And, with the way he handles horses, he probably really did teach their children to ride.

"When Boris first opens a bottle of vodka, he first pours long and slow, then stops with a quick motion—then pours another, only not as long, then four more, each shorter than the previous one. The last is just a drop. He then holds his glass up as though making a toast to someone or something, closes his eyes, and only then takes a swallow."

"The seven members of the Czar's family!" exclaimed Kim.

"Precisely." Buzz agreed.

"Now please tell me about Bob," Kim requested.

"Well, Bob was rather quiet and kept pretty much to himself until we started going to the opera regularly; now he's the life of the party. I think I remember that I told you about the time the three of us went to see Boris' friend who was the choreographer for Bolero."

"Oh, yes!" responded Kim. "That's when the opera was sold out, but Bob knew the manager, so got you all some super seats."

"Well, apparently after that incident, Bob realized how much he missed the camaraderie of his fellow musicians, and the people of the theater. It seemed like when we were invited to the post-performance parties, he began to live again—to come out of his shell, so to speak."

"Do you know how he hurt his hand in the war?"

16

"Like Boris, Bob doesn't like to talk about it."

"Oh, you men are all alike!" said Kim with exasperation. "The men who have interesting lives don't want to talk about themselves, and the ones whose big event of the day is nicking themselves while shaving, can't seem to speak of anything else! Well, tell me something about Bob, anyway! What's he look like? What nationality is he?"

Chuckling, Buzz replied, "He's from England or Scotland; he studied music in Paris and went on to play at the Opera—until the war. Then he joined the French Foreign Legion. I saw several medals in his trailer once, so he must have seen some action."

"So another lost ship finds safe harbor in the circus!"

"That's a good analogy. I never thought of it that way, but you could very well be right." Buzz gazed pensively out of the train's windows.

"Please don't stop now! What does he look like?" Kim pleaded as she positioned herself more comfortably on the faded, dirty seat.

"Well, I'll tell you if you quit constantly interrupting me," Buzz said with an attitude of mock authority.

"Oh! I promise! I won't do it again," Kim laughed.

"All right! But no more interruptions!" he acquiesced, in a deep voice. They grinned at each other.

"Let's see," began Buzz, "He must be about six feet tall. I'm 5'10," Boris is over six feet. Bob's taller than me, but not as tall as Boris, so I would guess about six feet. He has ash-blond hair, blue eyes, and an oval face with a fair complexion. He carries himself militarily erect—probably from his stint in the legion. And he has a slight Scots' burr. He looks like an English earl—except when he's in his working overalls."

"Well, what did he do at the circus?" blurted Kim

"I thought you promised you'd not interrupt anymore," Buzz shot back quickly, grinning wickedly at her.

"That didn't count! I had my fingers crossed!" Kim replied just as quickly, with a giggle.

Buzz broke out laughing, and Kim's laughter joined his.

"I'll have to keep an eye on your fingers, I see." Buzz was still laughing. "Bob would fix things, or make new equipment to use in the acts. I guess you could call him a handyman."

"How did the three of you get together and become such good friends?"

"I asked Boris if he would teach me to work with the horses and ride like he did. He said he would if I would teach him to fly a plane. We shook hands on it, and we've been close friends ever since."

"And Bob?"

"One morning, over a cup of coffee, Boris and I were discussing the need to change the flying act because of the sagging gate and..."

"Sagging gate! Was the tent falling down?" Kim asked, bewildered. "Or is that more circus talk?"

"Yeah, that's more circus talk. It means that the ticket sales at the entrance gate were not what they had been."

"Well, I didn't know! I'm sorry. That's why I asked," Kim retorted with a sheepish grin.

"Now, where was I?"

"You and Boris were talking about a saggy gate."

"Not 'saggy.' Sagging, sagging!"

"I'm sorry!" Kim lowered her head and looking up at Buzz through her lashes like a puppy being scolded, trying unsuccessfully to stifle a giggle.

"To make a long story short, Bob overheard our conversation and joined us at our table. He suggested one of the planes being shot down and coming back like the phoenix—I think I already told you about that. Bob drew the whole plan out for us, down to the last detail. That cost us a few francs, I can tell you!"

"Bob charged you and Boris for his plan?"

"No; that was free. What we had to pay for was the tablecloth he drew it on. Now he carries a notepad and a pencil."

They laughed again.

Buzz noticed the sun was lower in the western sky, and its light was beginning to stream through the window, causing Kim to squint slightly. Buzz reached over her, pulling down the shade enough to block the hot rays. He could smell her perfume; it was elusive, but one he was sure he'd never forget.

"Thank you," she said shyly.

Looking down the aisle, Buzz became aware of the porter approaching, carrying a small table and followed by a boy balancing a tray of food.

"Pardon, Miss Kimberley. Your aunt thought you and your gentleman friend might wish to have some tea and sandwiches," the porter reported as he placed the table between them. He stepped to one side, and the boy, dressed completely in white, deposited the tray and its contents on the table. It held four beef sandwiches cut neatly into triangles, a pewter teapot, two small china tea cups and their saucers, and matching sugar and cream containers.

Buzz watched the boy, who looked to be about fifteen, as he laid out the napkins and silverware. He continually stole surreptitious glances at Kim, obviously smitten. When the two had completed their duties and exited, Buzz glanced down at the table settings. Kim's napkin appeared to have been freshly laundered, and at just that moment. Her silverware looked newly minted by the silversmith. Everything in front of her was placed in mathematical precision, as if for the Queen of England. In contrast, his utensils seemed to have been laid out during the San Francisco earthquake, the napkin was crumpled, and the silverware looked like it had been used by the entire British army.

Buzz looked up at Kim. She, too, had noticed the inequitable setting of their table and, eyes dancing, was valiantly biting her lip to stop the inevitable giggle.

"Well, the boy does seem to be a good judge of character," he commented.

They both dissolved into laughter as Kim reached for the teapot. "How do you like your tea?" she asked, as she began to pour. "One lump or two, with cream or without?"

"Just one lump and a little cream, please," Buzz replied, still smiling at the disparity of their table settings. "Your aunt and uncle must have a well-developed spying organization, to know where you are and who you're with," Buzz teased.

"I consider it as a system of guardians rather than of spies," Kim countered, as she began to sip her tea.

"You're a wise young lady."

"Actually wiser than I've been pretending to be."

"Pretending?" Buzz's eyebrow rose questioningly.

"Well," Kim confessed, "I find that most older people, especially men, look askance upon a young woman who attempts to carry on an intelligent conversation with them. So I just play the part of a giggling schoolgirl. But I don't feel that way with you, Buzz—or 'something like that!'." The last phrase was accompanied by an elfin smile.

"I know what you mean! I had the same problem with some of the officers when I was in service—but I didn't have the sense to pretend."

They ate in silence, each wrapped in their own thoughts. After the tray was removed, Kim said somewhat diffidently, "Buzz, I hope you don't think I didn't want to hear the rest of your story, but I really wanted to be able to picture your two friends. Now I can, so please continue. I'm really anxious to hear the rest."

"All right, if you're sure I'm not boring you. Well, let's see—I think I was trying to hold up the tent with the ax handle. Following my shouts, Boris and Bob were able to cut me free of the canvas cover. We all took a couple of deep breaths, and then we split up—Boris to the horses, Bob to the prop tent, and I to the planes.

"Running to the airfield, I passed the main office where I was knocked head-over-heels. When I stopped rolling, I looked into the frightened eyes of one of the Rico brothers who was sprawled on the ground about three feet from where I had landed. The Rico brothers were roustabouts, who'd been hired about two weeks earlier. By the time I got to my knees, he was up and running across the airfield, carrying a large canvas bag over his left shoulder. Then I heard Jack yelling, 'Buzz, stop them! They emptied the safe! They stole everything!'

"I looked toward the office where Jack was standing in the doorway with blood streaming down his face; behind him was the big two-door safe, its drawers hanging out. A lot of the performers, including

Boris, Bob and myself, kept our savings there along with the circus money. We thought it was safer than banks, with the world finances as they are."

"Stop them if you can, Buzz!" Jack yelled, and tossed me a Belgian .44 pistol. I was still on the ground, so I propped my elbow on my knees, held the pistol with both hands, and fired. He was running in a straight line, about seventy-five yards away, and I saw the dirt kick up about fifty feet short. I re-cocked the gun and took aim. This time, when I fired, he faltered and went down on one knee. I cocked the gun again, and took aim to fire a third time then there was a huge explosion in my head. That's all I remember."

"Oh my God! What happened?" Kim interjected, her eyes round with excitement.

"Well, as I said, there were two brothers. While I was concentrating on the one with the bag, I didn't notice the other one coming up on my right side behind me. He whapped me in the head; it must have been with something heavy because I woke up three days later in a Paris hospital."

"Did you hit the one with the bag?"

"Boris said I must have because he found blood where he'd gone down, but they got away with all the money, leaving a lot of people broke. Apparently the Ricos knew the safe would be open Monday morning because that was payday, so they set the fires to cause a diversion. It sure worked," Buzz concluded ruefully.

"What about the circus? Was it a total loss?"

"The big top was saved, as well as the horses and the other animals. Bob organized a rescue party and salvaged most of the props and costumes, but the planes were lost to sparks falling on their canvas. The insurance company said they wouldn't cover the theft, and would only cover the rest if Jack would auction off what was left of the circus. Then they would pay the difference. I think Jack had taken out that kind of policy because it was cheaper, but that's Jack for you.

"The auction is to be held a week from today. I asked Boris to sell my .45-70 rifle; hopefully it'll bring enough to buy my two horses."

Kim, astounded, asked, "Jack is selling your horses? How can he do that?"

"Well, they belong to the circus, but they're the ones I always rode in the acts. One is a white Arabian, and the other is a black Polish Arabian," Buzz answered.

The two companions were startled when the train compartment was suddenly bathed in brightness. They looked up, and, reassessing their surroundings for the first time in a while, realized the porter had turned on the overhead lights. Instinctively, they glanced out the window and only then noticed the dark purple mountains outlined by the red-orange glow of the setting sun.

"Oh! I didn't realize it was so late," exclaimed Kim. "I need to go to my aunt and uncle for directions to where we're staying. Perhaps you'll come see me?" she said hopefully.

"Yes, I think I could do that. I'd like that!" Buzz watched attentively as she walked up the aisle and disappeared through the doorway. *Yeah, I sure would like that!* he thought, marveling at how quickly he'd become so comfortable with someone he'd met just a few hours before.

Kim walked as quickly as she could while maintaining the ladylike poise she'd been taught in school.

"Oh, phooey on what Miss Crone (her erstwhile instructor of etiquette) would think of me," thought Kim, as she broke from a quick, close-stepped pace into fast, long strides just short of a run.

Her aunt and uncle's compartment was merely three cars from where she and Buzz had been seated, but it suddenly seemed like a mile; the aisles were full of people and their baggage. There may have been just a few passengers preparing to depart, but to Kim each car had become an obstacle course. At long last, she arrived at compartment 3B, and could see Aunt Jane and Uncle George through the aisle windows.

The older couple jumped when the door slid open with a bang. Kim rushed in breathlessly and plopped down in the empty seat next to her Aunt Jane, gasping for breath and attempting to speak simultaneously and not succeeding well at either task.

"Calm down, Kim! Catch your breath, and then tell us what you want," Aunt Jane counseled, trying to quiet her own reaction to the sudden interruption. Aunt Jane was the type of woman who could have organized a sing-along while the Titanic was sinking. Although only in her mid-forties, her thick hair was silver-gray, and she always wore it in a neat bun at the nape of her neck. Her sharp, sparkling blue eyes didn't miss much, but had a soothing effect all the same. The fine lines on her face bestowed a look of strong character and wisdom rather than age. In her loosely tailored traveling dress, one could see she still retained much of her elegant, girlish figure—all five feet of it.

"Good heavens, girl! Get hold of yourself!" commanded Uncle George with asperity. A striking man of about fifty, he had a full head of black hair graying at the temples and a rather long, sharp-featured face. His dark eyes were framed by heavy brows and the deep lines acquired by staring at the seas in the wind and sun for many years. He spoke precisely in his deep voice, and could have taken command of the Titanic while his wife led the sing-along.

"What's gotten you so upset?" asked Uncle George, taking Kim's hand, so tiny in comparison to his, which would obviously have been more at home pulling heavy lines aboard a ship than pushing a pencil at a desk.

In her emotional state, Kim failed to notice the change in the motion of the train, even when the constant swaying ceased, and it came to a complete standstill. "Oh, Aunty! I met the nicest young gentleman, and I need a map of how to get to where we're going to be staying! Would you please draw one up for me so I can give it to him? Please? It's very important to me, it really is!" Kim gushed all in one breath.

"Why, I'd be glad to, dear," Aunt Jane replied, reaching into her traveling bag as she spoke.

"What's the fellow like? How does he make his living? What's his family like?" Uncle George demanded. "Good people, I hope. They'd better be!"

"Oh, shush, George!" remonstrated Aunt Jane. "You sound like my father when I first met you! Here's your map, dear." She tore the paper from the pad and handed it to Kim.

"Thank you, Aunt Jane," Kim said as she gave the smiling woman a grateful hug and kissed her cheek. She turned to Uncle George and laughingly kissed his forehead. "I love you both!" she called over her shoulder as she ran out of the car.

"Come right back, because we get off at the next stop— Peshawar," Aunt Jane called.

23

"I will!" floated back to her.

"Did your father really ask those questions about me?" George asked.

"Of course!" Jane replied.

"What did you tell him?"

"I gave him the same answer Kim just gave you," she replied serenely.

"Oh. Well, I guess that's the best answer you could have given," George said thoughtfully, as he began the prolonged ritual of lighting his pipe.

As she entered the next car, Kim suddenly remembered Buzz having said he was departing the train at the station before Peshawar, which was where they were. "I have to catch him before he gets off," Kim ordered herself aloud, as she felt a cold chill down her spine. She raced down the aisle, jumping over suitcases and dodging people.

She heard the train's whistle, and the floor beneath her gave a sudden jolt, nearly knocking her off her feet. The car began swaying from side to side as it gained momentum.

"Oh, no! We're moving! I've lost him! Maybe I was wrong; maybe this wasn't his stop! Maybe he didn't get off yet!" She jerked the door of the car open, and rushed to the seats where they had been sitting a short while before. His seat was empty. She suddenly felt ill as her stomach muscles clenched and a pain flared in her chest.

"He's gone! How will we ever see each other again? He won't know where to find me," she whispered despairingly under her breath as she crumpled the map in her right hand.

"Can I help you, ma'am?"

Kim turned to the voice and saw a steward facing her with a concerned expression.

"Oh, yes, please! There was a young man in this seat. He was about 5'10" tall; light brown hair needing a trim, He had hazel eyes, a slightly sunburned complexion, and a small scar over his right eye. His smile was warm, and he has nice teeth. He had large hands, but they were slender, like an artist's. He was wearing a tan shirt, tan jodhpurs, and tall-laced boots, like a pilot would wear. In fact, he is a pilot! Oh, yes! Also, he had a leather jacket, and carried a large, canvas duffel bag."

"Oh, is he a relative, or…" inquired the steward.

"No. No, we just met today. Why?" asked Kim.

"I'm sorry. You described him as though you'd known him for a long time."

"Somehow, it seems that way," Kim murmured.

"Are you Miss Kimberley Smith?" Another steward, a bit older, was approaching.

"Yes, I am," she replied, trying to regain her composure.

"Mr. Mark Kramer said I was to give this to you." He placed a small cloth bundle in her hand, bowed respectfully, turned, and left her to herself. She recognized the cloth as one of the linen napkins from their lunch tray, neatly folded and tied with a small piece of string. She slowly untied the string and opened it.

"My Dearest Kim," she read. *My Dearest Kim,* she thought—*not Dear Kimberley,' but 'My Dearest Kim.* Her heart began to beat faster. "Will you have dinner with me when we meet again? Yours always, Buzz." *Not "Sincerely, Mark Kramer," but "Yours always, Buzz."*

She unrolled the napkin the rest of the way and found the oddly shaped gold cross and its chain in her hand. She remembered Buzz saying, "My father said I should give it to someone special someday."

"He'll find me. I just know he will. Someday, somehow, he'll find me!" Kim said softly, determinedly, as she sank into the seat where he had been and cried with mingled hope and disappointment.

———

Buzz still stood on the small platform by the tracks with his leather jacket draped over one shoulder and securely grasped the well-worn strap of the duffel bag in his right hand. He watched forlornly as the red and green lights on the rear of the train slowly receded in the smoke that spiraled crazily, and disappeared into the cold darkness of the night.

"Sir! Sir! Did you leave something on the train?"

"Huh?" Buzz, startled, turned to the porter who had spoken.

"I asked, sir, if the gentleman had left something of importance aboard the train."

Buzz turned and stared pensively into the darkness where the tracks disappeared beyond the station's lights. "Yes, I believe I did. I believe I might have left the most valuable treasure I could ever seek."

"Perhaps if the gentleman looks hard enough, he will find it again," replied the porter.

"By God, boy, you're right! I will look! No matter how long it takes, or where I have to travel, I will find that treasure again!" Buzz took the young porter's hand and pressed a coin into it. Then he took a deep breath, filling his lungs with the cool night air, and squared his shoulders as if marching off to battle. He slung his duffel over his right shoulder, stepped off the platform, and advanced toward the station house.

— Chapter Three —

HARRY WHITECLIFF

Upon entering the station house, Buzz let his glance sweep the room. The space was about twenty by thirty feet, with a double door on the train side of the room and an identical one directly across, leading to the street. There were four large windows—one on each side of the doors. On Buzz's left sat the station master, wearing a cap which looked as though it had been awarded to him when he was a much younger man. It tilted over his round, dark face with beady black eyes, and a bulbous nose perched atop a bushy mustache, which bore the remnants of meals past. His dry, cracked lips looked as though they never smiled, except perhaps on his birthday, which today obviously was not.

Directly in front of him was a narrow, tall desk holding a dirty desk lamp, encrusted with the soot from the passing of many trains, a stack of papers, and a telephone; behind him was a wooden cabinet with forty or so square pigeonholes, all but three of which were empty. Number eight contained what seemed to be a lunch box, number ten a key with a dangling brass tag, and number thirteen contained a white envelope.

The other side of the room had enough wooden benches lining the wall and filling the center of the room to seat fifty to sixty patrons. A small door bore four signs, one of which Buzz understood to read Gentlemen.

The walls and ceiling may have been white eons ago, but were now a dull, yellowed gray. The whole, joyless room was dimly illuminated by a very small bulb hanging over the clerk's desk by a fuzzy cord and a six-bulb chandelier in the center of the ceiling, only one bulb of which was burning. The room had the brilliance of a crypt.

Suddenly, the two street-side doors swung inward, sending the night air wafting through the room creating little clouds of dust that swirled across the floor to dissipate at Buzz's feet. Standing there, with a hand on either door, stood a man, no less than 6'2" tall. He sported a spotless white suit, highly polished black shoes, a black belt, and a wide-brimmed white hat with a black silk band. At his neck was a red and black paisley cravat. His long face was enlivened by glistening, light-blue eyes and a broad smile.

"Mr. Mark Kramer?" he inquired with precision.

"I am he," Buzz answered. "And you?"

"Harry Whitecliff," he said, removing his hat and placing it in his left hand which also held a slim, ebony walking cane, tipped on both ends with silver bands. He hurriedly crossed the room to Buzz, hand outstretched in greeting.

"I left a message for you, but it is still in the mail slot. No matter; it just read that I might be late. I saw the train leaving, so I take it you didn't have to wait long."

"No, no, I just arrived," Buzz hastened to reply, finding himself responding to Whitecliff's firm, sincere handshake. Buzz at once felt comfortable with this man.

"Here, let me take your bag. We'll go to the hotel which is just across the street; then after you get settled in your room, we'll have something to eat."

"Yes. That will be fine. I am a bit hungry," Buzz said.

"Good! Then we can get acquainted," Whitecliff replied. "This was, at one time, a supply depot for the British army. It saw a lot of action, but, as you can see, it's dead now,"

It sure is dead, thought Buzz.

The hotel was, as Whitecliff had said, directly across from the station house, a three-story building in good repair—unlike some of the other buildings farther down the street. If not for the light from the hotel lobby, the six streetlamps, and the glow from what looked to be a pub at the end of the street, the blackness of the night would have been unremitting.

"The boy will show you to your room where you can freshen up. I'll wait in the lobby for you," Whitecliff said as he handed Buzz's duffel bag to the bellboy who greeted them at the door.

The hotel was as different from the railway depot as day from night. The lobby was well-lit by a sparkling chandelier and ornate wall sconces. There was even a small, pleasantly tinkling fountain in the center. The night clerk, dressed in a dark gray suit, stood behind a carved, highly polished counter. He greeted Buzz with a smile, and handed a key to a barefooted young boy, about eleven or twelve years of age, wearing a white turban, maroon velvet jacket, and white pantaloons who led Buzz to a gilded cage-type elevator. After entering, the boy closed the gates ceremoniously and manned the controls as if he were commanding a ship. As they rose, Buzz noticed that the second floor was dark, but the third floor, where the elevator stopped, was well-lit.

After the ceremony accompanying the opening of the gates, the bellboy ushered Buzz down the hall to his room. He opened the door, turned on the lights, put Buzz's duffel bag on a stand, and returned to the hall. He then bowed from the waist and, making a sweeping motion with his arm, ushered Buzz into the room.

Buzz reached into his pocket to retrieve some coins for a tip.

"Oh no, sir! No tip, no tip!" remonstrated the boy. "Mr. Whitecliff already took care of that!"

"Does Mr. Whitecliff stay at the hotel?" asked Buzz.

"Oh, yes; Mr. Whitecliff occupies the whole second floor. If you need anything, just call the desk," the boy said, motioning to a telephone on a nightstand by the bed.

"What is your name?" Buzz asked the boy.

"Kim—like in the book," he answered proudly. With that, he bowed deeply while backing out the door and closed it. Buzz heard his small bare feet retreating down the hall.

Buzz surmised that Kim was referring to Kipling's book.

Well, he mused, *two Kims in one day! That's strange.*

The room was quite pleasant—freshly painted tan walls, a white ceiling with a large fan turning lazily in its center, and one large window. A bed, a nightstand, a small dining table and two chairs, a large wardrobe, and to his surprise, a full bathroom completed the comfortable furnishings.

After quickly freshening up, Buzz retrieved the key from the table and locked the door behind him. As he approached the elevator, he changed his mind and decided to use the stairs to stretch his legs a bit.

Upon reaching the second floor, he found it still dark; the doorway was barred with a floor-to-ceiling gate made of iron bars, inside which hung a large padlock.

So those are Mr. Whitecliff's quarters. I'll bet they're interesting, Buzz thought with a tinge of curiosity.

Seeing Buzz striding down the steps, Kim ran quickly over to meet him. "Oh, sir! I'm sorry! Please forgive me!"

"That's all right, Kim. I didn't ring the bell because I wanted to walk; I need to stretch my legs. I was sitting for a long time on the train," Buzz explained. "When I return, you can take me up in the elevator."

"Oh, thank you!" Kim bowed gratefully.

"Well, if it's all right with you, Mr. Kramer, we'll proceed to get something to eat," Whitecliff proposed as he motioned to the door with one arm.

"Yes, that would be fine," Buzz remarked, and they exited the hotel and descended the steps. Whitecliff turned left, and Buzz followed his lead.

"That bellboy seems to think a lot of you," Buzz commented.

"Kim's a fine lad. I arranged a position for him at the hotel after his mother and father were killed. It's an extremely sad story; I'll tell you about it some other time. Let us speak of more pleasant things tonight," Whitecliff said with a quiet, matter-of-fact air.

As they walked, each commented on the weather. A warm breeze was stirring the puddles in the street, and the clouds were giving way to the stars and a rising crescent moon.

Buzz asked about the large buildings lining the street. Whitecliff told him that they were warehouses that had been used by the British army, but most were now deserted. The three at the end of the street across from the pub in which they were to dine now belonged to his company—H. W. Import & Export, Ltd.

The sign hanging above the doorway at their destination read Fife & Drum, with a colorfully executed painting of the said items beneath the wording. Whitecliff held the door open and, as Buzz entered, he felt as though he had somehow been transported to a pub in the heart of London. The air was heavy with the smells of tea, rum, ale, and fried fish. There were a number of round tables and a few booths in addition to a bar. The bar itself was about 20' long, with ten or twelve stools arranged in front of it. Behind it was a large assortment of liquor and several pump handles for beer and ale. A large mirror, etched with the same fife and drum that graced the sign above the door, showcased the bar's offerings from behind. It was all very clean and highly polished. The bar was manned by a heavy-set man with a round face that encompassed a large smile and merry, twinkling eyes. He had bushy gray hair and side-burns that curved dramatically to the bottom of his jaw. He wore a pristine white shirt, and a once-white apron permanently dappled with the stains from samples of his wares.

The tables were nearly filled by what looked to be old, retired soldiers who had stayed on after the conflicts. These jolly groups were being served by one barmaid who was probably in her sixties. She couldn't possibly have acquired the girth, graying hair, and wrinkles she proudly sported in less time than that.

"Why, Mr. Whitecliff, you're later than usual. Do you wish a pint to start with, sir?"

"Yes, Bess, that would be fine. I would like you to meet Mr. Mark Kramer. Mr. Kramer, this is Bess, the finest barmaid in town," said Whitecliff with a jovial air.

"Oh, Mr. Whitecliff, how you do go on! You know I'm the only barmaid in town!" laughed Bess, dropping a small curtsey.

"I'm pleased to meet you, Bess," Buzz replied with a smile.

Tankards were raised in gestures of a toast as they passed among the seated patrons. Bess led the way to a square table against the back wall. There were two chairs on either side, and it was the only table with a linen cloth. It was adorned with a small, handmade, brass-and-wood plaque carved with H. Whitecliff and decorated with gold leaf.

"I take it you've eaten here more than once or twice," Buzz remarked as they were being seated.

"Would the young gentleman fancy a pint, or would he rather something stronger?" Bess asked Buzz.

"Oh, a pint would be fine, thank you!"

"Bess, bring us two orders of your finest fish and chips, also," asked Whitecliff, leaning back in his chair and placing his hand on Bess' shoulder. He then leaned forward toward Buzz, and as though he was divulging a state secret, began, "They have the best—"

"I know," Buzz interrupted with a grin. "The best fish and chips in town!" They all enjoyed a hearty laugh.

The tankards of ale soon arrived. Raising his, Whitecliff proposed a toast. "To a pleasant future—or if not pleasant, at least interesting!"

"I'll drink to that," Buzz replied, clanking his tankard against Whitecliff's.

The ale was dark with a light, golden head of foam, and had a somewhat bitter taste with sweet overtones. It was just slightly cooler than room temperature.

"Do you like it? Bart, the owner brews it," stated Whitecliff with a nod toward the man behind the bar. "Oh! Here comes our good Bess with the fish and chips." He leaned back in his chair expansively, stretching out his arms in what seemed to be a welcoming gesture.

Bess placed before each of them a large, steaming hot platter that contained deep, golden-brown fish and mounds of crisp fried potatoes. Bess retrieved two bottles from her large apron pockets—one labeled Malt Vinegar and the other Hot. She deposited them in the center of the table along with napkins and silver beside each plate. Taking up the now empty tankards, she retreated through the maze of tables after inviting them to "enjoy your meal, gentlemen!" Whitecliff picked up his utensils, nodded, and then the two began to eat.

Armed with his own instruments, Buzz parted the white meat of the fish closest to him. The meat flaked away from the row of bones which Buzz lifted out in one piece, and discarded on the extra plate brought by Bess when she had returned to replenish their ale. The steam released when its encasement was breached carried the aroma of the perfectly baked fish to Buzz's nostrils, causing his mouth to water in anticipation. The texture was that of cake, and the flavor was mildly of fish, but not inordinately 'fishy.' The potatoes were firm and crunchy, and seasoned to a turn.

Buzz reached for the bottle labeled 'Hot,' but Whitecliff gently stayed his hand. "You may wish to reconsider this time," he cautioned, smiling. Buzz returned the bottle to the center of the table, and took up the malt vinegar. "A wise choice," said his companion, continuing to partake of his meal.

They dined in comfortable silence. When they had both finished the delicious feast, Bess cleared the table, brought a large ash tray, and a serving tray holding a decanter of wine and two glasses. Upon Whitecliff's approval, Bess poured each glass three-quarters full and, placing the decanter on the tray, left them to their quiet enjoyment.

Whitecliff lifted his glass for another toast, and Buzz raised his. "May we each propose a toast in silence, and may it be well for the other." They clinked their glasses and sipped the pleasingly warm wine.

Whitecliff opened the humidor and took out a long, dark cigar, sliding it toward Buzz. "Cigar? They're Havanas."

"Yes, thank you. I haven't had a Havana in some time."

They clipped the ends of their cigars with a cutter hanging from the side of the humidor, and lit up simultaneously with matches from a holder on the ash tray.

Whitecliff leaned back in his chair and directed a smoke ring toward the ceiling, cigar in his left hand, and glass in his right.

"Now, Mr. Kramer, we can talk. I'm sure you have some questions."

"Well, what type of plane will I be flying, and where? Also, why did you send for me in particular? I'm sure you could find pilots around here. After all, you don't know anything about me."

"You'll be piloting a Fairey Flycatcher. It was designed for the British Navy to use on aircraft carriers. It's a 400hp Armstrong Siddeley Jaguar IV engine, which can attain a speed of 133 miles per hour at 5,000 feet altitude. Yet, by virtue of the trailing edge flaps, it can drift in to land at only forty-seven miles per hour."

"Damn! That's a fairly new model. What shape is it in? Is it wrecked? If so, how bad?" Buzz asked without sarcasm.

"The plane is new, just out of the crate. One of the things I want you to do is to put it in order. I have all the manuals and tools you'll need. To answer your other questions—well, maybe tomorrow. It's late, and you've had a long day. I should be getting you back to your room so you can get some sleep; we'll be leaving early in the morning to go through the Khaibar Pass," Whitecliff said.

"I've heard of the Khaibar Pass," Buzz replied. "It has quite a history!"

"Yes, it certainly does. And tomorrow, you'll see it first-hand. Would you care for another glass of wine?"

"No thanks. I've had plenty, and frankly your idea of getting some sleep is suddenly very appealing."

"Fine. Oh, Bess," Whitecliff called, motioning to the barmaid.

She brought a small tray holding a pencil and the tab, which Whitecliff signed.

They wound their way through the tables, with Whitecliff pausing to shake hands and exchange friendly banter with some of the other patrons on the way to the door.

As he stepped out into the street, Buzz noticed the sky was crystal clear, dotted liberally with stars, and the moon shone brightly. The warm breeze still gently rippled the puddles. Whitecliff stepped a little way into the street, and looked both ways intently as if he were looking for some-one or some-thing. Then he shrugged and returned to stand beside Buzz.

"Shall we go?" he spoke quietly, tucking his walking stick under his left arm as one would a swagger stick. They began walking back to the hotel with Whiteside on the street side, Buzz next to the buildings.

"Mr. Whitecliff, you were definitely right!"

"Oh? In what way?"

"It has been a long day, and that bed is going to feel very good. And I also agree that that is the best fish and chips in town—Even if it had been served in the heart of Lon..."

POW!!

Buzz crumpled to the ground like an empty overcoat.

A noose was thrown over Whitecliff, pinning his arms to his sides. Two dark figures grabbed him by the arms, and another came from behind and quickly tied a gag over his mouth. Two more quickly came out from a nearby alley way, grabbed his ankles, and jerked his feet out from under him.

The jerking, squirming figure of the man in white was carried roughly into the nearest alley way and dumped unceremoniously on the wet pavement. The two attackers holding his arms switched their vise-like grips to his wrists. The rope around his chest was cut, and his arms were jerked roughly out to the side, as were his legs. Spread-eagled, he'd never felt so helpless in his life.

"Now you die, infidel!"

Whitecliff turned his head toward the rasping growl and saw a masked man dressed all in black, his eyes gleaming with triumph and hate. He was raising a sword over his head, which reflected the moonlight.

Suddenly, the moon was blotted out for a split second. The sword clattered, clanking, to the pavement, and the man in black disappeared. There was another thud, followed by a groan; Whitecliff's left arm was free, and then crunch. His right arm was released. He felt the grip on his right leg lessen somewhat, so he jerked it loose and kicked the figure grasping his left in the face. He was now totally unencumbered.

Rolling to his left, Harry felt for his walking stick and picked it up as he leapt to his feet. With the handle in his right hand and the shaft in his left, he gave a sharp twist and drew out a twenty-eight-inch blade of the finest Toledo steel.

Whitecliff caught sight of Buzz vaulting a dark figure on the ground to snatch up the fallen sword and slice one of the attackers in black across the mid-section. The man dropped his weapon and, clutching his stomach, dropped to his knees.

Buzz spun around to face Whitecliff, blood streaming down his face, teeth clenched, and a look in his eyes that made him very glad that they were on the same side.

Three more attackers came rushing in from the street, and Buzz rushed toward them as Whitecliff turned to the three remaining of the four who had held him captive. The closest made a thrust, which Whitecliff sidestepped and then sank his foil in the man's throat. The would-be assassin staggered backward, his hands trying vainly to stem the flow of blood. He made a loud gurgling sound. The one in the middle charged in, swinging at Whitecliff's head. Ducking, Whitecliff sank his weapon into his opponent's right thigh, causing him to stagger. Then he kicked him from the side, causing him to sprawl directly in front of the third man, who tripped over him and fell at Whitecliff's feet. He then planted his blade at the base of the man's neck between his shoulder blades and, like a matador dispatching a wounded bull in the ring, thrust the blade home.

Whitecliff turned to Buzz and saw that his ally was down on one knee, fending off blows from two adversaries. The third was crumpled up against the wall, holding the stump where his right hand had been. He was sprawled next to the sword that Buzz was groping for. Finally he was able to snatch it. He grabbed the weapon, and parried, knocking the sword of the man to his left upward. Coming up off his knees, he ran the blade to the hilt just beneath the attacker's ribcage, to exit under his shoulder blades. Then Buzz turned to face another opponent only to see him disappearing expeditiously into the street, to be swallowed by the shadows.

Whitecliff turned again to the alley, and could just make out the man with the leg wound limping stumblingly down the alley and melting into the night. He went quickly to Buzz, who was still standing at the entrance to the alley, dazed, with the sword still in his hand. He guided him gently but rapidly to the hotel, stopping only to retrieve his hat.

"Good God, man! What did you hit them with?" he asked Buzz wonderingly.

"Buckets of sand. All I could find on the street were two fire buckets full of sand."

"We'll both stay at my place tonight; it will be safer. I'll have Kim bring your bags."

They entered the hotel quietly to avoid waking the desk clerk, who was sleeping peacefully with his head propped up on his left arm. Whitecliff tiptoed over to Kim, who was curled up in a large, overstuffed chair next to the elevator. He shook him gently and, raising his forefinger to his lips, roused him from his dreams. Kim rose silently, and Whitecliff motioned him to follow.

"We'll take the stairs. They're quieter," Whitecliff whispered.

Reaching the second-floor landing, Buzz handed his key to Kim, who dashed up the stairs. Whitecliff reached through the bars of the gate to open the large padlock. By the time the two of them were through the gate, Kim had returned down the stairs, the sound of one patting themselves on the cheek with an open hand coming from his unshod feet.

Buzz snapped the padlock shut with a sharp click while Whitecliff unlocked the door to his quarters. Once inside, they all felt safer—even Kim, although he didn't know yet what he felt safer from.

Whitecliff stepped around the room, turning on the lights. For the first time since the fracas in the alley way, Buzz noticed that the front of his once spotless white suit was covered with dirty water stains and spatterings of blood, and the back was nearly black with mud and tar. His hair hung in disarray from under his still white hat, down into his eyes. Then he slowly took in his surroundings. The large room was eccentrically decorated. On the floor was a lion skin with paws outstretched and mouth agape, its yellow eyes glaring; next to a high-backed chair beside the window was a smoking stand fashioned from an elephant's foot. A zebra hide graced the wall, in the center of which were two short Zulu spears behind a shield; a number of skillfully carved African masks surrounded it. Another wall was lined top-to-bottom with hundreds of books.

Buzz's expression prompted Whitecliff to speak. "As you can see, there are advantages to being in the import-export business. One can enjoy one's wares before selling them."

"Mr. Whitecliff, who were those men and what did they want?"

"Well, first of all, I can't very well have the man who just saved my life calling me mister. I would like it very much if you would call me Harry."

"My friends call me Buzz, and I would be pleased if you would join that group."

"Thank you, Buzz."

"And you, Harry." The two men shook hands and smiled.

"Kim, please take M...Buzz's things to the blue room and draw him a warm bath," Harry directed. "Meanwhile, Buzz, let me pour you a large scotch, and I'll take a look at that nasty cut on your head." He motioned Buzz to be seated at a small rattan table.

Carrying a small black valise, Kim re-entered the room and placed it on the table. He opened it and quickly and efficiently laid out some of the contents on a white cloth—a roll of gauze, some cotton wool, a pair of scissors, a small bottle of alcohol, and a bottle of iodine. His matter-of-fact manner made Buzz wonder how many other business associates Harry had patched up.

Harry said, "Hmm—that's a bad cut, but it seems to have bled well. That's good; it helps to keep the dirt out. This is going to sting a little," he warned as he poured alcohol on the wound.

"Ooh," Buzz groaned slightly.

"Where was I? Oh, yes. Those gentlemen are part of a new organization they call the Dark Shadow of God, and they refer to themselves as Shadow Men. They were about to deprive me of a place to put my hat when you, in such a timely fashion, threw sand into their plans. But that's enough for now. We have a long day ahead of us tomorrow, and we'll have plenty of time to talk then."

"To the Khaibar Pass," said Buzz, raising his glass in a toast.

Harry raised his glass, and Kim raised his hand as though holding a drink. In unison, they said, "To the Khaibar Pass."

— Chapter Four —

THE KHAIBAR PASS

Someone was gently shaking Buzz's shoulder. He thought he heard a soft voice calling, "Dear, it's time to get up. Your coffee is ready." He reluctantly opened his eyes and blearily blinked a few times to clear the fog of sleep.

As his mind traveled from dreams to reality, the figure standing beside his bed changed from a beautiful dark-haired girl holding a cup of hot coffee to a young boy with a big grin holding his pants. "Wake up, Mr. Kramer, wake up!" It was not the Kim of his dreams, but Harry's 'Little' Kim. Damn!

Buzz threw the covers aside and got up. He noticed his pants felt clean and fresh as he pulled them on, and the shirt Kim offered was also cleaned and pressed. His socks were clean and his boots highly polished as well.

"I think you made a hit with Kim."

Harry was standing in the doorway holding a big silver serving tray, upon which was a large, steaming silver urn, two oversized cups and saucers, and a silver sugar bowl and cream pitcher. The intoxicating aroma escaping and filling the room had to be that of authentic Turkish coffee.

Harry was dressed in a safari jacket, jodhpurs, high-laced boots, and a pith helmet, all white but his boots, belt, and hatband. Around his neck was a black scarf with silver pinstripes.

"The boy stayed up late last night to wash, mend, and press your clothes," Harry informed Buzz, smiling affectionately at Kim.

"He did a really fine job polishing my boots, too," Buzz commended.

Looking at the young boy standing so straight and smiling so proudly, Buzz knew that Kim's work had been done out of friendship, not as a service for which he expected to be paid. So rather than reaching for a tip, Buzz offered his hand, which Kim shook gratefully. "Thank you very much, Kim. And please call me Buzz. If you don't mind, may I call you Little Kim? I know someone else with that name.

"Oh yes, Mr. Buzz, of course! Thank you!"

Buzz shrugged and thought ruefully, *Well, I guess that's better than Mr. Kramer.*

Harry poured a bit of coffee into a small cup, filled it the rest of the way with cream and, adding two lumps of sugar, handed the cup to Kim, who sat on the bed. Then he poured for himself and Buzz and sat across from Buzz at the table.

"Well, gentlemen, while we have our coffee, I'll give you our itinerary," Harry announced. "First, we stop at the pub and pick up food for the trip. Then we take the truck, which is parked in the warehouse across the way, to Jamrud, where we'll join the caravan—"

"Caravan!" Buzz interjected with a start. "You mean like in the old days, with camels and such?"

"Well, something like that. Now there are trucks and horse carts, but the reason is the same; there's safety in numbers. There will be armed guards also. It's very unwise to travel the Pass alone. Bandits," Harry reported.

"Oh. Well, in that case, I'd better unpack my pistols and my newly acquired saber," Buzz said thoughtfully.

"What kind of firearms do you have?" Harry asked.

"I have two .455 Webleys."

"Good choice. I'll carry the same, plus a couple of .303 British Enfields."

"Bet there are a lot of those around here," Buzz observed.

"Yes. Unfortunately, many are in the wrong hands."

They left the hotel for the pub at 6:30, and the sun was already casting long shadows. The puddles in the roadway were now golden instead of silver, and even the warehouses seemed smaller and less menacing.

They walked in silence; the only sound that of the footfalls of the two men, and the creaking of the baggage cart being pushed by Kim.

When they passed the site of last night's melee, Buzz saw that the only remaining evidence was two mangled fire buckets, a scattering of sand, and several patches of dried blood. Buzz started to ask, "Where are the—"

"They take care of their own," Harry replied.

"Oh."

The silence was unbroken the rest of the way to the pub.

When they reached the Fife & Drum, Harry held the door open for Buzz and motioned for Kim to leave the baggage cart, and come in as well.

As Buzz's eyes adjusted from the bright sunlight to the dimness of the pub, he noted that very little had changed since the night before. Some of the same patrons were at the same tables, but were now lifting tea instead of tankards of ale to their lips and Bess was busily serving platters of kippers and hotcakes.

As they made their way through the pub, Whitecliff noticed someone who had not been there the previous evening. Pausing briefly he placed his hand on the man's shoulder, and inquired, "Ned, I didn't see you here last night—is everything all right?

"Doing fine, guv! Top o' the mornin' to ya!"

"And you, Ned."

Rejoining Buzz, he remarked, "Another old soldier--come over here. I want you to meet Paddy. He's the best—"

"Don't tell me, I know. He's the best barkeep in town," Buzz interrupted with a smile.

"Paddy, this is Buzz Kramer, a very good friend of mine."

"I'm proud to meet you, Buzz," Paddy said, as he wiped his hands on his apron and put out his hand.

"Paddy, I'm going to need some essentials," Harry declared.

"Well, in that case, let's go back to the store," Paddy replied, leading the way to the rear of the pub. They passed through a colorful beaded curtain hung across a small doorway. Paddy pulled the cord leading to a single light in the center of the ceiling, illuminating the small room.

Buzz's mouth fell open; he was astounded at how much could be packed systematically into a room of that size. From top to bottom, wall to wall, ceiling to floor, and in the aisles between the glass shop-cases, were guns of all types; swords, knives, canteen covers, shirts, pants, canned goods, saddles, bridles; ammunition of all sorts, and even a small section just for tobacco.

"If Paddy doesn't have it, you don't need it!" Paddy chortled with a gleeful, self-satisfied smile.

Harry ambled over to the tobacco section. "Paddy, I'll have a couple of boxes of cigars—you know, the usual. Buzz, "Do you want some cigars? Paddy has a good selection."

"I'd like to, but I'm a bit short on funds, right now."

"If you wish, I can put it on my account, and we can settle up later," Harry offered.

"Well, then, I will have a box of cigars. No, wait! I think I'll try a pipe instead. I'll take one of those briars and that meerschaum." Buzz pointed to a pipe, the bowl of which was carved with the head of a tiger. "And a package of nice-smelling tobacco. Also, may I see that little pistol?" Buzz turned to the counter behind them. "I noticed it when we came in."

"Oh, yes, of course! It's a Star, semi-automatic, .380 caliber; a very fine gun, made in Spain. There are also four extra magazines and five boxes of shells, plus a leather holster," Paddy announced in his best salesman's voice, and then placed the box containing the pistol on the counter.

Buzz picked it up; it felt good in his hand. There was a molded thumb rest on the left grip, and the right had slight finger indentations. The pistol had good balance, and would fit a small or large hand well. The action worked smoothly and easily, and the hammer could be cocked and uncocked with very little effort.

"How much?" Buzz inquired.

"Four pounds, nine shillings," Paddy answered.

"Make it four pounds even and you've got a deal," Buzz returned.

"Done!" Paddy replied with alacrity.

"Now, may I see that little dagger?" Buzz asked, pointing to a dagger with a six-inch blade. Paddy handed it to Buzz, handle foremost.

The sheath was of red patent leather with a silver cap at the point which was finished with a bead of gold. A half-inch silver band around the top completed the ornamentation. On the back was a loop of leather for carrying on the belt. The blade, held by spring tension, was capped with a silver hilt which stuck out about an inch on either side of the handle. Both thickness and width tapered to a point, one of which curved up, the other down. Each was capped with a gold bead to match the sheath. The handle was of silvery gray Mastodon ivory, adorned with a snake holding a golden orb in its open mouth carved around the inch thick shaft. Buzz slipped the blade, which bore a light scrolling of inlaid gold, from its encasement. It had been made in Toledo, Spain, and both edges were as sharp as razors. Buzz hefted it for balance and found it perfect.

"How much?" he asked Paddy.

"Two pounds, six shillings—but for you, two pounds even."

"Sold!" Buzz exclaimed triumphantly.

Buzz nudged Harry lightly with his elbow to draw his notice, and then nodded toward Little Kim, who was standing between them, gazing wistfully at the wonderful things in the glass cases. Harry gave a slight smile, and nodded his approval.

"Little Kim," said Buzz, putting his hand on the boy's shoulder to get his attention. "I would like you to have this dagger. But there's an old custom in my family which states that giving someone a knife would sever the friendship. I will sell it to you for the smallest coin in your pocket."

The boy's eyes widened. His mouth an '0,' he stared up at Buzz in adoring wonder. "Really?" he asked, softly, breathlessly.

"Yes, really," Buzz replied, smiling.

Little Kim jammed his hand into his pocket, pulled it out, thrust his clenched fist toward Buzz, and slowly opened it. The now open hand revealed a polished pebble, a dead beetle (in several disjoined pieces), and a small ball of twine. Not one coin rested there. Little Kim dropped his hand dejectedly in front of him. Yesterday's wondrous treasure was today's worthless junk. He felt the chance of having that marvelous dagger of silver and gold quickly fading. He looked up at Buzz, trying to hide his disappointment, but a minuscule bit of dampness shown at the corner of each eye.

"I'm sorry, sir, but I don't seem to have any coins," the boy confessed with the slightest quiver in his voice.

"Oh, I see something I need more than a coin. If you could bear to part with it, that nice ball of twine is just what I need."

"Yes, of course! I believe I could do without it if you need it. Of course, it is of the finest silk, you know," Little Kim informed him with the air of a shrewd camel dealer.

Buzz gingerly lifted the ball of string from the boy's open palm, and ceremoniously deposited the item of trade in its place.

At that moment, Little Kim seemed to increase in stature by at least a foot.

Harry stood smiling, arms crossed in front of him. "Gentlemen, that was a fine transaction. Kim, would you get the food and drink from Bess and meet us at the warehouse?"

Little Kim placed his new dagger firmly in his sash and practically danced to the kitchen.

Harry settled up with Paddy, and he and Buzz made their way to the warehouse.

The large doors were rolled back on the middle building of the three owned by Harry. 'H. W. Import and Export, Ltd.,' was stenciled in red, trimmed in gold across the front of each. Inside was a large, square-nosed truck with dual wheels in the rear, its engine idling. As Buzz and Harry approached the rumbling machine, Buzz saw it was a dull, brownish-gray in color. On the doors, Harry's company logo was painted, not in red and gold, but in flat black. The bed was approximately 20' long with a canvas cover the same color as the cab.

There were two men who, judging by their dress, were locals, working busily; one cleaning the large headlamps, and the other checking the tires. Buzz assumed they were employed by Harry.

"Buzz, would you help Kim load our gear into the back of the truck? I have to check the manifest," Harry asked.

Buzz could see Little Kim pushing the cart across the road at a fast walk. "Be glad to, Harry," he answered.

Buzz met Little Kim halfway and helped him push the cart up the incline to the warehouse. As they passed the running board, Little Kim dropped off a large thermos and a bag which Buzz figured contained their breakfast.

Buzz hoisted Little Kim up onto the tailgate, then handed his duffel up to him to be stowed among the already packed boxes and bundles. Harry's kit bag was handed up next, leaving only the two Enfield .303 rifles, four bandoliers, and two cases of ammunition.

Damn, Buzz thought, *are we going for a drive, or to fight a war?*

"Don't put the rifles in the back, we need them up front. The bandoliers, too," Harry yelled.

"I guess we're going to war," Buzz mumbled.

Oops! Buzz bent over to pick up a bandolier he'd dropped. He happened to glance at the underside of the truck. "Wow! What a set-up," he said under his breath.

"We'd better hurry, boys, or we'll miss the convoy!" Harry called.

The two hurried to the cab of the truck as the locals came around to close up the back.

Buzz opened the door and Little Kim climbed in, taking the foodstuffs with him; then he boarded with the rifles. He placed them just inside the door, and the bandoliers next to them. The door closed with a hollow bang.

Harry was already behind the wheel, watching his side-view mirror for his men to give the signal that everything was closed up and tied down. Harry had draped his jacket over the back of the seat, revealing his .455 Webley in a shoulder holster and twelve extra cartridges in the loops on the straps.

Little Kim sat in the middle, his legs straddling the gearshift. Buzz imitated Harry and took his jacket off to drape it over the rifles, exposing the brace of pistols in his shoulder holsters.

Little Kim looked at Buzz, and then turned toward Harry. He puffed out his chest and patted his newly acquired dagger, obviously pleased with himself.

"Oh, Mr. Harry, Bess said to give you this," Kim said, handing him an egg.

Harry tossed it out the window and up in the air; it landed with a splat on the roof of the cab. "For good luck. An old custom," he explained.

One of the men motioned to Harry, indicating that the cargo was properly battened down, and they could proceed.

Harry revved the engine a couple of times, dropped the gearshift into low, causing Little Kim to part his knees and let out the clutch. The truck slowly moved out of the warehouse and into the sunlight.

The entire pub seemed to have turned out to cheer them on, as if they were a parade of one vehicle.

Harry shifted to second gear and honked the horn twice. They were on their way at last.

Turning right at the hotel, Harry again tapped the horn twice in response to the manager, who was waving vigorously.

Buzz wondered if they were waving goodbye or good riddance.

They were in third gear now, and traveling about thirty miles an hour down a fairly smooth road.

"We'll meet the convoy at Jalalabad. The British army will check our cargo against our manifest and make sure all vehicles have sound tires and are in good running order. They don't want any delays due to breakdowns; things are a little touchy in Afghanistan right now. Amanullah Khan, their leader, wants to be European in that he wants better education for his people and emancipation for women. His proposals caused his popular support to erode and totally enraged the Muslim religious leaders," Harry explained.

"Do you think we'll run into any trouble?" Buzz asked.

We have a British escort through the Pass, so once we get off the road to Kabul at Jalalabad and head north, we should be all right," Harry replied.

After driving for about a half-hour, the trio came to an intersection where a line of ten vehicles of various types was waiting. They pulled into the last place in line, apparently completing the convoy of eleven—excluding the military personnel who were to accompany them.

A sergeant approached the truck. "Oh, Mr. Whitecliff. Welcome, sir. Do you have anything that's not listed?"

"Yes, sergeant. I just noticed that I have an item that I forgot to declare on my manifest. Would you dispose of it for me?" Harry asked seriously. "I wouldn't want there to be any problems."

"That's very good of you, sir. We wouldn't want anything illegal going through the Pass." The sergeant accepted a bottle of twelve-year-old Scotch from Harry, and then stamped his papers and said, "You're good to go, Mr. Whitecliff."

Buzz grinned and said nothing.

Who is this Harry Whitecliff, and what is he? Buzz wondered. *Why would he need the silent-running exhaust system he has installed under this truck? Right now, he's using the standard system, but all he has to do is flip a switch. And the auxiliary gas tanks, too. Well, there's something strange going on; I wonder what I've gotten myself into. I guess I'll find out when Harry's ready to talk. Meanwhile, I'll go along for the ride and keep my eyes open.*

"Here we go," Harry announced, interrupting Buzz's musings.

The line of vehicles began to move forward, and soon it was their turn. Four motorcycles roared by, two on either side of the roadway, driven by Indian soldiers with rifles strapped across their backs. A military car bearing a Vickers machine gun mounted on a crossbar in the middle of the vehicle pulled into the line behind them, occupied by three Indian soldiers and the smiling recipient of the 'unmanifested' bottle of Scotch.

"What do you know about the Khaibar Pass, Buzz?" Harry asked.

"Practically nothing. I've seen Lady Elizabeth Butler's painting of Dr. William Brydon, the sole survivor of the massacre in 1842, and wondered what it was all about."

"Well, it's a long and rather involved story, but it is important to understand the history of the Pass in order to understand the current problems. So get as comfortable as you can; I'll put on my professor hat, and class will begin."

Harry paused, collecting his thoughts, took a deep breath, and began. "The Khaibar Pass has been coveted by and fought over by the Persians, Greeks, Mongols, Russians, Afghans, and the British for literally centuries. It is the key point for controlling the Afghan border and passage between the East and the West. Regarding your question after seeing the painting of Dr. Brydon—the first Anglo-Afghan War lasted from 1838 to 1842, and was turning sour for the British by 1841.

"The British commander, General Elphinstone, reached an agreement with Mohammad Akbar Khan which provided for the safe exodus of the British garrison and its dependents from Afghanistan. In January of 1842, the column of more than 16,000—4,500 military personnel, both British and Indian, and as many as 12,000 camp followers—began their journey to what they thought was safety. As they struggled through the snow in the Pass, the Ghilzai warriors attacked them. From behind rocks and the ledges along the steep walls of the thirty-mile long pass, the so-called 'warriors' massacred nearly all of them. Three quarters of them were civilians, mostly unarmed women and children."

The next several miles were traveled in silence, as if to pay tribute to the fallen. Buzz was thinking how horrible it must have been to see your husband or father shot down before your eyes, or to stumble over your wife with your child in her arms lying in the snow stained red with their blood. What a ghastly waste!

After some time had passed, Buzz asked, "Who owns the Pass now?"

"I'm not sure anyone owns the Pass, but the Treaty of Gandamak, which was signed in 1879, left the Pass and its occupying clans—the Pashtun, Afridi, and some others—under British control. The British are now responsible for the safety of the Pass."

He continued, "The Pass is about thirty-three miles long, from Jamrud, India, to just beyond the old Afghan fort of Haft Chah, where it opens onto the Lowyah Dakkah plain, which stretches to the Kabul River. Going from its northern entrance, the Pass gradually rises to Fort Ali Masjid, where the Khaibar River leaves the Pass to the south. For five miles from Ali Masjid, the Pass becomes a canyon not more than 600 feet wide, flanked by steep walls anywhere from 600 to 1000 feet high. North from Zintara village, the Pass becomes a valley a mile or more wide, with forts, villages, and cultivated fields. About ten miles west of Ali Masjid, lays Landi Kotal Fort and cantonment. This is the highest point in the pass, about 3500 feet, and it's very important as a market center and as an alternate route to Peshawar. There, the summit widens out northward for a couple of miles. The main pass, though, goes down from Landi Kotal to Landi Khana, where it runs through another gorge and enters Afghanistan territory at Towr Kham and winds another ten miles down the valley to Low Yah Dakkah. It has a caravan track, a hard-surface road for trucks and cars, and the British opened a railway in 1925. That has 34 tunnels and 94 bridges and culverts. And that's the Khaibar Pass!

"Whew! I hope I didn't bore you," Harry remarked, taking a deep breath and exhaling noisily. "It's been a while since I've given that lecture."

"No, no, professor," Buzz chuckled, "you did well. But this is so different from what I expected. I'd assumed the Khaibar Pass was a narrow canyon, but this is a lot like some of the valleys near my home in New Mexico. The rocky terrain, the clumps of grass here and there, the sparse, shrub-type trees; even the grayish-brown color. It makes me kind of homesick."

Buzz continued, "What does Khaibar mean, Harry?"

"It means across the river, or divide," was Harry's reply.

As the road curved sharply around a rock outcropping, Harry veered close to a cleft in the rock, removed a small packet from his shirt pocket, and tossed it into the opening.

"Another old custom for good luck?" grinned Buzz.

Harry was silent.

Kim spoke up. "Sirs, would you like some tea?"

"I think someone is hungry. Kim, will you serve up the tea and cakes, please?" Harry requested.

As Kim handed him a light blue enamel cup of steaming tea, a high-pitched shriek startled Buzz, nearly causing him to spill the hot liquid in his lap.

"That's the whistle for the Khaibar Express," Harry commented. He followed the example of the convoyed vehicles in front of him and applied the brakes, then geared down to a full stop. The signals flashed brightly as they waited for the train to pass.

"I think this would be a good time to eat," Harry said. "We may be here a while—until the train goes through the crossing ahead of us."

Watching the passenger cars go by, Buzz thought longingly of someone he'd met just yesterday. Somehow, with everything that had happened since, it seemed like a long time ago. *Could she be on that train?* he wondered. *Will I ever see her again?*

A nudge from Little Kim interrupted his reverie.

"Oh. Thank you," said Buzz, taking one of the cakes. When he bit into it, his mouth was filled with unexpected flavors. The cake had the texture and flavor of corn bread, or perhaps an English muffin, but was filled with cheese. The tea was equally exotic and delicious. Sipping the tea sent his taste buds scrambling again, to try to identify the magnificent flavor. It seemed to be a black tea, with strong overtones of mint, and maybe a hint of apple.

"This is really good!" Buzz exclaimed.

"I thought you'd like it," Harry remarked, smiling. "Well, here we go again." Harry quickly finished his last bite and slowly let out the clutch; the convoy slowly moved on.

Not much was said for the next few miles. Buzz daydreamed of New Mexico and Kim; Little Kim admired his fine new dagger—and Harry? Well, Harry thought about whatever someone like Harry thinks about.

~ Chapter Five ~

THE DECISION

They stopped to unload some boxes at a trade center on the outskirts of Jalalabad. Buzz and Little Kim stayed near the truck but took the opportunity to stretch their legs, while Harry took care of the paperwork and picked up food for the remainder of their journey.

"Let's load up, boys! We have a long way to go, and it's already past noon!" Harry cried.

"Where do we go from here?" Buzz questioned as he climbed into the cab and closed the door.

"From here, we head north on the road to the old lapis lazuli mines; they're some of the oldest in the area. Lapis is a semi-precious stone that has been mined there for more than four-hundred years. After a hundred miles or so, we turn off and head west through Khawak, then we turn southeast along the Paghman Mountains to the Bahmian Valley," Harry replied, deepening his voice and gesturing as though he were a tour guide.

"I'm glad I asked—I think!" Buzz said, grinning.

They pulled away from the loading docks and drove west on the road to Kabul for about half a mile, and then turned right, heading north. Buzz again thought of New Mexico as he gazed out over the plains toward the mountains. The tall trees from the foothills to the tree line and the snow-capped peaks rising above them were evocative, and he realized ruefully that he was rather homesick.

"Oh, look!" Buzz blurted excitedly, pointing to a small herd of gazelles running and leaping across a gully.

"They look like they're on springs, the way they bounce," Kim said, wide-eyed.

"Look at the horns on the one in the front! He must be the leader!" called Harry.

51

"They remind me of the antelope at home, only the gazelles' horns are longer," Buzz commented.

Harry soon said, "Kim, why don't you serve up some lunch? I bought cheese, bread, cold tea, and pistachios, and I had our thermos filled with hot coffee." He turned to Kim. "Oh yes, I also got some candy and sweet-water for you."

"Thank you Mr. Whitecliff," Kim replied gratefully.

"Pistachio nuts, cheese, hot coffee! Some of my favorite foods! Thank you, Mr. Whitecliff," Buzz echoed gleefully. "Little Kim, why don't you make use of that fine new blade of yours to slice up some bread and cheese and put together some sandwiches for us. I'll pour the drinks. Coffee, or tea, Harry?"

"I believe I'll have coffee, while it's still hot. Thank you."

"Little Kim, what'll you have?"

"I have my sweet-water, Mr. Buzz."

Kim handed Buzz and then Harry a cheese sandwich. Harry placed his atop the dash, on the linen Bess had wrapped around their morning cakes, while he steered and drank his coffee. Buzz took his sandwich in his right hand and his coffee in his left. Kim wrapped both hands around his sandwich, and held his bottle of sweet-water between his knees.

They ate in companionable silence, each lost in his own thoughts. Buzz was thinking of 'his' Kim, as well as what he might be getting himself into; Kim was remembering his family; and Harry wondered how to best answer Buzz's many questions, both spoken and implied.

Buzz broke the silence long enough to compliment Kim on the sandwiches. "You make a good sandwich, Little Kim—thick on the cheese, thin on the bread."

"Thank you, Mr. Buzz."

The quiet resumed, disturbed only by the rumbling of the truck as it traveled the velvet-smooth gravel road. Buzz could see the dust swirling behind them in the side-view mirror. It reminded him of the smoke snaking behind the train as it had carried Kim away from him into the darkness. He wondered, *"Will I ever see her again?"* Interrupting his reveries, Buzz noted, "This road seems to be smoother than the road we were on to Kabul. Is it because it's not used as much?"

Harry replied, "Well, it's seldom used and it has good drainage. Gentlemen, there are three shrubs up ahead that look to me to be in dire need of moisture. May I suggest we each bestow upon them our windfall of coffee and sweet-water, so to speak?"

He eased the truck to the side of the road and stopped near the bushes. Each chose a parched shrub to which he delivered his gift of life, after which they strolled, relieved, back to the shade of the truck.

"Kim, I think this would be a good time to review your lessons, don't you?" Harry inquired as he sat down on the running board of the truck.

"Yes sir," agreed Kim, and lowered himself to a cross-legged position directly in front of Harry.

Buzz sat on a rock some ten feet away, where he could observe the lesson in spelling or math without distracting Kim. The situation reminded him of his mother schooling him in the open air.

"Kim, I want you to describe what you saw when we got out of the truck. Now—no looking back, keep looking at me. I want you to tell me everything you think is of importance," Harry instructed Kim with a stern look.

"Well, sir, there are tracks of a truck stopping here about four days ago, judging by the wind erosion of the tire tracks. There are the tracks of a man wearing European boots. He walked from the road to the shrubs, and met a man coming from the mountains to the east, who was wearing worn English army boots."

"And?" Harry probed.

"This is probably used as a meeting place, because there is no cover for at least two-hundred yards in all directions except for the three shrubs. There isn't any place for ambush or eavesdropping. Also, this is the first place like this I've seen since we turned onto this road. Everywhere else had small trees, clump grass, shrubs, or ravines that someone could hide in."

"What else?"

"The wind is coming from the east at about five to ten miles per hour with a coolness that could mean a sudden drop in temperature. It could be a forewarning of rain by tonight."

"Is that all?"

"Well, no sir, but I..." Kim's voice trailed off as he nodded toward Buzz.

"It's all right. He's one of us," Harry reassured Kim.

"Well, I saw what looked like the reflection of the sun off binoculars in the foothills due east of us, at the tree line where the two hills form a *V*—the two hills that are in line with us here, and the three shrubs." With that, Kim leaned back with a sigh.

"Very good, Kim. You missed the cigarette stub by the small rock where the two men met, though. It looked to be Turkish," Harry gently reprimanded, one eyebrow raised.

"Oh! I'm sorry, sir."

"Be more careful next time; something like that could be very important. Now let's get back in the truck and be on our way; it's getting late. Kim, I'd like you to ride in the back. I had a mat fitted up for you, and you can open one of the side flaps so you can see out. Buzz wants to talk, I imagine."

"Yes, Mr. Whitecliff." Kim gathered up his bottle of sweet-water and bag of candy, and scurried into the back of the truck. Buzz helped him fold back a corner of the canvas tarp and tied it into place. Kim smiled at Buzz and gave him a long, slow wink. Buzz grinned and winked in return, and then climbed into the cab and slammed the door. Their journey continued.

"What was all that about back there? When you said let's review your lessons, I assumed it would be regular school stuff. That sounded more like cloak and dagger. Good Lord, man, that's just a small boy. What are you trying to make out of him?"

"That small boy has already killed two men and is hunting a third." Harry saw the amazement on Buzz's face as he continued. "Kim's real name is David, and his father was an army physician—retired—who married a beautiful Indian woman from a highly influential family. About four months ago, the three of them and their driver, Sabu, were on their way to a mission in Northern Afghanistan when they were waylaid by three men in black."

"The Shadow Men," muttered Buzz.

"Yes, the Shadow Men. They shot the driver and Kim's parents for no apparent reason, with no warning. Kim was asleep under some blankets and, thankfully, was overlooked. From his place of concealment, he saw them take his mother's locket and his father's ring and ivory-handled service revolver as souvenirs. Kim watched them ride away at a trot, as though they knew the bodies wouldn't be discovered for some time.

"It was getting dark when he crawled out from his hiding place, and his sorrow turned to anger as he covered the bodies with blankets and poured petrol around the car from the spare can in the boot. He hoped the smell would deter the jackals and hyenas.

"As the sun slipped behind the mountains, Kim could see the glow of a campfire in the direction the three men had gone—about a mile away. It could have been a goat herder, but it could also be the three making camp for the night. Not knowing which, Kim unpacked his .310 BSA rifle he used at military school and a handful of cartridges. His father had let him bring it to hunt rabbits, but he was hunting bigger game now.

"When he reached the camp, he could see it was the three who had murdered his father and mother and his friend, Sabu. He remembered hearing soldiers say they would hollow out the tips of their bullets to make them expand when they hit and do more damage. Using his penknife, he made six dum-dum bullets, as the soldiers called them.

"One man was tending to the horses, and the other two were sitting by the fire. When one stood up to replenish the fire, Kim shot him in the midsection; the other jumped up and was shot in the chest, knocking him over backwards. The third man leaped on his horse and fled into the darkness. The first man was holding his stomach, trying to reach his horse, when another bullet struck his right leg, taking him down, just a few feet from the horses. Kim levered another shell into the rifle and walked into the firelight. The two wounded men were astounded to see just a small boy emerging from the night, and not a score of men. Kim retrieved the locket and ring at gunpoint, hung their rifles from the saddles, and took a water bag from one of the horses. He passed the two men, who had their hands outstretched, thinking the water was for them.

He slowly poured the water on the fire, extinguishing it, leaving only the slight glow of the now rising moon. Kim mounted one of the horses, and leading the other, rode away, listening to the screams of the two men who realized what he had done; jackals are afraid of fire.

"He rode through the gates of the Franciscan mission after midnight and told his story to Father Sebastian, the presiding abbot. Only then did he collapse, sobbing, into the father's arms."

"The poor kid! How did you come by him, Harry?"

"Kim was put into my care for several reasons. One, his father and I were close. Two, he tried several times to run away from his home and people in India."

"Run away from home! Why?" Buzz asked.

"David—or rather 'Kim,' the name he wishes to go by now—wanted to come back to Afghanistan to find the third assassin."

"The one who took his father's ivory-handled revolver," Buzz said flatly.

"Yes, that's the one. Apparently he was the leader. And the third reason that he's with me is that I can teach him how to survive while keeping an eye on him until he gets over this obsession. Oh, yes—there's a price on his head. Not much, but enough that a greedy person might turn him over to the Shadow Men.

"Who the devil are these Shadow Men—some kind of religious fanatics?" Buzz demanded.

"They hide under the guise of religion. Though they say they work under the shadow of God, that's just a cover. They're nothing but glorified bandits. They're no more Muslim than I am. Since this revolt is between the tribes and Amanullah Khan, everything around Kabul has been thrown into chaos. One side or the other has forcibly taken most of the tribes' fighting age men, leaving the small camps and villages in the north virtually undefended.

"The Shadow Men are mercenaries from Russia, China, India, Tibet, Persia, Afghanistan, and Germany. It's the Germans who concern us at this time. We think they're the instigators and supporters of the Shadow Men, because much of their equipment is of German origin and most of their leaders are German. We think there's more to this than just plunder, although that probably helps pay the bills. But there must be another reason, too, because it's too well organized to be just a bunch of bandits."

"What's this 'we' stuff? You keep referring to 'we' and 'us.' Who are the good guys?" Buzz asked impatiently.

"Oh, some of the tribal heads. And me, naturally, because of my business," Harry answered carefully.

"I suppose British intelligence doesn't give a hoot what goes on here," Buzz said with a tongue-in-cheek smirk. "And I'm sure someone who has death-gripping battles in dark alleys, breezes through border checkpoints, drives a truck identified by a broken egg on the roof and is rigged to run silently for long distances, who leaves little packages behind rocks under shrubs out in the middle of nowhere—and I don't think those packages contain 'Grandma's Christmas pudding'—no, I'm sure that person has absolutely nothing to do with British intelligence." Buzz looked at Harry from the corner of his eye. Harry, although looking straight ahead in total silence, grinned like a little boy who's gotten caught with his hand in the cookie jar.

They drove a few miles without speaking, then Harry noticed Buzz lighting his pipe again. "There are some matches in the bag. I guessed you would run out soon, so I picked up a half-dozen boxes when I bought the food," Harry noted. "The way you keep relighting your pipe, I figured you would need some."

"Thank you. I usually smoke cigars, but I thought I'd try a pipe for a change. I don't seem to be able to keep the darn thing lit."

"Young ladies seem to prefer the aroma of a pipe to the odor of a cigar. Like perhaps a young lady on the train?"

"How'd you know?" Buzz blurted with a surprised look.

"There are two things that change a man's smoking habits—his health or a woman. You're too young for health reasons, so it must be a woman. And the way you watched the train leave the station, I assumed she was on it."

"Well, you assumed right. We met on the train and talked for hours, but I don't know much about her—except that her family owns a shipping line in France and she came to Afghanistan for some kind of pilgrimage at some mission with her aunt and uncle."

"Oh, the Smiths!" Harry surmised.

"You know them?" Buzz exclaimed.

"I met them briefly last year at the San Rafael Mission when I was doing some trout fishing in a nearby stream. Father Sebastian introduced us. Nice people. The mission is only sixty miles or so from the aerodrome."

"That's not so far. Maybe I could stop in for a chat sometime if I've nothing else to do," Buzz said nonchalantly while hoping Harry couldn't hear his heart pounding. Then he switched the topic, asking Harry, "Just what is this job that you have in mind for me? I'm beginning to think it isn't just putting a plane together and teaching someone to fly it."

"Well, we do have a more important mission in mind for you than just fixing an airplane."

"What? Besides, you don't know anything about me!" Buzz replied, somewhat aggravated.

"Let's see," Harry began. "Your father was a fine gunsmith and your mother was an opera singer, but lost her singing voice due to illness; she died two years before your father, who was murdered. You were rushed into military service by your neighbors so there wouldn't be any immediate repercussions. In France, you were at the front for a short time, where you rescued a wounded messenger dog by crawling out to it—under fire—and dragged it back to safety. The dog died, but the message it carried was vital to our side.

"You were transferred to the Air Service where you were assigned to the ground crew, but flew as an aerial photographer. You not only took the photos, you worked in the darkroom. Because you did extra duty for the pilots, they taught you to fly. After the war, you joined the circus, became a stunt-flyer as well as a knife thrower and sharpshooter, just to name a few things. You enjoy the opera, and are invited to most of the après-opera affairs where you have become acquainted with many of the high society people. You also know your way around the lower rungs of society, such as the roustabouts and the pickpockets.

"During the fire at the circus, you kept a cool head, saving much of the canvas structures, and prevented a worse disaster by rolling the powder wagon into the pond. Yes, you had help from your friends Boris and Bob, but it was through your quick thinking that it was done. And now you're here. I could give more details, but I really don't think they're necessary."

"Wow! Okay you know quite a bit about me. But what's this so-called mission you brought me here for?" Buzz asked again.

"There's trouble rumbling in Europe. Mussolini is building up Italy's army—and its navy, too. There's a new political party developing in Germany that's pushing for an arms buildup beyond what the Treaty of Versailles permits. And Japan's warlords are sharpening their sabers. We think the Germans are doing something here, but we don't know what, and that's why we sent for you. You're known only as a stunt flyer, a circus person."

"So I won't be taken seriously," Buzz stated dryly.

"Exactly!"

"Again, I ask, why me?"

"We need someone to do more than fly around taking pictures."

"Taking pictures?" Buzz interrupted as he unwrapped the cheese and cut himself a good- sized slice.

"Cut me some, while you're at it, please," Harry requested, glancing at the delicate operation Buzz was performing while using the dash as a table.

"I have a complete darkroom, with trays, chemicals, film, paper, and a Kodak camera in a crate in the back. We need someone who can take and interpret photos, someone who can organize the tribes to repel these bandits—perhaps even lead them. That's why I picked you, Buzz."

"Damn, Harry! What makes you think I can do all that?"

"Last night you could have run for help or to find a weapon. Instead you improvised and charged to my aid with buckets of sand, of all things. You didn't wait for someone to tell you what to do—you just did it. You saved my life, Buzz. I'll never forget that," Harry said, his face solemn. Then he announced,

"The aerodrome is just over this hill." He stretched back into the seat with a sound somewhere between a sigh and a groan. He chuckled wearily. "I don't know which are heaviest—my arms or my eyelids."

~ Chapter Six ~

THE AERODROME

A s the truck crested the top of the hill and began its descent into a valley about a half-mile long, and perhaps half as wide, the sun was rapidly sinking behind the mountains, hurrying to the west, selfishly dragging the last rays of light with it.

Midway into the valley, Buzz could barely make out the varying hues of dark-blue-shadowed outlines of buildings in the distance. The scene resembled bombed-out villages he'd seen during the war. By the time they reached the valley's floor, the sun had gathered its remaining rays and fully disappeared. The truck's headlamps lit only a narrow corridor through the night. A rabbit leaped confusedly into their path, zigzagged to and fro, and then quickly fled into the darkness and safety.

The road seemed bumpier, but it may have been only that the roughness of the ride was no longer softened by conversation.

At the farthest reach of the lights, a jackal stopped momentarily and watched their approach. Then, with a look of disgust on his ugly face for their encroachment on his territory, he faded, wraith-like, into the covering shadows.

Buzz thought they must be approaching the aerodrome. The truck's lights revealed an old oil drum, a tire leaning against a pole, and the front half of a truck similar to the one in which they were riding with flat tires and a missing hood. A strange, large shape at the fringe of the light caught Buzz's interest.

Just then, the headlights swerved sharply to the right and came to rest on a small structure. The truck came to a halt, and the evening quiet engulfed them.

"This is it, gentlemen! This will be our home for the next few days," Harry announced, and then called, "Kim."

"I'm awake, sir!" came the immediate reply.

As Harry disembarked, he slung his rifle over his left shoulder, and Buzz followed his example.

The building they faced was about twenty feet wide, made of wood that had been painted a dull gray (or had perhaps naturally weathered through the years of wind, sand, and sun.) It stood on stone pillars a foot or so off the ground. A three-foot-wide door bearing a massive padlock occupied the center of the front wall, flanked by single, broken windows. A small porch with two upright posts supporting the slanting roof gave a tenuous warmth to the otherwise cold, bleak edifice.

When the trio stepped onto the stairs up to the porch, the old wood creaked and groaned like an old man being awakened from a long, deep sleep. Harry inserted a large key into the lock; the resulting snap as the shackle opened was startlingly loud. The door slowly swung open, screeching like an untuned violin. At the same instant, they felt a cold wind blowing across their faces. Something was blown or flew in front of the truck's lights, causing a fluttering shadow. Then there was a flash of lightning and a crack of thunder.

"Spooky!" Kim barely breathed.

"Yeah," Buzz agreed just as quietly.

Harry broke the spell, announcing emphatically, "We need to get some light in here to save the truck's battery."

To the right of the doorway was a small table under the window, on which rested two kerosene lamps. Harry lit both of them, leaving one on the table to illuminate the room and the way to the truck; the other lantern he hung inside the canvas enclosure of the vehicle.

"I think it would be best to sleep in the truck tonight. It looks like a nasty storm is brewing," Harry suggested.

Noticing the large holes in the roof and the stars that were being blotted out by the rapidly approaching clouds, Buzz hurriedly agreed.

Following Harry's instructions, Kim pushed certain boxes to the end of the truck bed, and Buzz and Harry stacked them inside the building. After unpacking about half of the cargo, they had exposed enough room to set up three cots. Buzz covered the boxes and parcels they'd placed inside the building with a large tarp to protect them from the burgeoning storm.

When Buzz had nearly completed the job to his satisfaction, he noticed a reflection of the lamplight off two pieces of broken glass in the far corner of the dock and was amazed by how much they resembled two large eyes. Then the reflections blinked twice at him and disappeared. He quickly decided the boxes were covered well enough, picked up the lantern, closed the door behind him, and stepped with purposeful alacrity to the truck.

Just as he climbed in and pulled the tarp closed, thunder cracked and the rain poured down. It was as though someone had turned on a large tap. "Looks like we finished just in time," Harry observed.

"Damn! Does it rain here every night?" Buzz asked.

"Not every night, but this is the rainy season. It shouldn't cause any problems; the ground dries quickly."

The truck began to rock gently with the wind, and the rain beating on the canvas cover created such a roar that Buzz barely heard Kim telling him that his cot was ready.

As soon as Buzz removed his boots, it seemed as though all the strength flowed from his body. With his last remaining bit of energy, he lay down and pulled the covers up to his shoulders. The din of the storm drowned out any thoughts of the last two days, dragging him into a deep, uncomprehending sleep.

——— ———

"Mr. Buzz! Mr. Buzz!"

Kim was calling his name while gently shaking his shoulder with one hand. The other hand held a scalding-hot cup of coffee.

"Good morning, Little Kim, and bless you," Buzz said gratefully as he took the coffee from Kim. "Oooh, that's good! Truly the nectar of the Gods! The elixir of life! What time is it?"

Grinning, Kim told him.

"Quarter after ten! Holy cow, I didn't mean to sleep this late! What time did you fellows get up?"

"Oh, we've been up since about seven, but Mr. Whitecliff wanted you to sleep as long as you needed. That's why he had me set up your cot back here—so we wouldn't wake you."

"Well, I appreciate that. I'm up!"

"Yes, sir. Mr. Whitecliff said to tell you that breakfast is nearly ready."

"Okay. Tell him I'll be right there."

One side of the tarp across the back of the truck had been tied back, allowing the warm sunlight to penetrate the otherwise dark compartment. As Buzz laced up his boots, he could see the mountains across an airfield checkered with clump grass. A gentle breeze bent the tops of the grass and lifted a light haze of dust; the moisture from last night's rain had already disappeared.

Jumping down from the truck bed, Buzz squinted in the bright sun and looked around to identify that large shape he'd noticed the night before. *Aha! That's what it is!* Buzz thought. *It's a steam roller. The Brits must have brought it here to roll out the airstrip. I'll bet Calliope Bob would love to play with that!*

Laughing quietly, he heard Harry call, "Breakfast's on the table!"

Buzz leaped over the two steps and onto the porch, entered the building, and halted, stunned. "Wow!"

The floor had been swept. A four-foot square table Buzz hadn't seen the previous night was set up in the center of the room. The table was set for three, with military-type place settings and military precision. There were tin plates, large, sturdy knives, forks, and spoons. The spoons looked as though, if the need arose, they could be used to dig foxholes. Kim was pouring coffee from a pot that looked to have been used as a weapon in some war or other; the cups were the ones from the truck.

The mantle over the fireplace had been dusted and was now adorned with the two lanterns, one on either end. In the center was a bottle that had at one time contained a good Scotch whiskey; now it held red, yellow, and orange wildflowers, neatly arranged. On the wall above the fireplace hung an airplane propeller. The lingering dust particles glimmered in the sun's rays shining through the openings in the roof. Buzz figured that there must have been quite a cloud raised during the attack by broom and dust cloth.

Harry was standing over a gasoline stove, wearing a hastily fashioned dust cap and apron, tending something in a large frying pan.

He jabbed meat of some kind with a large fork, causing it to spatter and hiss, releasing a mouthwatering aroma into the morning air.

"Darn, Harry! You'll make someone a good wife!" Buzz joked.

"Oh, go on! I'll bet you say that to all the pretty girls," Harry replied in a simpering falsetto as he spread his apron with one hand and waved the fork in a girlish way.

"The two of you have done wonders while I slept. And thank you for that extra sleep, too. I didn't realize how tired I was until I laid down," Buzz said, seating himself at the table.

"We thought you could use some rest after your long journey," Kim replied proudly, scooting his chair to the table. Harry placed the frying pan in the center of the table and, sitting down, remarked, "I think that after the last few days, a silent prayer is in order." The three heads bowed, each giving thanks in his own way.

When they had raised their heads and taken their utensils in hand, Harry spoke. "I'm going to have to leave you two to fend for yourself for a couple of days while I visit some of the tribal camps in the area to set up a meeting of their leaders. You should find just about everything you need in the crates; I'll see if I can bring back a dozen or so chickens."

As he accepted the bread Harry passed to him and in turn gave some to Kim, Buzz enthused, "Yeah, fresh eggs and bacon would be good!"

"Don't get your hopes up for bacon. The people here are of Muslim beliefs, and they don't eat pork," Harry reminded him.

"Oh! That's right! Well, what is this marvelous concoction that Mrs. Whitecliff cooked up this morning?" Buzz asked as he transferred some of the food from the frying pan to his plate.

"Diced potatoes, cured goat meat, and of course, my special secret seasonings," Harry replied, pleased.

"This really is delicious," Buzz acknowledged, chewing thoughtfully. "What are your special seasonings? Come on, you can tell us. We won't give it away."

Harry leaned over the table after looking around the room as if to establish that he could not be overheard divulging top secret plans, and beckoned his two companions conspirationally nearer. He spoke in a stage whisper. "Well, I splash in a little coffee and add a few drops of lemon juice—gives it that extra little 'bite,' you see. You can add cheese and onions or garlic, too. It depends on my mood and what happens to be on hand."

"Well, whatever you did, it sure is good," Buzz whispered back.

They laughed, enjoying themselves and their meal.

"Little Kim and I will see what we can do about fixing up our living quarters while you're gone. What about water? Is there any around here?" Buzz asked. "I can't imagine the Army putting an aerodrome in a dry hole—at least, I hope not."

"I'm told there's a well here someplace, but for your immediate needs there are two five-gallon cans of water by the porch," Harry answered.

They continued eating with the usual chitchat. "How did you sleep?" "Do you think it will rain before nightfall?" and other small talk to fill the silence. At the same time, Buzz was wondering how he would fix the roof, Harry was musing on his upcoming meetings, and Kim was pondering how he could politely ask for the last bit of hash without seeming greedy. When they'd finished their meal, Kim cleared the table while Buzz helped Harry load his personal gear into the truck.

The two men shook hands and Harry clambered into the cab and started the engine. Leaning out the window, he quietly spoke a few words of caution. "Never venture far from your weapons and cover." And with that, he backed the truck onto the road, saluted, and drove off in the direction from which they had come. Kim was boiling water for the dishes, which were stacked neatly in a dishpan that seemed to be from the same war as the coffee pot.

"How about if I wash and you dry?" Buzz asked.

"That sounds good to me, sir," Kim answered quickly, grateful that his work would be cut in half.

With the kitchen work finished, Buzz slung his rifle over his shoulder and grabbed a hot cup of coffee. Kim opened the door and, with an exaggerated bow, ushered Buzz out to lead their expedition to find roofing material. Buzz thrust his cup outward, as though it was a sword, and they marched in step.

Once outside, the troop of two found sheets of metal roofing scattered around the perimeter of the grounds.

"Hey, Little Kim, we're in luck! Looks like the wind just blew the roof off, and I think it's all here. Some pieces are bent a little, but we can straighten them out—all we'll have to do is nail them back on."

"There's a box with some tools in it. I think I saw a package of nails in it, too, sir."

"Good. You get the tools and some nails, while I gather up the tin. It looks like I can just stack it up against the building and pull each sheet up as I need it."

"What can I do, sir?"

"Why don't you scout around and look for some glass to replace the broken panes, and some wood to patch the hole in the wall. We need to keep the rain and the critters out, as much as we can."

"Yes, sir!"

As Kim scurried around the corner of the building, Buzz noticed his bare feet. "If you have boots or shoes, put them on. There's a lot of broken glass and nails lying around here," Buzz called.

"Yes, sir. I will, sir," came a muffled reply from inside.

As Buzz adjusted the rifle, he remembered Harry's parting admonition. Carrying this rifle up and down a ladder and working on the roof would be awkward, so he figured it was time to strap on his Webleys.

As he entered the building, Kim was pulling on his boots. "I'm hurrying, sir."

"Oh, you're fine. I just came in for my pistols. In fact"—Buzz paused for a moment, seeing the Star automatic lying next to the Webleys. "Have you ever shot a pistol, Little Kim?"

"Yes, sir. I shot my father's revolver many times!"

"Well, this is an automatic. You just pull the hammer back and pull the trigger. This lever on the side is the safety. I'll show you more about the gun later so you'll know how to care for it."

Kim eagerly threaded his sash through the holster loops and proudly slipped the Star into it.

"Now, don't shoot that unless you have to! It's not a toy!" Buzz cautioned seriously.

"Yes, sir! I understand, sir," Kim replied quickly, snapping to attention and giving a smart salute, his eyes beaming with pride.

Buzz adjusted his shoulder holsters and picked up the hammer and nails that Kim had placed on the table. "I'll take these while you look for the glass."

"Yes, sir."

As they went out, Buzz carefully placed the rifle just inside the door, where it would be easily accessible if needed.

Kim was out of sight before Buzz even stepped off the porch. He envied the little soldier being the first to explore, but decent shelter had to come first. His own exploration of the aerodrome would have to wait. Buzz estimated that eight sheets of roofing had been blown off the building and, while standing atop a large boulder behind the structure, could see seven sheets scattered within a fifty-foot radius.

Before climbing down, he surveyed the surrounding area. About ten feet from their building stood another the same width, but perhaps twenty feet longer; another of the same dimensions stood next to that one. There were also the remains of a large structure that had been partially destroyed by fire. Buzz figured that was the hangar; the Brits must have set fire to it as they vacated the site. A windmill stood about thirty feet behind the building next to theirs, swaying gently in the wind—but the vanes weren't rotating. Since there was a large water tank on a platform beside it, he assumed the well was there and that the small building next to the water tank was probably the shower.

As he jumped down from his perch, he saw a ladder against the building next door. "Good! This won't take as long as I thought," he muttered. "I might be able to have this done by lunchtime!"

After the better part of two hours had passed, Buzz drove the last nail into the seventh sheet of tin roofing, sat on the peak, and admired his handiwork. It looked good except for the gaping hole on the end that was still waiting for the missing eighth sheet. "Maybe I'll find Little Kim, and he can help me find that last piece of tin. We might even have this done by lunch—if we have a late lunch." He laughed to himself with satisfaction. "I wish I had some tar to seal the seams."

"Yeoww!"

It was Little Kim!

POW!! POW!! —POW!! POW!!

"Little Kim! Little Kim!" Buzz yelled as he slid rapidly down the ladder, clamping his feet on the outside of the uprights. He ran onto the airfield. The row of buildings was eerily quiet, except for the rustling of the wind. "Little Kim! Little Kim! Where are you?" he yelled again, on the verge of panic.

"In here!" came the answering call from the second building. Buzz raced toward the structure with guns drawn, leaped onto the porch, and kicked the door open. It slammed against the wall, spraying shattered glass across the room. He dashed in a few steps and paused in a half-crouch, guns ready, his blazing eyes scouring the room for whatever it was that might hurt Kim.

"I'm all right, sir!"

Buzz looked toward the little voice. Kim was standing against a post in the center of the room, the pistol still smoking in his right hand and his new dagger in his left.

"Cobras," he said, nodding toward three outstretched bodies, one of which was still twisting in its death throes. The boy was pasty-faced, gasping, in deep quivering breaths, shaking violently. Suddenly, he dropped his weapons and ran to Buzz, who dropped to his knees and caught the shaken boy in his arms. "Thank God you're all right—thank God you're all right!"

Kim wrapped his arms around Buzz's neck and broke into uncontrollable sobs. "Let it out, Kim, let it all out," Buzz soothed, holding him closer and stroking his hair gently.

They stayed clenched in each other's arms for what seemed like an eternity, yet an instant. After a while, Kim released his grip from Buzz's neck and began to wipe his tears from Buzz's leather coat with the sleeve of his jacket. "I'm sorry, sir," he said, embarrassed.

"For what?"

"For crying."

"Don't be! It's good for a man to cry once in a while; it helps cleanse the soul. I've seen men cry before, during, and after battle. I cried when my father and mother died, and I've cried at other times, too."

"Really? You cry?" Kim was astounded.

"Sure. It's not good to keep things locked inside; that does things to a man. Sometimes holding everything in will make him mean. It does a person good to talk to someone or just cry once in a while. Now tell me what happened!"

"Well, after I found some glass panes that had fallen out of one of the windows in the back of this building, I thought I would look around."

"What did you do with the glass?"

"I put it over there," Kim said, pointed to several pieces of glass neatly stacked by the wall, next to the door. "I guess I'll have to find some more," he remarked, referring to the shards scattered across the room from Buzz's precipitous entry.

"No; I think we'll just board it up," Buzz returned sheepishly. Kim grinned. "Now, back to your story! What happened?"

"Well, I started to move those boxes over there," he explained, pointing to several wooden crates in the corner near the dead cobras. "That big one struck at me, but he didn't bite me—he just tore my jacket. I shot him. Then the other two started to crawl toward me, so I shot them. I missed on the second shot."

Buzz examined the carcasses; all three had been shot in the head. "That's still some good shooting, Kim!"

"Thank you. My father taught me."

"He sounds like he was a good man."

"He was, sir! He was!" A shadow passed momentarily over the boy's face.

Buzz spoke quickly. "Well, get the glass and let's head back."

After showing Kim how to replace the glass panes using the old metal wedges, he looked for that elusive last sheet of roofing. "Ah! There you are!" Buzz exclaimed as he noticed a shiny bit of tin peeking out from under a tangled brush pile. He tugged the sheet free with caution, remembering the snakes. At the same time, he uncovered a board that looked as though it would be just the right size to cover the hole in the wall.

In less than an hour, the roof was completely mended and the board was in place. "Hey, Kim! I finished the roof and the hole in the wall. How are you getting along on the windows?" Buzz called as he came through the door.

Kim was just sweeping the last of the old glass into a neat pile. "I finished putting the glass in, but I cracked one. Should I take it out and find another?"

"Nah! It gives the place some character," Buzz answered, laughing and patting Kim's shoulder.

Buzz looked at his pocket watch. "We did real good, Kim. It's only a little after two and we've finished all the repairs. I only wish I had some tar or something to seal the roof."

"That's a pretty watch, sir!"

"Thank you. It's been handed down in my family for generations. I'm told it was originally made for a duke. It plays a tune on the hour if you move this little lever, but I don't do that very often because it always seems to go off at an inopportune time."

"Oh, I would really like to hear that! Could you set it so it will play the tune sometime?"

"Sure! I'll set it now, and we'll hear it at three o'clock," Buzz replied, grinning.

"What does it play?"

"The beginning notes of *Beethoven's Fifth Symphony*, and then it chimes the hour. Kim, old man, why don't we throw some sandwiches together, grab a canteen, and do a little exploring?"

"That sounds like fun! Let's do it!"

"The first thing I want to see is that steam roller," Buzz remarked, as he fixed two bread and cheese sandwiches.

As Buzz stepped off the porch, he turned and looked back at what might be their home for the coming weeks, or even months. *Well, it's better than it was last night, with the wind and the rain blowing through. And, it's sealed against critters—walking or crawling types,* thought Buzz, with some satisfaction.

"I'll race you to the steam roller!" Kim yelled, jumping off the porch and streaking toward the machine.

"I won!" he announced triumphantly, slapping his hand on the big rear wheels.

"Hey! That's cheating! I didn't even have a chance to get started!" Buzz protested, laughing.

"That wasn't cheating, that was strategy!" Kim rejoined, throwing out his chest and locking his thumbs into imaginary suspenders.

"Oh, great! Now we have a politician in the ranks!"

Kim laughed delightedly. It seemed that the incident with the snakes and the resulting good cry had released the tremendous tension inside that small body. Now he was an eleven-year-old boy again. Granted, a very mature eleven-year-old—but now full of fun and pranks again, as he should be. Buzz was pleased.

"Darn, Kim, this is a 1925 Fowler! This thing's almost new, as steam rollers go!"

"What's it used for, sir?"

"I'm sure this one was used to roll the airfield smooth."

"How does it work? Did you ever run one?" Kim asked.

"I never ran one myself, but I watched the operation of one on a road in France. The big roller in front is like the front wheels on a truck; it steers it either right or left. Those two chains"—pointing, as he spoke—"go back to the steering gear. When the operator turns the wheel to the right, it pulls on the right chain, and it turns right. Same for the left. The yoke that is attached to the axle on each side and crosses over is a big roller-bearing that the roller itself pivots on. The big wheel on the left side of the engine spins, so if you want to run something else, like a pump or a saw, you just run a belt from that wheel to it. And the two rear wheels are flat, like the front roller, so all together they'll roll an eight-foot path."

"That's all very interesting, sir, but does it have a whistle?"

Buzz shouted with laughter. "Yes, it has a whistle, and yes, you can blow it—if and when we get it running!"

"Hooray!!" Kim yelled, his eyes shining.

"It's getting late. Why don't we check out the building where you shot the cobras? I think that was the mess hall.

"I'd better get rid of the dead snakes, sir."

"It's okay; I'll take care of them."

As they walked toward the building, Buzz looked down the row. Their structure had probably been the officers' quarters; next was the mess hall, and then what was probably the barracks. Next to that stood a square building adjoining a tall wooden tower, which had four large poles topped with an enclosed windowed room. *That must be the control tower*, he thought. Last but not least was the fire-ravaged hangar.

The mess hall looked different than it had a few hours earlier; the sun had been higher in the sky and the room had been bright. Now, the sun was beginning to slip behind the surrounding mountains, so the light was a bit grayer and the shadows were a bit longer. The only things in the main room were two chairs and three wooden crates in the corner near the dead serpents. In the kitchen, a poker lay on the floor among several empty boxes and biscuit tins. On one wall was a closed cabinet, heavily padlocked. Buzz deftly dispatched the lock with a quick twist of the poker, popping it open with little sign of damage.

"Where'd you learn that, sir?"

"Working with 'Maestro, the magician.' He taught me a lot about locks."

"Oh, wow! You worked with a magician?"

Looking inside the cabinet, Buzz exclaimed, "Well, well! We seem to have hit the jackpot! Two bottles of rum, one of Scotch, and one of gin. They're only half full, but they're still quite a find! This stuff must have been pinched from the officers' quarters by one of the cooks, and he couldn't take it with him without getting caught."

"Is that good, sir?"

"Yes, Kim, it's good. We'll have hot tea with a small shot of rum tonight after dinner, to relax."

Kim let out a sudden squeal and jumped back.

Buzz wheeled around, guns drawn, to see Kim standing on top of a box.

"Rats, sir! Rats!"

Buzz saw several long skinny tails disappearing under some debris.

"I opened that door, and a bunch of rats jumped out! At first, I thought they were more cobras!"

"Well, it looks like you found the pantry. There are still some canned goods in it. We won't know what until we open the cans, since the rats have removed all the labels. Should make fixing a meal rather an interesting adventure."

They both laughed gaily.

Later, after a strange but ample meal of beans, spinach, and cheese, topped off with a mug of hot tea and rum, they climbed gratefully into their cots. They felt secure in their new home. As Buzz closed his eyes, rain began to patter down, beating a tattoo that soon became a roar on the newly repaired roof. There were only a dozen or so small leaks. The man smiled to himself—a job well done. He drifted off, dreaming of flying with 'his' Kim.

The next morning, after a breakfast of fried beans, goat meat, and coffee, Buzz went out to inspect the hangar. He began by checking out the plane in the front area. "Damn! An old 1917 Fairey Campania two-seater sea plane converted for land use," Buzz muttered.

"Can you make it fly, sir?" Kim asked excitedly, as he came running up.

"Did you finish the dishes already?" Buzz asked, eyeing him quizzically.

"Oh, yes sir! Washed and put away, like we agreed. You cook, and I wash and clean up," Kim answered, accompanied by a snappy salute. "Can you make it fly?" he repeated.

"Well, it looks airworthy. It just needs an engine and some air in the tires," Buzz observed as he ran his hand gently over the fuselage.

"Look, sir! Here comes the truck!" Kim pointed excitedly at the vehicle cresting the hill.

"Harry's back earlier than we expected; I hope that means everything went well. I hope he brought some chickens, too. It sure would be nice to have some eggs for breakfast," Buzz commented, striding toward the truck as it came to a halt a few feet in front of them.

"Harry! Did you have a good trip?"

"Yes, I did, Buzz."

"Hello, sir," Kim cried as he ran past, headed toward the rear of the truck. "Hooray! Mr. Buzz, he brought some chickens—and two goats!"

Both men grinned.

Then Harry quietly said, "The tribal leaders want to meet with us this afternoon. We'll know then what kind of support they'll give us, if any."

"It doesn't sound like they care much one way or the other about these Shadow Men. I don't know if I want to get mixed up in other people's problems if they don't want to do anything about them," Buzz commented disgustedly.

"Just stay calm," Harry advised. "Let's talk to these men before you make any hard and fast decisions."

"All right, we'll talk." Buzz glanced over his shoulder at the Fairey Campania. "Not to change the subject, but is this the plane you were talking about?"

"Heavens, no! We have a little time," noted Harry, glancing quickly at his watch. "Let me show you what we have to work with. Follow me."

Harry led Buzz through the fallen timbers and rubble on the hangar floor to the back wall. There he moved a box, exposing a large ring. He tugged on it sharply, and there was a grating sound, as though someone had thrown a bolt latch open.

"Help me move this work bench," Harry asked Buzz as he started to push it to the side. As they pushed, the wall slid open, groaning and screeching, to reveal a large room dug into the hillside. Buzz could see some shadowy shapes in the dim light.

"That's good enough."

Harry stepped inside. He lit two lanterns and handed one to Buzz, who held it high and commented, "What a neat arrangement!"

To the left, mounted on a stand, was an airplane engine; behind it was a small machine shop with a lathe and drill press. On the right side were a fifty-five-gallon drum and some bolts of cloth; against the wall stood fifteen or twenty Martini-Greener riot shotguns. But what really caught Buzz's attention and brought forth a gasp of admiration, was in the middle of the room. There, in all its glory, was the neatest little compact bi-plane he had ever seen.

"Is that the Fairey Flycatcher?"

"It is," Harry replied, trying not to sound smug.

"Do you have enough gas for it?"

"There are five-hundred gallons in an underground tank. We also have several cases of ammunition and a few bombs."

Harry looked at his watch again. "It's getting late, and we still have to unload the truck."

Reluctantly, Buzz helped Harry close the opening in the wall and replace the bench and boxes as they were. Then they proceeded to quickly unload the truck's cargo.

~ Chapter Seven ~

COMMITTED?

The truck rambled on for the better part of an hour, each occupant engrossed in his own thoughts. Harry wondered how he could persuade Buzz to stay and help overthrow the Shadow Men of God; Buzz speculated about getting mixed up in a tribal war he knew nothing about. If he stayed, he might find Kim—but then again, he could get himself killed essentially for nothing. "Well, hell! I damn near got myself killed in Paris," he mumbled.

"Did you say something, Buzz?" Harry asked.

"Huh? Oh, no. I guess I was just thinking out loud. Will we be there soon?"

"The camp is just over the next hill. Are you all right back there, Kim?"

"Yes sir. But I'm having a hard time thinking of names for all the chickens and the goats," he replied.

The two men laughed.

"I wish all my problems were just that difficult to solve," Harry observed, still laughing.

"I'm with you on that," Buzz agreed.

They rode in silence for the next few minutes. Then Harry said, pointing to a cluster of tents and ancient stone buildings, "There's the camp ahead, gentlemen. It was an oasis used by some of the Silk Road caravans years ago."

"May I look around, sir? Maybe I can find something from China that might have fallen out of their packs!" Kim asked excitedly, his eyes dancing with merriment.

"There may be some boys and girls here your age. Perhaps they'll help you look," Harry replied, glancing over his shoulder at Kim.

"Oh, that would be great! Thank you, sir!"

Buzz inquired urgently, "Kim, you did leave the Star pistol back at the base, didn't you?"

"Oh! Yes, sir, I did. I put it in your duffel bag, like you told me."

"Good man," Buzz commended, obviously relieved.

The truck was met by a swarm of children that appeared to be eleven or twelve years of age down to perhaps two. Kim jumped off the truck as soon as it came to a stop and quickly mingled with the noisy, laughing horde.

As Harry stepped down from the cab, he scooped a large bag of hard candy from under the driver's seat. A loud cheer went up as he began distributing it generously to the joyfully outstretched hands.

"The universal peace offering!" Buzz called over the din.

"Yes. I wish it could be this easy with them," he said, nodding toward a group of five or six stern-faced men approaching them from a large, striped tent.

A rather large man weighing close to two-hundred pounds pushed his way through the group, leading the way to Harry and Buzz. His hurried gait caused his faded blue cotton robe to flare open, revealing an almost pink shirt tucked into a wide, brown-leather belt from which was suspended a wicked looking leather whip from his left side. Completing his apparel were grayish-white pants bloused into a pair of dusty-black high boots.

"That's Akbar; he's sort of the leader of the tribes in this area," Harry whispered quickly to Buzz.

"Harry! My good friend! I'm glad you could come. And this must be Mr. Kramer. Harry tells me your friends call you Buzz. I hope to have that honor someday," Akbar greeted them in a gravelly voice, hoarsened by years of dust, sand, and wind.

He took Buzz's right hand into both of his large, strong, leathery ones and shook it sincerely.

Buzz was immediately taken with the man. His friendly smile was encased by puffy cheeks, and his flashing dark eyes smiled too, from their frame of wrinkles. Akbar's short beard was dark and laced with gray, matching the hair protruding stubbornly from under his white turban. Buzz had the distinct impression that the man's frown would be as forbidding as his smile was welcoming.

"I'm pleased to meet you," Buzz responded.

"What's the situation? Will the tribes help?" Harry asked Akbar anxiously, in low tones.

"Not good, Harry. They're afraid—and I can't say I really blame them. We don't have anything to fight the Shadow Men with," answered Akbar, just as quietly.

"Did you tell them we have an airplane?"

"Yes, but you need to talk to them. Maybe the two of you can convince them to fight," Akbar urged as he moved to stride purposefully between the two men.

Taking each by an arm, he guided them through the entrance of the tent, followed closely by the group of somber men. Inside, all was nearly dark. As Buzz's eyes became accustomed to the dimness, he saw a circle of cushions in the center.

Akbar seated himself cross-legged at the far side of the circle, motioning Harry to sit to his right and placing Buzz to his left. The other men followed. It was eerily quiet; not a word had been spoken. The men sat on the cushions and crossed their legs, never taking their eyes off Harry or Buzz. Finally Akbar spoke.

"Gentlemen, given our present situation, I suggest we dispense with normal protocol and get quickly to the business we have come together to discuss. This is Mr. Harry Whitecliff and his friend, Mr. Mark Kramer. They're here to help us fight the Shadow Men."

The questions immediately came thick and fast.

"How many men did you bring?"

"Do you have any machine guns?"

"Tanks! Do you have tanks?"

"Horses! We need horses!"

"Airplanes! That's what we really need—airplanes!"

"Yes, airplanes. And bombs, too!"

"Gentlemen! Gentlemen! Please! Let Mr. Whitecliff speak!" Akbar motioned commandingly for calm.

Harry began to rise, and then thought it would probably be better if he remained seated at the same level as the men he so desperately wished to persuade to join him in his endeavor. "Mr. Kramer and I came here to seek your aid in fighting the thieves and murderers who have been terrifying your camps and homes."

The babble broke out again.

"Why are the English suddenly so interested in the welfare of the people of Afghanistan?"

"Do you or do you not have troops with tanks and airplanes?"

"Stop! Stop! Gentlemen! One at a time, please!" Akbar intervened. "Abu Abd al Hakin Hashim—you wish to speak?"

"Yes. I believe I can speak for all of us," Hashim said, looking quickly to the other men who unanimously nodded their approval. "What forces do you bring with you?"

"Well, at this time, we have an airplane, which Mr. Kramer will be piloting, and we—"

"You mean you have one—only one—airplane? And only one man to fly it?"

"As of right now, yes, but—"

Hashim spoke in sarcastic consternation. "The Englishman wants us—old men, women, and children—we, who only have a few old black powder muskets and swords and no horses to wield them from—we are to…"

Buzz could see that the men were getting angry and frustrated, with a wild look in their eyes. He began to unbutton his coat to make access to his revolvers easier in case the situation worsened, and they were needed in order to fight their way out of something that looked like it could become a riot at any moment.

Hashim continued, "The Englishman and his friend, with their one airplane, want us, together with our women and children, armed with sticks and stones, led by us old men with swords and canes, to lead a charge against the Shadow Men. The Shadow Men!—who are armed with Mausers, and are mounted on the finest horses in Afghanistan—most of which were once ours!"

Before Harry could reply, a boy of perhaps sixteen came limping quickly into the tent and hurried to Akbar. He whispered urgently into Akbar's ear, causing him to leap up, exclaiming, "Men! A party of seventeen Shadow Men is coming this way. We can continue this meeting later, but I think it best if we stay quietly in the tent. Otherwise, we may be seen leaving," he instructed with authority.

"The truck!" Harry exclaimed. "They'll see my truck!"

Akbar responded quickly. "Kashar!" he addressed the boy who had sounded the alarm.

"Yes, Father?"

"Take care of the truck."

"Yes, Father." Kashar rushed from the tent, intent on his mission.

"What can a mere boy do to hide a truck in just a few minutes?" Harry whispered to Buzz, who was equally bewildered. Buzz just shrugged.

"They're coming through the village now!" someone breathed.

The men rushed quietly to the far side of the tent, where they peeked out of small openings.

"Look! They have women with them!" Akbar reported quietly.

"Young girls, maybe fifteen to eighteen—and they're tied together," Harry noted softly.

"They probably took them from some of the southern tribes and are taking them north to sell," said one of the men near Buzz.

"What if they want to take our daughters?" asked a small man with a frightened look in his eyes.

"Well, they'll not take mine," Akbar announced grimly.

"How can you stop them? You don't have guns or horses!" bemoaned another man from the opposite side of the tent in a loud whisper.

"Shhh! They're going to ride by our tent!"

80

Everyone stood silently by their peepholes—some in suspenseful anticipation, others in obvious terror.

Harry and Buzz unsnapped their shoulder holsters.

"Where's Kim?" Harry asked Buzz suddenly, his body turning rigid with fear for the boy.

Buzz replied swiftly, urgently, "The last I saw him, he was playing with the children on the other side of the tent."

"Shhh! They're right outside!"

Within seconds, an enraged yell erupted nearly on top of them. "That's my father's gun! You have my father's gun! You killed my father!"

The crowd of men in the tent stood frozen in place, their hearts seeming to momentarily pause in sympathy—or fear.

Harry could see Kim running toward the lead Shadow Man, his face contorted, his fists beating the air in unbridled anger.

"It's that English doctor's pup! I'll finish him this time, for sure!" the leader swore.

As Kim reached the man on horseback, he was kicked in the face by the sole of the man's boot. The boy went flying backward and sprawled on the ground, bleeding profusely from his nose and mouth. The rider reared his black stallion menacingly over the small inert body.

"David! David!" Harry cried as he bolted from the tent. He dived on the boy and rolled with him just as the sharp hooves came down where Kim had been. Harry's shoulder was grazed, his jacket ripped. The horse reared again, and Harry reached for his revolver. To his dismay, it wasn't there; it had fallen from the holster when he dived for Kim. He clutched the boy protectively in his arms, scrambling backwards desperately away from those thrashing, threatening hooves.

POW! The horseman, still clutching the reins in one hand, grasped his throat, eyes bulging in an astonished stare, as blood bubbled from his lifeless lips. He fell backwards, pulling the horse off balance and into the other riders. The horse and its rider fell clumsily into the confused mass of men and horses, taking two more down with them. The other horses, in their attempt to escape the flailing hooves of their companions, were out of their riders' control.

POW! POW! POW!

While frantically searching the area for his own revolver, Harry could see Buzz crouched in the classic gunfighter's stance, blazing away into the melee. The girls were screaming with fright; the horses were rearing, whinnying, and pawing the air, eyes wide with fear and confusion. The Shadow Men were furiously attempting to regain control of their steeds, and at the same time attempting to unsling their rifles.

Buzz, carefully, but with deadly accuracy, downed a man with each shot.

POW! POW! POW!

One of the hapless riders fell just a foot from Harry and Kim, who were still on the ground. Harry was still seeking his pistol, but would not let go of Kim. Kim let out a squeal at the sight of the cold, blank, staring eyes and the small round hole in the middle of the fallen rider's forehead and broke from Harry's grip.

POW! POW! POW! CRACK! CRACK!

Rifle fire, Harry thought. CRACK! A geyser of sand sprayed up at Buzz's feet. POW! POW!

Four horsemen broke from the dust cloud raised by the frightened animals, seeking to escape. Buzz holstered his now empty guns and grabbed the knife from his boot. With a deft throw, he buried the blade just below the ear of the last rider.

Suddenly, Harry saw a dark figure on foot, sword raised high, running toward Buzz, who was unaware of that particular danger, since he was ruefully watching the escaping horsemen.

"Buzz!—behind you!" Harry yelled, but was unheard above the din.

"Sir!"

Harry turned to see Kim, who had just retrieved the ivory-handled revolver from his father's assassin. "Here, sir!" Kim cried as he tossed the gun to Harry, who caught it in midair and snapped off a shot.

As Buzz turned at the sound, the sword-bearing figure tumbled at his feet, startling him. Looking quickly back at his friend, Buzz gave him a grateful thumbs up.

SNAP! It was then they heard the unmistakable crack of a whip.

Buzz and Harry looked up to see one of the riders flip off his horse and fall to the ground. He looked like a hanged man being cut down.

"I had a feeling Akbar would be good with that whip," Buzz yelled.

Buzz ran rapidly to the fallen Shadow Men, and wrenched a rifle from the pile of bodies. He turned and dropped to one knee, bolted a round into the chamber, and set the sights for what he judged to be about a hundred yards. He took a deep breath and slowly exhaled as he drew down on his target. CRACK! Dust kicked up a few feet in front of it.

Damn! Mausers are set for meters, not yards, he mentally scolded himself, and reset his sights.

"If they get around that outcrop of rock, we'll lose them, and they'll bring the rest of the Shadow Men back to kill us all," Hashim yelled.

Buzz gave him a cold look and took careful aim at the fleeing man. CRACK! One more rider tumbled to the ground almost instantly.

As the last rider neared the outcrop, someone cried, "He's getting away! We're lost."

Buzz looked back. Again, it was Hashim.

Just as the man reached the outcrop, CRACK! The rider's arms flew up as he jerked out of the saddle and rolled down a slope to the edge of a thirty-foot drop off. The men watched the body fall to the ground, bouncing only once.

Buzz got up, and faced the tribal leaders. "They now have 483 Shadow Men, and we have seventeen horses and rifles. The odds are now more favorable," he commented wryly, then said, "Harry, we need to talk! Now!"

"Sir!" came a triumphant cry from Kim. "I found your pistol!"

Akbar methodically untangled his whip from the neck of the fallen Shadow Man, and then helped the other men corral and calm the frightened horses.

Harry had Kim untie the captive girls and get them some water. He hoped that, being young and small, the boy wouldn't be a threatening figure, and so would be able to calm them. God only knew what they'd already endured, and the previous few minutes were enough to traumatize anyone.

He strode to the large flat rock on which Buzz was seated, busily reloading his pistols. "I again find myself thanking you for saving my life," he said quietly and gratefully, extending his hand as he approached.

"Oh, that," answered Buzz casually shaking Harry's hand. "Hell, I had to do that so you'd be there to shoot that guy who was about to split my skull," Buzz retorted, casually shaking Harry's hand.

"I see. You planned ahead."

"Yeah, or something like that," answered Buzz, grinning.

They both laughed quietly, companionably.

Buzz asked, "Where in the hell did you get the pistol to shoot him with? Kim didn't find yours until after the fight."

"Kim recovered his father's pistol from the first one you shot— their leader—and tossed it to me just in time. So part of the credit for your life goes to Kim."

"He's your nephew, isn't he?" Buzz inquired, making it a statement instead of a question.

Harry sat down next to Buzz and slowly, thoughtfully took out his cigar case. He offered it to Buzz, and then took one himself. He waited while Buzz lit his, and then lit his own, and took a long, slow, deep drag. He blew a large smoke ring. He paused for a few more moments, seemingly arranging his thoughts, and then spoke quietly.

"Yes. His father was my brother. How did you know?"

"He resembles you somewhat. And when you called him David, and dashed to his aid the way you did, I knew he wasn't just a bellboy to you."

"My brother and I joined the Queen's service when the war first broke out. Since he was already studying medicine, he went into the medical corps, and then into—"

"Intelligence?" Buzz interrupted.

"Yes."

Harry looked beyond Buzz, toward the mountains, his eyes unfocused, peering deeply into the past.

"John and I were both stationed in India, where we served throughout the war. Afterward, we volunteered to stay there since we had few close family in England."

"Did you marry?"

"Yes. As a matter of fact, John and I met our future wives at the same military ball—he, a charming Indian girl whose family was of royal lineage; me, an English girl from an old military family. Our weddings were performed together. It was quite a sight--a British military and an Indian ceremony side-by-side. A year later David was born and, the following month, I was also blessed with a son. We named him Richard. He was quite a handsome boy."

"Was?" Buzz spoke very softly.

"Malaria. Six months after Richard was born, malaria spread through the area like the scythe of death. It took both Edith and our little Richard. I nearly joined them, but I pulled through somehow. Sometimes I wish I hadn't."

"I've heard malaria is something you never fully recover from. Is that true?"

"Yes. Once you have malaria, you'll always have it. Months, even years, may go by between attacks. Then, suddenly, without any warning at all, it lays you over like when you first got it—high fever, cold chills, delirium—the works."

Harry suddenly straightened as though he had just awakened. "I'm sorry! I didn't mean to ramble on like that. I usually don't do that."

"Hell, Harry, don't be sorry; it's good for friends to know each other. Besides, it helps to let one's feelings come out in the open once in a while. I might pour it all out on you sometime—you never know."

"I would be honored if you did, Buzz."

Harry paused a bit, and then spoke. "Now, I think it's about time I tell you why I brought you here. I didn't tell you before, because I had to be absolutely certain that you were right for the job."

"Right for what job? I thought I was brought here to fly an airplane and teach flying."

"Buzz, that's just a small part of what's needed here. Those old men elected by the people of England and France to run their governments have got their heads up their hats. They can't—or don't want to—see what's happening in the world. They actually believe that we fought the war to end all wars. Hell, Buzz, all it did was sow the seeds of another war.

"Mussolini, with his black shirts, is now dictator in Italy and wants a new Roman Empire. Stalin blazed a bloody trail to the top in Russia, and now he has his eyes on Poland. Japan needs raw materials, such as oil, iron and coal—so they're sniffing around the Far East for weak spots—Manchuria, maybe even China. Even that beer-garden upstart, Hitler, is slowly but surely rising to power. I read *Mein Kampf*: he just wants the whole world.

"We know that General Hans von Seeckt, the commander of the German army, is quietly and skillfully violating the clause of the Treaty of Versailles that forbids them an army of more than 100,000. They're secretly training men and developing equipment on foreign soil, such as Russia, and, we think, Afghanistan."

"The Shadow Men of God."

"That's what our information leads us to believe. We also think these raids on the tribes are to help to finance part of this project—whatever it may be," replied Harry.

"Who is this 'we' you keep referring to?" Buzz asked, feeling that he already knew the answer.

"The Secret Intelligence Service—MI6. We're a small unit of the War Ministry. We're underfunded and unappreciated. There are some in Parliament who want to disband us because they feel that spying on other countries is ungentlemanly. Of course, we're not the only ones with that problem; we have ties with intelligence forces in France and the Colonies."

"The Colonies?" Buzz said quizzically.

"The Colonies. The United States."

"Oh!" Buzz chuckled at the British terminology.

"So this endeavor is backed by the British government?"

"Well, not exactly," Harry replied, hesitantly.

"What do you mean, 'not exactly'?"

"The home office doesn't think there was enough evidence to support an operation in Afghanistan. They especially don't want to get involved in the civil war that's going on here."

"So you're doing this on your own? Just you, yourself, against 500 Shadow Men?" Buzz's face and voice were expressionless.

"Pretty much so. But if you join me, that'll double our odds," Harry cajoled with a hopeful smile.

"Are they all like the ones we met today, or are they seasoned German soldiers?"

"Some of the leaders are German officers, but the majority are ragtag mercenaries."

"In other words, they could be an uneducated, superstitious lot."

"Yes, I guess one could say that."

"Do they have any planes?"

"None have been spotted."

"Where's their main camp or fort?"

"As of now, they're in small, scattered bands."

"Can I bring on two more men—if they'll come—to fight with us?" Buzz asked.

"Bob and Boris?" Harry questioned, beginning to hope in spite of himself.

"Yes. You know of them?"

"Yes. If you can get them to come, I would be more than happy to have them aboard," Harry said with cautiously mounting enthusiasm.

"Can we expect any help from those men?" Buzz nodded toward the tribal leaders who were still milling around the fallen Shadow Men.

"I can vouch for Akbar, but I don't know about the others."

"Why is Afghanistan so important?"

"If Germany or Italy gains control of Afghanistan and the Khaibar Pass, one of our major supply routes to India and other Far Eastern holdings would be cut off."

They looked up as Akbar approached. "We've gathered up all the horses. What do you want us to do with the bodies?"

"What about the girls? How will they get back to their homes?" Buzz asked.

"They don't want to go home. They're disgraced by having spent a night with men other than those of their families—and no chaperones. They are on their own now."

Akbar saw Buzz's puzzled expression and tried to explain. "That is the custom and the tribal law in most of the area."

Buzz shook his head, not trusting himself to speak.

Akbar continued, "Oh, yes. Here's your knife, Mr. Kramer. I wiped it clean. That was the neatest throw I've ever seen."

"You were no slouch with that whip. And I'd be honored if you'd call me Buzz."

"It would be my honor," Akbar replied, as the two men shook hands.

Then Buzz quietly asked Harry, "While you help Akbar finish up here, may I have an hour or so to think things through?"

Harry nodded, turned, and walked back to the rest of the men with Akbar.

While Harry conferred with the group, he continued to be aware of Buzz, still sitting quietly on the rock near the gully, overlooking the surrounding countryside. He watched quietly as Buzz stared off toward the mountains for a time, drew in the sand with a stick, or lay back and watched the clouds, wondering what he was thinking.

Probably how to get out of this mess, and get back to Paris as quickly as possible. He was starting to realize what a fruitless project he was trying to take on. Three, maybe five men against five-hundred, or as Buzz had so recently figured, four-hundred and eighty-three. Even with an airplane. The Shadow Men might even have planes that he didn't know about. The odds against his success were tremendous.

Suddenly, Buzz jumped up, brushed himself off, and began striding purposefully toward Harry, but stopped short, gazed at the ground for a moment in deep thought, and kicked a rock, then changed direction and went to the girls. There were sixteen of them sitting in a close-knit huddle.

"What in the world is he up to?" Harry muttered to himself.

"Did you say something, Harry?" Akbar asked.

"Oh, no. I was just thinking aloud."

"Hashim wants to divide up the guns and horses now so he can get back to his camp before darkness falls."

"We'll wait for Buzz," Harry said, still watching him. He was now with the girls.

"Why do we have to wait for him? He's not one of us," Hashim called out angrily over the others.

"We'll wait!" Akbar replied gruffly as Buzz left the girls and started toward him.

I'd better meet Buzz halfway, away from the others, so Hashim won't have the privilege of saying 'I told you so'—not for a while, at least, Harry thought.

Buzz immediately asked, "Harry, do the spoils of war apply here?

"Well, yes—I guess. I don't see why it shouldn't," Harry answered in astonishment.

"Can I choose and train my own troops? Can I plan my own method of attack? With your approval, of course."

To each request, Harry nodded numbly.

"And you'll give us your support, Akbar?" Buzz inquired of the tribal leader.

Akbar, with a grin that lit up his entire face, nodded vigorously in the affirmative.

"Good! Then let's get started!" Buzz replied, grinning back.

Harry and Akbar rushed to Buzz thumping his back and shaking his hand, overjoyed. But the celebration was interrupted.

"Akbar, I have to leave now. I'm going to take the black horse and a rifle," Hashim shouted.

"Excuse me, gentlemen," Buzz said, as he quickly broke away from Harry and Akbar. "Hashim, take the rifle and the horse of the rider you shot."

"But I didn't shoot anyone!" came the puzzled reply.

"Well then, I guess you don't get anything."

"What? But, but..." Hashim stammered, livid, and then threw open his robes, exposing a large curved dagger in his sash.

Buzz planted his feet and crossed his arms over his chest, resting his hands lightly on the butts of the Webleys.

The other men of the tribal group hurriedly stepped away from Hashim. For a few seconds, the scene was eerily like a standoff in the streets of Tombstone.

Hashim, defeated, turned with a huff and nearly stumbled over his own donkey, which had been brought from a grove of palms where it had been left when Hashim had earlier arrived on it. Kashar held the animal courteously, while his owner mounted, accompanied by the uproarious laughter of the remaining tribal leaders. Highly insulted, he prodded the donkey cruelly and disappeared as speedily as possible.

"Whew! I'm glad that's over! Hashim is not to be trusted—and I don't think this is the last we'll see of him," Akbar commented wryly.

"I'll bring the truck around so we can load some of this booty," Harry said.

"Akbar," Buzz began, "we want to take everything—clothes, boots, everything in the saddlebags. Would you ask the other men to get rid of the bodies where they won't be found?"

"My truck! What happened to my truck?" Harry roared.

Everyone ran to the other side of the tent where they found Harry sitting on the ground, holding his sides, tears streaming down his face from laughter. He was pointing at a wreck of a vehicle with the doors hanging open, hood up, one tire flat, and a lush bush growing from the engine. There was enough sand, inside and out, to give the appearance that it had weathered several sandstorms.

The spectators joined in Harry's delighted laughter.

"Kashar, you sure did a bang-up job of taking care of the truck! No wonder the Shadow Men didn't give it another thought!" Buzz said to the boy as he patted him on the shoulder.

"Don't worry, Mr. Whitecliff. I'll have it cleaned up in no time!" Kashar averred while basking in the congratulations he was receiving from all sides.

~ Chapter Eight ~

STRATEGY

Harry drove back to the airfield slowly so that Akbar, Kashar, and his daughters Yasmin and Hasna, each of whom was riding alongside and leading a string of horses, would be able to keep pace easily. He was intent, too, on missing the potholes in the road to give the once captive girls, who were ensconced in the bed of the truck, a more comfortable ride.

"Akbar's daughters ride well," Buzz remarked, breaking the silence of the last ten minutes.

"Yes, they do. Akbar has taught them well," Harry replied, then asked, "What's going to be your strategy, Buzz? You seem as though you've come up with something. Am I right?"

"Harry, we both know that if we had taken on those men in an open field—not packed together the way they were—the outcome would probably have been different. We might have gotten five or six of them before they'd have cut us down. It was sort of like the Greeks at Thermopylae. Even though the Greeks were heavily out-numbered, the Persians could only send a few men at a time because of the confined fighting area. From what I saw, those men were just hired killers— probably uneducated and full of superstitions. I'm hoping to be able to play on that, using showmanship."

"You're suggesting circus tricks?" Harry didn't seem surprised.

"Yeah—something like that," Buzz replied, grinning ruefully to himself. "I guess that whenever I hear the phrase 'something like that,' I'll think of the pretty girl I met on the train who was trying to seem naïve."

"Good Lord! It just hit me! What are you planning to do with a truckload of young girls? Are we going to try to find homes for them?" Harry inquired in consternation. He was nearly speechless.

"Oh, no—I've already figured that part out. They're going to be our army—our fighting force."

"What?" Harry was even more confounded. "Buzz, they can't do that! They're just young girls who don't know anything about fighting! They'll be killed, to say the least!"

"Harry, I didn't paint any pretty pictures back there when I asked them if they wanted to join us. I told them we would teach them to be soldiers—teach them to fight and kill the Shadow Men. Not one of them hesitated; they said they had nowhere to go. Besides, they'll have the best instructors—Boris, Bob, Akbar, you, and me—the five best teachers of sneaky warfare in the land! And speaking of Bob and Boris, we need to get a telegram off to them as soon as possible."

Still reeling, Harry said, "There's pencil and paper in the glove box. Write up something and I'll send it tonight."

"You're driving back tonight?"

"Yes. I need to send the telegram and get more supplies. We have an army to feed now. And I'll take Kim back with me. He needs to be with his family now that his mission is accomplished, and I think he'll stay home this time."

"I'll sure miss the little guy!" Buzz confessed, choking up.

"I'm going to miss him too, but he needs to be with the rest of his family in India. There's no need for him to be in harm's way anymore."

"Yeah, you're right," Buzz agreed, as he grabbed the pencil and paper from the glove box.

Bob, Boris:

I found myself in the middle of a small war. If you don't have anything better to do maybe you can join the fun.

Ha, ha. Buzz

"Send it to Jack. He'll know where to find them," he instructed Harry, handing him the message.

They rode the next few miles quietly, the only sound that of the truck mingled with the voices of the teenagers in the back until Harry broke the silence by observing, "You know this plan of yours is absolutely buggers. There's no way you can beat an army of five-hundred armed killers with a handful of teenage girls."

93

"Four-hundred and eighty-three," Buzz replied, not even turning his head from the side passenger window.

"Oh, well, that's not so bad then," Harry said mockingly. Then he thought, *Who am I to question a man who can take on a band of cutthroats armed with no more than a bucket of sand and win? He might be able to pull the bloody thing off after all.*

After a few minutes, Buzz asked, "Do you think the men from the camp will keep us informed on the whereabouts of the Shadow Men, or will they just tell them where we are?"

"I honestly believe they'll help us—especially after that display of firepower today."

"And the teamwork," Buzz added.

"Some will help us out of respect and others out of fear, I suspect."

"I don't trust Hashim, Harry. It seemed as though he was trying to turn the others against us just before the shooting started."

"Buzz, I think you showed force and determination when you challenged him. These people respect that."

"Well, let's hope we can keep their respect."

He propped his feet up on the dashboard, using his knees as a writing table. The remainder of the journey was silent as Buzz alternated between staring out the window and then jotting notes on a pad. Harry was making facial expressions and moving his lips as though talking with someone not at the present time in the vehicle.

When they arrived at the airfield, the sun had just slipped below the mountain tops, bathing the valley in an eerie, reddish glow.

Akbar tethered the horses on the grassy airstrip while Kashar and his sisters found water for them.

The 'spoils of war' were taken to the mess hall where Buzz suggested that the girls sleep in the officers' quarters, since they were already rat-, snake-, and rain-proofed, and that the men spend the night in the control tower.

94

"The truck's unloaded, and all your gear—and Kim's—is in the back. Are you sure you're up to that long trip back through the Khaibar Pass after all that happened today?" Buzz asked, concerned.

"I'll be all right; David's fixing some coffee to take with us. I want to send the telegram as soon as possible, and I'll need to get more supplies. We have many more mouths to feed."

"Oh, I think it will be awhile before we starve. We have a lot of cans of something or other. We're just not sure what they are," replied Buzz, grinning.

"Well, I need to know how the war around Kabul is going. If Amanullah loses to Bachcheh Saqow, we could be in big trouble. Saqow isn't friendly toward the British." Then he quickly said, "Here comes David with the coffee. I guess we'd better be going."

"I have the coffee, sir, and I packed some bread and cheese, too," Kim reported, placing the items on the floor of the cab.

"Well, Little Kim, I'm going to miss you," Buzz said, extending his hand to the boy.

"I'll miss you too, sir. And you can call me David now, sir," said David as he shook Buzz's hand. Then they gripped each other in a long, strong hug, and Buzz felt warm rivulets of moisture rolling down his cheeks. He wasn't sure whose tears they were.

As the truck pulled away, David leaned out the window and called back, "I'll take really good care of my dagger, sir!"

"And I'll make good use of my fine ball of silk string, David."

Buzz watched the lights of the truck until they disappeared into the darkness beyond the hill. Then he paused momentarily, drew a deep breath, squared his shoulders, and began to prepare for the new challenges ahead.

The curtain of darkness gave way to morning, like the opening scenes of a dramatic opera. A rabbit hopped warily out from a clump of grass to nibble hungrily on a pink flower. A small bird gracefully glided to perch atop the steam roller and began its joyful aria. The morning breeze gently stirred the tall grass, causing the strands to move in rhythm like the ripples of a quiet lake.

95

Bang! Bang! Bang! "All right, girls! It's time to get up. Rise and shine!" Buzz yelled, banging enthusiastically on the door to the officers' quarters. "It's six-thirty! I let you sleep late this morning only because you had a hard day yesterday. I want all of you dressed and outside in ten minutes—no exceptions."

As Buzz stepped down from the porch, feeling rather smug, he saw Akbar standing by the mess hall with his son. Kashar's eyes were wide with surprise at Buzz's outburst of orders. Akbar stood with his arms crossed, a huge grin on his face, eyes dancing with glee.

"Well?" Buzz asked as he approached the two.

"You make a good sergeant, but will you make a good officer?" Akbar questioned in reply.

Instead of answering directly, Buzz turned to Kashar. "Kashar, I want you to make a list of the girls—name, age, can ride a horse, cook, or shoot a gun," Buzz instructed.

Kashar looked at his father, who nodded approval. "Yes, sir," he replied softly, quickly leaving to obey.

"Akbar, would you join me in a fresh cup of coffee?" Buzz inquired, motioning to the mess hall. Akbar nodded and followed Buzz into the building.

"Pull up a chair; I'll get the coffee. Do you take anything in it?"

"No. I think it will be best to drink it black and strong this morning."

"Would you like some breakfast?" Buzz called from the kitchen. "I made enough for everyone—at least, I hope I did. I've never cooked for a small army before."

"Yes, I would. You must have risen early."

"Well, I didn't sleep too well last night," Buzz confessed, grinning ruefully as he placed a tray on the table. "Help yourself while I get the coffee and some biscuits."

"It smells good. What is it?" Akbar asked.

"It's beans and something and another something; there aren't any labels on the cans. I recognized the beans, but I'm not sure about the other two. They smelled and tasted all right, though."

Buzz poured their coffee, and they raised their cups in the manner of a toast.

"Ahh!" Akbar sighed with satisfaction. "There are not many things better than the first cup of coffee in the morning."

"I agree," said Buzz, sipping from the steaming mug in his hand.

"Mmm, this is good! Your 'something' and 'something' is very tasty!"

They finished their meal with dispatch and pushed the plates aside. Buzz refilled their coffee cups.

Akbar took a long swallow, and then leaned back in his chair. He looked directly into Buzz's eyes, and solemnly asked, "What is the reason you asked me to join you, other than coffee and breakfast?"

Buzz waited for a few moments before answering. If he did not explain his ideas carefully, Akbar would not stay to fight. He also felt instinctively that if Akbar didn't join them, no one else would, and all would be lost. He had to get this right. A lot depended on the next few minutes!

Drawing a deep breath, he began. "Well, I've taken on the task of defeating five-hundred Shadow Men with only a bunch of kids and a couple of airplanes—and I'm not even sure the planes will fly."

Without changing his expression, Akbar corrected him. "Four-hundred and eighty-three. Do you have a plan?"

"Yes, I have a plan, but it depends on the help of many others." Buzz hesitated, wishing he had answered more forcefully.

"At least you have a plan; that's more than anyone else has. What do you have in mind, if I may ask?" replied Akbar, leaning forward and crossing his arms on the table.

Buzz was praying that Akbar wouldn't, in the next few minutes, dismiss him as a lunatic with his head in the clouds. He began to explain, mentally crossing his fingers for good luck. "If we can train these girls to fight like soldiers, and with the help of some circus showmanship, we may be able to take small bands of fifteen or twenty by surprise. If we can put the fear of God into them, they'll lose the will to fight."

"In other words, you want to make the Shadow Men think they are being attacked by demons or other unknown terrors," Akbar stated thoughtfully as he refilled their cups.

"Yes! That's exactly what I mean! But we need the help of the tribes to keep us informed of the location of the Shadow Men, and their numbers. Also, we need your help to train and command our ragtag army. That's the plan; we'll have to work out the details as we go."

"What if we lose?" Akbar leaned back in his chair, frowning.

Buzz met Akbar's eyes with a look of steely determination. "If we lose? That means that I will have let all these people down. They've put their trust in me, and I don't intend to do that! I'll need help with the local customs and religion. I don't want to step on anyone's toes, but there can't be anyone stopping in the middle of a battle to say a prayer."

"You need not worry; I'll take care of the things you ask." Akbar continued to lean back in his chair, his face an expressionless mask.

"Do you have any questions, or is there anything you want to add?" Buzz asked. He fervently wished he knew what Akbar was thinking—the man had the best poker face he'd ever seen.

Akbar pursed his lips, staring thoughtfully at his cup for some time. He shook his head slowly, and answered, "No. Not at the present."

The door suddenly opened with a bang, breaking the tension. Kashar entered hurriedly.

"I have the list you wanted, sir." He handed Buzz a sheet of paper, and snapped to attention.

Buzz took the list and glanced at it briefly. "Very good, Kashar. Please have the girls come in and line up at the kitchen for their breakfast, and have the first two in line help you serve. There's coffee and water, and you'll find cups, plates, and utensils on the counter."

"Yes, sir!" Kashar exited the mess hall and returned immediately with the girls close behind.

"Let's go outside, where it will be quieter, to check the list of our recruits and figure out how we can best use whatever talents they have," Buzz suggested. Akbar quickly vacated his seat and rushed toward the door.

Buzz thought, *Whoever walks through that door first will be in command.*

Akbar reached the door ahead of Buzz, grasped the knob, and hesitated. Their eyes met for a tense heartbeat, each realizing what was at stake. Then Akbar smiled gently, opened the door, and stood back, motioning for Buzz to pass him.

Buzz stepped calmly outside, but felt like doing handsprings across the runway. He had won Akbar's support.

"There's a table and some chairs in the officers' quarters. We can draw up some sort of duty roster there," Buzz said, walking toward the building. Akbar followed three steps behind. Buzz stopped, half-turning toward Akbar. Akbar stopped. Buzz said nothing, just waited silently. Nearly a minute passed before Akbar nodded, smiled, and stepped forward to stand beside Buzz. They strode the rest of the way in step.

— Chapter Nine —

GETTING ACQUAINTED

Buzz and Akbar cautiously made their way through the makeshift bedding strewn about the floor.

"The first thing that has to be done is to restore the barracks and make them rain- and critter-proof. And we have to do the same for the mess hall," Buzz rattled off. "The officers' quarters were made to house six officers, not eighteen girls. Besides that, I don't relish the thought of spending any more nights in the control tower than necessary."

"I heartily agree," Akbar replied, sheepishly rubbing his back.

They sat together at the small table in the middle of the room. Buzz placed the list on the table and took a pencil from his shirt pocket.

"We saved these girls from a life in brothels one day, and we're training them to be killers the next. Last week, they were playing with dolls; next week, they'll be 'playing' with guns." Buzz grimly shook his head.

Akbar reached across the table, grasped Buzz's hand, and squeezed it. "Believe me, my friend, you're doing the right thing. With us, they'll have a better chance to grow up and have a decent life."

Buzz nodded, sighing. He knew Akbar was right, but that didn't make him like the situation any better. He squared his shoulders.

"You're right, I guess. Let's see what we have to work with." He peered at the list. "Oh, good! Kashar had them fill it out themselves. That should tell us something about each of them."

"How do you figure that? They were just answering some questions."

Buzz slid the sheet across to Akbar. "See for yourself."

- Kashar, 16 - I can ride and shoot and sew

- Hasna, 18 - Ride, shoot, cook, sew

- Yasmin, 19 - Ride, shoot, cook, sew
- Rima, 16 - Cook, sew
- Amber, 15 - Cook, sew
- Hana, ~~15~~ 13- Sew
- Nudar, 17 - Ride, cook
- Zayna, 16 - Would like to learn
- Sara, 15 - Cook, sew
- Jehan, 16 - Cook, sew
- Sagirah, 14 - Cook, sew, want to shoot
- Ara, 17 - Cook, ride
- Basima, 15 - Cook, ride a little
- Hala, 16 - Sew
- Anan, 16 - Cook
- Israt, 15 - Cook, shot gun once
- Zohra, 17 - Cook
- Ara, 18 - Rides (Father raised horses)
- Kebira, 13 - Takes care of goats and chickens

"I see a lot of cooks and seamstresses, and a few riders. Not much to work with," Akbar said, looking questioningly at Buzz.

"Over half of them are unable to read or write. Notice those that are in the same handwriting as your daughter Yasmin; she wrote their answers for them because they couldn't. Zayna was probably betrothed at an early age to someone of means since she wasn't taught to do any housework. Hana may be a problem, because she wants to be something more than she is—see where her age was changed? Probably because she lied about it and Amber or Nudar corrected her. They're sisters or they're from the same village. Over all, they seem eager to learn."

"You're very observant of people." Akbar's gruff voice held a hint of admiration.

"I picked that up in the circus, being around the crowds for so long."

Akbar, leaning precariously back in his chair, only smiled and folded his hands behind his head. "What now?"

"Well, we need to—"

The door opened, and Kashar briskly entered and stood at attention. "We've finished breakfast, sir, and the girls are cleaning the mess hall. What do you wish me to do next?"

Buzz motioned Kashar to wait and turned to Akbar. "I'd like you to oversee the repairs to the barracks. There are some nails and tools in those boxes by the window."

He turned back to Kashar. "Kashar, have Zohra, Kebira, Sagirah, and Hana meet me at the mess hall. Akbar, where do you want your girls?"

"Have them wait for me at the barracks."

"Yes, sir!" Kashar dashed from the room, forgetting to close the door behind him.

"And for God's sake, watch out for cobras! We've already killed several," Buzz yelled after him.

"I'll tell them," Kashar yelled back. The word 'sir' came floating back as a quick afterthought.

"It looks as though we've started," Buzz said as he and Akbar stood on the porch watching Kashar instruct the girls.

"He's a good boy. I'd like to make him my aide, unless you have other plans for him," Buzz stated, looking inquiringly at Akbar.

"He would do well," Akbar answered proudly. "Shall we face our recruits?"

"Yeah, I guess we'll have to sooner or later," Buzz answered. "Into the valley of death strode the two." The men laughed companionably as they walked to meet their troops. Buzz stopped at the mess hall, and Akbar continued on to the barracks.

"Why were we told to wait here? Why can't we be with the others?" asked one of the younger girls as Buzz entered the mess hall.

"What's your name?" Buzz asked sternly, looking directly into her eyes.

"Uhh! Uhh! Oh! I'm Hana," she stammered and retreated a couple of steps in confusion.

"Well, Hana, Kashar sent you here because I told him to. I need someone to get the kitchen in shape."

"What if I don't want to do kitchen work? I want to fight, not cook!" the girl replied defiantly, taking a step forward.

"You have two choices; One, you can leave. Two, you can stay. If you choose to leave, we will give you some food, water, and some matches."

"What are the matches for?" Hana inquired haughtily.

"To build fires. We're forty miles or more from any other encampments or wells, so you'd be making at least three camps. The fire keeps the jackals away—most of the time."

The other girls stared at one another, wide-eyed.

Hana swallowed noisily, and then asked mildly, "What is the other choice?"

"The other choice is that you stay, follow orders, and learn to be a good soldier. If you disobey an order, you will be shot," Buzz said matter-of-factly. "You can give me your answer tomorrow. Meanwhile, if you want to eat, you will work in the kitchen today."

He paused for a second. "Anan."

"Yes!" Anan stood quickly erect.

"That's 'Yes, sir!'"

"Yes, sir!" the girl responded, trembling.

"How good a cook are you?" Buzz asked, softening his tone.

"I have been told I was good many times."

"How many can you cook for?"

"Ten to fifteen—uh, sir. But sometimes my little sisters help, sir."

"Can you read and write, Anan?"

"Yes, sir," was the proud rejoinder. "My mother taught me!"

"Anan, I'm going to put you in charge of getting the kitchen ready for use. Have lunch ready when you can. It's not going to be easy, because the cans of food don't have any labels, so do the best you can. I'm going to assign Sagirah and Hana to help you. Hana, Sagirah, Anan's in charge, so help her and do what she tells you."

Buzz paused, giving his instructions time to be absorbed. "Are there any questions?"

"What about me?" Kebira asked. Anan quickly nudged her. "Oh! Sir."

"Kebira, I see from the list that you take care of goats and chickens."

"Yes, sir." She looked at him, frightened but determined to do her part. Her innocent, dark eyes were huge.

Buzz thought of what the Shadow Men had had in mind for her and his stomach tightened. He spoke softly. "We have some chickens and a couple of goats in the back. I want you to look after them. Fix their pens and check on their food and water. Whatever they need, you will be responsible for."

"Oooh! I'd like that, sir," the girl replied happily.

"All right, girls, get to work. Anan, if you need me, I'll be at the hangar." With that, Buzz turned on his heels and marched out.

He arrived at the hangar and quickly entered its haven. Once inside, he allowed himself to slump. "Wow! What the Hell did I get myself into, now?"

"Sir?" Kashar came running into the hangar. "My father said I was to stay with you."

Buzz straightened. "Yes, Kashar. I want you to be my aide—help me and run errands, things like that."

"Oh, yes sir!" Kashar spoke as if thanking someone for giving him a large piece of gold. His chest swelled, and he seemed at least two inches taller.

"I want you to help me move this wall," Buzz said.

"Move the wall?" Kashar repeated, puzzled.

"You'll see. First, let's move the workbench. You pick up that end, and we'll carry it to the other side. Watch out for those fallen timbers. This will be the next building we'll work on. Set the bench down in this clear spot."

As Buzz brushed his hands together to remove some of the dust, he surveyed the damage to the hangar. "Kashar, I don't think this building was destroyed by fire; I think it was dismantled and made to look as if it had been burned. Look." Buzz ran his hand over one of the timbers leaning from the remains of the rafters to the floor. "No soot. This wood was painted to appear as if it were burned. The British are good at deception."

"Why would they do that? Oh! Sir!" asked Kashar.

"To make anyone passing by think it was destroyed and that there wasn't anything of value remaining here."

"Oh. I see."

Buzz mused, nearly to himself, "Still, I wonder why the roofing and the lumber from the other buildings wasn't hauled off before now?"

"There wasn't much time between when the British left and the fighting started in Kabul; that's when all the young men were taken. So that didn't leave anyone to take it away except the old men and women," Kashar explained.

"That makes sense. Hey! Look! Hanging from the end of that beam! An electric light," Buzz exclaimed joyfully. "Maybe the generator is still around here someplace! But enough sightseeing—let's get that wall moved."

Buzz excitedly went to the area where the work bench had been. He moved the large box and pulled the ring to release the latch as he'd watched Harry do earlier. He began pushing the section of wall to one side. "Kashar, give me a hand." The two pushed the sliding wall as far as it would go, and then proceeded to do the same on the other side.

When they finished, there was an opening of forty feet, exposing a large natural cavern, which had been enlarged by hand, in the hillside behind the hangar. Kashar's mouth dropped in astonishment at the sight before his eyes.

"Yeah, Kashar, I felt the same way when I first saw this. Wow! But as much as I want to explore that room, we need to clear a path so we can move the Flycatcher out. That will give us some room to move things around and establish some order," Buzz said. "I want you to find some tools. We need shovels, brooms, pry bars—anything we can use to clean up this mess. I'm going to check with your father to see if he can give us some help."

He left the hangar, leaving Kashar to a task nearly every sixteen-year-old boy savors—searching unexplored territory for mysterious, interesting new items. As he neared the barracks, he saw smoke billowing from the open windows and the door. His heart thudding, he raced toward the building only to skid to an abrupt stop when he realized that the smoke was dust—huge, foggy clouds of it. Laughing in relief, he slowed to a more sedate pace.

Still grinning, he mounted the first step to the porch and was met by a dusty, disheveled Akbar. Stumbling, eyes tearing, wracked by deep barking coughs, he took Buzz's arm and motioned to a bench at the edge of the landing field. He was unable to speak. They seated themselves, and Buzz waited patiently for Akbar's coughing fit to cease. "Are you all right?" he asked. "Can I get you a drink of water?"

"No, no. I mean, yes, I'm all right. It's the dust; I had to get some fresh air. Buzz, I'm telling you, if those girls fight like they clean, the Shadow Men won't have a chance. I told them what needed to be done and the older girls, with me saying no more, took charge. One group found some brooms and started sweeping, another few took the bed frames out back to clean them. My daughter Hasna discovered some mattresses in a back room." Akbar was obviously proud of the work his girls had accomplished.

"How are the mattresses? Are they any good?" Buzz asked, stifling his merriment. Akbar's face was bright red from coughing, and liberally streaked with the tracks of the tears that had run from his streaming eyes.

Akbar replied, with as much dignity as he could muster. "Most seem to be in fair shape, although a few of them had a good part of their stuffing removed by the local animals—probably for nesting material. The girls are hanging them on some lines they rigged behind the barracks and are beating the dust out of them. What conditions did you find in the hangar?"

"Not too bad. It wasn't damaged by fire; it was just made to look that way. All we have to do is bolt it back together like a big jigsaw puzzle, and that's why I came to find you. I need to see if I can borrow some of your troops to help."

"Buzz, I don't want to take any of them from the barracks now. The way they're all working together, they'll probably be able to sleep there tonight," Akbar responded thoughtfully.

"I think you're right. Let's get that area finished. We can go on to the hangar full-force tomorrow."

"Mr. Akbar, sir." Nudar cried, running toward the men on the bench. "Look what we found in some boxes in the little room." She held up a dingy, almost white towel in one hand, and a bar of soap in the other. "And there are a lot of empty boxes." she continued.

Buzz explained, "Those boxes are probably footlockers. They go at the end of your beds, and you can keep all your personal things in them."

"Oooh! That would be nice," Nudar said longingly. She quickly gathered the towel and soap, raised one hand in a salute of sorts, and ran back toward the barracks.

Buzz said, "We should quit early enough for the girls to take showers. Get rid of some of the grime," he added, watching dust fluff off Nudar as she returned to the barracks.

"There's a shower?" Akbar exclaimed hopefully. "I might partake of that myself after the girls have finished."

"Of course," agreed Buzz, hiding a smirk.

"They don't need me there right now, so perhaps I can help at the hangar," Akbar suggested.

"That would be good. Maybe we can clear a path to push the plane out."

Suddenly they heard a loud clanging. Clang! Clang!

"What the..." Buzz leaped up from the bench with a start.

"It's coming from the mess hall!" Akbar yelled.

They men raced to the mess hall and slammed through the door, prepared for a calamity. Instead they were met by a strange but pleasant aroma. Four smiling girls stood proudly behind the serving counter. Hana was waiting to hand out bowls; Zohra, ladle in hand, stood next to a large pot of something; Kebira was cutting bread into slices, and little Sagirah was ready to pour coffee into the waiting cups.

"Lunch is ready, sirs," they said in unison.

"Like the ladies said, 'lunch is ready,'" Buzz said. The two men looked at each other and burst out laughing.

"I'll go tell the others," Akbar said and left, shaking his head.

"Your table is by the window, sir. If you'll be seated, Hana will bring your tray to you."

"Thank you, Zohra." Buzz pulled his chair up to a table decorated with a jar containing an array of wild flowers. There were two stained but clean placemats across from each other, and the utensils were placed in an orderly fashion on them.

Hana carried a tray to the table and served Buzz efficiently and quickly. He noticed with some dismay that she would not look at him, but kept her gaze downward. She finished and held the empty tray stiffly at her side. Still refusing to meet his eyes, she asked, "Will that be all, sir?"

"Yes, Hana. Thank you."

"Sir?" Hana spoke in a near whisper, meekly.

"Yes, Hana?"

"I would like to stay—if you'll let me."

"I would be very glad for you to stay." Buzz was greatly relieved.

"Oh, thank you, sir! And I'll be a good soldier. I promise."

"I know you will."

The girl at last raised her eyes to meet Buzz's. Her face was radiant, and she practically bounced across the room to her station.

Buzz peered questioningly at the bowl in front of him, wondering what it was and hoping it would be edible. He prolonged the suspense, and took a tentative sip of coffee, finding it strong and good. *Well, here goes*, he thought as he dipped his spoon into the thick, dark-brown liquid. As the spoon stirred the contents of the bowl, some strange-looking green and orange bits appeared, surfing to the top of the liquid, then disappearing beneath the surface. He slowly, carefully, brought the spoon to his lips and, with a deep breath, thrust it into his mouth. He swirled it experimentally for a moment, then chewed and swallowed.

"Zohra, step over here for a moment. No, wait. I want all of you to come."

The girls marched to him and stood at attention. Each of them wore a worried expression.

Buzz took another spoonful with gusto. "This is excellent! You girls did an outstanding job. How did you do it?"

Letting out the breath she didn't realize she'd been holding, smiling, Zohra complied. "Well, sir, first we had to run the rats out and straighten up the boxes that were scattered all over. Hana and Sagirah found the dishes and the pot and pans. I didn't know how to work the stove, so Hana built a fire pit out of rocks, and we boiled some water in the big pots to clean the dishes in." As each girl's name was mentioned along with her accomplishment, she beamed with pride.

"Sagirah found some numbers on top of the cans and noticed that there were a lot of cans with matching numbers. She can read and write. She opened two cans with matching numbers, and they were both peas— so she opened one of each set of numbers, and now we know what is in them. There are even some peaches and chocolate. I didn't put any peaches in the soup, but I did put a little chocolate in it. We thought maybe everybody could have hot chocolate and peaches before we go to bed.

We didn't sweep the floor yet, because we saw all the dust in the barracks, so we'll sweep after lunch. Oh! And Kebira brought in a big pitcher of goats' milk. She said the goat was about to burst from not being milked for so long. She helped with the dishes, too." Zohra inhaled deeply, and stopped suddenly, her eyes wide, her cheeks red with embarrassment. She had rattled on because of her pride in her team's accomplishments. She covered her mouth with her hand, hoping Mr. Buzz wouldn't be cross.

Buzz smiled with amusement and satisfaction. He was as proud of Zohra and the other girls as they were of themselves. "You all did a fine job, but you'd better get back to your posts. I think I hear the rest of the troops coming."

As Akbar entered the mess hall, Buzz called, "Over here, Akbar. Sit with me."

As Akbar was seating himself at the table across from Buzz, Hana placed his meal before him.

"It's really good," Buzz said, noticing Akbar's hesitancy. He took a bite of bread, and grinned reassuringly. "It really is. The girls did well."

After everyone had eaten, they returned to their interrupted projects. Buzz and Akbar began cleaning a pathway for the plane using pry bars, shovels, and a wheelbarrow Kashar had discovered in a pile of rubbish.

At last the way was completely cleared. The three men stood just outside the hangar and admired their work. Then, grinning, without a word, and only one thought in mind, they dashed for the plane.

"Akbar, you push the right wing; Kashar, you push the left. I'll push the tail and steer," Buzz yelled, as he scurried to the rear of the plane. The Flycatcher resisted their efforts at first, but finally gave way to their persistence and rolled reluctantly onto the field.

"She's a pretty little airplane," Kashar exclaimed. "All silver, with that yellow stripe across the body behind the seat where the driver sits. But it looks bent in the middle, like it's been sat on!"

"No, Kashar, it's not bent. It was designed that way, probably to make it more maneuverable—the same reason the lower wing was set back so far from the upper wing," Buzz explained. "And that's called a cockpit. It's where the pilot sits, not the driver."

"It's got a machine gun on each side," Akbar observed.

"Yeah!, they look like .303 Vickers. God! I can't wait to fly her, but we need to get the base in shape first. Let's see what's in that big room. Kashar, bring the clipboard and a pencil," Buzz requested as he walked toward the dimly lit area where the plane had been.

"Are you ready to take notes, Kashar?"

"Yes, sir!"

"All right. Let's start with the engine on the stand. One Rolls-Royce Eagle."

110

"Is that one word, or two?" asked Kashar.

"What?"

"Rolls-Royce?"

"Two words, with a hyphen in the middle."

"Oh," Kashar replied, as he proceeded to write it down quickly.

"Just spell things the best you can, for now," Buzz suggested. "We can figure it out. Okay, here we go—a machine shop with one lathe, one drill press, one grinder, a gas welding set, and various hand tools. Next, one drum of..." Buzz paused, leaning down to hold his lantern close to check the label on the drum. "Airplane dope, lacquer-type, and two bolts of fabric."

"What's airplane dope, sir?" Kashar was curious, since he had never heard of that before.

"It's a thick, clear lacquer that's used with that fabric to patch holes or tears in the airplanes."

"Buzz!" came an excited cry from Akbar. "I think I've found a generator!"

"Where are you?" Buzz called in return, trying vainly to spot the other man in the dim light of the large cavernous room.

"On the other side of the room."

Buzz and Kashar went carefully and quickly toward Akbar's voice and saw him leaning from an opening in the back wall, waving his lantern frantically.

"Here! I found a couple of rooms back here, and one has what looks to be a generator." Buzz and Kashar took a shortcut, climbing rapidly over some precariously stacked crates to reach Akbar. "Here, in here," the bearded man barked unceremoniously, leading the way through a large doorway into a room measuring about ten feet by twelve.

Buzz excitedly exclaimed, "It is a generator! It's just like one of the ones we used for backup power at the circus. Kashar, see if there's any gas in that tank," he said, pointing.

Kashar dashed to a rack holding the fifty-gallon tank Buzz had indicated, unscrewed the cap, and lifted out the dipstick. "The stick shows almost full, sir."

"Great; maybe we can light this place up," Buzz responded happily as he sat his lantern by the engine. He opened a valve by the glass fuel bowl on the carburetor. They all watched, fascinated, as it filled with gasoline.

"Do you know how to run one of these?" Akbar asked.

"Yeah, I helped run the ones at the circus when storms knocked out the power. Well, here goes. Let's see if this thing will start."

From a hook on the wall, Buzz took a three-foot piece of rope with a large knot at one end, wrapped it around the starter pulley, grasped the knot securely, and pulled sharply. The pulley spun, the exhaust coughed, but it didn't start. Buzz tried it again and again and again until finally, after the eighth attempt, he plopped wearily onto a nearby crate, panting.

"Damn! I was really hoping it would start without any problems," he spat, disgusted.

"Maybe it's not getting gas," Akbar suggested.

"Sir?" interjected Kashar.

"Maybe it's getting too much gas?" Akbar questioned.

"I don't think that's the problem, Akbar," replied Buzz.

"Sir?" Kashar interrupted again.

"What do you want, Kashar?" Buzz snapped impatiently.

"What does this loose wire go to?" He raised the wire in question.

"That's why it wouldn't start! The coil wire was disconnected, so there wasn't any spark." Grinning sheepishly, Buzz said, "I'm sorry I snapped at you, Kashar."

Buzz quickly plugged the offending wire into its receptacle and cranked the starter again. This time the motor coughed, popped, and belched black smoke, but still refused to start. Buzz coiled the rope around the crank again, and pulled. This time, the engine started and ran smoothly.

"Well, here goes." Buzz closed the electrical switch. "Kashar, flip that switch on the wall next to your head."

Kashar obediently moved the switch up and down. Still no light.

Akbar looked at Buzz in bewilderment. "What do you think is wrong?"

Buzz shook his head, perplexed. "I don't know. The mice could have chewed the wires, which means we'll have to rewire the whole thing."

"Sir, the lights are on in the big room," Kashar called out from the other side of the hangar.

The two men looked at each other in chagrin.

Laughing, Buzz said, "On the other hand, it would probably be easier just to change the light bulb."

"You think so?" replied Akbar. All three whooped with laughter.

"Where's the other room you found?" Buzz asked, still chuckling.

Akbar led the way. "It's over here, but it's locked."

"That shouldn't be a problem." Buzz grabbed a large screwdriver from a nearby work bench and snapped the lock with a single, strong twist, then flipped the hasp back and pushed on the door. It opened less than six inches, and then stopped with a thud.

"Something's blocking the door; let's put our shoulders to it," Buzz said. "Ready? One—two—three!" They threw their bodies against the door, succeeding in moving it only another inch or so. "Again! One—two—three—heave!" This time, the door opened an additional six inches.

"I think I can squeeze through there, sir," Kashar ventured.

"Good boy," Buzz complimented him. "Feel around on the wall for a light switch."

"I found it, sir." They heard a sharp click. "This one works. Some boxes have fallen in front of the door, blocking it. I'll have them moved in a couple of minutes, sir."

"Be careful, Kashar," Buzz and Akbar said practically in unison.

Suddenly, the door slammed shut, and Buzz and Akbar heard loud scraping and banging on the other side.

113

"Kashar, are you all right?" Akbar yelled.

The door opened slowly, and there stood Kashar, grinning and obviously excited.

"I'm okay. I had to move these two heavy boxes." He motioned to the two crates of Enfield rifles behind him.

"It's the arms room!" Buzz exclaimed. "Those two cases hold British .303 Enfields, Mark I. Twelve to the case, so that's twenty-four. Those sealed tins on that shelf contain the ammunition; looks to be about 10,000 rounds. And there are two tins of .455 Webley pistol cartridges, too."

Buzz eagerly opened the lid of a large case sitting on the floor in the corner of the room. Inside was a Lewis machine gun with ten .303 magazines neatly packed around it. "This must be the machine gun for the other plane."

"What's in these cases?" Akbar asked, pointing to ten cases stacked by the wall.

"From the markings on them, I'd say they each hold two twenty-pound bombs," Buzz answered. "That should give us some bite!"

"What are those things piled up in the corner behind the door, sir?" Kashar inquired, his eyes darting around the room, trying to take in everything at once.

"Parachutes."

"There are so many of them," Akbar commented. "I wonder what we can use them for."

"We'll only need three or four," Buzz replied. He had turned away from the stack of parachutes, but returned to stand in front of them, deep in thought. A smile spread slowly across his face. "Parachutes are made of white silk. We have all those seamstresses in our ranks. By gobs, we'll have white silk uniforms! Gentlemen, we can start preparing our troops for war!"

~ Chapter Ten ~

ALL FOR ONE, ONE FOR ALL

"**O**h, here you are, Buzz. I've been looking all over for you." Akbar said, climbing the last few steps to the top of the control tower.

"Shhh!" Buzz whispered, with a finger to his lips. "Stay low and come over here."

Akbar crawled on his hands and knees to the corner where Buzz was crouching. Whispering in return, he asked, "Who are we hiding from, and why? And what's that on the end of your rifle barrel?"

"I'm hiding from the girls because Hana and I are playing a trick on them. It's a silencer on the end of the barrel. I worked out the design, and made it in the shop last night."

Akbar snorted gently, still whispering. "But what does that have to do with—"

"Shhh!" Buzz hissed again. "Here comes Hana now."

The men peeked over the railing and watched little Hana strutting to the shooting range, which was set up in front of the control tower so the shooter could be viewed by an instructor. Eight piles of sandbags were placed eight feet apart in a row at the edge of the airfield. A hundred yards across the field toward the mountains were the targets— black boards eight inches wide and four feet tall, that would fall back when struck properly. Attached to each was a parachute cord, which ran back to the shooter for resetting.

As she approached the girls milling around the rifle racks, waiting to begin their training session, she called out, "I can outshoot any of you!"

"You can't shoot, Hana," one of the girls replied.

"Besides, that's just a wooden training rifle you're carrying," another girl said derisively.

"This is a magic gun! Watch!" Hana retorted.

As she took aim, Buzz quietly eased his rifle over the railing of the control tower.

"Bang!" Hana cried.

Akbar watched as Buzz moved with the recoil of his rifle. He was astonished to hear only a muffled 'phfft.' One of the targets on the other side of the airfield fell.

Buzz bolted another shell into the chamber, and waited for his cue from Hana.

"Bang!" Another board dropped, with the same, strange 'phfft.'

This was repeated three more times. Hana smugly shouldered her wooden rifle and marched back to the mess hall, leaving the stunned girls with their mouths gaping in total consternation.

The two men in the control tower were rolling on the floor, holding their sides, trying valiantly to stifle their uproarious laughter over Hana's 'magic,' when Kashar thundered up the stairs.

"Sir! One of the lookouts signaled that three trucks are approaching the five-mile marker."

"It could be Harry," Akbar surmised.

"It could be someone else, too," Buzz answered. "I don't want to take any chances. Kashar, sound the alarm!"

Kashar rushed to the large iron triangle hanging by the steps and complied. Clang! Clang! Clang!

As the alarm rang out, Akbar disappeared down the stairs. The girls grabbed their rifles and bandoliers from the racks and ran to their assigned posts.

"This is not a drill!" Buzz yelled through a megaphone. "I repeat! This is not a drill!"

In a matter of seconds, the airfield looked deserted, but from the tower Buzz could see Akbar positioned in the rocks with the Lewis gun, covering the road leading into the aerodrome. Hasna and her rifle team dispersed themselves into the three buildings below him, and Yasmin was in the cockpit of the Flycatcher, manning its two machine guns, aiming by signaling two other girls at the rear of the plane next to the rudder and telling them to push the tail left or right. The rest of her team was scattered throughout the hanger.

Kashar stood tense, with his rifle at parade rest, waiting anxiously for orders.

Buzz removed a pair of binoculars from its compartment under the railing and scoured the area. As he watched for another signal from the lookouts, he hoped it was Harry. He hadn't heard from him since he watched the truck disappear over the hill more than two weeks ago. He'd wondered, without mentioning his thoughts, if Harry and Little Kim—David—had been ambushed on the way back. He spotted a flash from a signal mirror and translated out loud for Kashar's benefit.

"Two trucks, one trailer, mile marker one. If that's Harry, why would he have two trucks?" Buzz mumbled. "His truck is big enough for the supplies we need. Maybe he'd have two, but why the trailer?"

"Are you talking to me, sir?" Kashar asked.

"No, just thinking out loud."

The following minutes seemed more like an hour. They heard the faint whine of a truck engine as it labored up the steep hill. Slowly, the volume increased, as the vehicles drew closer to the base. Buzz trained his glasses on Akbar. "They should be in his line of sight by now," he narrated to Kashar. "Ah!—he sees them! He's giving the signal that they're friendly. It's Harry, Kashar. It's Harry!"

"Sir! Another signal from the lookout!"

Buzz turned his glasses to the new incoming flashes and read, "Two men, horseback, mile marker five. Kashar, take a message to your father. Tell him to stay at his post until the all clear bell sounds. And give this one to Harry as soon as he arrives." Buzz tore a hastily scribbled message from the clipboard in his hand and shoved it at Kashar, who grabbed it and dashed down the steps.

Buzz replaced the binoculars, picked up his Enfield, and followed. As he ran past Hasna, he shouted, "Stay at your posts until the all clear!" He yelled the same instructions to Yasmin as he raced through the hangar on his way to the corral.

Buzz saddled the black stallion and galloped to intercept the incoming riders.

117

"We're here at last," Harry announced as the truck began the descent toward the aerodrome.

Boris asked, "Where is everybody? I thought you said there would be at least twenty people here."

"I don't know! It looks like everybody's gone," Harry replied. He was as bewildered as Boris.

"Look!" Boris exclaimed. "There goes Buzz, riding across the field. Where the hell is he going?"

As soon as the truck stopped, the two men jumped out and were met immediately by Kashar, who thrust a paper into Harry's hand. "Mr. Kramer told me to give this to you right away, sir."

Harry—

Move the trucks behind the hangar. You've been followed.

Buzz

"Mr. Kramer went after two riders who followed you, but he left before the other message came in," Kashar informed Harry, worriedly.

"What other message?" Harry demanded.

"That there are twenty more riders a mile behind the first two. He left without taking extra ammunition. He only has five shots," Kashar answered in a panic. "He only knew of two."

Buzz rode to a narrow gully at the end of the airfield, which opened into a deep ravine. He rode low in the saddle, so as not to be seen from the road, for about a quarter mile, and then dismounted quickly and peered carefully over the rim.

The ground was nearly flat all the way to the foothills a mile away. To his left was the rocky ridge that all but circled the airfield; to his right the plain tilted abruptly upward to disappear over the horizon. A light breeze blew from the southeast. The vegetation was sparse—just patches of short grass and two spindly wild rose bushes; hardly enough cover to hide a rabbit, much less a man.

118

Buzz smiled with satisfaction. His calculations to intercept the two unknown riders were right on. About a hundred and fifty yards away, two men in black rode at an easy lope, watching the ground for tracks.

"Gotcha!" Buzz whispered to himself as he raised his rifle and took aim.

Ka-pow! Ka-pow! The second shot rang out almost before the echo from the first one faded; the two men fell from their horses nearly simultaneously.

Buzz scurried to his horse and led it back up the steep slope. While remounting, he noticed with surprise that one of the Shadow Men was trying to gain his horse, so he unslung his rifle and snapped off another shot. The man jerked, and then slid down the side of his horse, and dropped to the ground.

Leaping into the saddle, Buzz raced to the fallen men and was on the ground before his horse had fully stopped. Rushing to the last man to fall, revolver in his hand, he rolled the body over, prodding it with his foot. The man was dead. He saw that his first shot had been stopped by the leather cartridge belt across the man's chest. His companion had been killed with the first shot.

Buzz was startled by the crack of a rifle and the whine of a bullet passing just inches over his head. Turning toward the sound of the gunshot, he saw a mass of black with galloping hooves beneath. Shadow Men! They were cresting the hill, about two-hundred yards away, and wasting no time.

"Damn! These two were scouts for a bigger party. I'd better make a stand here rather than try to cross the open ground back to the ravine. With ten or twenty rifles firing at me, someone might get lucky." Speaking aloud to himself somehow made it seem as though there were someone else with him; he didn't feel so completely alone to face the charging horde.

Buzz acted with alacrity. He jerked loose the cinch, pulled the saddle from the nearest horse, and threw it to the ground. Stripping the two Shadow Men of their cartridge belts and rifles, he placed the bodies on either side of the saddle and jumped behind his newly made 'fortress.'

Taking up one of the Mauser rifles, Buzz began firing as fast as he could bolt the rifle, dropping an enemy rider with each shot. He stopped only to empty a stripper clip of its five rounds into the magazine with his thumb. The rapid firing resembled one of the acts in the circus— only now his targets were flesh and bone, and returned fire.

The bullets sounded like a swarm of hornets around him. The dead Shadow Men on either side of him twitched each time they absorbed the impact of a projectile. Chips of wood and leather from the saddle hit him in the cheek; sand kicked up in front of him, stinging his face like hundreds of tiny needles. He felt a tug at his right foot as a 'hornet' stung his left shoulder, and another his right ear.

The charging mass was only fifty yards away. Buzz was drawing his Webleys.

Suddenly, gunfire was coming from the right. In the distance, Buzz could hear the muffled sound of the Lewis gun.

Akbar and the girls, Buzz thought. Jumping up, he began blazing away with his pistols. The murderous crossfire stopped the onslaught of the men in black, almost as if they had encountered a wall. A trailing dust cloud, spurred on by a light breeze, caught up with the Shadow Men, enshrouding them in a brownish-gray fog.

All firing ceased. The silence was deafening, broken only by the neighing of the frightened and wounded horses. Then the cloud of dust enveloped Buzz; he shielded his eyes with his arm until it had passed.

When he lowered his arm, he confronted the carnage of war. Dead men lay on the ground in front of him, one with his foot still in the stirrup. A downed horse was trying vainly to rise again. Buzz's attention was drawn to a lone Shadow Man wavering on his mount, slashing at a phantom enemy with his sword despite the spreading crimson stain over his chest. It was evident he was no longer a threat. His near-lifeless eyes looked toward Buzz unseeingly as he tried to lift his sword again. The effort proved too costly. His arm dropped to his side as his fingers relaxed in death, and the sword clattered to the ground. The dead man's eyes slowly closed, and he fell forward, draping himself over his saddle, and then slowly slipped to the ground beside his sword. The battle was over.

"Akbar! Send four girls after the runaway horses! We don't want any to make it back to their camp," Buzz shouted.

Akbar chose his four best riders and sent them in pursuit of the escaping horses, and then he and the remaining three girls rushed to meet

Buzz." I hope I didn't spoil your party, but I thought this would be good training for the girls. It looked like you had everything under control," Akbar remarked with a welcoming smile. He dismounted and put the Lewis gun on the ground.

"You old fart. If you only knew how glad I was to hear the Lewis gun!" Buzz said, hugging Akbar gratefully.

"Your two friends came with us, but Yasmin said she saw them ride off before our shooting started. I'm afraid they disappointed you, Buzz," Akbar reported solemnly.

"Oh, they're not cowards. They must have had a good reason to ride off," Buzz replied hastily. Akbar just shrugged his shoulders.

"Sir, we counted only seventeen bodies." Nudar announced breathlessly, running up to stand near the two men

"I was afraid of that."

"Afraid of what? What's wrong, Akbar?"

Akbar only said, "We had better get you back to the base and have your wounds attended to. Your shoulder is bleeding heavily."

"Damn it, Akbar! My shoulder is fine. What's wrong?"

"There were twenty riders—and there are only seventeen bodies. Three of them must be riding back to their camp, and they got too much of a head start for us to catch them. They'll surely return with a larger party tomorrow," Akbar explained in dismay.

"Oh! Well, I wouldn't worry too much about that if I were you." Buzz grinned and pointed over Akbar's shoulder, where two riders were approaching at a fast trot, leading three horses.

"Sir," Nudar came running to them again, "it's the two new men. It looks like they have the three missing Shadow Men."

Still smiling, Buzz said, "Like I said, they must have had a good reason to run off."

"Buzz, I owe you an apology. I'm sorry that I implied that your friends were cowards," Akbar said with deep concern.

"No offense, Akbar. You don't know Bob and Boris like I do, but you soon will. Come, let me properly introduce you."

As Buzz began walking toward his two old comrades, he noticed that his right foot felt strange.

"I think this is what you're missing," Akbar said with a grin, handing Buzz the heel of his right boot.

Buzz laughed. "I thought I felt something hit my foot."

"You were very lucky; an inch lower and the bullet would have taken your heel. Save it. I can fix it when we get back to the base."

"Thanks, Akbar, I'd appreciate that."

Suddenly, Buzz was spun around unceremoniously by Boris, who held him at arms' length.

"Good God. Look at this lad, Bob. Bloody ear, bloody shoulder, hair a mess, face streaked with sweat and peppered with sand and chips of wood."

"He looks like he's been fighting circus fires again," Bob added, laughing.

"Before you start the 'How do's' and the 'How are yous,' Buzz, let's get our horses and head back. We're starving," Boris boomed.

Beep! Beep! Beeeep!

"Here comes Harry with one of his trucks," Buzz noted, as he pointed to a truck rapidly approaching, seemingly trying to out-run the large cloud of dust behind it. Harry was perching on the passenger-side running board, waving vigorously.

"Hey, who's driving?" Buzz asked.

"That's Ned. He drives for Harry from time to time," Bob answered.

"He looks familiar, somehow," Buzz commented.

"He said he spends much of his time at the Fife and Drum; maybe you saw him there. He's a real nice chap. We had a long talk during the drive up here. He was a mechanic at the base until it closed, and then he retired from the service and just stayed here because he said he didn't have anywhere else to go. We hit it off real good. I think it's the first time he felt like talking to anyone like that since he mustered out over a year ago."

Just as Bob finished, the truck came to an abrupt stop alongside the four men. Harry jumped off the running board, camera in hand. "Buzz, I want you to stand over there, in front of the dead Shadow Men." Harry ordered. Then, as an afterthought, he said, "With your revolvers drawn."

"What the hell for? I didn't shoot these men for the glory of it!" Buzz snapped.

"Just do it! I'll explain later."

Reluctantly, Buzz walked over and stood by the fallen men, and removed his pistols from their holsters.

Following Harry's hand signals, everyone else moved to the side. He shot the scene from three different angles. "Now a shot with everybody else in it—there, that's good." The camera clicked again.

Harry motioned to the man in the truck. "Ned here said he can get rid of the bodies, so let's load up." Ned acknowledged the introduction by leaning out the window and giving a casual salute.

"I want everything off the bodies except their undergarments," Buzz cried.

Harry looked at Buzz, frowning quizzically.

"Just do it. I'll explain later," Buzz said with a slight smirk. "And no, I'm not being ghoulish."

Lowering his voice to a near-whisper, Buzz spoke to Akbar. "Do you think we should have the girls doing this?"

"Yes. This is a good way to weed out the weak from the strong. And quit being such a mother hen."

The grisly task was set upon and completed without a word spoken. Ned and the three girls boarded the truck—one of the girls in the cab with Ned, the other two on the running boards.

As the truck rumbled off, the other four girls returned, leading the runaway horses.

"As soon as we get back to the base, I need to tend to your wounds—again," Harry told Buzz, mounting one of the horses.

~ Chapter Eleven ~

THE ODDS CHANGE

L ittle was said during the ride back to the base. As the party approached the hitching rail in front of the mess hall, Harry called to Buzz, "Let Akbar take care of your horse. I want to tend to your shoulder so it doesn't get infected." He stepped up onto the porch, and waited for the wounded man.

"If you don't need me for anything right now, I think I'll see to the injured horses," Akbar said.

Harry acknowledged the request with an affirmative nod.

"Boris, why don't you and Bob go with Akbar? Maybe you can help," Buzz suggested, handing his reins to the tribal chief.

"You don't want us to watch while Harry operates on you, right?" Boris asked, grinning.

"You're right," Buzz answered, and they all laughed.

"Here, Boris," Bob said, quickly handing over his reins. "Take my horse with you. I want to get a closer look at that steam roller."

Everyone scattered to their own tasks. Harry prepared to patch up Buzz; Bob eagerly began to inspect the steam roller; Akbar and Boris gently led the horses to the corral. The four girls, in somewhat of a daze from the earlier events, followed behind the horses.

"Sit at that table by the window where there's more light," Harry instructed Buzz. "I'll get the first aid kit; have one of the girls in the kitchen heat up some water." He returned shortly with Basima close behind. The girl was carrying a tray laden with two cups of fresh coffee, a large basin of hot water, and a bottle of rum. She was smiling, as was usual for her.

Buzz had once commented to Akbar, "That girl has the warmest smile. Her whole face seems to glow and her eyes twinkle."

To Buzz's dismay, when she saw him with blood dripping from his fingertips, her smile immediately vanished, her face blanched and she grimaced with fear for her friend. "Oh, sir! You're hurt!"

"I'll be all right, Basima. Just put the tray on the table and go on back to the kitchen," Buzz said gently, trying to comfort her.

She quickly placed the tray, bobbed a tiny curtsey, and then ran from the room, sobbing.

Harry spoke gruffly, concerned for both Buzz and the girl. "Let's get that shirt off," he said, pulling a large pair of scissors from the first aid kit.

"Whoa! Don't cut it off, Harry. I'll get it. I only have two shirts, and this is my best one."

Harry shook his head and carefully helped Buzz remove his Sunday-go-to-meeting shirt, as Buzz had labeled it.

"Basima," Buzz called, "would you bring some soap and a towel?"

Buzz gingerly cleaned himself up as well as he could as Harry laid out the implements he would need on a clean linen cloth.

"Does your shoulder hurt that much?" Harry asked, with a worried look.

"I hardly noticed it on the field, but it burns like hell, now," Buzz replied.

"It'll feel better when I get the dirt and sand out of the wound," Harry remarked, gently swabbing the fleshy groove two inches from the base of Buzz's neck. When he poured alcohol on it, Buzz winced.

"Sorry!"

"That's okay. It has to be done."

"Your ear looks all right; the bullet just nipped it. The bleeding kept it clean. I won't bandage it, but I will put some salve on it. It'll help speed the healing process."

"Thanks, Doc."

"Is that too tight?" Harry inquired as he brought one end of a gauze strip across Buzz's chest and the other from under his arm.

"No. It feels fine."

"Good. Put your finger here."

Buzz put his finger where Harry indicated as he tied a knot.

"Now, let's have that rum," Harry said. They drank the remaining coffee in their cups, and Harry refilled them with the amber-colored elixir. They clinked their cups in a toast and drank. Buzz took a long, deep, grateful swallow. He could feel the welcome warmth gently embracing him like summer morning's sun, and sighed contentedly. At long last, he relaxed.

"Sir?"

Buzz was somewhat startled by Basima, who'd quietly appeared beside him holding his other shirt. "Sir, I brought you your clean shirt. I just took it off the line. It's still warm from the sun."

"Why, thank you, Basima." He carefully slid his arms into the still warm garment. *Bandages and salve help heal physical wounds, but soap and water and a clean shirt soothe the spirit,* Buzz mused to himself. He took another tiny sip from his cup, savoring it.

"I'd not drink any more rum if I were you. It may have a stronger effect than usual due to the blood loss," Harry cautioned.

"Yeah, I think you're right. I think I'll have coffee instead."

"Buzz, why don't you find your friends and take them to the officers' quarters? I'm sure you have a lot to talk about. I'll have some food brought to you." Harry paused for a moment, and then said, "Oh, by the way! You have far surpassed my expectations in what you've accomplished here. I'm very pleased."

"Thank you, Harry. There were a few difficulties, but everyone worked hard, and things seem to be coming together now."

Buzz left the mess hall and looked around for his cohorts. He found them together, approaching the building he had just vacated. They had timed their arrival perfectly, correctly figuring that Harry had had enough time to tend to the patient.

He led his companions to the officers' quarters, and each pulled a chair to the table. Boris pulled off his boots, noisily exhaling a long, drawn-out sigh. Bob removed his jacket, hung it over the back of his chair, sat down, and lit a cigar. Buzz tiredly plopped down and gently massaged his shoulder.

"Hurt much?" Bob asked.

"Oh, it's much better. Sore, but better."

"Well, let's get to it. What's this war you said you got yourself into?" Boris inquired.

Buzz responded, "Didn't Harry explain anything to you?"

Boris answered somewhat impatiently, "We arrived last night, unloaded from the train, and were wined and dined."

"At the Fife & Drum?"

"Yeah, I think that was it. Then we went to a hotel, slept, got up, and went back to the tooter and banger place for breakfast. After that, it was on to the truck, which was already loaded, then here—just in time to see you arguing with your neighbors."

Bob interrupted. "Harry said you would tell us about what's going on here."

"I don't know if you've heard about the civil war that's going on here. It's mostly in the area of Kabul."

"We read something about it in the Paris newspapers. It doesn't look like the good guys are doing so well," Bob said. "Is that what you're involved in?"

"No. But that war has taken all the fighting-age men from this area, leaving it undefended from these Shadow Men, who are really gunmen from all over, hired by the Germans."

"I thought I saw several different nationalities in that pile of bodies. What in the hell is Germany doing here?" Bob inquired, puzzled.

Three sharp raps on the door forestalled Buzz's reply. "Come in," he called.

Kashar entered the room carrying a tray of goat cheese, biscuits and jam, and a steaming pot of coffee.

"Just set it on the table, Kashar. Gentlemen, this is Kashar. He's my aide. If you need anything, just ask him, and he will help you. Thank you, Kashar. You may go now."

"Looks like a sharp lad," Boris commented.

"He is. He's Akbar's son. Only sixteen. That limp of his probably kept him from being drafted." Buzz paused for a moment. "In answer to your question, Bob, as Harry explained it to me, the high command in the army is developing new and better airplanes."

"I thought Germany wasn't supposed to have any planes under the Versailles Treaty," Bob commented quickly.

"Not to change the subject," Boris interjected, "but this cheese is excellent. Try some, Bob. Now, back to the Hun air force."

"They're not. Some of the Brits think they're setting up secret air forces in other countries, including Russia and Afghanistan," Buzz said worriedly.

"And the guys in the black robes?" asked Bob.

"Those are mercenaries going under the guise of the Shadow Men of God. There were about five-hundred of them, all armed with German Mausers."

"*Were* about five-hundred?" Bob questioned.

"Counting the skirmish today, there should be about four-hundred and sixty. These men have been terrifying the small tribes around here; they plunder their horses, food, and livestock, and now they're taking their young girls to sell at the Russian border. A bit over two weeks ago, we rescued sixteen of those girls, aged thirteen to eighteen." Buzz paused, and stood to refill their coffee cups.

Bob rose, and slowly paced to the window, sat on the sill, and stared pensively into the sunlit world outside, cradling his unheeded cup in both hands.

Boris leaned back in his chair, his cup in one hand, the other tucked securely into his belt. His feet were propped on the table. His face was grim.

Buzz resumed his chair and took a tentative sip of coffee. "I figure if we can get those two planes to fly, we can use surprise and showmanship. You know, circus tricks. I think we can beat them."

"How many men do you have? A hundred, hundred and fifty?" Boris inquired, taking a swig of coffee.

"Well, not counting Harry, Akbar, and myself, we have Kashar and eighteen girls," Buzz responded quickly, hoping to slip the hugely uneven odds through the conversation unnoticed.

Boris' feet slammed to the floor as he rocked forward in his chair. Coffee splashed from his cup and spewed from his mouth like a Roman fountain, baptizing the table.

Bob's eyes and mouth opened wide, and his cup dropped to the floor, shattering, sending coffee and cup fragments in all directions.

"You're proposing to fight five-hundred—"

Buzz corrected Boris, "No, four-hundred and sixty,"

"Oh, sorry. Four-hundred and sixty well-armed cutthroats, with three men—"

"It would be five men, if you two join us."

"Three men and eighteen young girls. What are you planning to do, use mirrors?" Bob asked sarcastically.

"Well, yes, as a matter of fact!—something like that," Buzz replied softly.

Harry was reaching for the door, preparing to enter the room, when he heard the outcry from within. He very gently withdrew his hand from the knob and backed off the porch and down the steps as though they were made of eggs. When he reached the ground, he executed a sharp 'left face,' and beat a hasty retreat to the mess hall.

"You must be still suffering from that nasty knock on the head you got from Rico."

"Boris is right! You must be out of your bloomin' mind. Even if you had eighteen seasoned fighting men—men!—it would be impossible. With eighteen girls—just kids, at that!"

"They're good kids! They've come a long way in the last couple of weeks; you saw them fight today!"

"Oh, hell, Buzz. When we got there, there were probably only five or six left. You'd already chewed them down. And besides, Akbar more than likely got most of them with the Lewis gun."

"Look! Before you make any decisions, at least let me show you some of the stuff we have to work with," Buzz was almost pleading.

129

"Well, show us what you have to work with. I mean, it's not as though we have a pressing dinner engagement or anything," Bob acquiesced.

Buzz wasted no time ushering the two men out the door, closing it firmly behind him. He quickly stepped ahead of his companions, who were warily waiting at the foot of the steps. "Okay, I guess I'm the tour guide. Coffee or souvenirs, gentlemen? Right this way," he gaily cried.

"Hmmpff, what? Oh, Ned!" Harry was startled from his reverie. "I didn't hear you come in. Yes, I will have a cup of coffee, thank you." Harry reached for one of the two steaming cups that Ned had brought to the table.

Ned spoke softly, trying to lift the spirits of 'Mr. Harry.' "When I saw you gazing out the window, there, I said to myself, 'Ned', I said, 'There's a man who looks as though he needs a cup of java in his hand.' That's what I said to myself, I did—so I brung you one over. Oh, and the girls in the kitchen said to tell you that lunch will be ready in about an hour or so."

Harry replied, smiling pensively, "Good. And thank you for the coffee. Now that I think about it, a cup of coffee is comforting when one is alone, or is thinking about things."

"Yeh, guv'nor. I guess 'cause one usually drinks with his friends, so he relates to that."

"When did you get back? I didn't see you drive up," Harry inquired.

"I drove in on one of the back trails. I was dragging some brush behind the truck to cover the tire tracks. It kicks up a lot of dust, and I didn't want it to get all dusty here. I back tracked our tire tracks for several miles, and then I used the brush to wipe out our tire tracks as well as their hoof prints, so's anybody'd have a hard time finding us."

"You're a fine man, Ned. That was good thinking."

"How's your boy doin' with his friends?" Ned asked, pointing to the three figures exiting the hangar.

130

"I don't know. They weren't too happy when they found out we're fighting a force at almost twenty-to-one odds—and our own should be playing with dolls instead of guns."

"Oh. Doesn't sound good."

"No, Ned, it doesn't. I don't know if Buzz will persuade his friends to stay, or if they will convince him to leave." Harry nervously lit his cigar.

The two men stood by the window, sipping their coffee, as they watched the three men walk from the hangar and approach the Flycatcher. Boris stood, arms crossed over his chest, solemn. Bob lit a cigar and seemed more interested in blowing smoke rings than in what was being said. Buzz was making swooping motions with his hands, obviously describing the flight of the plane, and then began drawing figures in the dust with a stick.

"It's like watching one of them silent moving pitchers," Ned commented.

"Yes. Only they have printed captions on the screen to tell what's being said," Harry replied.

"Is Mr. Kramer Italian?" Ned asked.

"No. Why?"

"Well, he sorta talks like one, waving his hands about and all."

"Yes he does," Harry said, amused.

"Look. The other two are going back into the hangar, and Mr. Kramer is going over to that hitching rail," Ned observed, watching Bob and Boris disappear into the building.

Buzz leaned on the rail, legs crossed. He took out his pipe, lit it, crossed his arms over his chest, and calmly puffed away, watching the smoke waft lazily into the atmosphere.

"Mr. Whitecliff, sir." Ned said, breaking the suspense.

"Yes?"

"Instead of me driving the truck back like you hired me to do; I would like to stay on with you, sir."

"Ned, you know the odds against coming out of this alive, don't you?"

"Yes, sir. But, you see, sir, I have this illness that I could go anytime. The way I see it, it would be better to go on a battlefield with a .303 Enfield in my hands than at Paddy's place with a tankard of ale."

"Glad to have you aboard, Ned," Harry said, shaking Ned's hand. "But we'll have to ask the others."

"Look, here they come," Ned said in a loud whisper.

Harry and Ned watched Buzz lead the way to the mess hall, up the steps, and in the door. Buzz held it open for his companions and, when they'd entered, softly closed it. Not a word was spoken. The clatter in the kitchen stopped abruptly. The room was completely silent except for the scrape of the chairs as the trio settled themselves at the table.

"Sagirah." Buzz broke the silence. "Is there any tea?"

"Yes, sir. I just made a fresh pot."

"Good. Please bring us three cups."

"Yes, sir."

"Well, gentlemen, what do you think? Can it be done?" Buzz asked.

"It's iffy as hell, but I think we could do it. Don't you, Boris?" asked Bob.

"It sure as hell won't be easy, but yes, I think so. You have fine horses, and if these girls are as good as you say, I think I can make something out of them—with Akbar's help, that is."

"I already have some ideas," Bob said excitedly.

"Your tea, sir." Setting the tray on the table quickly, Sagirah scampered off.

Bob removed a silver hip flask from his pocket and poured a generous amount of golden liquid into each cup.

The three men rose in unison and raised their cups, which then came together with a resounding clink.

"All for one, one for all."

~ Chapter Twelve ~

RENEWING OLD ACQUAINTANCE

"That was a good meal, Buzz. You and Akbar have done wonders with these young ladies."

"Thank you, Harry, but we can't take all the credit. They work hard, and they're eager to learn," Buzz replied.

"Is everyone finished eating?" Everyone nodded in the affirmative, and Buzz waved his hand in the air to catch the attention of the kitchen staff so they could clear the tables. Then Harry made an announcement.

"Before we get to the business at hand, I believe you've all met Ned?" Everyone agreed. "Well, Ned has asked if he can stay and help fight. I told him I would have to see what you gentlemen think."

Harry, who was seated at the end of two tables that had been pushed together, turned to Akbar. "Akbar?"

"I like him," Akbar answered, turning to Boris.

Boris was leaning on his elbows, hands folded in front of him on the table. "I don't know him very well, but what little I do know, I like. What about you, Buzz?"

Buzz, sitting at the other end of the table, was staring at his half-cup of tea, slowly rotating it around and around with his fingers. After some thought, he looked up. "After seeing how he handled the situation with the dead bodies today, I think he'll work out very well. Bob, what do you think? You spent several hours with him in the truck coming up here, so you probably know him better than any of us."

Bob leaned back in his chair and laced his hands behind his head. "He knows this area like the back of his hand and, as a man, I like him."

"That settles it. I'll have him join us." Harry called, "Ned, would you come over here? And bring your chair."

Ned, who had been sitting with Kashar and some of the girls on the other side of the room, responded immediately to Harry's invitation.

The new recruit was about five-feet, seven inches tall, with narrow shoulders. He had a well-developed paunch, probably from the ingestion of a few too many helpings of 'the best fish and chips in town.' He had a face that was round, with deep lines around the eyes from years of squinting in the bright Afghanistan sun. His plump cheeks were the color of a pale cherry, the tip of his nose was that of one fully ripened. His 'salt and pepper' hair had receded past the top of his head, and was shaggy over the ears. His over-all complexion was of the paleness of a not-well man. He walked in a military manner.

"Ned, put your chair between Bob and me and sit down. I talked to the rest of the boys, and they've agreed to have you come aboard. Welcome."

"I thank ye, Mr. Whitecliff, sir—and you gentlemen, too," Ned said diffidently, and scooted himself in at the table.

Buzz caught the attention of the kitchen staff again, and asked for more tea. The girls quickly responded by bringing another tray holding cups, a pot of tea, a basket of hot biscuits, and a jar of jam.

"Cigar, anyone?" Harry asked as he passed his silver case first to Akbar, who politely refused, then to Boris, who smiled as he took a Havana. Buzz held up his pipe, Bob took one, with a gesture of thanks, and Ned accepted gladly. Harry removed a cigar, and passed his tip cutter to Boris, who cut the tip off the cigar he had taken, and then passed it to Bob. When it came to Ned, he said that he was okay, as he bit the end off his. Harry clipped his, and they all lit up; Buzz his pipe, and the others, save Akbar, their cigars.

"What's this thing with a pipe? That's the second time I've seen you smoke one. I can't believe you turned down a Havana," Boris remarked.

"Did you meet a girl that likes pipes?" Bob asked teasingly, giving Buzz a quizzical look.

"Damn! Why does everybody think I fell in love or something, just because I decided to start smoking a pipe?"

Harry said nothing; he just sat back in his chair, put his hands behind his head, and smiled knowingly as he puffed his Havana.

"Well?" Bob and Boris chorused in unison.

"Well…" Buzz hesitated. "I did meet this girl on the train, and we hit it off pretty well. That's all."

"And?" the two friends chimed again.

"I kind of like her!"

"Kind of?"

"All right! I love her, and I want to ask her to marry me—when I find her."

"When you find her?" Boris snorted.

"This man lived in Paris, the city of romance and light, where some of the most beautiful women in the world live. Does he fall in love with someone there? No! He has to find someone on a dirty train traveling through the middle of nowhere. Then he loses her!" Bob exclaimed, gesticulating wildly, his hands flying through the air like frightened birds taking flight.

Clink! Clink! Clink! Harry rapped his cup with a spoon, rescuing Buzz from further discussion.

"Gentlemen, I think we should get down to business. Buzz, I know you're wondering why you hadn't heard from me for over two weeks. Well, I didn't know of a sure way of getting word to you without giving your location away."

"Harry, where in the hell is the gas for the planes? You just told me that there were at least five-hundred gallons of gas here, but you didn't tell me where," Buzz countered, piqued.

"I didn't tell you where because I don't know—I just know that it's here. I was hoping that you would have found it," Harry explained.

"I can help you chaps there, because it was my job to hide the pipe when we shut the field down," Ned piped up. "Actually, there's twenty-five-hundred gallons, not five-hundred."

"Well, maybe you know where the spark plugs are for the Fairey Campania?" Buzz asked.

"Sorry, guv, don't have any."

"None at all? Not even the old ones?"

"Nope. Pete, our supply sergeant, could get us just about anything, but he couldn't get those plugs. He even sent the old ones to the other bases to see if they could match them. Nobody had any. Pete said some car maker in Germany bought all the surplus plugs."

"Damn!" Buzz thought quickly. "Bob, do you think truck plugs could be used?

"Too small."

"What if I made an insert on the lathe to make them fit?"

"Maybe, but I doubt the spark would be hot enough."

"Gentlemen, gentlemen," Harry broke in. "You can worry about the planes later. Buzz, Akbar, how is your training program coming along? Will you be able to make a fighting force out of what you have?"

Buzz looked as though he'd seen a ghost. "Harry! Are you telling me that what we have now is all we're going to have? That none of the tribes are going to help us fight their war? Is that what you're saying?" By this time, Buzz was standing, leaning forward onto the table, his weight resting on his outstretched arms. His chair lay on its back, where it had clattered to the floor when Buzz had leapt to his feet.

The room rang with silence. All eyes were on Buzz, then Harry.

Harry leaned back in his chair and put his hands in his lap. He looked calmly at Buzz, who was waiting impatiently for an answer. "Yes, I'm afraid that's the way it is—at least for now."

"What do you mean, 'for now'?" Buzz asked angrily.

"That's why I took those pictures today. I'll set up the darkroom tonight, and make some prints to show your victories to the tribal leaders. Maybe then they'll help."

"When?" Buzz demanded.

"If Akbar will meet with some of the leaders and set up a meeting—maybe in two or three days," Harry replied.

"I'll go at first light tomorrow," Akbar said.

Buzz drew a deep breath. "Thank you," he said to Kashar, who had righted his chair and placed it under him as he sat down.

136

"Akbar, aren't you a leader of these people? Can't you get them to help us?" he asked, frustrated.

"Buzz, at one time I was the leader of the largest tribe in this area. But wars and illness have taken all but Kashar, my daughters, and me, so I don't have much say anymore. Don't think badly of these people; they were once the lions of the fields. Now, after years of fighting, they are worn down to gazelles that run from the jackals and hope they don't become their meal. The Afghan people have been fighting since before the time of Alexander the Great. They're just plain tired!"

Boris motioned Kashar to come to him, and whispered in his ear.

"Yes, sir." Kashar ran from the room, beaming.

"I'm sorry I blew up at you, Harry. I know you're doing your best, but the reality was a slap in the face," Buzz said in a calmer tone.

"Just don't make any definitive decisions until we have a meeting; maybe then things will be different. Why don't you show your friends around some more, Buzz? Akbar and I need to talk about tomorrow."

Buzz nodded and started to walk away, then stopped. "Oh, Ned. We'll have to find you a place to bunk."

"Oh, that's all right, Mr. Buzz, sir. I'll use my old quarters. I had a nice little room in the back of the hangar while I was stationed here."

"I guess you know this place pretty well."

"Like the back o' me hand, sir."

"I'd like you to show me all the nooks and crannies tomorrow, Ned."

"I'd be mighty proud to, sir," Ned answered, snapping to attention.

"Well, Bob and Boris are waiting outside for me to show them around some more, so until tomorrow…" Buzz downed the last of his tea and went out the door.

Closing the door behind him, Buzz stood on the porch in total disbelief. At the hitching post in front of him were Boris, mounted on his black stallion, Tasha; Bob was atop his gray mare, Grizela; and next to

137

them was Kashar, holding the reins for Flamme Blanc and Diable Noir. Buzz cleared the porch in one bound and was beside his beloved steeds in a split second. With an arm around the neck of each horse, he hugged one, then the other. The tension of the day melted away with tears of joy. The horses' bodies quivered with excitement, and they caressed Buzz's face tenderly with their velvety soft muzzles.

"Who do you think missed who the most?" Boris asked Bob, grinning.

"From where I sit, it looks to me like a flat-out tie," Bob returned happily.

"You bought both of them. How can I ever thank you?" Buzz was laughing and crying.

"Oh, I think we'll be able to think of a few ways," Boris replied.

"I didn't think you'd be able to sell my rifle for enough to buy both horses," Buzz said, a look of wonder on his face.

"Mount up, and we'll tell you all about it as we ride. These horses need to stretch their legs; they've been cooped up far too long," Bob instructed, and took Diable's reins from Kashar. After Buzz mounted Flamme, Bob handed the reins to him.

"Thanks. I'll ride Flamme out, then change over and ride Diable back. Maybe I can keep them both happy." He was grinning like a kid who just got what he'd asked for on Christmas morning.

"Lead on, MacDuff! Let's ride!" Bob whooped.

"Yes, show us the marvels of this land you wish to spill blood upon," Boris called.

"We'll ride across the landing field to the mountains, then swing around across the flatlands and be back here by dark," Buzz told them. "Let the tour begin!"

Then he cautioned, "Whoa, boy, whoa. We may have a hard time holding the horses to a lope," Buzz said as he struggled with Flamme.

"Yeah, but we can't just let them run. After that long trip, they have to loosen up their muscles first," Boris said.

"Okay, you two. What's the deal with the horses?" asked Buzz.

"You're a hero back at the circus," Boris explained.

"A hero? What?"

"When you shot the Rico brother who was absconding with the money, you must have hit him pretty good. Two days after you left, his brother brought him into the hospital and gave himself up, in order to save him. He said he had tried to patch him up, but he kept getting worse. He had no choice but to get him to the hospital, in order to try to save his life." Boris was obviously enjoying telling Buzz the surprising outcome of their previous adventure.

"So, everybody got their savings back, and Perry was able to prove, without a doubt, that he had nothing to do with setting the fire, so the insurance company had to cover all damages. That's why you're a hero!" Boris heartily pounded Buzz's back.

"That was one hell of a shot you made! Three-hundred and thirty-seven feet! I measured it," Bob commented.

"That's all fine and dandy, but it still doesn't explain how you were able to bring the horses here," Buzz insisted.

Bob took up the narrative where Boris had left off. "Perry gave them to you as a reward—plus he saw to it that you received the award the insurance company had put up for the capture of the Rico brothers. With the reward money and the recovery of your savings, you now have a tidy sum waiting for you in Paris."

"What about you and Boris? You fellows risked your lives in that fire, too."

"You don't have to worry about us; old Jack took care of us, too. Plus, he gave us all the pyro supplies that were in the trailer that Boris rode down the hill into the pond. Since everything was in sealed containers, the only things lost were a few rockets."

Boris chimed in, "He even pulled some strings to get us a traveling circus pass so we'd be able to pass through customs. And, if I'm not mistaken, he paid for the trip here. Do you think Jack and your Mr. Whitecliff have something going on that we don't know about?"

"Not that I know of," Buzz answered.

"Well, if nothing else, we can put on one hell of a fireworks show," Bob said, throwing his arms wide.

The three reached the foothills and turned north. The sun was slipping behind the mountain peaks, casting shadows on their rocky sides and in the crevasses, creating a cold, mysterious atmosphere.

"That cloud of fog hanging between those two peaks. Is that a canyon through the mountains, or what?" Bob asked, pointing to the area in question.

"I don't know; it's been like that ever since I've been here. I always wanted to explore it, but I've never found the time," Buzz replied.

Bob spoke with an exaggerated shudder. "It sure looks sinister!"

"On a lighter note, this is really pretty country, in a rough sort of way," Boris commented.

"Yeah. It reminds me of my home in New Mexico, only it seems to rain more here. Harry said that this is the end of the rainy season. It rains just about every other night, but by the next morning, the ground is nearly dry."

"Enough of the tour guide routine. Tell us about this girl you met on the train," Boris demanded.

"And lost," Bob added.

"Did you use the old ploy, 'May I sit in the seat next to you since the car is full?" Boris inquired, grinning hugely.

"No, Actually, it was the other way around. The car was practically empty. I was looking out the window when I heard a sweet voice ask, 'Sir, is this seat taken?' I looked around, and there was this stunning girl pointing to the seat across from me. Well, of course I said, 'No,' so she sat down."

"What does she look like? Is she pretty?"

"Well, of course she's pretty," Boris chided. "Have you ever known Buzz to go with anyone who wasn't? She is pretty, isn't she?" he asked Buzz, suddenly having second thoughts.

"Yes, very. She's twenty-two, a little over five feet tall, maybe a hundred and ten pounds, very pleasantly proportioned. Her hair is like black silk. Her skin is like cream, not pale, but of that soft rosy hue it has just before it turns to butter. It's kind of the light tannish glow of someone that spends a lot of their time outdoors. She has an oval-shaped face, with a little nose that has a cute upturn at the end. Her lips are like rose petals—not a deep red, but a soft, pinkish-red."

"Her eyes—what color are her eyes?" Bob asked.

Buzz answered dreamily, "Her eyes are sort of pale green, but they become darker, almost emerald, when she's excited, and they sparkle and dance when she laughs. She giggled a lot."

"Giggled?" Boris and Bob asked in unison.

"Yeah. When we first met, she giggled and used the phrase 'something like that' after just about every other sentence. She told me later that she put on a silly young girl act when we first met because most people expect girls her age to act like that. But she's very intelligent, and can ride and shoot, too. She can hold a conversation with a poor man, or a rich man alike. Kim had the cutest way of acting like she was pouting—she'd push out her bottom lip, and wrinkle her brow."

Buzz paused, startled, and exclaimed, "Damn. We're back at the base already."

The three men rode the rest of the way in companionable silence. Buzz's thoughts were, of course, of Kim, while Boris and Bob reminisced about similar memories of loved ones in their own pasts.

As the men unsaddled their horses, Bob turned to Boris. "Boris, I think we should help this man find the girl he loves so."

"I agree. Let's make a pact."

"Agreed. All for one, one for all," and the three clasped hands.

"After we finish grooming the horses, let's take a look at the Flycatcher." Bob said.

"I'd like to talk with Akbar before he leaves tomorrow, so why don't you and Buzz check out the plane without me. I'll join you when I can," Boris rejoined.

"I believe you'll find Akbar with Harry in the officers' quarters," Buzz said, pointing.

"Thanks. I'll meet you two for dinner," Boris said, as they parted company.

Buzz petted his two recently returned equine friends one more time, and he and Bob strolled over to the Fairey Flycatcher. It looked smaller, somehow, sitting on the runway, than it had when it had been in the hangar.

"What do you think of her? Look at her wing structure. I'll bet I could have wowed the crowds at the circus with this," Buzz said as he gently ran his hand over the fuselage.

"It sure is compact. Have you flown her yet?" Bob asked.

"No, not yet. I found the manuals and some spare parts for it, but I haven't found any gas—at least not enough to fly it."

"How are the guns? I see it has two." Bob was fascinated with the plane since he'd not seen this particular model before.

"Two .303 Vickers. I set up a target a hundred yards across the airfield and set the guns up to converge on it," Buzz explained.

Bob's eyes opened wide. "Isn't that a little close for a fighter plane?"

"Maybe for aerial combat, but I don't foresee any of that. I think most of what I'll be doing will be ground strafing. The manuals have the plane listed as the 'Flycatcher MKII Prototype.' Since it was originally designed for aircraft carriers, this little jewel only needs a hundred and fifty feet to take off and land. It has a service ceiling of nineteen-thousand feet, and the combat range is three-hundred and eleven miles. But I think we could squeeze a few more miles out of her without the four twenty-pound bombs."

"You said it's a prototype. What makes it different from the other model Flycatcher?" Bob asked, peering curiously into the cockpit.

"I'm not sure, but I think it's the starter motor and the hydraulic brakes. I know that adds more weight, but it cuts down on ground crew to start and shortens the runway needs," Buzz said, pleased.

"How soon do you think you can have it in the air, and how many pilots do you have?"

"Hopefully, Ned will have gas in her tomorrow morning, and we should be in the air by noon. As for pilots—you, Boris, and me. Three."

"You know, for some strange reason, that answer doesn't surprise me!" Bob said, laughing and shaking his head.

"Actually, I'm supposed to train more pilots, but it's going to be rather difficult in a single-seater. I wish we could get that two-seater flying," Buzz said, nodding toward the Campania.

Clang! Clang! Clang!

"There's the dinner bell. Let's eat," Buzz said, "and hit the sack early. We had a long day, and we've got a lot to do tomorrow."

"I'm for that! I'm beginning to droop, myself," Bob agreed, and the men hastened to the mess hall.

— Chapter Thirteen —

THE BEE FLIES

The following morning at dawn, Akbar left on his mission to persuade the other tribal leaders to unite their forces with the group at the air base to defeat the Shadow Men. He was hopeful, but not overly confident, that he would be successful.

Soon after his departure, everyone gathered at the mess hall for a hasty breakfast, and then gathered around the Flycatcher. Some brought their coffee and biscuits with them. Harry arrived carrying his breakfast in one hand, coffee in the other, and a white napkin over one arm. The girls were still in their aprons. Little Basima, wearing her ever-present smile, brought up the rear. She was lugging a large pot of coffee for refills.

"Blimy, it looks like a ruddy English picnic!" Ned commented, startled, when he glanced up from his task of filling the plane's fuel tanks.

Buzz, who was inside the cockpit checking the controls, looked up when Ned spoke. "You're right, Ned, it does," he agreed, grinning. "Let's hope we can give them a real show."

Three of the girls were sitting on a tablecloth spread on the grass, and others were perched atop the steam roller swinging their legs gleefully. Kashar was sitting comfortably cross-legged; Boris was leaning nonchalantly against the hitching rail, contentedly puffing a large cigar. Harry was seated on an overturned crate, with another in front of him, adorned with the unfurled napkin. His cup and plate had been precisely placed on the cloth.

The mountains were bathed in the morning sun, with just a few wispy white clouds in the bright blue sky. *With a change of costume, this would be a perfect setting for Monet*, Buzz thought.

"All right, everybody! Stand clear of the prop!" Buzz yelled from the cockpit. "Bob, be ready to pull the wheel chocks." Buzz snapped his safety belt closed, tested the brake and flap pedals, and

144

checked the gauges. Everything looked good. He signaled thumbs-up for good luck, pulled out the throttle and turned the ignition switch on. With a deep breath, he jabbed his thumb onto the starter button.

"Ur-rur-rur-rur," came from the engine.

Suddenly, Buzz knew exactly how Marco, the aerialist, had felt when he tripped and fell flat on his face in front of 400 circus patrons when making his grand entrance after a glowing, five-minute introduction.

"Uh, Bob, I think the battery's down. I guess we'll have to start it the old way—spin the prop by hand," Buzz stammered, red-faced. He quickly switched the ignition off to prevent the engine from firing prematurely while the prop was being moved to the starting position.

"Switch off," Buzz called to Bob, who moved the prop into position so he could pull it forcefully enough to get it spinning and ignite the starter.

As soon as Bob was ready, he yelled, "Switch on."

Buzz immediately flipped the switch and yelled back, "Contact."

Bob pulled down and to the side, quickly stepping away from the arc of the propeller, which spun three times. The engine coughed and sputtered, then stopped.

"Again," Buzz cried.

"Switch off."

"Switch on."

"Contact."

Puff—Puff—Pop!

"Switch off."

"Switch on."

"Contact."

Puff—Pop—Puff—Puff!

This continued for a half-hour. During the last ten minutes, Bob was in the cockpit and Buzz manned the prop.

Finally, Bob spoke. "Buzz, I don't think she's getting any spark."

Buzz, gasping, replied ruefully, "Well, I'm losing my spark! What do you think it could be?"

"Well, it could be the mag needle, or…where did everybody go?" For the first time since they'd begun, Bob looked around. They were alone on the field.

"Damned if I know." Buzz too, looked around in surprise.

"Oh, they all left!" It was little Basima, who was standing by the wing still holding the coffee pot. "Mr. Whitecliff went to his quarters, Mr. Boris and Kashar are looking after the horses, the girls said they had work to do, and Mr. Ned went to the back of the hangar to do some work, but I think he's really taking a nap," she said with an elfish grin. "Would you like some coffee?"

"No, thank you. Not right now!"

"Good! Then I can leave, too!" She skipped merrily away, leaving the two men even more alone.

"Well, Bob, I guess we just can't hold a crowd the way we used to." They both laughed, and then Buzz returned to the business at hand. "What were you saying about the mag needle?"

"Sometimes when an engine sits for a long time, it loses its spark like a magnet loses its magnetism. If we can crank the engine fast enough and long enough, it may build up again."

"Well, we sure can't do it by hand. What if we pulled one of the trucks alongside and hooked up a cable from the truck battery to the plane's starter?"

"You know, I think that might work. You get the truck, and I'll find some cables," Bob said as he climbed down from the cockpit.

As Buzz drove the truck next to the plane, Bob met him with cables draped around his shoulders. "Where did you find those?"

"They were hanging on the wall in the hangar. They look like this is what they were meant to be used for."

Buzz grinned with satisfaction. "Great. Maybe we'll get her started yet."

146

Bob smiled back. "I'll hook her up, you get in the cockpit."

"Okay." Buzz clambered in behind the controls. "I'm shutting the gas off so she won't flood. Let me know when you're ready."

"Ready."

Buzz pressed his thumb firmly against the starter button, and held it there a full five minutes by his watch. The starter motor whined loudly and continuously, at an extremely high pitch. The backwash from the spinning propeller felt good on Buzz's face. At the end of five minutes, he removed his thumb. The propeller spun for a short time, then stopped.

Buzz met Bob's eyes, asking silently, *Should we do it?*

Bob didn't speak; he just closed his fist and raised his thumb.

Buzz turned the gas valve on, set the choke, and eased out the throttle. He flipped the ignition switch on, and jammed his thumb on the starter button again. The engine whined—and whined—and whined some more. Time seemed to stop, yet it seemed like forever. All at once, there was a loud pop. Again, 'Pop!' And another! The sound of a seeming explosion, accompanied by a cloud of black smoke crouped from the exhaust, and the engine roared.

Inwardly, Buzz was screaming, *She's started! She's alive!* He was elated. He quickly adjusted the choke and checked the gauges silently—gas, —okay. Amp meter—okay. Oil—twenty pounds. He yelled out, frustrated, "That's too low!" The needle suddenly jumped to where it should be, indicating the correct pressure. Buzz sunk back into the seat and sighed. "Oil pressure—okay!"

Bob had already unhooked the cables and moved the truck. Now he was waiting for Buzz's signal to remove the chocks.

The signal was joyfully given, and the feisty little plane rolled onto the airfield as though it owned it. Buzz taxied down the field, finding that he'd regained his audience, all whom were cheering and waving with enthusiasm. Harry, in particular, seemed to have momentarily lost his English reserve. He was in front of the officers' quarters, leaping in the air, his hands clasped above his head, waving his congratulations with abandon.

Buzz reached the end of the field, turned his plane into the wind, idled the engine down, and ran through a short mental checklist. When

147

he looked up, he saw the crowd standing quietly. He could almost feel their tension. Then he thought of the other things that should be checked—control cables, wing bolts, engine mounts, struts, and more. He looked again at the waiting crowd.

"Oh, what the hell! The show must go on!" He released the brakes and pulled back on the throttle. The Jaguar IV nine-cylinder engine revved its 400 horsepower with a loud roar and bounced down the runway, picking up speed every foot of the way.

On the sidelines, prayers were mumbled and fingers were crossed.

Buzz's eyes darted from the runway to the airspeed indicator, to the oil pressure gauge, to the runway, and back again. Then he thought of the hub nut that held the prop. He fervently wished he'd checked it.

"This is it!" he said, and pulled back on the stick. Suddenly, he was no longer bouncing, he was floating on a cloud—his cloud. At last he was in the air again. He was home!

He circled the field a few times and did some banks and wide loops, but nothing that would inadvertently strain the engine or the structure of the plane. After fifteen minutes of general flying, Buzz brought the plane in for a good but somewhat bouncy landing, and taxied triumphantly to the hangar. Everyone was waiting with breathless anticipation.

Their little army now had an air force!

Bob leapt onto the wing beside the cockpit and began questioning and congratulating Buzz as he pounded him vigorously on the back. "How did she handle? Did the engine act up? You looked good from the ground."

"She flew like a dream; the engine ran smoothly. The only thing to complain about is that she's slow to respond to a left bank, but I think I can correct that by adjusting the control cables."

Bob was so pleased by their success that he couldn't abide being idle. "While you're tinkering with the plane, I'll get Ned and see if we can start up the steam roller and roll the airstrip."

"That would be greatly appreciated. I felt as though I was riding a bucking horse."

"You looked great up there—just like old times." Buzz turned, to see that Boris had climbed onto the other wing to shake his hand.

"What do you mean 'like old times'? You'd think we were a bunch of old men," Buzz retorted, and the three of them broke into hearty laughter.

As Buzz climbed down from the cockpit, he was besieged by the entire group of girls. They all wanted to touch him, perhaps with the thought that some of the majesty of flight would transfer to them. Few had ever seen an airplane fly. They jumped up and down excitedly, clapping their hands and giggling with joy. Some even hugged the plane.

"That flight not only raised the plane; it raised everyone's spirits—including mine," Harry said, as he clasped Buzz's shoulder and shook his hand vigorously. "I was beginning to doubt the venture but, by God, now I think we can do it."

"Well, I hope you're right—even though I'm not completely sure what we're doing," Buzz answered.

"You will be, soon," Harry replied with a raised eyebrow. "How soon do you think you'll be able to do some reconnaissance flights?"

"Bob, Ned, and I will do some maintenance and check flights today. Then, if everything's okay, I should be able to start tomorrow morning."

"Good. After dinner this evening, I would like to go over a flight plan with you."

A short time later, Buzz mused, "I wonder how accurate this gas gauge is. What do you think, Ned?"

"Well, Mr. Buzz, sir, we had a two-seater fighter here that would show empty on the gauge and still have about ten gallons in her. Then, on the other hand, that bloomin' Campania sittin' over there would read a quarter of a tank, and they'd be landin' her on fumes."

"Thanks—I think."

"Hey, Buzz. The book says there's a screw in the back of the gauge for adjustments," Bob reported. He was sitting cross-legged on the ground with the maintenance manual in his lap. "It tells you to empty the tank and refill it, setting the needle the way you want it to read—empty at ten, five, two, or even zero gallons."

"Well, if the needle moves with each gallon put in, I can mark the gauge for the first quarter of a tank," said Buzz.

Ned wore a puzzled expression as Buzz and Bob discussed the fuel gauge.

Buzz explained, "I don't like surprises at five-thousand feet."

"Oh. Well, I was just wonderin', guv. I guess that makes sense, now that I think of it."

"How's it going, boys?" Boris asked, as he and Kashar approached. "Is there anything we can do to help?"

At that moment, little Basima ran up to them, carrying her coffee pot and three cups. "Mr. Buzz, sir, Mr. Whitecliff said to tell you that all the British insignias have to be painted over, and do you want some coffee? He didn't tell me to ask you about the coffee—that was me asking. So will you, and do you, and if Mr. Boris and Kashar want some, I'll get more cups, sir."

Buzz, slightly befuddled, smiled and said, "Yes, Basima, we'll have some coffee, and thank you. And, yes, we'll paint over the insignias."

"Good! I'll get Mr. Boris and Kashar some cups, unless they want to use Mr. Bob's and Mr. Ned's cups. Then I'll get cups for them instead."

The men, now thoroughly confused, just looked at each other, shook their heads, and grinned.

"Uhh, okay!—whatever you say Basima," Buzz mumbled.

The girl dropped her habitual small curtsey, turned, and skipped merrily off to the mess hall to bring more cups for someone.

"Whew!" Buzz laughed. "Boris, you and Kashar want to paint? I'm sure Ned can find you some paint and brushes—right, Ned?"

"You bet, guv—I can get them any size brush and any color of paint they want."

Boris glanced at Kashar, who grinned and nodded. "Sounds good to us. In fact, I have some ideas for this old bird," he said, pointing to the Flycatcher.

Basima was back. "Here's the two cups, and I brought you some sandwiches since you didn't come in for lunch."

"Thank you, Basima."

"You're welcome, I'm sure," she replied cheerfully, curtseyed again, and skipped quickly back to the mess hall—probably to brew more coffee.

The men worked steadily, uninterrupted, for the next few hours, taking the plane into the air for short flights at intervals after making various adjustments. Since the paint was still wet, Boris complained about the test flights, but to no avail.

When the dinner bell rang, the men—except for Boris, who was still engrossed with his painting—drank a toast, coffee cups raised, to a job well done. Four repaired to the mess hall for dinner, leaving Boris to complete his work.

———

"That was a good meal," Buzz said, as he scooted his chair away from the table.

"Don't you want to stay and play a few hands of cards, guv?" asked Ned.

"No, I'd better not. Harry wants to talk to me about doing some recon flying tomorrow. And, besides that, I want to leave Afghanistan with something to show for it," Buzz replied, laughing.

As he was leaving the mess hall, he met Kashar, who was coming in. "Hi, Kashar. Where's Boris?"

"He's still painting. He wants to finish tonight so it will be dry by morning. I'm going to take his dinner out to him."

"Well, I won't bother him, then." Buzz closed the door behind him and walked quickly to his meeting with Harry.

As he entered their quarters, he found Harry leaning back in his chair, a cup in one hand and a Havana in the other. He was watching several smoke rings make their wobbly way to the rafters.

"Come in, Buzz, come in! Sit down, and have a cigar and a cup of tea. Oh, that's right!—you smoke a pipe now."

"I'll take you up on both. I still like a good cigar now and then," Buzz replied, as he poured a cup of tea for himself and refilled Harry's cup. "I'm glad you were able to enjoy that fine meal tonight."

"It was exceptionally good. Actually, I had forgotten all about dinner, but Basima brought a plate and a pot of tea. She said she knew I was here and she didn't want me to miss my dinner—and I was to eat every bit, especially my vegetables." Harry laughed.

"That little girl is special! She looks after everyone, and her smile can brighten the darkest room," Buzz commented, smiling.

Harry's expression grew serious. "Is the plane ready to fly? I mean, is it the way you want it?" He sat forward, his elbows on the table.

"She feels fine in the air; I think I can safely take her on a long flight without any trouble. The only thing that isn't finished is the painting, and Boris said he would have that done tonight."

As Buzz spoke, he pulled a chair to the table and sat across from Harry. "Thank you," he said, accepting the proffered cigar. After clipping and lighting it, he blew a large smoke ring, which floated lazily to perch over Harry's head like a halo before fading slowly into oblivion. Buzz smiled to himself; somehow he didn't feel that was the appropriate symbol for Harry Whitecliff.

"Buzz, I'd like you to do some recon for me tomorrow. The entire trip would be about two-hundred miles in all."

"That shouldn't be a problem."

"Good. Do you know how to use an aerocamera?"

"Yeah. I operated one during the war. You want me to take some photos tomorrow?"

"Yes. I figure that would be a good way to familiarize our people with the area. Akbar and his family know it well, but the rest of them don't have any idea. The girls only knew the area around their own camps, and Boris and Bob need to learn the terrain as well. But, most importantly, what I really want you to watch for is signs of the Shadow Men. We haven't any idea of their present whereabouts."

"Well, show me the flight plan," Buzz said.

Reaching to the floor, Harry grasped a large roll of maps, which he quickly placed on the table, securing the four corners with the knife, fork, dinner plate, and teapot, which remained from his meal.

"So that's what Afghanistan looks like. This is the first time I've seen a large map of it. All the others I've seen were from small travelogues," Buzz commented, rising from his chair to get a better view.

"Here's where we are now." Taking up a pencil, Harry pointed to an *X* marked on the Bahmian Valley at the base of the Hindu Kush Mountains. "Those are the ones to the west," Harry said, pointing to the mountains across the airfield. "What I would like, or would suggest, is that you fly due east to the Paghman Mountains; that's about seventy-five miles. You'll see a road that runs along the foothills. Follow that road north for about seventy-five miles, and you'll come to a com—"

"Isn't that Kabul—east of us, over the Paghman Mountains?" Buzz interrupted.

"Huh? Oh, yes. Those mountains act as a barrier between us and the revolt. Now, where was I? Oh, yes. Follow the road north," Harry instructed as he retraced a line he'd drawn with his pencil, "to a small complex of buildings—some new and some old. It was formerly a watering stop for the Silk Road. The new buildings were erected by the British to store supplies during the last Afghan war. Then you fly due west for fifty miles or so, until you see an old mission."

"Is that—?" Buzz questioned, hopefully.

"Yes, that's where the Smiths are visiting. You'll be back at the Hindu Kush Mountains. Just fly south and follow the mountains back home. Altogether, I imagine the entire flight to be two-hundred and seventy-five miles, more or less. How long do you think it will take?" Harry sat down and relit his cigar.

Buzz too sat, propping his feet on the table. He puffed his cigar a few times as he rocked the chair back on its rear legs. "Well, let's see— the manual states that the maximum speed is a hundred and thirty-three miles per hour—but I don't think I should fly at that speed on her maiden flight. She should be broken in at between ninety and a hundred miles per hour, which would be a good speed for photos. Let's see, two-hundred and seventy-five miles would take about, hmm..." Buzz intertwined his fingers behind his head and puffed a few more times on

153

his cigar, gazing into the rafters above. "I should be able to make the flight in three to three and a quarter hours."

"Good." Harry was pleased, but still concerned. "If you're not back in four hours, I'll send out two search parties—one over the northern route and the other, the eastern."

"That's encouraging, I think." Buzz said, frowning slightly. "If I take off at eight tomorrow morning, I should be back by eleven or eleven-thirty at the latest."

"Yes, you should be back in time for lunch. Now, what do you say we relieve Ned of a few coins at the card table?" Harry asked, as he scooted his chair away from the table and picked up his hat and cane.

"Good idea. I feel lucky," Buzz replied, following Harry out the door.

The morning sun was casting long shadows across the field when Buzz, Harry, and Bob stepped from their quarters, each sipping a steaming cup of coffee, supplied by Basima. Their attention was drawn to a small group gathered around the Flycatcher.

"Boris," Buzz called to the man leaning wearily on the hitching rail. "Boris! What's all the commotion about?"

Boris turned to face the trio. Buzz noted the multicolored paint spatters on his friend's hand as he greeted them, as well as a smudge of blue on the tip of his nose. His sleep-starved eyes gave away his all-night effort, but he wore an expression of extreme satisfaction.

"Top of the morning to you," Boris said, raising his cup in a token toast.

"Good morning, sirs." Kashar greeted them sleepily. He was lying on the ground and had obviously just awakened.

"Look, Mr. Buzz. Look at what Mr. Boris and Kashar did to your plane," Hala said, pointing excitedly at the Flycatcher.

Smiling in anticipation, the crowd moved aside to give the men an unimpeded view of the little plane. The three of them stood stock still in amazement. Buzz advanced slowly, his mouth agape, and his eyes wide.

154

"Well?" Boris challenged, smugly sipping his coffee.

"Boris, you've outdone yourself." Buzz stood, arms akimbo, nearly stammering. "I've seen the work you've done for the circus, but this is absolutely outstanding!"

"Ara, run and get the camera!"

"I already have it, Mr. Whitecliff, sir."

"Good. Thank you, Ara. Everyone, gather around the plane—I want a picture of this," Harry said, moving his arms as though he were herding sheep. "Leave an open spot for me. I'm setting the timer so I can get in it too." Harry adjusted the tripod, and after setting the focus and timer, he dashed to his spot.

All stood absolutely still, grins pasted on, for what seemed like long minutes but was only seconds. The timer whirred and clicked as the lens flashed open and closed, capturing the little group standing in front of the plane. In the center of the photo, where there had once been British insignia, was now a circular field of light blue punctuated by a caricature of a yellow bee with black stripes. On its head was a flying helmet and goggles; boots decorated the ends of its spindly legs, and a white cape flowed toward the rear of the plane. The bee angled downward, with its antennae, wings, and rear legs swept back as if it were in a power dive. The right arm was crooked at the elbow, the hand grasping a sword, and the left was outstretched, holding a blazing pistol. On the face was an expression of stubborn determination.

At last, they had a symbol of their own.

"Mr. Whitecliff, sir. Would you like some coffee?"

Harry gazed down at the little figure who had tugged his sleeve. "Yes, Basima, I would. In fact, see that everyone has a cup. I would like to propose a toast."

As soon as everyone had been served, Harry held up his cup and said, "To the bee that flies over Afghanistan!"

Laughingly but determined, came the rejoinder as each raised a cup and cried as one, "To the bee that flies over Afghanistan!"

— Chapter Fourteen —

RECONNAISSANCE

"There's the foot of the Paghman Mountains and the road ahead." Buzz was again talking to himself. He found that, on long flights, such conversation whiled away the time and stifled loneliness. As he approached the road, he took additional photos. Then, instead of banking to the left and flying north, he pulled the stick back, climbed nearly straight up, performed a tight loop, and made a spiral dive, pulling out just a few hundred feet from the ground. He flew north, and then ascended to his previous altitude of five-thousand feet.

"Ooh!—if I had only had you when I was flying in the circus, we could have packed the crowds in there every day!" he said admiringly to the little plane.

"Let's see, the next reference point is the group of buildings," Buzz mumbled, looking at the smaller map Harry had given him. "Wow!—is that what I think it is, standing on that high cliff?" He hurriedly uncased his binoculars. "By Jove, it is! It's an ibex! Look at those long, backward-curving horns. That really is beautiful!—'by Jove,' did I just say 'by Jove?' —I must be hanging around Harry and Ned way too much—I'll have to start being more careful about the company I keep!"

"Hmm!—I wonder what he's looking at so intently. He's not paying any attention to me at all—he's looking at something in that little grove of cedars. There it is! He's watching a snow leopard," Buzz said as he focused his glasses on the sleek animal slinking toward the ibex. Like a flash, the ibex turned and, with the grace of a ballerina, bounded up the mountainside, ledge to outcropping to ledge, and quickly disappeared through a cleft.

"Boy is Mr. Leopard ticked—look at that long tail of his twitch! Now he'll have to settle for moles or shrews instead of a big, fat ibex. Damn! I just saw something I'll probably never see again, and I forgot to take pictures. That was really stupid."

"Hmm, looks like some one- and two-story buildings about two miles straight ahead. How much film is left in the camera?" He checked. "Six shots left. Then I'll have to change the roll."

"I'll drop down to a thousand feet and take four shots—one from each direction. I'll take one from directly above, too. Looks like there's been some activity down there recently—lots of horse and vehicle tracks in the streets."

Buzz flew over the compound, taking photos with each pass. The layout of the buildings much resembled the area in which Harry's warehouse was located, except that instead of a hotel and train depot, this grouping had two very old buildings, one of which lacked a roof. As Buzz banked the Bee westward, he noticed an area just west of the warehouses where there were a large number of burned-out campfires.

"I'd better take a photo of that—it could be important," Buzz mused as he flew over the campsite. After returning the plane to its westerly course, he placed a fresh roll of film in the camera.

"Interesting rise of rock about two miles ahead." As Buzz approached the rocks, he could see the sun glimmering off what might be a pool of water. "I may as well get a photo of that, too."

After taking the photos, he replaced the camera in its rack, and took the Bee to an altitude of five-thousand feet, and then leveled off, heading west.

"Well, let me check the map and see what's ahead. Hmm— there's a small mountain or a mound of some sort. There it is. It's too small for a mountain and too big for a mound. It looks like a flat-top butte like we have in New Mexico. After that, there's nothing for about thirty miles. No, wait.—half-way across, there's a symbol for water. It must be another well. I'm almost over it. I'd better get the camera ready—two shots will do it. It's kind of a pretty spot, nice place for a picnic.

Once past the butte, there's nothing but sand as far as the eye can see. The map doesn't show anything of interest until the mission, except maybe that well or water-hole, whichever it is."

"I wonder if I'll see Kim at the mission. Hell, she and her aunt and uncle have probably returned to France by now. It's been weeks since I saw her on the train."

Buzz said nothing more to himself for a while; he just daydreamed of Kim. *He pictured the cute way she would stick out her bottom lip when she faked a pout, the way her eyes would twinkle when she'd laugh, and that silly phrase, 'something like that.'*

I wonder if she's wearing the cross I gave her? he thought. Suddenly, he stiffened. *What if the porter hadn't given her the message and the cross? What if he'd kept it for himself? After all, it was gold. I'm sure he gave it to her; he seemed like a decent fellow. But if he didn't, she'll think I left without saying anything. She'll think I was lying to her about wanting to see her again. I'll beat that little thief of a porter to a pulp!*

He began to laugh at himself. Here he was, about to start a war over maybes. *When I get back to France, I should be able to look her up easily enough. There can't be that many "Smith and Smith" shipping companies there.*

Buzz chuckled to himself and remarked aloud, "Buzz, old boy, I do believe you have fallen in love with this girl."

"Oops—almost flew past the watering hole." Buzz banked to the right and descended to 1,000 feet. "There's the water hole, surrounded by bushes and one tree. Those ruins next to it look like it might have been a small fort at one time. Damn! There are those burned out campfires again. Must be the same group of travelers. I'd better take a shot of this place, too."

Buzz continued toward the mission. Daydreams of Kim filled his mind—the two of them riding, flying, dancing. He even thought of asking for her hand in marriage. *The top of that butte I flew over has such a great view. I can picture it—just the two of us, sitting by a softly glowing fire, the full moon above, maybe just enough clouds in the sky to make it interesting, a warm, soft breeze gently brushing her hair and carrying that perfume she wears toward me. I'd take her soft little hand and a night bird would sing, and I would say, "Kim, would you marry me?" And she would blush and quietly say, "Yes, Buzz, I will marry you." Then we would embrace.*

He woke with a start from his reveries, realizing that the mission was only a mile ahead, and reminded himself sternly that he was here to take photos. As the Bee passed over the centuries-old buildings at 2,000 feet, then again at 1,000, Buzz snapped photos from all angles.

Then he saw someone running madly out of the gates into the open. Was it—? He grabbed the binoculars and rapidly focused on the wildly waving figure. "It is! It's Kim! She's still here!" he yelped with glee. His heart was pounding with elation.

He could see her jumping up and down, waving both arms. Buzz took the Bee into a power dive and leveled off a few feet from the ground. He flew past Kim, slowing nearly to a stall, and snapped a picture of her.

Then he sped up, gained altitude, and executed the finest stunt flying he had ever performed. Loops, rolls, dives, and even things he had never attempted previously; he did them all, plus maneuvers he didn't know he could do. There are times when a man has the right to show off, and this was one of those times.

Buzz saw a small field just on the other side of a ridge in front of the mission that looked large enough to land the plane. He began to approach it, but then thought, "I look like a bum! I need a shave, my hair is shaggy, and my clothes are a mess. It would be better if I'd come back tomorrow after I've cleaned up."

Disappointed but joyfully anticipating his plans for the following day, he performed a few more loops and waved goodbye by dipping his wing.

He headed back for the base with his head in the proverbial clouds. He pulled the throttle out and flew the Bee at her max, rushing to prepare for tomorrow, so he could fly back early and have as much time as possible with Kim.

I think she was wearing my cross; something at her throat shined in the sunlight, at least. I wonder if she feels about me as I do about her. Atop that butte would be a nice place to take her. We could have a nice lunch, enjoy the quiet (except for the song of the birds), and the whisper of the wind—a gentle wind, of course. But that would be too long a ride by horseback from the mission. Damn. I wish that two-seater was flyable. That butte would be a good place to propose; there would be no interruptions. Hmm, me getting married and settling down. I wonder just how much she would want to settle.

Such thoughts floated in and out of Buzz's mind until he came in sight of the airfield. Then he cleared his head to concentrate on landing the Bee. "Where's all the smoke coming from? Is one of the buildings on fire?" Buzz asked himself aloud as he circled the base. "Well, how about that. They got the steam roller running. Well, at least they got it smoking. Unfortunately, the smoke is blowing across the field. Oh well, they say all clouds have a silver lining. At least I can tell the direction of the wind. It's coming from the northeast, so I'll pass over the field and land from the south."

He was able to make a good landing in spite of the smoke and the roughness of the field. After coming to a stop, he taxied to the hangar where Bob, Boris, and some of the others were waiting. As soon as the engine was cut, they all came running to greet him.

"How did she fly? Did you have any trouble?" Bob asked as he assisted Buzz in unbuckling his seat belt.

"Did you see any Shadow Men?" Boris queried.

Grinning, Buzz said, "In answer to your questions, gentlemen, the plane flew like a bird, or should I say like a Bee." Buzz pointed to the insignia and nodded in grateful acknowledgement of Boris's artistry. He continued, "No, I didn't have any trouble, and no, I didn't see any Shadow Men. Now, where's Harry?" he asked as he began unbuttoning his coat. Before he could receive a reply, he felt a tug on his sleeve.

He glanced down to see Basima standing there with her ever-present coffee pot. "Would you like a cup of coffee, Mr. Buzz?"

Chuckling, he said, "Yes, Basima, I would love a cup of coffee. Thank you."

Boris then said, "Harry's with Akbar in our quarters. He sent word that he'd like to see the three of us as soon as you got back."

"Well, let's go." Buzz handed his empty cup back to Basima. "What's with the steam roller? Do you think you can get it working?" he asked Bob.

"Everything looks good except a valve that was shot—probably to disable it. Ned said he thinks he knows where another one is. He's looking for it now. I think all that black smoke is from the firebox being used as a depository for oily rags. Makes one hell of a smoke screen, though."

"Yeah, I know. I had to land in it!"

"Sorry," Bob apologized, grinning.

"Well, here we are, gentlemen, at the lion's den. Let's see what the old lion has to roar about," Boris said as he held the door for the other two men to enter.

"Buzz. How was your flight?" asked Harry as he and Akbar stood to greet them.

"Oh, it was fine—no problems."

"Were you able to get some good photos?"

"Yeah, I think I got some good shots. Let me know when you develop the film. I'd like to have a couple of them enlarged," Buzz requested.

"The Smith girl?" Harry asked with a smile.

Buzz nodded his head, his grin sheepish. Then, after hesitating a bit, inquired, "Akbar, how was your trip?"

Akbar shook his head ruefully and replied, "Not good."

"Pull up some chairs, gentlemen, and Akbar will tell you of his meeting with the elders," Harry instructed.

"To get to the point, the elders won't help us in any way," Akbar reported.

"What? We're risking our lives to help them, and this is what we get?" Boris growled.

Harry could see anger beginning to overwhelm the three men. He raised his hand, and said, "Calm down, gentlemen, calm down. Let Akbar finish, then I think you'll understand their decision not to join us. Go on, Akbar."

"The fighting around Kabul isn't going well for Amanullah, who is friendly to Westerners. If Bachcheh Saqow, the leader of the revolt, seizes Kabul and gains control of Afghanistan, the tribes that help us could be punished severely. I know you're wondering 'what about us— what about our little army'—if Amanullah loses. Most likely, we will not only be hunted by the Shadow Men, but by all Afghanistan."

The men sat in silence for a few moments, absorbing Akbar's information. Finally, Buzz asked, "Now what?"

Harry spoke calmly, though defeat hovered in the air. "As some of you know or have guessed by now, my purpose here is not just to help

161

these people fight the Shadow Men. I feel there is something greater developing here than just raids on small tribes." He paused briefly to relight his cigar and take a sip of coffee.

"Then what are we here for, if not to fight the Shadow Men?" Bob asked in frustration.

"To fight the Germans," Harry returned quietly.

Boris was taken aback. "To fight the Germans? Hell, I thought we fought and beat them in the Great War."

"We did, Boris, but the German general staff was not obliterated by the Treaty of Versailles. In 1922, the Berlin government arranged the Treaty of Rapallo with Moscow; German officers had already made dispositions to manufacture tanks, shells, and aircraft in the Soviet towns of Lipetsk, Saratov, Kazan, and Tula. At Lipetsk, all-metal aircraft are being developed and tested. Our people there say—"

"Your people!—you mean spies?" Boris interrupted.

Harry fixed him with a cold, piercing stare and continued, "Our people say that at times, more planes take off than land. They think the Germans are secretly setting up hidden airbases in other countries where their pilots can learn to fly under differing conditions. I have reason to believe that one of those air bases is here, somewhere in these mountains. And I also believe that when the time is right, the Germans will offer their aircraft and a fighting force of at least five-hundred armed horsemen to Bachcheh Saqow to aid in the overthrow of Amanullah."

"By armed horsemen, you mean the Shadow Men? Buzz inquired.

"Yes. The Shadow Men."

"What interest would Germany have in Afghanistan?"

Harry spoke with sorrowful resignation. "Well, Bob, they hope to gain control of the Khaibar Pass—the gateway to the East and India. I'm sorry I brought you into this mess only to have it end this way."

"End this way? You're calling it quits?" Bob exclaimed, his voice rising.

"I don't think we have much of a choice. If there is an airbase here, we don't know where it is. We don't even know where the damn Shadow Men are. From what Akbar tells me, it may be only three or four

162

weeks before Kabul falls, and then we may be in the position of having to fight our way back to India. Even after we sell our war booty and with the few pounds I have, there may not be enough money to pay your way home. The home office didn't want to get involved in another Afghanistan war, so this is my personal venture."

For a few moments, the room was enveloped in silence. Then Buzz spoke thoughtfully. "Harry, would you give us some time to think about this some more before you tell the others that our army is being disbanded?" Nods of agreement came from both Boris and Bob. Buzz continued, "At least a couple of days."

Struggling against hope, Harry agreed. "Yes, of course. Well, if there aren't any more questions, let's have some lunch."

As they were leaving the officers' quarters, Buzz stopped Harry and asked, "Would you mind if I used the plane tomorrow?"

"Of course you can, Buzz. I hope to meet this wonderful girl someday," Harry replied, his eyes twinkling.

"Thanks, Harry!" Buzz said gratefully, shaking Harry's hand vigorously. Seeing Ned on his way to the mess hall, he leaped off the porch, and ran toward him, yelling, "Hey, Ned, wait up. I heard you used to give haircuts. I need one!"

"Glaring at the rain isn't going to make it stop; besides, your breakfast is getting cold. Come back to the table and finish eating," Boris called to Buzz, who was standing in front of the window with his arms folded, gloomily watching the monotony of the falling rain.

Slam!

All heads turned toward the door, where Harry was struggling against the force of the wind to close it. "Sorry!—I didn't mean to startle you. The wind blew it out of my hand." As he spoke, Harry shook the water off his raincoat and hat. "The wind makes the raindrops sting when they hit your face. Are the planes secured?"

"The Bee is in the hangar behind closed doors, and the two-seater is tied down the best we could," Bob answered.

"What about the lookouts?"

"I called them all in—except for Kashar in the tower," Boris replied.

"Good. Now, if you gentlemen have finished your breakfast, please bring your cups over here. I have something to show you." Harry said as he removed some photos from an oilcloth pouch, and laid them on an empty table.

"Oh, thank you, Basima. I could use a hot cup of coffee right now," Harry said as he accepted a steaming cup.

Harry remained standing as the others seated themselves, and fanned the 8 x 10 photos across the table. "As you can see, Buzz took some nice clear shots of the locations I'd asked for, and then some."

Buzz quickly picked a photo from the array on the table and smiled. It was the shot he'd snapped of Kim as he had flown low and slow.

"Buzz, I thought you might want an enlargement of that one," Harry said with a smile, and handed Buzz another photo, which had been made into a close-up of the shot he held in his hand. She was wearing jodhpurs, tall black boots, and a white blouse partly covered with a vest. His cross graced her throat. Her face glowed with a huge smile.

"Thank you, Harry. You do well in the darkroom."

"May we see the reason you kept us up late while you polished your boots, Buzz?" Bob asked.

"You should see the Bee. He shined every bloomin' thing on it— even waxed the props!" Ned chimed in.

"Sure. Here," Buzz said, passing the photo to Bob.

"I believe I would curse this storm too, if it was keeping me from someone like that," Bob commented and, grinning, passed the print to Boris.

"Very, very nice, Buzz," Boris remarked and passed it to Akbar and Ned.

"She looks like a princess!" Ned said in awe.

"Yes, she does," Akbar agreed.

"Oh, she's pretty, Mr. Buzz, sir." Basima softly breathed as she refilled their coffee cups. "Are you going to marry her?"

164

"Well, I—" Buzz stammered.

"Gentlemen, it's the other photos I asked you here to view," Harry interjected.

Buzz welcomed Harry's intervention. He didn't really know how to answer that question just yet.

Harry continued, "If you look closely at the shots of the building, you'll see a lot of tire tracks and hoof prints. Those buildings haven't been used for at least two years, but they now seem to be the hub of some activity. And the two sets of campsites shown in these photos," Harry said as he pointed to the relevant prints, "seem to indicate a large party of horsemen either going toward, or arriving from, the northwest."

"Shadow Men?" Boris questioned.

"That's my belief," Harry replied. "I was thinking that perhaps Buzz, after visiting with his lady friend, could fly over that area again and find out which direction that party is headed."

"I'll do that, Harry, as soon as the storm lets up," Buzz agreed.

"We have extensive coverage of the mission for reasons we all know, but I just brought these two for now," Harry noted.

Buzz, grinning like a bashful boy, slid down in his seat.

Harry indicated a point on one of the prints. "Something in this shot caught my attention—see, near these rocks—a shape that doesn't look natural." The men saw a shadowy form. "I enlarged that portion and, as you can see, it's two saddled horses. Now, the question is, who do they belong to, and why are they apparently being hidden in the rocks?"

The men were silent. Harry sat down and lit a cigar. Boris pensively sipped his coffee; Bob pulled the photo closer for a better look; Akbar leaned far back in his chair and rested his chin on his chest. Ned stared deeply into his cup. Each man had only one thought, and each was hoping someone else would speak and propose another, less sinister, reason for the presence of the horses.

Buzz finally broke the seemingly interminable silence. "I know what you're all thinking—it could be spies for the Shadow Men. When I fly up there, I'll be armed and cautious."

"But what would the Shadow Men want with a mission?" Bob asked.

"Maybe they think there're gold or silver crosses—or maybe they're after the wine in the cellar under the chapel," Ned suggested.

"Well, whoever they are, we won't know anything more until this storm quiets. Besides, it might just be that some of the guests staying at the mission went for a ride and stopped to enjoy a picnic or something, so let's not build monsters until we learn more about the situation," Harry instructed, trying to still his own fears. "Meanwhile, who wants to try to best me in a game of darts?"

"What do you say to Bob and me taking on you and Ned?" Boris asked as he rose from his chair.

"You're on!" was the quick reply. "And may the better men win—which will be us, of course."

"We'll just see about that, Mr. Whitecliff," Bob jibed. The four men strolled to the dart board, leaving Buzz and Akbar seated at the table sipping their coffee.

"Akbar, what are you going to do if we pack up and leave? Well, I guess I might as well say when we leave," Buzz stated. He was intensely concerned, for he had grown close to the older man and the rest of his army in the last few weeks.

"Buzz, I think you're probably right when you say 'when'," Akbar replied gruffly. "Harry said he has a friend in Paris who might take the girls and me as a circus act. It could be a new start for all of us, although it would be a very different life from what we've known, to say the least."

"He must mean Jack Perry. Jack's a good man—he'll treat you well," Buzz assured Akbar.

"Oh, you know this man?"

"Yes—very well. Boris, Bob, and I worked with Jack for a number of years. The circus is like one big family. I think you and the rest of the troops will like it there."

"Do you really think so?" Akbar felt deeply responsible for the girls so recently freed from captivity, as well as his own son and daughters.

166

"Oh, yes. When I first started with J…"

CRASH!! —WHOOSH!!

Every eye abruptly pivoted to the door, where they saw a man on all fours, struggling feebly against the force of the wind and rain. He rose halfway, and then staggered forward, fell prone, and rolled onto his back, obviously exhausted.

"My God! It's Father Sebastian," Harry gasped.

— Chapter Fifteen —

FATHER SEBASTIAN'S MESSAGE

Buzz laboriously forced the door closed against the storm.

"Quick! Take him into the kitchen—it's warmer in there. Someone get blankets, the first aid chest, and a bottle of brandy. Hurry!" Harry ordered.

The girls were rapidly dismissed from the kitchen, and the men proceeded to remove the priest's sodden garments. They dried him off gently, and then vigorously rubbed his cold, clammy skin to warm him.

"Here're the blankets and the brandy," Buzz said, handing the blankets to eager hands. "Bob's bringing the first aid chest."

"Good chaps," Harry said, as he took the brandy.

The priest was wrapped like a mummy and seated next to a warm oven. Harry administered the brandy to the semi-conscious man a few drops at a time. Father Sebastian's eyes fluttered, and then slowly opened. He gazed dazedly around the room. He sighed, "God bless you."

"Anan," called Harry, "was there any porridge left from breakfast?"

"Yes, sir—there was a little bit."

"Good. Warm up a bowl with some milk and lots of honey. That'll give him some strength."

"What do you think happened? Do you think he was thrown from his horse?" Buzz asked.

"He looks more like he's been severely beaten," Boris said.

"Beaten? Who in the he—I mean, who in the world would beat a priest?" Bob asked.

Harry took the warmed porridge from Anan, and said, "Here, Father, eat this. It will give you strength," and he gently fed the injured man. After eating nearly all of the warm, sweet concoction, the priest reluctantly succumbed to exhaustion, and fell asleep. There were many questions, but they would have to wait.

Harry spoke softly. "I'll need someone to hold him while I put a couple of stitches in that cut over his eye."

"You're going to do it while he's asleep?" Buzz asked as he gently placed his hands on the man's shoulders.

"As severely as his face is battered, I don't think he'll feel much of anything. Just to be on the safe side, though, I want you to hold him."

Buzz watched closely as Harry sewed the laceration closed. It reminded him, somehow, of watching his mother patching his trousers when he was a child. Buzz could feel Father Sebastian's body tense when Harry tied the knot.

"Bob, would you hand me the bottle of iodine from the chest?— No, not that one, the smaller one next to it. Yes, that's it—thanks. The rain seems to have cleaned his wounds quite well, and there don't seem to be any broken bones in his face—just a lot of bruises and abrasions. That lump on his forehead will need a cold-pack," Harry said in a low monotone as he applied iodine to the open wounds. "From that bruise on his side, it appears that he may have some broken or cracked ribs. We'll bind them after he awakens."

"He sure doesn't look like any monk I ever saw in paintings or in books—you know, kind of short and round," Buzz commented. "I mean, he's built like a wrestler, or maybe a soldier."

Harry replied, still whispering, "He's the abbot at the Franciscan Mission. He was a soldier in the war. It was because of what he had seen and done that he became a man of the cloth. All we can do now is wait till he wakes; then perhaps we can find out what happened to him."

It was eleven minutes past eight o'clock that evening, by Buzz's watch, when someone called out softly, "He's awake."

Buzz pocketed his watch and rushed to the kitchen. There was already a crowd surrounding the priest.

"How do you feel, Father?" someone asked.

"Like that place I'm trying to stop people from going to," the priest replied, speaking with difficulty due to his injuries.

"Would you like some hot tea?"

"Yes, that sounds good. Thank you."

Buzz waited quietly until the tea had been served, but he could hold his impatient curiosity no longer. He dreaded the answer he knew he might receive, but he had to know. He asked the question that was on everyone's mind. "Father, what happened? Is everyone all right at the mission?"

"Let him tell it from the beginning. Please, Father, would you tell us what happened? That is, if you're up to it," Harry requested.

"Yes, I feel well enough. Oh—thank you, little one! Mmm, that's good!" said Father Sebastian. He sipped the hot, sweet tea gingerly, and then sat back and sighed, collecting his thoughts.

"It was yesterday. We'd just sat down for our evening meal, and Kimberly, a young girl who is visiting, was telling us about a flyer friend of hers when the gate bell rang. Brother John went to investigate. A few minutes later, the room was filled with men in black."

"The Shadow Men!" someone gasped.

"Yes, the Shadow Men. We were told to stay seated until the colonel came."

"The colonel?" asked Harry.

"Yes, a tall, slender man entered the room and introduced himself as Colonel von Schroeden."

Boris jumped from the counter where he'd been seated. "This colonel," he demanded harshly, "did he wear a monocle? Did he have a scar here?" As he spoke, he raked the back of his thumb down his left cheek.

"Yes, yes, he did. Do you know this man?" asked the priest.

"I spent the last days of the war in the prison where he was commandant. The man is evil through and through. He fancied himself a great swordsman. He would challenge prisoners to a duel and tell them that if they won, they would go free. He always chose those who'd probably never held a sword in their lives. The poor souls never had a chance. That coward would never choose one of the Cossacks. Yes, that's Colonel Wolfric von Schroeden for sure!" Boris leaned tensely against the counter, fire blazing in his eyes.

"Go on, please, Father. What of Kim and the others? Are they all right?" Buzz asked stridently, impatiently.

"Yes, they're all right—at least for now."

"Who beat you?" Bob asked.

"One of von Schroeden's henchmen—on his order. He wanted to know if the mission had any gold, and didn't like it much when I told him it didn't."

"Did you escape?"

"No, I was sent on a mission."

"A mission?" Several voices had spoken at once.

"Yes. Von Schroeden had all the guests who were there on mission work—the Smiths, Mr. Brown, Mr. Blomside, and a rabbi—write to their relatives asking for £5,000 in ransom, or they would die. The Smiths, Mr. Blomside, and Mr. Brown wrote theirs, which I have in my saddle bag, but Abrams, the rabbi, said he didn't have any relatives to send a letter to. Von Schroeden just looked at him and said, 'Oh. I'm so sorry.' Then he pulled out his pistol and shot the man with no more compassion than if he had been swatting a fly." The priest shuddered with horror.

"What of the ransom notes?" Harry asked.

"I'm to ride to the nearest telegraph office and contact the people who are to pay the ransom; then I'm to wait for the money. I convinced von Schroeden that I would need at least two weeks because of the fighting in Kabul, and the fact that I might have to ride to India. Then, of course, it would take some time for the money to be raised and sent. He said that, after two weeks, he'll begin shooting the hostages one by one. He also said that if there is any attempt to rescue them, they would all be shot before the rescuers could get past the gate." The priest's voice was hoarse with fatigue and fear for those he had left behind.

"Don't trust him!" Boris cried. "He told two French officers, whose families were wealthy, that if they would have their families send money to buy their freedom, he would allow them to escape. They did as he said, and one night he let them escape—right into a waiting machine gun nest. You cannot even think of trusting him!"

"I don't. That's why I came here." He looked directly at Harry. "I know of your activities here."

"Oh?" Harry stiffened.

"There's little that transpires around here of which I'm unaware." The priest, smiling slightly, spoke in hushed, urgent tones. "I'm hoping you'll help."

"Somehow, I have the feeling that you have some ideas, Father?" Harry asked.

"I have the seed of a plan, and I'm hoping you might be able to expand on it. Von Schroeden has the hostages locked in the wine cellar. That's a blessing for us, because there's a secret entrance to it from outside the mission. I think we might be able, somehow, to free those dear people through that entrance."

"Hmm, that's an intriguing thought." Harry pondered silently for a moment, and then turned to Akbar. "Akbar, do you think you and your son could ride to the mission and do some reconnaissance so we know more clearly what we're up against?"

"We'll leave tonight, as soon as the storm subsides," Akbar replied without hesitation.

Buzz jumped up. "I'll go with them!"

"No. We'll need you here to fly the Bee, if necessary. Besides that, Buzz, you're too involved," Harry retorted.

"Boris and Bob can fly the plane. I don't intend to do anything foolish! I didn't do anything foolish in the alley, or during the meeting with the elders, did I?" Buzz argued stubbornly. "I might be able to help with a plan to save these people if I can see what we're up against." In spite of himself, his voice quivered.

"He has a good point, Harry. I've known him to come up with some pretty outlandish ideas, but they usually worked. And he does a good job of thinking on his feet!" Boris remonstrated.

"I agree," Bob said adamantly.

Harry gazed thoughtfully at the three. "Perhaps you're right. All right. It would be better if the three of you went. Just don't ride that white stallion—it would stand out like a beacon," he said, giving in.

"I won't. I'll ride Diable," Buzz replied quietly. "Thanks, Harry."

A few impatient hours later, as Buzz, Akbar, and Kashar rode rapidly under a now star-studded sky, Buzz asked, "Akbar, do you know Father Sebastian very well?"

"Yes, we go back a few years. The first time I met him was when he sewed up a saber cut across my left arm."

"But you're not Catholic."

"Father Sebastian cares for anyone, Buzz, no matter what his faith. The man who cut me was in the cot next to mine, recovering from the slash I had given him. In fact, we lay there long enough to become close friends."

"Harry said he was once a soldier. Did you know that?"

"I thought he might have been. The Father once was invited to the yearly gathering of the tribes, when we swap stories and trade goods. Well, Father Sebastian came and brought some goat cheese made by the monks. (They do make very good cheese, by the way.) Anyway, a— bully, I think you would call him—of the group was always picking on the small or weak, and he tripped Kashar, who was much younger then. Before I could get there, Father Sebastian stepped between the two. The bully asked Father Sebastian if it was true that Christians turned their cheek if struck. He said yes, and got knocked to the ground. He got up and turned the other cheek, and again was knocked down. As he picked himself up again, I noticed him scooping something up in his hand. He looked the bully straight in the eyes and said, 'I have now fulfilled the commands of the good book.' Then he punched the bully in the jaw, knocking him backward ten feet into the crowd. The man came to several hours later with a broken jaw. I believe I was the only one who saw the Father drop a rock from his hand. I asked him about it later, and he said, 'Who am I, not to use the tools provided by the Lord?' And then he winked!"

"You know what, Akbar? I think I'm going to like Father Sebastian."

The sound of their laughter rang through the cold night air.

As they urged their horses to a faster pace, Buzz again questioned Akbar. "Do you know why people come to the mission? It's in the middle of nowhere. What's the draw?

"For different reasons, my friend. The rabbi was probably interested in the Khaibar Pass and hoped Father Sebastian could help. *Khaibar* means across the river, or divide. It's from the Aramaic *Habar*, which means Hebrew. Some believe that the seven lost tribes settled in the Pass."

"And the others?" Buzz inquired.

"They probably came for the solitude; to get away from everything for a month or so. The mission is known for its cheese and wine. The Father sometimes takes guests on archeological excursions, too. And the stream that runs by the mission has large trout, and the mountains are beautiful this time of year. It's left alone in times of war because of the good it does for all sides."

"Except for now," Buzz commented, scowling.

"Yes, except for now. But those thugs are outsiders," Akbar replied, somewhat defensively.

"How long before we get there?" Buzz asked.

"We should arrive just before sunrise."

The three rode silently on.

~ Chapter Sixteen ~

THE ENEMY CAMP

"**A**kbar! Kashar! Wake up! It will be light soon," whispered Buzz, as he shook his comrades.

"Huh? Oh, good morning, Buzz. What time is it?"

"Quarter till five."

"Thanks to your pocket watch's alarm, we were able to get two hours sleep," Akbar said, yawning. He stretched and sat cross-legged.

"Yeah, that watch comes in handy sometimes," Buzz commented. "Wouldn't it be nice to see Basima walking up with her coffee pot?"

"Yes. A cup of coffee would go well right now," Akbar agreed wistfully.

"Well, Father, at least we have some bread and cheese," Kashar interjected.

"Any activity down there?" Akbar asked Buzz as he crawled up to the top of the ridge partly encircling the mission.

"They're beginning to stir," Buzz said as he gazed through his field glasses. "Some are rebuilding the campfires, and others are fixing coffee."

"It would be nice of them to invite us down for a cup or two," Akbar declared, grinning.

"Yeah! And then they'd slit our throats."

"Why, Buzz, I didn't realize you were so picky."

Buzz chuckled, and then became more serious. "As far as I can see, the only guards are the three camped on the top of the ridge overlooking the pass that's been cut through it for the road to the mission." He continued to carefully scan the area with his binoculars.

"They probably figure there isn't a force large enough to be a threat for at least five-hundred miles," Akbar replied as he trained his glasses to the north. "Look, over there, on the other side of the mission. See the opening in the side of that cliff?"

"Yeah, I see," answered Buzz.

"Well, scan down toward the bottom."

"Yeah! There's a fence—and what looks like horses behind it. I did see a sort of box canyon there when I flew over. I'll bet that's where they're keeping the horses." Buzz now wore a satisfied, conspiratorial smile. He had an idea!

Akbar spoke again. "The two tents with the campfire between them must be for the guards—probably ten or twelve of them."

"How many do you think are in the camp just below us?" Buzz asked. "It looks like there are about twenty-five tents."

"Those are good-sized tents; they sleep maybe six or eight each," Akbar said, figuring swiftly.

"Yeah—about that! Damn! I wish we could see how many are in the courtyard. There could be two-hundred or three-hundred men there. We'd better put our field glasses up; the sun is starting to shine over the mountains and we don't want them to see the reflection," Buzz suggested.

Buzz suddenly felt a quick, urgent tug on his pant leg. It was Kashar. "Sir! I went to check on the horses. There are two Shadow Men looking at them!"

Buzz and Akbar looked at each other, startled, and then grabbed their rifles and scrambled down the slope, scurrying behind a growth of covering bushes. They saw two men in black; one was searching meticulously through Buzz's saddle bag, and the other was eyeing up Akbar's saddle with acquisitive admiration.

Akbar raised his rifle, but Buzz stayed his move, removed two of the newly manufactured silencers from his shoulder bag, and handed one to Akbar. He then quickly slipped his on the end of his rifle barrel and twisted, locking it onto the bayonet lug. Akbar did the same.

The two men stealthily took aim. 'Phfft!'—'Phfft!'

The Shadow Men slipped to the ground, still clutching their horses' reins. Akbar nodded toward his silencer and winked. "Nice!"

They looked at each other, grinned, and said in unison, "Coffee!"

As Buzz and Akbar donned the clothing of the dead Shadow Men, they instructed Kashar that if the two of them were caught he was not to try to rescue them. Instead, he was to ride as speedily as possible back to the base and report what he'd seen here.

Akbar suggested, "Let's take all the bread and cheese with us. We may be able to use it in trade, or something."

"Good idea," Buzz said, grinning. "How do I look?" he asked as he modeled his new attire.

"Fine," Akbar replied, grinning back, with a mock lecherous look on his bearded face. "Except that the butts of your pistols are trying to push through your robe—and that makes you look like a woman."

"Oh! Well, I wouldn't want to upset anyone." He adjusted his weapons. "How's that?"

"Much better—but you're not as attractive."

"Darn! I was hoping to get a date to the dance tonight."

"If you had, someone would have been greatly disappointed," Akbar laughed.

"Shall we walk in or ride?" Buzz queried.

"Let's walk in from the bushes as if we'd been doing our morning business, Akbar suggested.

"Let's go get some coffee!"

"Bring me some if you can," Kashar said.

"We'll try. In the meantime, keep your eyes open and be careful," Akbar cautioned gruffly. He did not want to embarrass either his son or himself by being openly affectionate, but he still had difficulty leaving Kashar alone in a situation he knew was dangerous.

"Let's enter the camp between those tents," Buzz proposed quietly, nodding at the two closest to them.

"Good. One of them has two cups hanging from a tent rope. I'll get them as we pass by," Akbar said under his breath.

"Yeah. Two men with coffee cups will look less like spies—I hope."

They strode out toward the camp.

"Got them."

"Good man."

"Hey, you two. Did you steal our cups?"

"Who, us?" Akbar questioned, obviously affronted. He looked sternly at their accuser, who had just emerged from the tent from which the cups had been acquired.

"Why would we take your cups when we have our own? See?" Buzz snapped at the recently awakened Shadow Man, holding up his newly procured cup.

"Oh, okay. I guess ours fell on the ground somewhere," said the black-robed man. He began looking under and around his tent.

"Well, so much for the mental capabilities of the enemy," Buzz wisecracked with a grin.

"There is not much organization. The tents are set up every which way, and the campfires are the same way—no order," Akbar commented.

"As are the weapons. Their rifles—mostly 8mm Mausers—are all either leaning against the tents or laying on the ground," Buzz noted.

"And their swords are either stuck in the ground for use as clothes hangers, or like that fellow's, being used to chop wood," Akbar observed disgustedly. "The air is a little strong here." Akbar wrinkled his nose.

"You're right! It reminds me of the circus—when Jack fired one of the animal keepers for not cleaning the cages for over a week. Careful! You nearly stepped in that," Buzz cautioned as he pulled Akbar aside.

"What was it?" asked Akbar.

"I'm not sure, but I don't think you would have wanted to step in it," Buzz answered as they nonchalantly made their way through the labyrinth of tents and half-clad, sleepy-eyed men. "There sure is a mixture of nationalities here. I think those were Greeks that we just passed, and there are some Blacks from Africa. The aromas of the different foods are beginning to overpower the animal odor."

"I'm not sure which I prefer, at this point," Akbar said from the side of his mouth. "I wish a brisk breeze would blow through; the smoke is really beginning to irritate my eyes."

"That group of Chinese is staring. Let's cut to the right, between those tents," Buzz murmured.

"Good idea," Akbar agreed, following Buzz.

"There's a man with some coffee," Akbar said, gesturing with his cup to a partially dressed man pouring dark liquid into his own obviously unwashed drinking utensil.

"Hey friend, could you spare us some of your coffee?" Buzz asked.

"No. And I'm not your friend."

"Our tent is out of coffee—all we have is some bread and cheese."

"Oh! Well, for that, I might become your long lost brother," replied the man with the coffee.

"Slice off some bread and cheese for our lost brother while I help him with our cups," Buzz instructed Akbar.

"We used the last of our coffee last night. I wish I knew when we're supposed to get more," Buzz lied as his 'brother' filled the two recently acquired cups.

"A supply truck is supposed to come tomorrow. Mmm, good cheese," the man said indistinctly through the huge portion he'd stuffed into his maw.

"Is that the one from the north?" Akbar inquired over a steaming cup.

"Nah! This is the one from the east."

"I heard that ten more men came in last night. How many does that make now?" Buzz asked, cautiously sipping his coffee.

"I was told yesterday that we had four-hundred and fifty-nine, so the ten will make four-hundred and sixty-nine. No, wait—two died of snakebite the other day, so that would be four-hundred and sixty-seven."

"Yeah, that's one of the problems with camping outside of the mission walls—snakes and scorpions. Damn, I hate them!" snorted Akbar in feigned disgust.

"What's it like behind those gates? We haven't been here long, so we never had a chance to go inside," Buzz said, looking toward the two heavy gates barring the courtyard.

"You haven't missed much. Oh, I guess it's a little nicer in some ways."

"Oh?—in what ways?" Buzz probed.

"More bread and cheese, brother?" Akbar asked solicitously.

"Oh, yah!—here! And take some more coffee."

"Now, what's inside?" Buzz inquired again.

"Well, let's see! For one thing, they have tarps strung from the building almost to the outer wall, giving them shelter from the sun and the rain. Some of them have straw to sleep on, which is better than this rocky soil out here," said their 'long lost brother,' kicking a rock into his campfire.

"I guess they use the whole courtyard, since there's—oh, how many men did you say were staying in there?" Akbar queried as he sliced another piece of cheese for their unwitting informant.

"The same as out here—a little over two-hundred; half on either side of the gate. At first I wished I was staying in there, but now I like it better out here. It smells better."

"Does anybody stay inside the mission itself?" Buzz continued his interrogation while pouring another cup of coffee.

"Just the colonel and his ten staff men, as he calls them. And the monks and hostages, too."

"I think we'd better get back to our tent. Our mates are probably wondering what happened to us," Buzz fabricated.

"Yeah, we have to go. Maybe we can come around for another cup of coffee sometime," Akbar suggested.

"Only if you have bread and cheese," the man remarked scornfully.

As they made their way back through the maze of tents and ropes, Buzz said, under his breath, "I think we've learned all we need to know, don't you?"

"More than I had dared hope for. I had—wait, don't go that way!" Akbar said urgently as he grabbed Buzz's arm. "Quickly! This way!"

"What's the matter?" asked Buzz tensely.

"Don't look back! Those men—the ones who were in front of us—are from one of the mountain tribes. They're a bunch of cutthroat bandits. The one with the scar across his face? I put it there."

"Do you think he recognized you?"

"I don't know. It happened a long time ago."

"Well, if you still remember who you slashed, I'm sure he still remembers who gave him that scar. Cut through that cloud of smoke between those tents!"

Buzz continued a running commentary as they moved quickly and unobtrusively without drawing undue attention.

"We've made it to the edge of the tents; now we just have a hundred yards across the field to the brush." Buzz turned, attempting to appear as though they were just going nowhere in particular. It was enough to see 'Scarface' following them, and motioning, as if waving to someone. "Damn!—He's following us."

"If we can make it to the brush, we might be able to lose him," Akbar said worriedly.

"Akbar—bend over as if you're sick. I'll act like I'm helping you to the bushes." A few tense moments passed before Buzz noted, "Okay, we've made it to the brush. Now let's see if we can make it to those rocks."

"Akbar. Stop or I'll shoot!"

"Damn! I was hoping it wouldn't come to this" Buzz swore as he drew his revolvers and spun around, only to see the man with the scar fall, eyes wide and mouth agape in surprise. He collapsed slowly forward onto the tangled mass of a thorn bush. Blood dripped from leaf to stem to leaf and pooled on a rock, leaving a bright crimson trail in vivid contrast to the dull, dusty green foliage.

Buzz and Akbar stared at each other in bewilderment.

"Kashar!" Akbar said in a loud whisper.

"The silencer! He used the silencer!" Buzz explained quietly.

Crouching low, the two men hurried to the edge of the brush and nervously peered through the entanglement of branches and leaves. "I don't think anyone noticed him," Akbar said, his voice hoarse with tension.

"I agree; no alarm has been sounded. Let's get him back to the horses," Buzz instructed.

Akbar dragged the body deeper into the brush as Buzz slung the slain man's discarded rifle over his shoulder and quickly obliterated the blood and the drag marks. When out of sight of the camp, the two men carried the body between them, and returned to their horses.

"Father? Sir? Did I do the right thing?" Kashar asked, his voice trembling.

"Yes! You did the right thing, boy, you did the right thing," Akbar replied, hugging his son fiercely, proudly. "You did the right thing!"

"You have a fine young man there, Akbar," Buzz complimented as he watched the scene between father and son.

"I know that, Buzz. Thank you!" Akbar's great paw of a hand still rested on Kashar's shoulder.

"What should we do with the bodies?" Kashar asked. He stood tall and straight, pleased with his father's pride in him.

"We'll wait until dark. Just before moonrise, we'll load them on the horses. The two lead horses can drag brush behind them, covering their tracks, and the prints of the three horses following will leave a trail of three apparent deserters. After four or five miles, where the ground is too rocky to trail us, we'll strip the first two we shot of all valuables and dump their bodies on the side of the trail," Akbar explained.

"I get it—the third deserter shot the other two and robbed them. We'll bury the third one a mile or so farther along so he won't be found," Buzz replied admiringly. "Now, let's get some sleep. We had a long ride last night, and we'll have another tonight."

"I'll take first watch," Kashar volunteered.

"It's good to be rid of those dead men," Kashar commented with relief. "It wasn't so bad in the daylight, but at night, they were kind of spooky. The light from the moon coming up over the mountains formed some weird shadows when we buried that last one."

"The horses are more at ease too, now that the smell of blood is gone," Akbar remarked.

"Mr. Buzz is so very quiet, father. Is he worried about his lady friend being held at the mission? Maybe I should ride up and keep him company."

"No, my son; stay back here with me. Let him ride ahead by himself. I have a feeling he's working on a plan."

"To rescue his friend?"

"In the short time I have known that man, I somehow don't think he is planning only the rescue of his Kim, but the total defeat of the Shadow Men!" Akbar declared, respect and admiration in his voice.

"But there are nearly five-hundred of them and just a handful of us. And most of our troops are girls," Kashar protested.

"Yes, I know it sounds impossible, but that's why I think he will devise a plan. And when he does, it will be so bizarre, it will be successful," Akbar replied, shaking his head and smiling with confidence.

The only sound during the remainder of the return to the air base was the sound of the horses' hooves.

— Chapter Seventeen —

PREPARING FOR WAR

Clang! Clang! Clang!

"They're back! They're back!" Zohra shouted, racing down the tower steps.

Phfoot!—Phfoot!—Phfoooot! screamed the steam roller whistle. Bob vaulted from its cab, nearly landing on top of Ned, who was hastily crawling out from under it.

In a matter of minutes, everyone had gathered on the field, shielding their eyes from the morning sun and anxiously watching the small, shadowy figures get larger as they approached. Harry was nervously slapping his leg with his swagger stick; Bob was pacing; Ned was wiping his greasy hands over and over with an oily rag; and Boris was rapidly puffing on his cigar, turning the surrounding air into a haze. The only sounds were the slapping of Harry's stick, the hissing of the steam roller, and the wind whistling softly but insistently through the Bee's guy wires.

"Why do they have two extra horses?" someone asked, adding another mystery to their already racing thoughts.

At last the returning men reined in their horses. As soon as Buzz dismounted, Harry began his interrogation. "Did you have a good trip? Any trouble? Did you get any information?"

"Coffee, sir?"

"Yes, Basima! I would love a cup of your wonderful coffee," Buzz replied. He took the cup in both hands, gratefully inhaling the aroma before drinking. "Ahh! Thank you! We missed you and your coffee very much."

"To answer your questions, Harry, we had a good trip; no trouble to speak of. All we did was walk into their camp, drink their coffee, ask some questions, and leave. Akbar and Kashar will fill you in on the

184

details. There are some things I need to check out, so if you'll excuse me..." With that, he handed his now empty cup to Basima and disappeared into the hangar.

"What the bloody hell was that all about?" Harry asked in bewilderment.

"He hasn't said more than two words since we buried the last body," Akbar commented.

"Buried the last body? Bloody he...! He spoke as if it were no more than walking across the road to visit the neighbors for tea and crumpets, and you talk of burying bodies," Harry yelled, his face reddening alarmingly.

"Harry, Kashar and I will tell you about it over breakfast and more of Basima's coffee. As for Buzz—I think he has something on his mind."

"Yeah, he's working on something," Boris agreed. "Bob, remember when he came up with that new routine for the clown act?"

Bob nodded in agreement. "He holed up in his tent for two days. But when he was done, he'd dreamed up one hell of an act."

———

"G'morning, gentlemen! Oh, thank you, Basima!—could you fix me a plate?"

"I would be glad to, Mr. Boris—sir."

"Has anyone seen Buzz this morning?" Boris asked, sipping his coffee.

"The last time I seen him, is when he asked me if I would mind if we traded bunks for a while. He said he would like to use my room in the hangar for a bit," Ned said.

"I hope that bit is over soon," Bob grumbled.

"Why is that, guv'ner?" Ned asked.

"Did anyone ever tell you that you snore? Loudly?"

"I do believe that subject has come up in conversation a time or two," Ned admitted, ducking his head and grinning with embarrassment.

"Buzz, asked me for all the aerial photos and maps of the mission yesterday," Harry remarked.

"He asked Ned and me about Nelly."

"Nelly?" everyone chorused in unison.

It was Bob's turn to duck his head. "Ned and I named the steam roller Nelly," he confessed sheepishly.

"Where's Father Sebastian?" Boris inquired.

"Last I saw, he was taking a breakfast tray to Buzz," Bob reported. "Oh, here he comes now," he added, pointing to the figure just coming through the door, carrying a cup.

"Morning, Father. Anything to report from the tiger's lair?" Harry asked.

"As a matter of fact, there is. He'd like all of you," he motioned to the six men at the table, "to come to the hangar when you get a chance. And, oh, yes—he also asked for 'Little Miss Coffeepot' to come, also."

"Little Miss Coffeepot?" Understanding quickly dawned on Akbar. "Oh! He means Basima," he said, chuckling.

"Let's go see what our mastermind has cooked up this time," Boris urged. Cups in hand, in parade-like fashion, they all followed the priest to the back room of the hangar.

"Gentlemen, glad you all could come. Please, pull up a crate and be seated—or stand if you prefer," Buzz greeted them gaily.

The room was new to most of the men. Ned had converted the storeroom into his own rather quaint living quarters. It had the basic comforts—a cot, and an upturned .303 ammo crate for a bedside stand. Atop the crate were a kerosene lamp and several books. Above the cot hung a large picture of the king, which Ned had enhanced by attaching three medals to it. Across the room, stood a large six-by-two-by-two-foot crate which had been up-ended, forming a tidy clothes closet. In it hung, in meticulous military order, Ned's uniforms—his highly polished boots residing beneath.

A board resting on two sawhorses served as a table and commanded the center of the room. Over this hung a single light bulb, its glare subdued by a green shade. One end held an assortment of aerial photos; an array of drafting instruments lay here and there on the table, and at one corner sat an empty coffee cup surrounded by many overlapping rings, giving evidence of the countless cups consumed previously. In the center were six 8 x10 photos which had been taped together to form a single large image of the mission and the area immediately surrounding it.

Buzz, red-eyed, unshaven, and uncombed, sat in the only chair. His feet were propped up on the table and he was leaning back against the wall, his fingers interlaced behind his head. Above him, a large square of white paper—probably the reverse side of a map—was pinned to the wall. On it was a pencil drawing of the mission and other points of interest surrounding the compound.

As the men entered, Father Sebastian, Harry and Kashar all proceeded to the left, and seated themselves on some ammo boxes. Ned, Bob, and Akbar perched on the cot, and Boris leaned against the doorway.

"'S'cuse me, sir."

"Oh, I'm sorry. I didn't see you, Basima," Boris said as he quickly moved aside to let the girl enter, her coffee pot firmly in hand.

"Heaven forbid. Please don't keep our 'Little Miss Coffee Pot' out!" Buzz exclaimed, grinning at her as he extended his cup. Basima's smiling face blushed as she shrugged her head into her shoulders, trying in vain to stifle a giggle as she learned her new title.

"Gentlemen," Buzz addressed them, as he paused momentarily to sip his coffee, "I believe I've worked out a plan to solve the dilemma at the mission. But first I must ask some questions. Father, you said there's a hidden tunnel into the wine cellar, but is there a way to get into the mission from the wine cellar—past the barred door?"

"Yes, I think it could be done. That old building is honeycombed with secret passages."

"Good. Harry, do you think you could haul the steam roller on its trailer? I think the trailer parked behind the stables is for it. Do you think you could pull it with one of your trucks to the mission?"

"My trucks could pull it, all right, but I haven't been over those roads in several years. Father, you know the roads better than anyone. What do you think?"

After a thoughtful pause, the priest replied, "There are a few rough spots, but nothing major. Yes, I think you could."

Buzz spoke again. "Boris, Akbar. Do you think the two of you could train the older girls to ride and fight on horseback in nine days?"

"I think we have ten days before the deadline, Buzz," Father Sebastian interjected.

"Yes, we do, Father," replied Buzz, "but von Schroeden would more than likely expect something on the last day. That's why I'd like to do this in nine—and, if for some reason, we need an extra day, we'd have it."

Boris looked at Akbar questioningly, his left eyebrow raised. Their eyes met, and each man nodded in agreement. "The girls are smart, and some already have the ability to ride," Akbar noted.

"From what I've observed of these Shadow Men, they fight more like rabble than trained soldiers," Boris interspersed.

"That brings up another question," said Buzz. "Boris, you said you knew this von Schroeden. What kind of military leader is he?"

"May I smoke?" Boris asked, holding up a cigar.

"You'll have to ask Ned. These are his quarters," Buzz replied.

"Why, of course, guv. In fact, I have one I started yesterday, here by my lamp. I'll join you!" Ned said companionably. Boris and Harry quickly lit up, too.

After somewhat ceremoniously lighting his cigar, Boris replied to Buzz. "As a leader, he isn't for crap; his ego gets in the way. He once stopped a truck convoy carrying five-hundred troops desperately needed for reinforcement at the front to look for an escaped prisoner. He went into a rage, yelling, 'No one escapes from me—no one!' After two days, the man's body was found under one of the barracks, where he'd apparently died from one of the many illnesses in the camp. Von Schroeden said that not even death could pardon the man, so he had the dead body tied to a post and shot. He's insane!"

"That's what I had figured. It's an integral part of the plan I've been working on to attack and defeat the Shadow Men." Buzz leaned forward on the table and looked into the attentive faces of the men before him.

Harry slowly exhaled cigar smoke, thoughtfully rolling his cigar between his fingers. Akbar solemnly returned Buzz's gaze. Kashar looked to his father. Boris blew smoke rings toward the light. Bob rubbed his chin and studied the diagram on the wall. Ned busied himself in re-lighting his cigar.

Father Sebastian was the first to speak. "You would be fighting fifteen-to-one odds!" he exclaimed in awe.

"Well, Father, actually, it will be closer to twenty-eight to one," Buzz replied.

"So what's your plan?" Harry asked.

"Well," Buzz began, as he rose from his chair and turned to the diagram. "Bob, Boris, and Akbar would ride ahead and take out the guards on the road—here." He pointed to a crude drawing of a tent and three stick-figures. "They would then take the guards' place around the campfire so everything would appear as it had been from the mission."

"Would we be using the silencers?" inquired Akbar.

"Yes," Buzz said. "And I'll make up a couple more of them. Once the guards are taken care of, Harry and Ned will bring the trucks here." Buzz pointed again to the diagram. "This stream is hidden from view of the mission by this ridge."

"Is that the ridge we hid behind?" Akbar asked.

"Yes," Buzz affirmed. "As you can see on the photos, the ridge would form a protective crescent between the trucks and the mission."

"It's the remnants of an old wall from years ago, when the mission was rather large," commented Father Sebastian.

"Father, you and Harry will rescue the hostages. Harry, you'll escort them back to the trucks; Father, you'll gather your brothers and subdue any Shadow Men staying in the building. Then you'll need to lock all the doors and windows so we can keep the main body of the Shadow Men massed together in the courtyard. Kashar, you and two of the girls will take Boris's, Bob's and Akbar's places as fake guards while they prepare for the next phase."

"Which is?" Harry inquired.

Buzz reached under the table and brought up a cone-topped, quart-sized oil can. "Bob, do you have anything in that stuff you got

189

from Jack that will send one of these about two-hundred yards? I need to fire these toward the mission from two depressions about a quarter of the way from the top of the ridge. See?" Buzz pointed with his pencil to two darker shadows on one of the photographs. "I packed one of these cans with some 35mm movie training films, took it a distance away from the base last night, and lit it. The part of the film that stuck out of the can burned with a flash, but the stuff inside just smoldered and poured out a thick, white, noxious smoke that burned my eyes and lungs."

"Like the gases in the trenches in the war!" Bob remarked.

"Exactly," Buzz agreed.

"What are the dimensions of the cans?" asked Bob thoughtfully.

"They're four inches in diameter and five inches tall, with another inch-and-a-half for the cone where the cap screws on. Each will weigh a bit more than a pound."

Bob pursed his lips, considered a moment, and then nodded decisively. "I think I can handle that."

"Good. Now, back to the timetable. Boris, you and Akbar will take your troop, under the cover of the ridge, around to the base of the cliff. There's a sort of road there. You'll have whichever girls you pick. Plus, we'll mount some kind of ghostly-looking figures dressed in the shadow robes we have on any extra horses. I figure that with the troops, the ghost riders, and the Bee flying in with her guns blazing and flames coming from the wings, we should scare the he…" Buzz caught sight of Basima sitting in the corner, "…heck out of them! And that should give you and Akbar something of an edge. Your objective is to keep the Shadow Men from their horses. Stampede them if you have to, but keep them separated!"

"How will you know the right time to fly in?" Harry asked.

Buzz quickly replied, "That will be your job, Harry. You'll be here"—he pointed again to the area with the three stick figures—"directing the whole operation with rockets. The gunfire should bring out the 'tent men' (I called them that for identification purposes) from their tents, giving me better targets to strafe and bomb."

"Bob," he continued, "you and Ned will be getting steam up in Nelly and hitching up the trailer."

"Trailer? What trailer?" Bob asked. "We don't have a trailer!"

"Here's a sketch of what I have in mind," Buzz said as he taped a drawing to the wall. "It's basically a steel box on four wheels with viewing slits and a gun port on both sides. In it are two of these."

As he spoke, he reached beneath the table and brought out a strange-looking firearm. It was like nothing any of them had seen before. He placed in the center of the table. "I took five of the Martini-Greener shotguns and welded them together with the barrels fanned apart to achieve a wider field of fire. When it's finished, it'll only take one trigger and one lever to operate. Each shot-shell has twelve .32 caliber lead balls, so that's a total of a hundred and twenty projectiles per volley. With two loaders and a gunner per gun, I figure we can get off twenty volleys per minute.

"Bob, after you crash through the gates, your team—with the war wagon and the Lewis gun in the cab—should be able to fire three-thousand projectiles a minute into a mass of men, who will already be in a panic because of the fires and the gaseous smoke fired in from these two positions." Buzz pointed to the two areas he had indicated earlier.

"It'll be like shooting fish in a barrel." Buzz paused and said, "That's it. Any questions or comments?"

"Yes. I have one."

"What is it, Harry?"

"If you don't take out at least two-thirds of the 'Tent Men,' as you call them, on the first pass, you'll have a hail of bullets coming up at you during the second strafing run. How will you overcome that?"

Buzz grinned tiredly. "Well, that's obviously something I'm hoping we can work out! Anyone else?"

"Yes," Kashar spoke up. "Do you have a plan for withdrawal or retreat?"

"Make for the trucks and drive for the base, or for the Khaibar Pass and India. If the Bee is still flying, I'll give you air support somehow."

Ned asked, "Wouldn't it be better to have the Lewis gun on the ridge?"

"I considered that, but I think it would be better mounted on Nelly to give the trailer support the way the infantry does for tanks."

"Yes sir, I see," Ned replied.

"Basima." Buzz softened his tone. "Do you have a question?"

"I would like to fire the gas bombs, sir."

Startled, Buzz spoke forcefully, "That could be very dangerous!"

Basima was adamant. "I know that! But I want to fight in this, too!—to help destroy the evil men who took me from my home! I know what they had in mind for me!"

The men were all taken aback by the fiercely determined expression on her usually smiling face.

"Okay, you can shoot the gas bombs, Basima," Buzz agreed reluctantly. "Any more questions? No? Then I suggest we start on this right after lunch. Thank you, gentlemen—and you too, Basima."

"More coffee, sir?"

"No. No more coffee for Mr. Buzz, Basima. He needs some Scotch to unwind so he can get some much needed sleep," Harry interjected firmly as he took Buzz's cup and poured a generous measure of Scotch into it.

"I believe you're right, Harry. I guess I am going on coffee, but I wanted to work something out. We have so little time," Buzz agreed wearily. He flopped down into the chair and gratefully drank. "Oh, that's good," he commented, and then sipped again. "You fellows will think it over, won't you? I mean—if you think there should be some changes, that's okay."

"Will you relax and get some sleep? You look like a death-eaten soda cracker," Bob snapped.

"A what?" In spite of himself, Buzz's eyes were beginning to close and his body was relaxing.

"Just get some sleep. We'll wake you in a few hours," Boris said. Since he was the last to exit the room, he closed the door softly behind him.

— Chapter Eighteen —

NINE DAYS' TIME

"Come on, Boris. We're going to the mess hall to discuss this over tea and biscuits," Bob yelled.

"Go on over, and sit with the rest—I'll see about the tea, and if there are any biscuits left over from breakfast," continued Bob, as he held the door for his friend.

"Sit down, Boris. Do you think Buzz will sleep?" Akbar asked, obviously concerned.

"We were just talkin' about how beat he looked," Ned observed.

"Oh, I think he'll be okay. It looked as though Harry's Scotch was already beginning to take effect when I left him," Boris replied.

"Here's the tea, boys. Nudar said they were out of biscuits, but they'll bake some up in just a few minutes," Bob reported, placing a tray laden with a steaming pot of tea, sugar, and cream in the center of the table.

"I don't think there's anything approaching Buzz's plan in the books at Sandhurst Academy," Harry commented

"It is rather out of the ordinary! Twenty-eight to one odds?" Akbar mused.

"Leading a bunch of kids and ghosts against seasoned fighters," Boris remarked, ruefully shaking his head.

"Using a steam roller for a tank?" Bob added.

"Can he make that five-barreled gun work?" Ned asked doubtfully.

"Of course he can! Buzz was a gunsmith, like his father," Bob answered in quick defense.

"Damned good one, so I'm told," Boris added, supporting Bob.

"Oh! I didn't know that!" Ned said admiringly. He somehow had the feeling that Mr. Buzz could probably walk on water if he chose. He was proud to call him his friend.

"Here are your biscuits, sirs."

"Thank you, Nudar. Just put them on the table, please," Bob said absently. His thoughts were racing.

Kashar chose a biscuit and slowly and methodically applied butter to it. Akbar leaned his elbows on the table, and rubbed his chin, staring into space. Boris leaned back and folded his hands behind his head, while watching the smoke from his cigar rise languidly to the ceiling. Ned traced the rim of his cup, around and around, over and over, with his forefinger. Father Sebastian sat with his hands folded in his lap, head bowed. Harry's eyes were focused on the whirlpool formed by his tea as he continually stirred the untasted liquid in his cup. Bob sketched something resembling a steam roller on a scrap of paper. The hall was quiet but for the clink of Harry's spoon. Then that too ceased, and only the sound of the wind remained.

BAM! Harry slammed his fist resoundingly on the table, causing his cup to jump and his tea to slosh. "By Jove, I think we could pull it off! It's so far-fetched, they would never expect anything like that," he declared excitedly.

"I think that welding a battering ram onto Nelly's front will help push the gates open," Bob mused, as he slid the paper over for the others to see.

"Push open, hell. I can adjust the speed, guv, so she'll do at least thirty or forty miles an hour!—and we'll smash those gates open!" Ned said. He slammed his fist into his other hand, then threw both hands into the air and fanned his fingers, simulating flying debris.

"They'll think they're already in hell when we crash through those gates and start spraying them with—how many rounds a minute did Buzz say? Three thousand?" Bob whooped, his eyes ablaze with excitement.

"Don't forget the gas bombs and fireworks dropping in on them, starting fires and filling their lungs and eyes with smoke," Kashar added.

"Boris, can't you just picture the look on those guards' faces when they see us leading a charge of screaming girls and ghost riders with our flag waving?" Akbar exclaimed, arm extended as though presenting a saber.

"It'll be like Wagner's 'The Ride of the Valkyries' —Dum te da dum ta, Dum te da dum ta, Dum Te daaaa, Dummm!" sang Harry, enthusiastically waving his arms as if he were conducting an orchestra.

"We don't have a flag," Boris reminded Akbar. After pausing momentarily, he vowed, "But, by God, we will—and uniforms, too."

Ned chimed in again. "Yeah!—there's some parachutes in the hangar that we can use, and a Singer sewing machine, Model 1641, still in the box!"

Father Sebastian's eyes darted from one speaker to another as he silently, gratefully mouthed the words, "Thank you, Lord!"

"The kicker will be when Buzz flies the Bee in from a dark sky, with flames flashing from its wings, and swoops over the guards and swings around the mission and strafes the tent men," Bob said excitedly, "and comes back to—" He halted, suddenly aware of a ghastly possibility.

"Yes," Harry pronounced gravely. "If he doesn't wipe out a large majority of them the first time, he'll be a sitting duck the second time around! If there are enough left of them to counterattack, we won't have a chance!"

"Mr. Buzz will work something out," Ned insisted, shaking his handful of biscuit. He popped it decisively into his mouth, and mumbled around it, "Yes, sir, I know he can." He injudiciously sprayed crumbs as he spoke.

"That's just one of the details that needs to be worked out. I think we should get started now on what we already know needs to be done," Harry suggested.

"Ned and I will start working on Nelly immediately," Bob said.

"Akbar and I will get the horses and the girls and start their training," Boris stated, eager to begin.

"The girls! We didn't talk with the girls about this! We need to ask them if they want to do this!" Harry exclaimed. "We can't expose them to such—"

"There is no need to ask, sirs. We already know about Mr. Buzz's plan—Basima told us about your meeting, and we listened as you spoke just now," Yasmin spoke up. As the oldest of the girls, she served as the spokesperson for the entire group. "We talked it over among ourselves, and we all want to be part of it—even though some, or perhaps all, of us may be killed. These men are bad and must be stopped. Besides, we want to help Mr. Buzz get his lady back!"

"With a fighting force like this, the Shadow Men won't have a chance. Let us prepare for war," Harry stated grimly. Brandishing his cigar as though it were a saber, he led the troops outside.

"Ned, let's start fortifying Nelly with some steel plates or whatever else we can find," Bob suggested, as he and Ned headed for the steam roller.

"Kashar, gather up the girls and meet Akbar and me at the stables," Boris cried over the din of excited voices.

"Mr. Ned. Mr. Ned, sir," Hala called as she ran to catch up with him.

"Yes, Hala?"

"Could you show me where the parachutes and the sewing machine are, sir?"

"Sure thing, lassie. They're in the hangar. I'll show you," he replied with an obliging smile. He called out to Bob, who was already climbing into the cab of the steam roller, "I'll be with you as soon as I show Hala where the 'chutes and the sewing machine are!"

"While you're in the hangar, get the service manual for Nelly, will you?" Bob yelled.

"Right-o, Bob," Ned shouted back.

"Father Sebastian, what do you say we go to my quarters and work on the rescue of the hostages?" Harry proposed, gently taking the priest's arm.

"Good idea," he agreed.

Harry turned and yelled, "Oh, Bob, will you have Buzz come to our quarters when he wakes?"

Bob merely waved his acknowledgement.

"Good Lord. Look at the time." Harry said. "I didn't realize it was so late!"

"The girls serving sandwiches and tea to everyone at their work sites saved a lot of time. What was the name of the girl who suggested it, again?" asked Father Sebastian.

"That was Anan, Father. She's one of the girls who do the cooking."

"You have some very talented people here, Harry."

"Yes, and I'm very proud of them," Harry replied with the air of a father whose children have been justifiably praised.

"Maybe I had better wake Buzz. Too much sleep can be nearly as debilitating as not enough," Harry commented, as he began to rise from his chair.

"I don't think that will be necessary—there he is now, talking with Bob," said the priest, pointing to the two men standing by Nelly.

Buzz turned with a bounce and, half-running, headed their way and took the porch in one leap. Opening the door, he turned and paused, looking over his shoulder. "It looks like Boris is going to perform a marriage." He stood, still gazing out the doorway.

"A what?" asked an astonished Harry.

"That's when he pairs up the riders and their horses. He says that it links the two; it's a sort of marriage of mind and spirit. Come outside and watch. You might find it interesting," Buzz suggested as he leaned against the building and lit his pipe.

The two men rather unceremoniously vacated their chairs, and rushed out the still-open door. Father Sebastian sat on the steps, while Harry perched on the porch railing. They watched closely as Boris and Akbar walked onto the airfield with the girls following behind in single file, each leading a saddled horse. Using a stick, Boris drew a line in the dirt and motioned the girls to lead the horses to the line, drop the reins, and step aside. They were then to form a single line. Basima, being so tiny, would be at the front, the others behind her in order of height.

Buzz spoke softly. "The way Boris explained it to me is that as he walks by the horses with a person, he places one hand on their shoulder to feel their reaction. Then he has them touch each horse as he watches the horse's eyes. There—watch him with Basima."

They were engrossed as they watched Boris lead Basima to the first horse. They paused, she stroked the horse's muzzle, and they continued down the line of horses. At the seventh horse, Boris handed Basima the reins and instructed her to embrace the horse's neck briefly. Then she led her horse over to join Akbar, who stood in the middle of the field. This was repeated until each girl had been paired with a mount.

Buzz, Harry, and Father Sebastian continued to observe as the last girl led her horse to the middle of the field to join her companions. Boris gave the order to mount, which everyone did in unison—except for Basima. Because of her small stature, she was unable to reach the stirrup. As she continued her vain attempt to follow Boris' order, Yasmin rode quietly up beside her and, reaching down gently, grasped the smaller girl's collar and helped her to her saddle.

"Yasmin is like everyone's big sister, isn't she?" commented Father Sebastian.

"Yes," Harry answered softly. "These girls are closer than sisters in many ways. Things happened to them that have made an even stronger bond than blood."

The girls formed a column of twos. With Yasmin and Basima in the lead, they rode toward the open valley.

"The girls probably don't want to have the men watching them as they ride for the first time for fear they may make mistakes and lose face," said Harry.

Boris and Akbar mounted their horses and rode toward the foothills.

"I'd bet those two are going to keep an eye on their brood from a distance," Buzz observed, smiling his approval.

"A couple of old war horses with soft spots for their troops," chuckled Harry as he stepped down from the railing. The other two men followed him inside.

"Buzz, Father Sebastian thinks he should return to the mission tomorrow," Harry said as they were seating themselves.

"Yes, Buzz, I do. This von Schroeden is apparently quite unpredictable. He may get restless if he doesn't hear anything for six or seven days; he may shoot or torture some of the hostages," the priest said anxiously.

"We want to hear what you think about him going back," Harry said.

"Well, it's like going back into the lion's den to see if the lion is still hungry, but it does make sense. Von Schroeden sent Father Sebastian to demand the ransom, or so he thought. But, Father, you can give us the latest information about what's happening inside the mission. I hate to see you go back, but you're right," Buzz agreed. He was engrossed, aimlessly drawing with his finger in some coffee that had spilled on the table.

Tap! Tap! Tap! "It's Bob, and it looks like he has his hands full," Buzz said as he rose to open the door.

"Ah, welcome. We never deny entrance to a man bearing tea and cakes," Harry cried jovially. He was leaning back in his chair, arms outstretched toward Bob and his tray of refreshments.

"Not to intrude, but I thought you might be thirsty now that Basima has joined the army. I also thought you might want an update," Bob announced, grinning.

"Here, let me help you with that tray," Harry said, carefully relieving Bob of the tray and setting it in the center of the table. "What's this update you speak of?" As he questioned Bob, he efficiently arranged the cups, and began to pour. "Oh, I'm sorry. I should have asked. Everyone want some?"

All accepted, and the men concentrated quietly for a short time on mixing their personal blends of cream, lumps of sugar and tea.

Buzz sipped from the steaming cup. "Ahh! That's good tea!" he said, leaning his elbows on the table and holding his cup directly below his nose. He inhaled the aroma appreciatively.

"Now," Harry demanded, "what's the update?"

"Well," Bob began, and then paused for a moment to clear his mouth of cookie. "Well, since I had some time, I thought I'd report on the progress being made. First of all, Boris and Akbar have returned from playing mother hens, and Akbar and Ned are in the arms room pulling out some shotguns. Akbar said there isn't enough time to teach the girls to shoot rifles accurately, so he's going to train them with shotguns. Akbar's daughters, and Kashar and Ara—the girl whose father raised horses—have divided the girls into troops of five or six, and have each taken a unit to teach them to ride. When I left Boris, he was preparing to make wooden swords out of some crating Ned found. I, myself, am waiting for the welds to cool so I can paint. Ned and I finished the ram on Nelly."

Harry was astonished. "Already?" he gasped.

"Yeah! Ned and I used the torch, and cut part of the frame off that old truck up the road, and welded it to the front of the steam roller. Oh, yeah—Buzz, Ned said that there are some steel plates in the weeds behind the stables, and he thinks there's enough for your war wagon. There may not be enough to cover the cab on Nelly, but we think we can sandwich about three inches of close-packed fine sand and gravel between two sheets of corrugated roofing. That should stop an 8 mm bullet. After I finish my tea party, I'll paint Nelly, and then Ned and I will start bulletproofing the ol' girl."

When Bob finally finished, he leaned back in his chair and sipped his tea with an extremely satisfied expression. He was proud of his comrades.

"It sounds like you have the makings of a fine fighting force here, Harry," said Father Sebastian, his eyes agleam with hope.

"Yes, it seems we do," Harry answered proudly, and then continued in a more subdued manner. "Father, let me suggest that I drive you to Anderab. I know the telegraph operator there; he'll give us copies of your supposedly sent messages, as well as the replies. They'll all be on official forms, and stamped and signed by an official operator. Then you'll have something to give von Schroeden to show that you sent the ransom demands and received replies."

"That sounds to be an excellent idea, Harry. When do we leave?"

"As soon as I attend to a few things and the girls prepare us some food and drink to take with us. It'll be a long drive." Harry rose purposefully from the table.

"I'll get the messages and the addresses to which they should be sent," said the abbot as he too stood.

"Bob, I'll walk with you to Nelly. I want to talk with you about installing the gas pipes on the wings of the Bee for the flame effect," Buzz announced as he scooted his chair back.

"Okay. Did I tell you Ned said that there's some quarter-inch gas pipe left from when the stoves were put in the kitchen? The way he talked, there should be enough to do the job," Bob replied.

"That's good. We've made a lot of progress—and this is only the first day; we just might be ready in nine days. What do you think?" Buzz inquired, warily hopeful.

"I'll be able to better answer that question in about six days," Bob rejoined.

"Okay, I'll ask again in six days," Buzz retorted, slapping Bob on the back. The two men quickened their steps toward the hangar and Nelly.

"Morning, Ned," everyone chorused.

"Morning, Mr. Whitecliff, Mr. Buzz, Bob, Boris. Where's Akbar?"

"He's checking on the horses. He should be here soon," Buzz answered.

"Yeah! Those horses kind of took a beatin' yesterday afternoon when you flew low over them with flames coming from your wings— spooked the hell out of 'em, it did. Blimey!"

"I know, Ned, but we have to get them accustomed to the plane and the flames, so they won't spook during the attack," Buzz explained.

"It wasn't too bad, though," Boris interposed. "Only four girls out of nine were thrown, and they remounted by the time Buzz made the second flyover."

"It looked as though the girls had established good control over their steeds by the third time. In fact, the horses seemed remarkably calm," Harry stated. "Oh, here comes Akbar now."

Akbar entered the mess hall, nodded a greeting to everyone, and sat. "Mmm, whatever they're preparing for breakfast smells good.— Huh? Oh! Thank you, Basima." Akbar sipped his freshly poured coffee and said, "It seems uncanny. How does that girl know when you want coffee?—sometimes, seemingly, before you know yourself."

The men all smiled in agreement as they watched Basima skip back to the kitchen. They felt as though they had become uncles to all of the girls, but there was something truly special about Little Miss Coffee Pot.

"Akbar, how are the girls coming with firing the shotguns from horseback?" Harry asked.

"Quite well, actually, Harry. I think they'll be ready with two or three hours more of intense training," Akbar replied proudly.

Boris chimed in. "After breakfast, I'm going to begin their saber training. In the short time we have available, I'm hoping I can teach them how to swing a blade without cutting off their horses' ears."

"Ned," Buzz said, "how's the war wagon progressing?"

"Well, sir—Mr. Buzz—I finished the welding late last night, and it's ready for inspection. If I may make a suggestion, sir—I think we should pad the insides some, and maybe make some leather straps to hold on to. It'll probably be a bumpy ride down that hill and crashing into the gate."

"That's a really good suggestion, Ned; see to it as soon as you can. I'll have the guns ready to install this afternoon," Buzz declared.

"Damn! I was really hoping we could have some sort of uniforms for the girls, but it looks as though there won't be enough time," Boris said, disappointed.

"Oh, I think they'll have uniforms, sir," Ned contradicted, grinning delightedly. He was obviously very pleased with himself.

"How? The girls have been busy every day. They've been training or working from daybreak until dark." Harry was as puzzled as Ned was tickled.

"Well, when I gave them that sewin' machine and those 'chutes, you'd a thought I was givin' them a pile of gold. Well, sir, they asked if I would run the generator through the night so as they could sew after dark. Well, I didn't say anything about it 'cause they wanted it to be a surprise," Ned divulged, a broad smile creasing his pale face from ear to ear.

"Damn, Ned! I hope you didn't use a lot of gasoline. That's only a five-hundred gallon tank, and we're going to need every bit of it for the Bee," Harry angrily exclaimed.

"No, sir! It's twenty-five-hundred!" Ned shot back, abashed.

"The report I have is five-hundred," Harry insisted.

"Yes, sir. If you say so, sir. Sorry, sir!"

"What's done is done, and there's nothing we can do about it now," Harry said sharply.

"Excuse me, gentlemen, but I'm going to gather up our riders and give them a crash course in becoming expert swordsmen on horseback." Boris interposed as he rose from his chair and hurriedly gulped the last of his coffee.

"Here comes breakfast, Boris. Won't you stay and eat?" Buzz invited.

"No, I don't think so. I want to get an early start so I can—damn, that looks good. Well, I don't want to hurt the girls' feelings," Boris remonstrated. He resumed his chair quickly and watched eagerly as a platter loaded with an extremely large omelet, graced with a strip of fried gazelle and liberally garnished with wild green onions was placed on the table.

"That is the biggest bloomin' omelet I ever seen," Ned enthused as he speedily tucked his napkin into the top of his shirt.

"What's the occasion, Israt?" asked Harry.

"Well, sir, Kebira has been taking such good care of the chickens—they have been laying their little hearts out for her—and the goats' bags are about to burst every morning. So we had to do something with the eggs and cream."

"Cream?"

"Yes, sir. We made a hot cream sauce to pour over your biscuits, if you wish it," Israt replied. She proudly stood aside to allow Sara to place a large bowl of steaming spiced cream beside the omelet. On top of the cream was a ladle, which slowly, very slowly, sank to the bottom of the bowl. Sagirah approached from the other side and put a large platter of hot biscuits on the already well-stocked table. All their coffee cups were rapidly and efficiently refilled by Little Miss Coffee Pot.

The mess hall became uncommonly quiet for some time—the only sound was the tapping of utensils against plates, cups being returned to their saucers, and eventually, sighs of satisfaction.

———— ————

"Buzz, over here," Bob cried, patting the space next to him on the step where he was seated. "Where have you been? Boris is about to start school."

Buzz sat down next to Bob. "I was checking the gas tank."

"And?"

"Well, the measuring stick shows just a hair above half—which by Harry's report is only two-hundred and fifty gallons or so. It's going to be damn close," Buzz said grimly.

Bob spoke quietly. "Maybe Ned's right! I sure hope so, anyway."

"We'll know for sure when we begin filling the Bee," Buzz replied, leaning back comfortably to watch Boris.

"All right," Boris boomed. "You've been divided into two groups by the color of your arm bands. There is a White team and a Black team. The wooden swords I have just given you have blunt edges and rounded points; the steel sabers you will be given later today will have very sharp points and edges. I will show you how to sharpen them so you can shave with them!"

"Sir?" A tiny voice was heard.

"Yes, Jehan?"

"Sir, we don't shave, sir!"

"Well, slice bread, then, dammit!"

A nervous titter was heard, and quickly extinguished.

Boris barely paused. "Hasna," he barked, "I want you to charge me with your sword as if I were one of the bad guys."

"Now, sir?"

"Yes, now. But do it slowly."

Hasna charged at a trot and met Boris with an overhead swing. He blocked it. She raised her arm across her chest and swung at him; again and again he blocked her blows. Then, when she brought her arm back to prepare for another blow, Boris moved his blade into her body from the blocking position, slashed across her midsection, and then thrust forward into her ribs. Hasna winced in pain, and dropped her sword to clutch her side.

Boris threw his sword aside and quickly held the girl to steady her, keeping her from falling out of the saddle. "Are you all right? I didn't mean to thrust so hard!"

"I'm all right—just a little sore. After all, I'm a warrior, not a china doll—sir."

Boris gave the young girl a quick hug and turned to the other warriors as he surreptitiously wiped moisture from his eyes, pretending it was beads of sweat from his brow. "Did you notice how my horse, Tasha, continually crowded Hasna's mount? I was guiding her with my knees as I taught you yesterday. That keeps your opponent off balance. Let's take a break. I want you all to find some cloth—towels, rags, or even some of those black robes we have—anything to wrap around yourself to soften the force of the blows. Dismissed!"

"You know, Bob, I think we're becoming a bunch of old fathers," Buzz remarked.

"Yeah, Buzz! A bunch of proud old fathers."

"Do you think we'll be ready in time?"

"Everything looks good to me, except for that second strafing of the tent men—we still don't have that problem figured out."

"I might have that solved," Buzz said excitedly. "I found ten or twelve inner tubes in the hangar, and I filled one with acetylene and oxygen. Then I wrapped some cloth around it to hold rocks and scrap iron for shrapnel. What do you think?"

"I remember when we filled balloons with that stuff and shot them with tracers. They made one hell of a bang," Bob recollected, chuckling.

"Jack wouldn't let us use it in the act, remember? He said it was too volatile—too dangerous! I have one filled and ready to try, but I need a way to detonate it," Buzz explained, his voice revealing hope and frustration.

Bob spoke with both exuberance and caution. "I have something in the stuff we got from Jack that should work. I'll get it, and we can try it on the other side of the airfield at lunchtime, when everyone's inside."

———

"Akbar, Boris—come on, sit down. We've been waiting for you," Harry called.

"It's good to sit at a table and have a hot lunch again. Oh, thank you, Basima," Boris said wearily.

"Thank you, Basima! What are we having? Does anyone know?" asked Akbar.

"All I know is it sure smells good, and it's hot! Those sandwiches served to us where we worked saved time, and it was a good idea, but that wind yesterday made them more 'sand' than 'wich,'" Ned replied, laughing, and holding his cup to be refilled.

"Where are the girls?" Harry inquired.

"They'll be here soon—they took the horses back to the stables," Akbar answered.

"Has anyone seen Bob or Buzz lately?" Boris asked.

"I saw them going into the hangar a short while ago, sir," Kashar responded.

"Speak of the devil—there they go across the airfield now," Harry reported, pointing out the window with his cup.

"What in the world are they carrying?" Boris asked.

"It looks kind of like a big, black doughnut," Ned stated wonderingly.

The occupants of the mess hall watched curiously as Buzz and Bob carried their mysterious burden to the opposite side of the airfield and disappeared into a ravine. A few minutes passed, and the two men resurfaced, racing out of the ravine as though the hounds of hell were at their heels. They leaped behind the rifle targets and stuck their fingers firmly in their ears.

"Gentlemen, I think we had better duck for cover," Harry suggested forcefully as he dove to the floor. His example was expeditiously followed by the others.

KA-BOOOM!!

Tink!—Crak!—Tink!—Crunch!—Tink! Various small, inanimate (hopefully) objects rained across the air field, and liberally peppered the windowpanes.

Heads slowly and cautiously rose above the level of the window sills, peering through the now spider-webbed panes. They observed, with great and awesome surprise, a large black cloud rolling skyward and two seemingly demented figures holding hands and dancing in a circle. They resembled two youngsters from the underdog squad who had, at just that very moment, succeeded .in kicking the winning goal of the soccer championship.

"What the hell was that?" someone asked softly, wonderingly.

"I do believe the royal artillery has arrived, gentlemen!" replied Harry gleefully.

— Chapter Nineteen —

THE SECRETS OF THE TUNNEL

"Looks like a storm coming in from the north," Bob remarked. "There. Did you see that glimmer of lightning?"

"Yes. Let's pray that it holds off until after the fight! Well, on the other hand, it might give us more cover," Harry replied.

The men sat quietly, being jostled about in the first vehicle of the two-truck caravan, watching the occasional flash in the distant clouds.

"Bob, do you think the ghost riders will be all right if it rains?" asked Father Sebastian.

"Father, the bodies are made of chicken wire and the heads are large, empty cans, so they should be okay," Bob assured him.

"The one you led across the field at full gallop last night was sure an eye-opener," Harry commented, grinning.

"Yes. I thought that cutting holes in the cans for eyes and a mouth was a nice effect, but lighting a red flare inside was the kicker." Bob was obviously proud of his inventions.

"Those riders gave me quite a start when I rode in from the mission last night," Father Sebastian said, smiling ruefully in remembrance.

"The girls sure looked smart in their uniforms when they paraded by us in formation, too. I don't think Boris and Akbar could have been prouder if they had been leading the Palace Guard," Harry said. "And those uniforms—the white turbans with black streamers, the white high-collar jackets, black sashes, and their white pantaloons tucked in their black leather boots! The girls outdid themselves. By the way, where did they get those boots?"

"Akbar said he and his family used to work in leather, so they worked after hours too, and cut down the captured Shadow Mens' boots. He also told me he found German stampings inside them," Bob recounted.

"I thought as much—where the boots came from, I mean. I suppose I shouldn't have jumped Ned about using the generator at night, but I'm not certain which is correct—Ned's twenty-five-hundred gallons or the report's five-hundred," Harry added as an afterthought.

"Oh, Harry, don't worry about it. We all know you're just an old crab," Bob remonstrated with a smirk.

"I don't think Harry is so old," said Father Sebastian, laughingly coming to Harry's defense.

"Thanks, Father! That makes me just a crab, right?"

Father Sebastian grinned wickedly in reply.

For some time, all that could be heard was the rumbling of the truck.

"Back off the trailer a bit more, Ned. Every time Kashar stokes the boiler fire, it belches out a mess of sparks," Boris ordered.

"He has to keep the steam pressure up so's she'll be ready to go when the time comes," explained Ned.

"I know, but we don't want any sparks to land on us—especially with all those inner tubes filled with acetylene, oxygen and gasoline in the back, just ready to ignite," Boris replied.

"That's right. I almost forgot about them," Ned said, easing the truck another fifty feet farther behind the trailer carrying the steam roller.

"How are Hasna and Yasmin doing with the horses?" Boris asked.

"I can just make out Yasmin in the dark; she seems to be doing fine. Her string of horses seems to be trailing well," Akbar replied, glancing out his side window.

"The same with Hasna, over here," Ned reported, checking his side mirror.

"These are the quietest trucks I have ever ridden in," Boris noted.

"Mr. Whitecliff had them rigged for jobs like this one. The truck ahead even has bulletproof plates that pop up when he needs them," Ned explained.

"Hmmpff! I didn't know the import and export business was so dangerous," Boris commented.

"I think he has a few side jobs once in a while," Ned replied with a devilish smile.

"Do you think the girls will be able to handle those guns in that little trailer all right?" Akbar fretted.

"Well, Buzz drilled them on loading and dry-firing for two days. When they did the live-fire exercises yesterday, Harry timed them and said they were loading and firing a volley every three seconds," Boris replied. "I think that was damned good!"

"They sure tore the targets to smithereens, too," Ned added.

"Did either of you see the double-barrel Buzz made by putting two of the Greeners together?" asked Boris.

"He showed it to me just before he put it in the plane; it's a nice piece of workmanship. I like the way he fitted the stock and forearm to the two guns, and one lever to operate both guns as if they were one," Akbar said.

———

"Ara?"

"Yes, Amber?"

"Are you afraid?"

"Yes, Amber, I am."

"Does that mean you're a coward if you're afraid?"

"I talked with Mr. Whitecliff about being afraid. He says that it's the brave soldier who goes to battle and does his duty even though he's afraid."

"Mr. Whitecliff said that?" Sara asked.

"Yes, he did."

210

"I bet he's afraid too, then, because I know he's brave," Basima chimed in.

"I must be really brave, because I'm very afraid," Sagirah said with the tiniest of smiles.

"Then Mr. Buzz must be scared to death, because I think he's the bravest of them all," Basima stated. They all giggled nervously.

"Father Sebastian said he would pray for us," Israt reported.

"But he's Christian and we're Muslim," Zohra noted.

"That's what I said; he said that didn't matter. He said that there are many roads with different names, but they all lead to the same God, and He hears us no matter what we call Him."

"I like Father Sebastian. He's a good man," someone said quietly.

"Ara?"

"Yes, Amber?"

"May I hold your hand?"

"Yes, Amber."

Amber gently slid her hand inside Ara's, and clutched it tightly.

"Let's all hold hands and pray," Ara suggested.

"Is everything all right back there?" Father Sebastian asked, pulling aside the curtain separating the cab and the rear of the truck.

"Yes, Father," several voices murmured.

"Yes. We're all right now," Ara said strongly.

"How are the girls, Father?" Harry asked, as he swerved deftly to miss a pothole in the road.

"About as well as can be expected, under the circumstances," he replied.

"Father, do you think there could have been changes made since you left there two days ago? Like how many guards, and where they're posted?" Bob asked thoughtfully.

Father Sebastian paused for a moment, and then replied confidently, "Nothing had changed in all the time I had been away; I don't think anything will have changed in the last few hours. But I noticed that von Schroeden seems to have become involved in something that seemed to be more important to him than the hostages. I overheard the word 'treasure' mentioned once, and when I put on a display of anxiety about the ransom being delayed, he just nonchalantly said to take another twenty-four hours if needed. It seemed strangely out of character, I thought."

"He might've heard some rumor about the Afghanistan treasure, possibly from the time of Alexander in these mountains. There are plenty of those stories batting about," Harry surmised.

"That could well be," agreed the monk.

"How are the hostages holding up?" Bob asked.

"Quite well. I didn't tell them about our plans for fear of a slip of the tongue, but I did alert the monks."

"Father," Harry asked, "where is the entrance to the tunnel?"

"In the cemetery."

"The one west of the mission?"

"No, in the small one for the clergy to the east."

"If I remember correctly, that's in the middle of a large, open field," Harry stated with dismay.

Father Sebastian replied ruefully, "Four-hundred years ago it was in the middle of a forest. Since then, the trees have been downed for construction or firewood. We'll have the cover of darkness and, from the looks of it, possibly a storm."

"How would I find the entrance, in case something—well, in case?" Harry groped for the right words.

"In case something happens to me? Is that what you're trying to say?"

"Yes, Father. Not that anything will, but—"

"On the northwestern corner is a large marble cross, overlooking a three-by-six marble slab. On it are inscribed the words 'Father Sanchez, 1613–1653.' Grasp the horizontal bar of the cross—one hand on each edge—and twist counter-clockwise until you hear a loud click; that indicates the lock has been released. On one of the corners of the marble slab is a carving depicting a pair of praying hands. Push on that corner. The slab will slide to the side, revealing steps that descend into the tunnel."

"So, you—" Bob began, but was quickly hushed by the priest.

"Let me finish."

"Sorry, Father."

"When you reach the bottom of the steps, you will find a long lever on your right. Pull down on it and swing it to the other side until you hear another click. You'll see the slab slide back into place when you do that. To open it from the inside, there's a large ring overhead. Pull down—again, until you hear a click—then move the lever back the other way. When you're outside, just push the slab back, and click. It's all done with balances and counter-balances; it's very ingenious. Any questions?"

"Was there a real Father Sanchez?" Bob asked.

"Oh, Father Sanchez was very real! According to church logs, he had a very interesting life. He spent twenty years in the New World, as it was known then, until the church transferred him here."

"So is he really buried there?" Bob queried.

"No. That's one of the many mysteries of the mission. The logs indicated that there was an attack by raiders from the north on June 14, 1653. It was the duty of certain monks to hide the sacred gold and silver objects while the others warded off the intruders. Father Sanchez was to care for the gold crucifix on the altar. During the attack, he was seen to take an arrow in the back while running, carrying the crucifix. He rose and continued on, but that was the last time he or the crucifix was ever seen—until a few months ago, anyway."

"What? His ghost?" Bob asked, wide-eyed.

"No," chuckled Father Sebastian. "I was exploring the tunnel one day when I came upon some loose stones in the wall. It looked as though there was an opening behind them. When I removed a number of them, enlarging the opening, I found a tiny little room. On the floor were the remains of an ancient mummified body with an arrow embedded in his back. Next to him were a gold crucifix and a few other items."

213

"The missing Father!"

"Yes, Harry. The missing Father Sanchez. Apparently he fled to the tunnel but, once inside, realized he might not be able to operate the heavy lever in his weakened state. So he painfully walled himself up in that small room. He has now finally been given a proper church burial."

"Wow, what a story," Bob remarked.

"You had better douse your lights, Harry. We're nearly there," warned Father Sebastian.

Harry slowly brought the vehicle to a halt and shut the engine off. The men sat in silence for a time, watching the flickering lightning in the distant northern sky and listening to the low rumbling of approaching thunder. The truck rocked sporadically with each increasingly powerful gust of wind.

"I wonder how long it will be before the storm reaches us?" Bob mused.

"An hour, perhaps an hour-and-a-half," returned Father Sebastian.

"Let's get those people out before it hits," Harry said anxiously as he opened his door and stepped out onto the rocky ground. Bob and the priest exited the truck from the passenger side and came around to stand beside Harry.

Phfft, phoo, phfft, phoo. The sound of Nellie's pulsating steam and the occasional reverberation of a mournful howl when the freshening wind blew through her pipes was now all that broke the silence.

"I'll get Boris and the others," Bob whispered, hurrying past his companions.

"The storm is approaching faster than I thought it would," said the priest with concern.

Bob returned, quickly and quietly. "We're ready. How's the time?"

"We're good. In fact, we're a bit early," Harry replied, peering at his watch while Bob held a match nearby, shielding the flame with his other hand.

214

Boris approached and spoke to Bob and Akbar. "We'd better be going. It's going to be hellish enough to shoot our targets in the dark, much less having to fight the storm, too." The three men shouldered their rifles, pulled the hoods of their black robes over their heads, and started off.

"Pardon me, sir," Kashar said as he rushed past Harry, trying to sling his rifle and don his robe while hurrying to catch up with the others.

"Do you chaps mind if I join you? It's a bit lonely back there," Ned asked.

"Sure, Ned. Let's all wait in the truck. The wind is a bit chilly," Harry suggested.

Inside the truck, the three watched the four black-robed figures fade into the cover of darkness, reappearing only in the blue flash of the lightning.

"I know a doctor in Paris who could correct Kashar's foot," Harry mused as he peered through the rain-speckled windshield.

"Wind's picking up," someone said as the truck rocked more violently. The men sat quietly, watching the incoming storm.

"It's kinda like being in the trenches, waiting for the whistle to blow, signaling for us to go over the top," Ned remarked, breaking the silence.

"Blowing that whistle was like ringing the death knell for so many of those boys," Harry observed sadly.

"Now, don't you go and load a bunch of grief on your shoulders, Mr. Whitecliff. We were in those trenches 'cause we was ordered there. We're here 'cause we want to be, not 'cause we were ordered, sir," Ned replied, punctuating his statement with a decisive nod.

"He's right, Harry," Father Sebastian attested solemnly.

"Thank you. Thank you both. I—"

Tap...tap...tap!

Startled, the men in the truck straightened, quickly alert.

Tap...tap...tap!

Harry lowered the window and glanced down.

"Basima? What are you doing out there?"

"I thought you gentlemen might like some hot coffee, sir."

"Hot coffee? Here? How?"

"Well, sir, I saw Mr. Bob and Mr. Ned use a little spigot on the steamroller to get hot water for making tea. Well, sir, I thought I could do the same for coffee. So I brought some coffee and my pot. Do you want some, sir?"

"Yes, Basima, and I think I speak for all of us," Harry said, leaning farther out the window. "Thank you!"

"It might have just a bit of the taste of rust, sir."

"That's all right, Basima. A little rust just gives it character. Thank you. Here—Ned, Father," Harry replied, passing the steaming cups to the others.

"Blimey! If this coffee had any more character, it would have a leading part in a Shakespearian play," Ned declared, gulping and attempting to clear his throat at the same time.

"It does have a rather—quaint taste," added Father Sebastian.

Harry took a sip, squinted, and pursed his lips. "Ahh! It's like the first taste of Scotch; after that, you acquire a taste for it. With that thought in mind, it's…" Harry took another sip, "really quite good."

"Basima, before you leave, give me another cup of that Shakespearian coffee," Ned requested, passing his cup to Harry.

"Now, get back in the truck, Basima. We don't want you catching a chill in this cold drizzle," Harry remonstrated as he passed the refilled cup back to Ned.

How ironic, Harry thought. *I'm worried about that little girl catching a chill; in a short time, I'll be worrying about her catching a bullet.*

"Look! There's a light."

"Where?"

"To the left."

"There it is again. That's two flashes."

Immediately, the three men were talking excitedly.

"There's one...two...three! That's the okay to move up," Harry noted as he started the truck's engine.

"I'll be getting back to my truck," Ned said, jumping out of the cab.

"Everyone hold on back there! We're moving out," Father Sebastian called to the girls.

Harry eased out the clutch, and the truck moved slowly and smoothly up the hill. The headlights weren't necessary; the flickering glow of the bonfire at the guards' camp was sufficient.

As the truck crested the hill, the view before them was exactly as the maps and photos had portrayed it—a large field, four to five acres in size, sloping gently up to the ridge. The guards' tent was silhouetted by the fire, and the entire area was well lit.

Harry made a large circle and parked the truck facing the way they had come; Ned followed his example and positioned his vehicle alongside Harry's.

Boris, Bob, and Akbar met Harry as he exited his truck. "You men know what to do," Harry stated as he fought the increasing winds while attempting to don his black robe. "The only suggestion I can make is to keep an eye on the fire." He indicated the blazing bonfire that was spewing showers of sparks and flames with each gust. "We don't want it to reach the inner tubes." He paused for a moment. "And have someone stay with the horses. We don't want them to panic in this storm."

"We already took care of that, Harry," Boris reassured him. "We'll take care of things here; you and Father Sebastian go bring those people out!"

"We're still a bit ahead of schedule," Harry noted, returning his watch to his pocket. He took a deep breath, straightened his shoulders, marched to the other side of the truck, and joined the waiting priest. Without a word, Father Sebastian took the lead, and the two men were quickly swallowed by the thick brush along the ridge.

As they shouldered their way through the brambles, there was a blinding flash, quickly followed by an earsplitting blast from above. The men instinctively shielded their eyes. Another streak of lightning was followed almost immediately by a clap of thunder nearly as great as the first. Then, the wind slammed into them in rapid, powerful gusts. The twisted bushes whipped back and forth madly, grabbing their clothing and slapping their faces.

Finally, they broke through the brush and were standing at the edge of the field. By now, the lightning flashes were coming fifteen to twenty seconds apart.

"Blast! It'll be nearly like walking across that field under a noonday sun," Harry yelled, leaning his head close to Father Sebastian's to be heard over the howls of the wind.

In response to Harry's comment, the priest looked across the field and toward the cliffs. To his dismay, it seemed Harry was right; the lightning was bright as day with an eerie blue cast. He could see the cliffs with their mysterious shadows, the tent of the guards' camp, the bonfire spraying flame and sparks. The mission itself seemed bathed in blue except for yellowish lamplight in two of the windows.

Suddenly, a gentle, satisfied smile played across his face. "Look!" he yelled, pointing to the cliffs.

Harry's vision followed the gesture of the cleric's outstretched arm since he was unable to hear his shout. Another flash of lightning showed, instead of craggy cliffs, a blue-gray shroud moving rapidly toward them. With the next flash, the camp had disappeared; even the glow of the bonfire had faded away. Yet another flash revealed the mission being engulfed by the encroaching cloud.

Then pouring rain roared down. It was as if they were in a monsoon. It was the kind of rain that washes out roads and turns gentle streams into raging torrents—the kind of rain that keeps planes from flying.

As soon as the wall of water reached them, they started down the hill at a rapid clip, fighting the weight of their rain-soaked garments. It seemed that every breath they took was more water than air. The fact that visibility was only a few yards was worrisome to Harry. He was concerned that they would miss the cemetery and end up at the mission walls. When he glimpsed the headstones at last, he breathed a mental sigh of relief.

The men made their way through the maze of stones, dodging the lashing limbs of the few trees in the small consecrated plot. The tortured trunks were bent nearly to the breaking point. At last, they came to the grave of Father Sanchez. "I'll turn the cross. As soon as you feel the lock release, push the slab aside," yelled Father Sebastian into Harry's ear.

Harry nodded and placed his hands next to the stone praying hands. He felt a thump, as though the stone had been hit by a mallet, and pushed. The slab moved with very little effort. When Harry stood up and peered into the gaping black hole, a stab of lightning dramatically exposed narrow stone steps descending to a small chamber. Then it was dark again.

The priest turned the cross to its original position, hurried past Harry, and scurried down the steps. Harry followed quickly and, as soon as he reached the bottom step, Father Sebastian immediately grasped a long iron bar with both hands and swung it upward. The slab rotated back into place with a grating thud and a sharp click.

The constant thundering outside the tunnel was now felt more than heard, and the ensuing darkness somehow seemed to have a calming effect after the nerve-wracking lightshow they'd just endured. The room smelled, not of mildew, as Harry had expected, but of stale, dry air.

Father Sebastian quickly illuminated his torch and proceeded down the tunnel. He ducked his head as he went, since the tunnel was only about three feet wide and not quite six feet high. Harry followed close behind, shining his light on the walls and ceiling. Even now, he was impressed by the meticulous craftsmanship used when laying the stone blocks. They seemed to equal the precision of the Notre Dame de Paris.

Father Sebastian paused at the opening to a very small room and bowed his head in a short prayer.

"Is this where you found Father Sanchez?"

"Yes."

"Father, you said you found other things with him besides the crucifix. What other things?"

The priest merely made the sign of the cross, and urged, "Come. We must hurry so you can get the hostages out under the cover of the storm." He turned and continued rapidly down the tunnel. They soon reached the end and faced a large, oval door of old, dark wood. After deftly removing a small round plug from its face, Father Sebastian peered through the opening.

He sighed in relief. "Good. They're asleep," he whispered. He replaced the plug, lifted a bar, and gave the door a sharp push with his shoulder. The barrier held its ground for a moment, and then opened with a sudden jolt and a subdued rasping. When it came to an abrupt halt, the sound of sloshing liquid could be heard.

The two men entered a large room lined with racks of wine bottles and stacks of kegs. The wall through which they had entered had eight large, oval wine kegs set into it. One of these, even when half-filled, was constructed to swing out on large iron hangers, thus exposing the tunnel from which they'd entered.

There was a large, heavy, square table in the center of the room which was at the moment arrayed with scattered cups, plates, and half a loaf of bread on a large platter. An oil lamp with its wick damped down, giving the faintest glow of light, dominated the table. Four chairs were positioned around it; and, in a fifth, slumped a man, his folded arms serving as a resting place for his head. He was snoring sonorously. In makeshift bedding on the floor were two more men and a woman.

"There are only four! There should be five!" Harry whispered urgently. The two men quickly flashed their lights in every nook and cranny. Only four.

"The girl, Kimberly. She's not here!" Father Sebastian rudely shook the man at the table. "George, George! Come on, man, wake up!"

"I'll wake the others," Harry said. As he crossed the room, his foot kicked an empty wine bottle, sending it spinning across the floor to crash into three other empties.

"Drunk! They're bloomin' drunk," Harry exclaimed in a loud, frustrated whisper as he picked up an empty bottle. "Looks like they each finished off a bottle—maybe two or three. Hell, who knows how many!"

"Father Sebastian, Mr. Whitecliff. What...who?"

"Shhh!" the men hissed.

"Quiet, Jane," Father Sebastian whispered. "We're here to get you out!"

"I'm sorry," was the whispered reply.

"Where's the girl? Where's Kimberly?" Harry demanded.

"Oh, God help us!" she cried, bursting into tears. "He took her away! He took my little girl away!"

"Who took her? Jane! Look at me! Who took her, and where?" demanded Father Sebastian.

Jane and the other hostages had been kept prisoners for nearly two weeks, not knowing whether the next day—or the next hour—would be their last. Then her beloved niece was taken away. She had been pushed to the breaking point but, a strong woman; she understood the need to regain control. Wrapping her arms across her chest, she drew her shoulders inward, took a deep breath, held it, and then let it out slowly. Gradually, she stopped shaking and her sobs subsided. Then she raised her head and opened her eyes. Her look of despair had changed to one of determination.

"I'm all right now. It was the colonel—Colonel von Schroeden. He and two of his men came in last night after dinner, and the two men grabbed Kim by her arms. Von Schroeden pointed at a cross she had hanging from a chain around her neck—the one a young man had given to her on the train. The colonel said, 'Someone wants to see you about that,' and they left, taking her with them. Oh, Father, you will save Kim, won't you? Please. Please!"

"We'll get Kim back," Father Sebastian promised, gently placing his hand softly on Jane's head.

"Jane, do you know where they've taken her?" Harry asked.

"No, no! I don't have any idea!" Despair was threatening again.

"It's all right. My brothers may say little, but they hear much. I'm sure I can find where they took her," the priest said soothingly.

Harry spoke urgently. "Father, we don't have much time! There are just forty-eight minutes left until the attack is to start. Do you have the dust bomb Bob made?"

"Yes, Harry, I have it," was the calm reply.

"Father! You're not going to blow up your mission, are you?" Jane asked, alarmed.

"No, Jane, of course not. It's just a small charge that will fill the room with a cloud of dust. When it settles, the room will look as though no one has set foot in here for months. It's just a little something to rattle the Shadow Men's nerves when they come to get you." The priest's eyes were twinkling with genuine amusement.

"Good!" Jane blurted with a satisfied smirk.

"Take everything that doesn't belong here—plates, cups, food, anything you brought in—and put it in the tunnel. Leave some rags or something to wipe up the water Harry and I dripped when we came in," instructed Father Sebastian.

"I got the other two men up. They're a bit wobbly, but I think they can make the trip," Harry reported softly, urgently.

"That would be Mr. Blomside and Mr. Brown. Do they know what we propose to do?" the abbot asked anxiously.

"Yes. I explained about the trip back, and told them to gather up the bedding and put it in the tunnel," Harry replied.

"Good. Here, take my torch. I won't be needing it," said Father Sebastian, handing his light to Harry.

"Jane, are you feeling well?" Harry inquired gently.

"You mean, am I sober? Yes, Mr. Whitecliff, I am. But you might have trouble with George; he's short on getting drunk but long on getting sober. You'll probably have to carry him out of here."

"Mr. Ahhh…"

"Brown, sir."

"And I'm Blomside, sir."

"Yes. Could the two of you carry Mr. Smith?"

"Oh, of course!"

"Yes, indeed! Happy to be of service."

"Look, Mr. Smith is coming around," Mr. Brown said.

"Hey! Look at all the theeshe people! Now we can sing!" boomed George, wavering between Mr. Brown and Mr. Blomside, who were trying valiantly to steady him. "All right, now, ever'body folla me!"

Harry looked questioningly at Jane; she hesitated for a moment, nonplussed. She drew a deep breath and resignedly ordered, "Sock him!"

Harry ruefully shrugged his shoulders, and 'Whap!!'

George's bearers caught him as he fell back and carried him into the tunnel with Jane on their heels. As she passed Harry, he handed her the extra torch and instructed, "Here, Jane. Take this and bring up the rear."

Father Sebastian, who was preparing to close the opening to the tunnel, made the sign of the cross and said, "God bless you all." He then gave a thumbs-up and added, "Good luck."

Harry executed a military salute and whispered, "See you in a few hours."

The keg swung into place and latched.

"Quickly, follow me," Harry urged, leading the procession at a fast pace until they reached the steps. "Lights out," he whispered. He pulled the ring until he heard the click and then pulled down on the bar. The stone moved about two inches, then stopped. He pulled harder. Nothing! "Give me a hand! Something's blocking it."

Brown and Blomside propped George against the wall and the three men pulled with all their might. Again, nothing. Then Jane joined them, and all four pulled desperately.

"It's moving," someone exclaimed. "It's moving, thank God!" The slab slid back, albeit reluctantly and the party hastily half-dragged, half-carried George out into the night air. Harry slid the slab into place and locked it.

To his dismay, the storm had subsided somewhat and the mission was visible, though just barely. They still had a chance to make their way to the brushy perimeter without being seen if the storm continued for perhaps another five minutes.

Without a word, Harry led the little group up the hill as quickly as he could, swiveling his head to be sure they kept up with him. They did; the two men carried George with uncommon ease. Soon they were at the top, then in the brush and, at last, in sight of the bonfire. The first phase of their mission had been completed.

~ Chapter Twenty ~

THE THREE-RING CIRCUS

"**K**ebira! Hana! Remember what I told you," Buzz admonished the two drenched girls. "When I give the signal, pull the wheel chocks free and get out of the way fast."

"But sir, you won't be able to take off in this storm. You'll get killed," Hana pleaded.

"She's right, Mr. Buzz. This storm is too bad! Please don't do it," Kebira sobbed. She tried desperately to stop Buzz from climbing into the cockpit of the Bee.

"I'm going to need more power to take off because of the extra weight and drag the rain is creating on the plane and the airfield. That's why I need to hold the Bee here with the brakes and wheel chocks—so I can build up the rpms to have enough speed for takeoff," Buzz explained, trying to reassure the frightened girls.

"I don't care about all of that! It's still too dangerous." Hana's words were muffled by the pounding rain and wind as the girls grasped the ropes to their prospective chocks.

Buzz adjusted his safety harness, set the throttle and choke, flipped the ignition switch on, and pushed the starter button. The 400 horsepower engine turned with a slow whine; then, with a cough, it sputtered and stopped. Buzz adjusted the choke and pushed the starter again. This time, five or six cylinders fired, and it loped for a few seconds. Suddenly, all nine cylinders fired and, with a cloud of smoke, the engine roared evenly. As Buzz made a last adjustment on the choke and slowly eased out the throttle, the sound of the engine increased from a low roar to a higher pitch. He watched the gauges attentively to be sure the engine was running properly, and then extended the throttle until the rpms reached the acceleration point he wanted. He raised his arm slowly, his eyes still glued to the instrument panel. The little plane began to bounce and shake, its tail lifting off the ground. Buzz quickly dropped his arm; the two girls jerked the chocks away. He released the brakes with a snap. The Flycatcher sprang forward like a racehorse from the gate.

The two girls watched fearfully as the plane splashed its way down the water-soaked field, the spray glistening as it passed an oil-burning runway light. The pitch of the engine was still rising as the plane fought for airspeed. The girls held each other's hands, watching the blue flames from the exhaust recede as the plane neared the end of the runway. It began to rise, and then returned to the runway with a splash. It tried again, flew a bit longer and higher, and then bounced down again.

The extra weight of the pipes and gas bottles for the flaming wing effect combined with the gallons of water covering the plane's skin was apparently just too much for the Flycatcher. But a sudden gust of wind finally gave the Bee the lift she needed, and the plane rose slowly off the ground, gaining just barely enough altitude to clear the bushes at the end of the runway.

The girls watched as the plane climbed steadily until it faded into the low overhanging clouds, continuing to listen to the drone of the engine. Their warm tears were soon diluted by the cold pellets of the rain drops. A blinding flash, then another, came from where the little plane had vanished into the clouds, followed by a clap and rumble of thunder. They could no longer hear the plane, no matter how desperately they tried. They looked at each other, unspeaking. Still holding hands, they ran for the mess hall. Once inside, they slammed the door and quickly sat at the nearest table.

Trembling, Hana asked, "Do you think the lightning hit the plane?"

"It wouldn't dare! Not with Mr. Buzz flying it!" Kebira replied.

"You're right! It wouldn't dare," Hana said with bravado. She wasn't sure if she was agreeing with Kebira, or merely attempting to reassure herself.

"What do we do now?"

"We wait."

"And pray?"

"Yes. And pray!"

"Do you know where Boris and Akbar are?" Harry asked Bob and Ned as they hooked the battle wagon to the steam roller.

"They just left with their troops to get in position for the attack," Bob answered.

"Basima and Israt should be in position to fire the gas canisters about now," Ned chimed in.

"I'm ready, too, sir."

Harry looked over at little Sagirah, standing at attention next to the gas-filled inner tubes, some as tall as she. The rockets were all placed neatly in their stands.

"We're ready, Mr. Whitecliff, sir."

Harry turned. Standing at attention by the open door to the wagon were Rima, Amber, Zayna, and Sara, all in their white uniforms, with gas-mask packs over their shoulders. They were smiling. Harry saluted them and nodded; the girls climbed into the wagon and closed the door.

Harry had a lump in his throat. He was extremely proud of his little army. They were more than just soldiers; they had become family to him. Now they were waiting patiently for him to send them to what could be their deaths.

"Harry, Ned and I are going to move the steam roller into position for attack."

"Wait, Bob!" Harry waved Bob back. "I think we should load everyone into the trucks and leave before they're onto us and give chase."

"Call off the attack? Why?"

"I've been thinking. The direction and force of the storm would place it at the airfield in full force about the time Buzz should be taking off. There's no way that little plane could fly through such a gale. Remember, Buzz said that timing is the key for the whole plan to work."

"Mr. Whitecliff, sir," Bob said calmly, coolly, looking Harry squarely in the eyes—"I have never known Buzz to be late for a curtain call. This will not be an exception. Now I'm going to help Ned bypass the governor and tie off the safety valve on the steam engine. That should give us the speed and momentum we'll need to ram through the gates."

Bob turned, and began to walk away, but stopped, turned halfway back, and said, "Buzz said to follow your signal rockets. I believe it was one for Boris to attack, two for us to move, and three for us to fall back to the trucks. It's your call, Harry." He continued on to the steam roller.

"Is there a problem, Mr. Whitecliff?" Mr. Brown asked.

"Yes, Mr. Brown, there is a problem," Harry answered somberly, continuing to gaze through his field glasses.

"What is the problem, if I may ask?"

"You may. We're concerned that our air force may not have been able to take off due to the storm. And even if it did, there's a great deal of doubt it could find us with the low ceiling overhead," Harry explained, still looking through his glasses.

"How many planes are in your air force?"

"One."

"One? When will the rest of your troops arrive?"

"There aren't any more." Harry's eyes remained glued to the field glasses.

"Good lord, man! You people must be insane. Attacking a force of four-hundred and fifty hired killers with five men and a handful of children is crazy! I've never heard of such a thing," Mr. Brown said in awe.

"And one airplane. Yes, Mr. Brown. We are completely insane," Harry replied sardonically.

"Why, that new group of sixty men that's supposed to arrive in the morning is enough to wipe out your little army."

"What's this about sixty men? When? From where?" Harry demanded.

"One of the Shadow Men was bragging about how they were growing in force. He said that sixty more were supposed to arrive this morning from the north," Mr. Brown replied, startled by Harry's sudden inexplicable loss of composure.

Harry quickly focused on the north road with his field glasses. Suddenly, his whole body froze as he sighted a group of at least sixty riders approaching at full gallop. "Good God! Boris was expecting no more than ten guards on foot, not sixty on horseback." He responded with dispatch. "Sagirah! Quickly! Fire three rockets!" Harry commanded.

"Three, sir?" she asked, hesitating.

"Yes! confound it! Three!"

Harry glared at his watch. It was only a few minutes until the attack was to begin; without air support, their little band would be cut to ribbons.

Whoosh!...Whoosh!...Whoosh!

"The rockets are away, sir, but I don't think they could have seen two of them; they went into the clouds and exploded. Should I do it again?"

"No, it's too late. They're already preparing to charge," Harry noted glumly.

"Don't they see the other horsemen?"

"Yes, Mr. Brown, they see them. Boris and Akbar are warriors; they would charge even if there were a hundred horsemen," Harry replied. He watched the lanterns light up in the ghost riders. Jehan, who'd won the honor by drawing straws, unfurled the white flag with the symbol of a fighting bee that was to fly at the head of the column.

Boris and Akbar drew their swords and pistols to lead the charge side by side. Holding their steel over their heads, the two men led their troop forward at a fast trot until they dropped their swords and broke into a full gallop. The white flag leading into the charge waved bravely and defiantly.

"Those fools! Those brave fools are riding to their deaths!" agonized Harry.

"What's that coming out of the clouds? A plane?" Mr. Brown yelled.

Harry swung his glasses to where Mr. Brown was pointing excitedly. "It's Buzz! He made it!" Harry exulted. "Thank God!"

"Is that the nice young man our Kimberly keeps talking about?" Jane asked.

"Yes, ma'am, that's the one. That's him!"

"Oh, my goodness! His wings are on fire! Is he going to crash?"

"No, ma'am. That's showmanship—just a stunt to scare the hell out of the enemy. And, I must say, it seems to be doing a bang-up job of it," Harry crowed as he watched Buzz swoop toward the riders.

The sight of the dark ghost riders with their flaming heads—and a burning airplane coming at them—had thrown the horses and their riders into an uncontrollable panic. Buzz strafed the chaotic mass as he flew into them, and then dropped two twenty-pound bombs as he passed over. The effect was devastating.

"Our troops are coming!" Harry yelled. "What a show! They're riding through the camp, cutting the guards down as they go. They didn't slow the charge one bit!"

"Sir! Mr. Buzz is flying toward the bivouac area."

Harry brought his glasses to bear on the rows of tents. Confused men, abruptly awakened by the explosions, were bursting from them, only to observe a burning airplane approaching with guns blazing and explosives plummeting to the ground. Some attempted to shoot at the plane; others retreated hastily to their tents. Most scattered in utter panic.

"Kashar! get the inner tubes ready. Someone take the cameras at my feet and get photos of this! Sagirah, send up two rockets now, and then help Kashar with the inner tubes," Harry commanded.

"Rockets away, sir."

Harry saw the steam roller begin to creep forward, and turned his focus on the fight at the corral. "Boris is fighting two at once," he reported, giving a blow-by-blow description of the battle to those nearby. "Behind you, Boris! Behind you," Harry yelled, somehow seeming to hope Boris could hear his warning shout. "Good old Akbar and his whip! He just jerked away the Shadow Man coming up behind Boris! Now Akbar just shot one and ran another through with his sword—both at the same time!"

"What about Boris?" someone asked worriedly.

"Wait! Oh, I see him! There are two riderless horses next to him, and he seems to be looking for another adversary. I see one of our people on the ground. She's standing!—it's Nudar, trying to fend off blows from another Shadow Man. No, wait—it's Nudar's horse! He came back for her. I've never seen anything like this! The horse just grabbed the

229

Shadow Man by the arm with its teeth, pulled him off his own horse, and trampled him into the dust. Nudar's back in the saddle now. Damn! Boris sure knows how to match horse and rider; I never saw such devotion in my life. Nudar seems to be okay. Ara is riding toward her. She handed Nudar her Greener, and now they're both riding back into the battle—Ara slashing, and Nudar blasting."

"Tubes are ready, sir. Should we roll them?"

"No, wait," Harry said calmly, glasses still trained on Boris and his troops.

"Hala, look out! That's it!—block...block...slash...thrust. Good girl!" Harry was waving his arm as though wielding his own saber.

"Mr. Whitecliff, look! The plane is coming around to fly over the tents again—only this time they'll be ready for him. Can't you warn him?"

"No, Mr. Blomside, I can't."

"But there are at least a hundred-and-fifty men ready to shoot at him; he can't fly through that barrage without being shot down. You must do something."

"I intend to, Mr. Smith." Harry panned his glasses over the bivouac area, which was now a scene of torn and collapsed tents and wounded or dead bodies. But, as Mr. Blomside had pointed out, there were at least a hundred and fifty—some standing, some kneeling—all with their rifles aimed at the oncoming plane. "Light the fuses and roll the tubes—now!"

"Tubes away, sir."

Harry began counting off the seconds as he watched the strange objects, which resembled nothing more than large donuts encrusted with nuts, wobbling their way toward the tents and men. "One thousand and one...One thousand and two..."

Swinging his glasses to observe the oncoming plane, Harry could see Buzz in the cockpit and knew that he shared the same tension—would the tubes explode before Buzz flew over, or as he did?

"One thousand and four," counted Harry. He watched the inner tubes bumping clumsily into the tents and the men—falling over on their sides. The men were laughing at what seemed to have been a feeble attempt to do them harm. Some were even lying behind the tubes, using them as shields and rifle supports.

Buzz was less than two-hundred yards away.

"One thousand and five..."

Kaboom!—Booom!—Kapow!

The inner tubes ignited almost simultaneously, with such force that men were flung, tumbling end-over-end, through the air. Rocks and scrap metal ripped holes through fabric and flesh, and gasoline spewed out, engulfing everything it touched in flame.

"Perfect! The Royal Artillery couldn't have done it better. It had the timing of a perfectly executed trapeze act," Harry said with a somber but satisfied smile as he watched Buzz fly in under the black clouds of smoke that had rolled skyward, guns blazing, cutting down the few men left standing.

When Buzz reached the end of his strafing run, he performed a tight loop and returned, guns still firing. Suddenly, the right gun, then the left, stopped.

"Oh, dear! He's out of bullets," Jane cried.

"Not quite," Harry announced. He watched as Buzz lowered the plane to just five feet off the ground and drew his Webley pistols. The group watched, mesmerized, as the plane flew at forty miles an hour, striking men unable to dodge the path of its landing gear and tumbling them end-over-end. Men fell in answer to the reports from the pistols as well. Twelve shots, twelve men. Then there were two louder blasts; three more men fell.

Buzz and his Greener, Harry thought.

The plane rose above the surrounding hills and into the diminishing clouds.

Harry rapidly refocused on the action around Akbar and Boris. Akbar seemed to have sustained a cut on his left arm; Boris was blood-spattered but didn't seem to be hurt. Ara, though, was bleeding badly, holding her right side with her left hand and cradling her shotgun in her right. Hasna was standing on her saddle.

Good God, Harry thought. *She's leaping from the back of one horse to another, as if they were stepping stones, hacking and slashing her way to Ara! She made it! She's helping her stay in the saddle and still wielding a mean blade. They're circling a cluster of unhorsed Shadow Men, and the one in the middle is waving a white rag of some sort.*

"Yasmin! I don't see Yasmin!" Harry said aloud.

"Who, Mr. Whitecliff?" Jane asked.

"Yasmin. She's Akbar's oldest daughter!"

He moved the glasses away from his face to wipe the sweat away, and then quickly replaced them to greedily follow the continuing battle. "Akbar! Akbar! Behind you!" Harry yelled. Then, he muttered with relief, "Good show!" He smiled hugely.

"What? What? What happened, Mr. Whitecliff?" Jane's eyes were wide with fear and excitement.

"Boris just speared a Shadow Man sneaking up behind Akbar with his saber, from at least thirty feet! Oh, my God! Fantastic!"

"What? What?"

"Boris just retrieved his saber from the back of the fallen Shadow Man at a full gallop and, in the same motion, came up to thrust the blade between the ribs of another charging enemy! Lord! These men are incredible!"

"Good! I see Yasmin's horse, but I don't see her! Where? Oh, thank God! There she is," Harry exclaimed with a huge sigh of relief. "She's off her horse, taking weapons from the prisoners."

Suddenly, to Harry's horror, two of the prisoners grabbed Yasmin and another slit her throat. Before her limp body crumpled to the ground, the sound of ten Greener shotguns rang through the air; some had been fired more than once.

"The bloody blaguards! And under a flag of surrender!" Harry's eyes blazed with fury and stung with tears.

Tweet!—Tweeet!! The whistle of the steam engine reverberated twice, signaling that Bob and Ned were within a hundred yards of the mission gate. There was no time to grieve now. With a heavy heart, Harry returned his attention to the battle raging below.

Basima and Israt began firing their gas canisters and fireworks into the court yard.

Some of the Shadow Men were trying to escape into the mission by beating down the doors, which had been barred by the monks. They were using a heavy bench as a battering ram, but were soon dissuaded from their efforts by the monks who were pouring scalding water on them from the windows above.

"Sir, Basima isn't firing her canisters. I'm going to see what's wrong!" Sagirah yelled, racing off to help her friend.

Tweet!—Tweet!—Tweet!

Harry focused on the steam roller. "Good lord! That thing must be doing fifty miles an hour," Harry cried in amazement. He watched as the roller, its power unleashed, raced toward the gates, splashing water twenty feet out of puddles as it passed. Bob was at the controls and Ned was in the makeshift turret, spraying the Shadow Men who had been stationed on the walls with the Lewis gun. The two of them presented a strange sight in their gas masks.

The whistle of the steam engine was heard again. Toot-ta-toot-ta-toot-ta-toot-ta-toot-ta-toot-too-too!

"I'll be damned. That's the first time I've ever heard the cavalry charge played on a steam whistle," Harry said wonderingly as he watched Bob unleash his rockets at the enemy.

"It almost looks like one of those clown cars in Jack's circus—" He paused as realization dawned. "That's why this whole operation seems familiar! Buzz modeled the whole plan after a circus act! First the bareback and trick riders, followed by the aerialists, and then the clowns in their noisy car pulling a trailer full of tricks. This is a blasted three-ring circus and I'm the bloody ringmaster!"

Harry noticed that the canisters were again being lobbed from Basima's position. His eyes clouded with moisture when he brought his glasses into focus and saw Sagirah cradling her wounded friend in one arm and firing the mortars with the other. She stopped only to dash the tears from her eyes.

Someone behind him yelled, "They're going to hit!"

Harry turned his attention to the gate just in time to see the steam roller explode through the heavy structure as though it were balsa wood, crushing, impaling, or bludgeoning everything and everyone behind it. The vehicle stopped with its front roller implanted halfway into the mission's wall.

Suddenly, the only sound was the drone of the Bee circling overhead. The same question occupied all their minds—"Are they all right or did the impact kill them?"

The chatter of the Lewis gun began again—then came the reports of a pistol. Bob and Ned were alive. Harry could see the Shadow Men closing in on the wreck of the steam roller. Steam was hissing madly from its burst lines and valves. "How long can two men hold out against that horde?" Harry asked himself.

The hatches on the trailer flung open and the barrels of the shotguns jutted out, firing point-blank into the wall of black robes and turning them red. The guns roared continuously, cutting the Shadow Men down like the scythe of death. With gas burning their lungs and stinging their eyes, fireworks exploding among them, and their bodies being ripped apart by lead balls, the army of the Shadow Men of God was no longer a fighting force; it had become a panicked mob.

"Mr. Whitecliff, there are some men running up the hill toward us," Jane cried, pointing down the slope at several approaching figures in black robes.

"Everyone grab a rifle and start firing on them," Harry yelled. "Don't fire from the same place more than twice—move around, so they'll think there are more of us!"

The recently rescued hostages and Israt, who'd returned after firing all her gas canisters and fireworks, retrieved the Mausers from the dead guards and immediately began firing from whatever clumps of rocks or brush they could find on the ridge. Harry and Kashar did the same with their Enfields. Harry concentrated his fire on the men approaching the position where Basima and Sagirah were huddled.

The small group's method of firing and moving gave the oncoming Shadow Men the mistaken impression that they were faced by a much larger company of troops. The fleeing men quickly threw down their arms and held up their hands, pleading, "Mercy, mercy. We surrender!"

"Lay face down and put your hands behind your heads, or you will be shot!" Harry yelled through a megaphone he had fashioned from a sheet of notepaper.

His strident command was followed with dispatch.

The shooting ceased in the mission courtyard, and Boris, Akbar, and their troops rode in from the corral to help where they were needed. It was over at last.

"Kim! Kimberly! Has anyone seen Kimberly Smith?" In all the commotion, no one had noticed that Buzz had landed on the small field where the trucks were parked.

"Are you Buzz? The young man Kimberly met on the train?"

"Yes, ma'am. And you are?"

"I'm Aunt Jane, and this is Uncle George. Oh, Mr. Buzz! You must save our Kimberly! You must bring her back to us!" Jane pleaded, clutching Buzz's arm in desperation. "They took her away from us!"

"Bring her back? Bring her back from where? Who took her and why?" Buzz was nearly stammering in panic.

Jane explained as best she could. "Those men in black—they came into the wine cellar, grabbed her, and took her away."

"I heard one of them say something about meeting the colonel tomorrow morning and taking her to the German," George reported.

"But why Kim? What would the Germans want with her?" Buzz was mystified.

"It seems to have something to do with that cross you gave her. It has some link with a lost treasure or something," Jane sobbed.

"That sounds quite possible," Harry interjected. "The German, as we know him, has an obsession with lost treasures. A year or so ago, a Frenchman was looking for one north of here and ran into some trouble."

"The monks may know something."

"Who are you?" Buzz asked the gentleman wearing a tweed jacket, who had just spoken.

"I'm Blomside, sir. This is my assistant, Mr. Brown. The monks seem to know everything that goes on inside the mission."

"Yes, we were hostages," Mr. Brown interjected, as if the situation had been the crowning point in their lives.

"Your horse, sir," Kashar said quietly, handing the reins to Buzz who leapt into the saddle and raced to the mission.

———

Buzz dismounted outside the mission walls and climbed over and through the wreckage that had once been a massive gate. Inside, the scene awakened the memories of the Great War he had fought so hard to bury. Bodies lay two and three deep, some still smoldering from the fireworks that had exploded in their midst. Little rivulets of blood trickled from the limp masses, forming small puddles that reflected the sunlight now shining through the scattered clouds. The lingering fumes of the burnt cellulose film made Buzz cough spasmodically. The odor of the film, blood, burning canvas, and gunfire was overpowering.

"Hello, Mr. Buzz, sir."

The small voice seemed out of place amid all the death and destruction.

"Oh, hello, Zayna. Is everyone okay?" Buzz asked as he tried to peer inside the gun trailer from which the voice had come. He couldn't tell who was who; all their faces were weirdly streaked with sweat, burnt gunpowder, and marks from their gas masks.

"We're all okay, except for Sara. I think she broke her arm when we hit the wall, but she still did a good job of loading."

"I'm sure she did. You're all very brave." Buzz's voice, trembling, seemed to catch in his throat.

"Thank you, sir."

"Where is Sara now?"

"She's in the mission, sir. The monks are fixing her arm. We're guarding the prisoners. I sure hope someone brings us some more shotgun shells before the prisoners figure out that we're out of them." Zayna sounded very tired, but was determined to accomplish the task she had been assigned.

Buzz looked at the row of prisoners sitting on their hands, backs against the wall. Their eyes had the dull look of men who no longer had the desire to fight—perhaps ever again. "I don't think they'll give you any trouble. You all did a fine job! I'm very proud of you!"

"Thank you, sir."

"Where're Bob and Ned?"

"Mr. Bob and some of the monks took Mr. Ned inside. He was hurt real bad, sir." Zayna replied. For the first time, her voice broke.

———

When Buzz strode into the mission, his heart sank. Laid out on a bench was Yasmin's body. A cloth had been laid over her throat, but it was horribly blood-stained.

"Buzz, your plan worked, but with some losses—as we had thought there might be. I'm so sorry!" He raised his tear-filled eyes from Yasmin, to see Father Sebastian approaching.

"Does Akbar know?"

"Yes. It was he who brought her in; then he went out to fight again."

"Did we win, Mr. Buzz, sir?"

Buzz turned toward the tiny, weak voice. Ara was lying on a table, her side heavily bandaged.

"Yes, Ara, we won! You were all very, very brave," Buzz commended her, gently squeezing the cold hand she attempted to stretch toward him. He looked at Father Sebastian, who shook his head in silence. Ara's eyes closed, as though to sleep—and her hand went limp in his. Buzz held the petite hand for a moment, and then softly placed it at her side. A monk reverently drew a sheet over her.

"Damn!" Buzz muttered under his breath. He drew his sleeve across his eyes and tried hard to swallow the lump in his throat.

"Your other friends are over here."

"Thank you, Father." Buzz followed the priest to the other end of the room, where Ned had been placed on a makeshift cot.

Bob rose from Ned's side and met Father Sebastian and Buzz as they neared.

237

"How is he?" Buzz asked.

"Not good. He took a bullet in the chest that was meant for me," Bob said, his eyes wet. "He doesn't have much time."

"Does he know?"

"Yes. He said he'd rather die on a field of battle for a good cause than on the floor of the Fife and Drum for a pint."

"Hey! Quit pussyfootin' around over there. Come here, where I can see you," Ned gasped.

"Hi, you old fart! How are you feeling?" Buzz inquired as he started to take Ned's hand. Instead, he drew back, and patted him gently on the shoulder.

"I feel just fine—(cough, cough)—for somebody with a bullet in their chest!—(cough)—Actually, I do feel good. I really (cough) mean it! This is the first time I feel (cough, cough) that (cough) I've accomplished some (cough) thing worthwhile. I thank you for letting me (cough) do that—(cough, cough, cou…)." Ned's face relaxed into a peaceful smile.

"This is a far, far better thing he has done, that he has ever done. It is a far, far better life that he goes to than he has ever had,'" Bob paraphrased as he gently passed his hand over Ned's eyes, closing them. The three men watched silently as Ned was covered.

"Father, do you know where they took Kim?"

"Yes, Buzz, my son. They took her to the old British storage depot east of here. They're supposed to meet someone tomorrow morning and take her somewhere north to the German."

"I know where that is! I flew over it a few weeks ago," Buzz said excitedly.

"Why don't you go now and find her? Maybe you can stop them, or follow them. We'll mop up here, and then we'll follow," Bob suggested.

"I'll have to leave right away to find her before they take her north. Does anyone know what she was wearing when they took her?"

"I do," volunteered one of the nearby monks.

"Brother Timothy," said Father Sebastian, "tell Mr. Kramer what you know."

238

"Yes, Father, of course. She was dressed in a long skirt, a white blouse, and walking shoes."

"Thank you, Brother Timothy." Father Sebastian turned his gaze back to Buzz. "Will that help you?"

"Yes, Father, it will—and thank you, Brother Timothy! Now, where is her room? She's going to need clothes suitable for riding!"

Father Sebastian spoke to his brother monk. "Brother Timothy, take Mr. Kramer to Miss Smith's room."

The monk then addressed Buzz. "I'll leave you with Brother Timothy, Buzz. I have much to do."

"Thank you for your help, Father," Buzz said gratefully.

The monk escorted Buzz to a door at the end of a long corridor, opened it, ushered Buzz in, and then waited in the hallway.

An overpowering rage engulfed Buzz at the sight of Kim's belongings scattered about in total disarray. Drawers had been jerked open, their contents strewn about haphazardly; bedding had been viciously ripped, and tossed aside. The thought of the Shadow Men violating Kim's privacy in such a way infuriated him.

He quickly found and gathered what he thought she would need if—no, not if, when—he freed her from her captors and dashed to safety. Buzz had stuffed everything into a discarded pillow case and started for the door, when the only thing in the entire room that hadn't been disturbed caught his eye. On a small table beside the bed were the white napkin and the note he had left for her on the train. The obviously cherished items were laid out neatly with a small bunch of wildflowers placed upon them. It was only then, as he paused in his fury that he noticed the fragrance of her perfume still lingered in the room. A sob of anger and frustration catching in his throat, he turned, and dashed past Brother Timothy and down the hallway.

"Bob, I'm going to pack up Flamme and Diable; then I'm riding toward the warehouses. Harry knows where they are. If I can, I'll hold up on signal mount. Akbar knows of it!" Buzz barked, staccato, as he hurried past his friend.

"Good luck!" Bob offered encouragingly.

"God be with you, my son!"

239

"Thank you, Father!"

As he was hurrying out the door, Buzz met Harry as he was entering, carrying Basima in his arms. His eyes were red, and his face, already covered with the grime of battle, was streaked with tears.

"Look, Buzz. Even in death, she still has her warm, happy smile."

Buzz stopped short, shocked and saddened. Wordlessly, he hugged Harry and softly touched Basima's face with one gentle finger.

"Thank you, Buzz; I'm all right now. Are you going to find Kim?" Harry fought to gain his composure.

"Yes, as soon as I get the horses packed."

"Can't you take the plane?" Harry asked.

"No, I can't. The field is too soft from the rain for the Bee to take off, and it'll be hours before it will be dry enough," Buzz explained. He mounted Flamme, and galloped up the hill.

"Is he going by himself?" Jane asked. "Doesn't he realize that thirty men took her?"

"He knows," Harry answered grimly, watching his friend ride away.

"Why, he won't stand a chance against those odds! He's only one man. There are thirty of them against him," George remonstrated in alarm.

"George, from what I've seen of that man, the odds are against the Shadow Men," Harry replied. "After all, there are only thirty of them against Buzz Kramer!"

— Chapter Twenty-One —

THE RESCUE

K im awakened from a restless, uneasy sleep, disturbed by a strange sound. The source seemed to be her dutiful guard. He was sitting at a table, his head buried in his folded arms, sound asleep and snoring loudly, croaking like a sick frog.

A kerosene lantern was fighting a losing battle for shadow rights with the rising morning sun's rays coming through the paneless window. The sunlight skimming across the floor highlighted tracks in the thick dust left by things that had walked, crawled, or slithered across it within recent memory. Kim shuddered to think that those creatures could still be in residence.

With the oncoming sunlight, Kim could now see parts of the room that had been hidden by the dimness of the lamp. One wall held the only door. It was closed. Opposite it was a wide window. The wall across from Kim had a large, faded map of Afghanistan tacked to it, and the wall behind her featured a large bracket, firmly affixed to the wall and the ceiling above. It was to this that her captors tied the leash, as they jeeringly called it—a half-inch wide leather strap that bound Kim's wrists together. One of the Shadow Men had firmly grasped the other end as they rode to this place on separate horses.

Kim reached up and lovingly fondled the strange gold cross that still hung around her neck—the one Buzz had given her on the train. Someone must have overheard her telling Aunt Jane and Uncle George Buzz's story about the treasure in New Mexico and how the cross might be a clue to finding it. These men, however, seemed to think it was a clue to treasure here in Afghanistan. Kim had tried unsuccessfully to convince them that it was a clue to a treasure found in the United States of America, far across the seas, but they wouldn't listen to her. All they would say was, "Tell your story to the German!"

They wouldn't even touch the cross, nor would they allow her to remove it. The cross, and their obvious fear of the German if anything happened to her—or it—was probably why she hadn't been harmed. So far.

Kim stood up quietly so she wouldn't wake her guard, and considered her chances of escape. She might be able to loosen the leash from the bracket if she stood on her tiptoes, and then she could sneak past the guard and out the door. But what if the door were locked? And if it wasn't, could she get past the twenty or so men she could hear downstairs?

Maybe she could jump out the window. *It's only about eight or ten feet*, she thought. Looking out the window, though, she could see six or seven men across the street near the horses they'd ridden on last night. Apparently they were preparing to ride again.

"I guess jumping out the window wouldn't be such a good idea. I'd probably break my leg or something like that, anyway!" she cautioned herself in a low whisper.

Trying desperately to think of a way of escape, she continued to gaze out the window. She noticed a hunchbacked old man in rags hobbling up the middle of the street. He was leading an old, lame horse and carrying what looked like a tattered, ancient tent and a pile of rags. She watched them make their way laboriously up the street until they passed from her line of sight. She felt sorry for them. Strangely, though, there seemed to be something familiar about the man.

Oh, well!—back to my chances of escaping! There must be something I can do, Kim thought. *I can't go out the window or the door—too many men.* Her mind raced.

"Get away from that car, old man!" Kim heard one of the Shadow Men shouting at the poor old man in the street. She tugged at her bindings to see more, but she could only view the tops of the Shadow Mens' heads.

"Don't hit me! Please don't hit me! I dropped my ball of silk string and it rolled under your car. I just crawled under to get it. I mean no harm. Please don't kick me again. I'll leave."

Kim heard the loud, jeering laughter of the Shadow Men. How she despised such bullies! *I wish I could help that old man*, she thought. She stopped in her tracks—that voice! Hadn't she heard it before? But—could it be? No, surely not.

Suddenly, the door to the room slammed open and Colonel von Schroeden entered. Without breaking his stride, he kicked the chair from under the sleeping guard, tumbling him unceremoniously to the floor. The man hit his chin resoundingly on the table as he fell.

"Untie her and bring her downstairs. We're getting ready to leave!" von Schroeden snapped.

As her guard loosened her leash, Kim could see blood running down his chin, where he had bitten through his lip. *Good,* she thought. *It serves him right.*

"Come on," the man said gruffly, jerking the strap roughly and nearly causing her to fall. He led her down the steps, past a number of men seated at a long table who appeared to be finishing their morning coffee. Their weapons were stacked in the far corner of the room, away from the door.

Then she was outside, evidently to be placed in a Mercedes touring car. The street looked different in the morning sun; when she'd been brought in last night, all she could see were dark shadows. Now she noticed six long, warehouse-style buildings, three on each side of a wide street, and narrow alley-ways between the buildings. Kim thought they might have been used by the trade caravans, or possibly as a military outpost. The entire area looked wholly deserted except for the building she was exiting.

To her left, up the street, she saw the old man and his horse. She suddenly remembered something from the train—something about an old cowboy and his lame horse. In a loud, bold voice, Kim shouted, "Oh Lord, let that old man be my savior!"

Her captors laughed uproariously. One of them said mockingly, "Oh, dear, we're shaking with fright!"

The ragged old man stepped from the shadows into the golden rays of the sun. Immediately, there was a sudden, muffled explosion and a large thick cloud of white smoke. From the midst of the white cloud, prancing forward, reared up on its hind legs, was the most magnificent white stallion Kim had ever seen. In the saddle was a man clad in white, draped in a flowing silk cape, both arms raised above his head. In his right hand was a glistening saber; his left held a pistol. His clenched teeth held the stallion's reins.

In spite of the perils of the present situation, Kim joyfully realized that she was living every young girl's dream—to be rescued from the jaws of death by a handsome knight on a white charger.

With the Shadow Men still in a state of shock, Kim quickly jerked the strap around her wrists from her captor's grasp, rushed down the steps, ran to the car, and leapt atop the rear seat.

Kim's white knight charged toward her with gun blazing and saber slashing. He swept her off the car, into the crook of his arm, and onto the saddle in front of him. In nearly a single motion, with a back-swing of his saber, he slashed the throat of the driver as he attempted to rise. When the revolver had been emptied, Buzz let it drop to hang by its lanyard and whisked another from a shoulder holster. The Shadow Men who had been holding the horses were falling with each blast of his revolver. As Buzz galloped by, Flamme neighed forcefully, scattering the other horses in all directions.

Kim looked over Buzz's shoulder to see men pulling the dead driver out of the way and piling into the Mercedes. "They're coming after us in the car!" she yelled in warning.

"Good!" was the reply.

Buzz turned a corner and sped down a narrow street; Kim saw the Mercedes take the corner on two wheels. Suddenly there was an explosion, and the vehicle flipped onto its top and slid into the wall of a building, followed by a spectacular display of sparks and debris from beneath it. When it finally stopped, it was rapidly engulfed in a huge ball of orange fire.

Turning away, Kim saw a three-foot wall at the end of the street. "Hold tight," Buzz said, and they flew over it. Kim instinctively leaned into the jump as though taking hurdles at the riding academy.

As they galloped from the town, the sounds of chaos died away until all she could hear were Flamme's reverberating hoof beats and the pounding of her own heart.

As they rode, Buzz carefully cut the bindings from Kim's wrists. She put her arms around him and snuggled her head against his chest. She could hear his heart beating too, and it seemed to be in tune with hers.

At first, they rode at a full gallop, but after they'd covered a mile or so they slowed to an easier pace. In contrast to their time on the train, they rode in silence. There are times when words aren't needed to express one's feelings—this was one of those times.

They continued on for two or three more miles until they came to a rocky rise. Buzz guided Flamme up a narrow path to the top, halted, slid off, and gently lifted Kim down.

"There's a horse for you on the other side of that rock, and a change of clothes and some other things you might need in the saddle bags. There's also a pool of water, if you want to freshen up. But hurry!—we probably don't have much time. I'll create a diversion to buy us a little more time. They should be here in ten or fifteen minutes—I can see their dust, and it's not very far away."

Kim found a black horse reined to a small tree near a clear pool of water. In the saddle bag was her riding outfit, along with a comb and mirror, some soap, and a towel. At the bottom of the bag she discovered a holster, gun belt, and a Star .380 automatic pistol with four extra magazines. In the saddle's scabbard was a rifle.

Not many men would think to bring a comb, soap, and a mirror to lift a woman's spirits, Kim thought. After a quick, albeit cold sponge bath and changing into clean clothes, she felt ready to meet whatever the next few hours would bring.

Kim could hear Buzz calling to her. "Make it quick! They're almost here." Then he added, "Bring that rifle!" She gave her hair a few more fast rubs with the towel and grabbed the rifle and a bandolier. As she came around the rock, she could see Buzz crouched behind a pile of small boulders, his rifle perched atop them. He indicated the oncoming dust cloud.

"They're not far!" she agreed.

"I fixed up a spot for you over there," Buzz said, pointing to a hollowed-out space in the rocks where he'd arranged a pile of grass for her to kneel on. "The sights are set for a hundred yards, which is about where those rocks are. We'll fire on them when they get to the rocks. Hopefully that will force them to dismount and hide in the rocks."

"Why would you want them to do that?" Kim asked.

"See the fuse connecting those little pockets along the rocks? That's a slow fuse. It'll set off small charges at timed intervals to make the Shadow Men think we're shooting at them. Meanwhile, we'll ride off the other side of the rise. I'm hoping it will be twenty minutes or so until they figure it out."

"Oh, I see. I think," Kim replied. "Good idea."

"Are you familiar with the Enfield Mark III rifle?" Buzz asked.

"Yes. My father has one."

"Good. Then you'll be okay. Well, it looks like it's show time— here we go!" Pow!—Pow!

Two shots rang out, and two Shadow Men tumbled from their saddles. Buzz glanced at Kim.

"They aren't men; they're mad dogs," she muttered grimly.

Pow! Another shot, another of the Shadow Men slid down, and off to one side. Kim struck another one, who fell backward on his horse with his arms outstretched. He bounced slowly along, his arms waving in rhythm with his horse's gait. Pow!—Pow! Only one dropped this time.

Buzz glanced at Kim sternly; they couldn't afford to waste ammunition. She nodded toward the approaching riders, and Buzz watched as the other one fell to the ground.

The Shadow Men turned their horses toward the rocks and dismounted behind them. Once concealed, the men rained a continuous hail of bullets at Buzz and Kim.

Kim fired a couple of shots while Buzz lit the fuses; then they carefully crawled to where they'd concealed the horses. As Kim mounted, she saw Buzz retrieving a long-rifle scabbard from the brush. He hung it on his saddle and then shoved her discarded clothing into his saddle bag. As they rode away, they could hear bullets pinging among the rocks where they had been; it sounded like hail hitting a tin roof during a summer hail storm.

"Our so-called return fire should start about now. I sure hope this buys us the time we need," Buzz exclaimed.

"Why didn't we just keep riding, instead of stopping here?"

"Kim, my horse has been in constant motion for two days, and you looked like you could use a lift. I'm praying that we can gain about a twenty-minute lead on them."

"I didn't know you prayed," she retorted saucily.

"Everyone does, I think—in their own way," he replied rather gruffly. "We have a good hour's hard ride ahead of us," he continued. "We'd better get a move on!"

"Where are we going?" Kim yelled. She found it difficult to hear over the sound of the horses' pounding hooves.

"There's a small butte ahead, about three-hundred feet high. We'll hold up there and make a stand. Beyond that is desert—nothing but sand for miles and miles. If they catch up with us there, we won't have a chance. In the rocks, though, we have a better chance of holding them at bay until help arrives."

"Who's going to help us?"

"Some friends," Buzz replied hopefully. "By the way, how many Shadow Men were with you?"

"I counted thirty."

"Well, we eliminated fourteen or fifteen in the village and six at the rocks, so that leaves about nine," Buzz calculated.

"I only saw fifteen to twenty at the rocks," Kim noted.

"That's true. But just before we left, I saw the rest riding up—about a half mile distant."

"Okay," Kim said. "Let's see if I have this right. We have to ride like a bat out of someplace really hot to a pile of rocks on the edge of a large desert so we can fight off twenty or so bloodthirsty men, whose sole purpose in life right now is to cut our throats—in the hope that we'll be rescued, eventually, by some unknown friends. Or something like that."

Buzz grinned. "That's right."

"Oh! For a while there, I thought we were in trouble!—I feel much better now," she replied with a supremely sarcastic smirk.

"I'm glad you feel better. By the way, your horse's name is Diable Noir. That means—"

"I know!—'Black Devil.' I like that. Is that the horse you rode in the circus?" Kim inquired.

"Yeah. This is Flamme Blanc—White Flame. I just call him Flamme."

"Have you had him long?"

"About two years."

"I thought so. You work well as a team."

"We'd better give the horses some water while I check on the bad guys," Buzz said as he slowed to a stop.

While Kim watered the horses with a canteen and a small pail, Buzz stood atop Flamme and scanned the horizon with his binoculars.

"Damn! They figured out our ploy sooner than I'd hoped. You ride on ahead; I'll catch up. I'm going to see if I can slow them down a little," Buzz ordered. He slipped the long 45/70 Martini out of the scabbard, walked to a mound of rocks, and set the sights for eight-hundred yards.

Hurriedly, he explained, "At the base of the highest butte, you'll see a narrow trail that winds to the top. I think it was used as a lookout, or for signaling, because I could see where some fires were made. Go, quickly. I'll be with you as soon as I can."

Riding away, Kim could hear the boom of the rifle again and again. *Oh, dear lord, please protect him. I love him so*, she prayed silently, tears streaking her cheeks.

After firing the first shot, Buzz grabbed his binoculars to see where he'd hit and saw a horse and rider tumble. Good, he had the range. He calculated that, as close together as they were riding, if he fired ten rounds into the group, he should bring down at least five or more and maybe cause enough confusion to slow them quite a bit.

Buzz looked over his shoulder to check on Kim and saw three riders coming fast from the opposite direction. Through his binoculars, he could see their black robes. *Shadow Men. They must be bringing news of the mission to von Schroeden!* Two of them veered off toward Kim, and one rode straight for von Schroeden and his men, who were shooting the hell out of a rock pile they had surrounded.

Buzz focused his glasses on Kim, who was between him and the other two riders. "Good God, she's riding straight toward them!" he said to no one in particular. "Doesn't she see them? Turn, turn away! Can't you see they're Shadow Men?"

When Kim was about thirty feet from the approaching riders, Buzz could see her right arm stretch out to them. There were two puffs of smoke; both riders tumbled out of their saddles and rolled into a pile. Kim leaped over them as if she were jumping steeples at a horse show.

"Good girl! Damn, what a woman!" Buzz crowed. Relieved and proud, he turned his attention to the third rider and took careful aim. Calculating the distance and the speed the horseman was traveling, he gently pulled the trigger. The messenger fell from his saddle, ten feet from von Schroeden.

Buzz knew he'd given his position away, but he felt he'd had to stop word of what had occurred at the mission from reaching von Schroeden and the German. He leaped to his saddle and urged Flamme to a full gallop toward the butte and Kim.

Buzz rode by the two men Kim had shot. They looked like a pile of dirty laundry. Buzz noticed that the horses' rifle scabbards were empty, and realized that he hadn't seen any guns when they were riding toward Kim. "That's why they didn't shoot at her; they were unarmed. I wonder why."

As Buzz approached the butte, he was seeing it up close from the ground for the first time. Its sides were steep and jagged, and it looked to be of gray granite. Nothing grew on them—not a tree or a bush or blade of grass. It was a large, bleak, gray mass of stone that had been belched out of the bowels of hell thousands of years ago. There were a few scraggly bushes at its base where the narrow trail to the top began.

When Buzz reached the base of the butte he saw the tracks left by Kim, so he knew she'd be waiting for him. He wished she could greet him with a nice hot cup of coffee, and his pipe, but that reverie was rudely interrupted by gunfire from below. Bullets began striking the rocks close by.

After he had ascended about two-thirds of the way up the narrow trail, Buzz saw that ten or twelve rebels had reached the bottom of the butte, and were firing at him. The path was narrowest at that point and gave him little or no cover. He felt like a moving target in a shooting gallery.

He suddenly became aware of gunfire from above. Two of the rebels pitched from their saddles; the rest dismounted and scattered, seeking cover. It was Kim, —she was giving him covering fire! Crack!—Crack! She was firing as fast as she could bolt her Enfield.

The last ten feet of the trail was a sixty-degree incline between two large boulders four or five feet apart. It then opened out to the flat top of the butte, which was sixty to seventy feet in diameter. The constant wind had swept away everything except a small pile of firewood and a few fist-sized rocks.

Diable was standing quietly, watching Kim, who was still firing her rifle from the cover of the rocks that had been placed beside the trail by some long-ago defenders. *I wonder how they fared*, Buzz wondered fleetingly as he grabbed his Martini, a bandolier, and a canteen. He ran to the rock parapet near Kim. "Could you use some water?" He handed the canteen to her.

"You always seem to know what a lady needs. Yes, thank you; mine seems to have sprung a leak," she said, nodding at the mangled remains of her canteen. "I put it on top of the rocks so it would be handy, and all of a sudden it exploded. It —scared the holiness out of me, but the spray of water felt good."

Standing behind one of the large boulders, Buzz peered into the valley below. He could see their adversaries scurrying from their horses to take cover behind any rock or bush they could find. Taking a quick count of the horses, he figured there were about twenty-five. Damn! That was more than he'd planned for. Then he looked down at Kim in her tight-fitting jodhpurs, dirty white blouse, and riding boots, surrounded by spent cartridges. *There's a lot of woman in that little body,* he thought. *I hope I can keep her alive.*

"Why do you think they're so quiet down there?" Kim asked, interrupting his thoughts.

"I'm not sure, but I think they might be waiting for the sun to wear us down. It's going to get hot up here."

"Oh, I see. That's nice of them! How much water do we have?"

"Well," he replied, "I packed two canteens on each horse, and a water bag for the horses on mine. Your losing one of them to a sharpshooter leaves us with three for us and one water bag for the horses. That should be enough."

"I'm sorry about the lost canteen, but this is my first war. I promise to do better in the next one," she said, looking up at him ruefully, eyes twinkling.

He looked at her, her hair plastered to her head with sweat which streamed down her face, cutting muddy little trails in the dust. "Will you marry me?" he asked quietly, his heart in his eyes.

"Yes, of course! I thought you would never ask."

"Well, a few things came up. There hasn't been much of an opportunity," he retorted, somewhat defensively.

"Procrastinator. Now don't make me a widow before I'm a bride."

"Damn! Engaged less than thirty seconds, and she's already telling me what to do."

Their eyes locked, each looking deep within the other; then they broke into simultaneous laughter, delighted with themselves.

"Kim, take the horses over by that pile of wood and bring the canteens and every bit of food you can find in the packs. Bring all the ammo and my cape as well; maybe I can make a shelter from the sun. Meanwhile, I'll keep an eye on our friends down there."

A short time later, they sat under the shade of Buzz's cape, dining on dried goat meat and cheese washed down with warm water. In years to come, they would remember this as their best meal ever—their first meal together as an engaged couple.

"Buzz," Kim asked, "What is so important about this cross you gave me? Why does this German want it so badly?" She fingered the cross hanging about her throat. "They wouldn't touch it, and they wouldn't allow me to take it off."

"Remember, there are three of them—the one you have, mine, and another, which is lost. Placed together in a certain position, the three of them show the way to a large treasure. But that's another—"

251

"I know, I know," she interrupted, laughing. "That's another story. I want you to tell it to me on some cold, stormy winter night."

"Uh-oh!" Buzz exclaimed, grabbing the binoculars. "That's what they were waiting for—more men. There're about a hundred riding in. Let's see if we can pick a few of them off before they can take cover. How many rounds do you have?"

"Ten for the rifle and thirty-six for my pistol," Kim answered, with a concerned expression.

"I have eight 45-70s and thirty-eight .455s. Here, take these matches and light a signal fire."

Kim grabbed the matches and ran to the pile of wood. As she lit the kindling at the base, she was startled by the roar of the Martini. Buzz fired three more times before she returned to his side and picked up her own rifle.

"Shoot the ones coming up the trail. I'll get the riders," he directed.

Kim could see four—Boom!—no, five riderless horses. She trained her attention on the men coming up the trail. Pow!—Pow!—Pow! Two tumbled down the side of the butte, knocking over several men who had begun to clamber up the rocks. Kim emptied the magazine and inserted her last one. *Damn. I only took out four of them,* she thought, chagrined. She fired again. *'Poofph!'* *"That was a strange sound,* she thought, as she bolted the next shell. ' Ka-booom!' Her face felt as though someone had thrown hot sand in it, her eyes blinded by the flash.

"Kim!—are you all right?" Buzz yelled.

"I think so, but my gun blew up."

"You must have had a short round that lodged a bullet in the barrel, making the next one blow. Use your pistol, but wait until they get closer." Having used all the 45-70s, Buzz unholstered his Webleys.

The Shadow Men were climbing the rocks hand over hand, their rifles slung over their backs. They looked like black ants. Buzz was methodically picking them off, one at a time, making each shot count. At thirty feet or so, Kim began firing her pistol as rapidly as possible.

The Shadow Men were now climbing over their dead comrades as bodies piled up on the trail and the rocks just a few feet below the two defenders. As Kim was inserting her last magazine, a head covered in black except for wild eyes, appeared just a foot from her face. Instinctively, she jabbed the eyes with two forked fingers of her right hand. Screaming loudly, the head and attached body fell back down the cliff, complaining all the way.

Kim stood up to get in a better position. There was a loud explosion in her head, and she went down with a thud. When she opened her eyes, her head throbbed abominably and she could see a man in black, an evil grimace splitting his face, aiming a rifle directly at her. His eyes suddenly widened, then lost all expression and slowly closed. He fell limp at her feet, a knife embedded in the base of his neck. Unable to locate her pistol, she snatched up the fallen man's rifle.

When he'd used the last round in his revolvers, Buzz drew his saber. He thrust through the chest of one Shadow Man, and slashed the throat of another as he withdrew the blade. He looked up. Standing atop one of the boulders was a Shadow Man—and Buzz was squarely in his sights. Pow!—the man in black pitched forward and crumpled to the ground.

Startled, Buzz quickly glanced toward Kim, who was bolting another shell into the newly acquired Mauser. She said, "I love you." He replied, "I love you, too. Thanks," and turned back to face the trail.

Before him poised von Schroeden, saber in hand. The leader of the Shadow Men slashed at Buzz, cutting his shirt from shoulder to waist but barely scraping his flesh. Buzz fended off another slash to the left and backed away, taking defensive action against von Schroeden's onslaught.

Kim shot a Shadow Man rising from the trail and bolted the shell out—but the bolt wouldn't close. She looked down at the empty chamber. That had been her last round, and there were three—no, six— Shadow Men coming over the top of the ledge. Seeing that Kim was unarmed, they drew their sabers and approached her, grinning victoriously.

Oh, God, please don't let it end like this. Let Buzz and I have some time together. In desperation, Kim picked up some of the fist-sized rocks lying about the butte and began pelting her adversaries. She hit one squarely in the face, tumbling him backwards into a black heap. Another was struck in the chest and staggered back a few steps, but recovered to raise his saber. He gave forth a blood-curdling yell; the others followed

253

suit. They charged, swinging their sabers over their heads, screaming, "Kill! Kill!" Kim continued to throw rocks as fast as she could, but the men, dodging the missiles, came on like a black wave of death.

All at once, sand and gravel was spraying upward in two rows which were racing toward her attackers, who began to twist and jerk spasmodically. With a loud roar, a bi-plane flew over Kim's head, barely missing the two large boulders. She could see a bee painted on the fuselage. *His friends did come, thank God!*

The plane banked and came back, flying straight at Kim. To her astonishment, the guns were blazing away at her. She dove unceremoniously to the ground. *No, no, I'm on your side!* The plane flew past and she rolled over, shaking her fist. "You idiot! You fool! You...you wonderful, marvelous angel." Her fist opened to wave gleefully, gratefully at the plane as she watched it climb. It left behind five bodies—the men who had scaled the back of the butte and intended to shoot them in the back. Kim blessed the pilot a few more times.

Von Schroeden could see that the lack of sleep and a full day of battle were taking a toll on Buzz, who was using mostly defensive, rather than offensive, moves. *It's only a matter of time*, the colonel thought. *The defenders of the butte will be at my mercy.* He made a vicious thrust toward Buzz's midsection.

"Gotcha!" cried Buzz. He sidestepped and slid his saber in a twisting motion along von Schroeden's blade until it caught the guard. A quick twist to the right wrenched von Schroeden's weapon from his grasp, and Buzz followed through with a thrust through his midsection. *This is the bastard who caused Kim so much hell*, he thought. He twisted his blade and performed a downward thrust upon withdrawal.

Von Schroeden gazed down at his bloody hand with which he was trying to hold himself together, and then looked at Buzz with more disbelief than pain in his eyes as he sank to his knees, before falling forward onto his face.

Looking upward, Buzz saw the Bee coming in slowly across the top of the butte with Bob at the controls. As the plane passed no more than ten feet over Buzz's head, a bundle dropped toward him. Landing only a short distance away, it spilled its welcome contents—a Greener shotgun and another bandolier of shells.

Buzz grabbed the supplies and ran toward Kim, who was picking herself up off the ground, yelling and pointing wildly behind him.

"Buzz, they're coming up the back side!" Reaching her side, he thrust the gun and ammunition into her hands. "Here, you take care of the back, I'll take the trail."

Kim threw the gun up to her shoulder and pulled the trigger. Nothing happened. "Buzz, it won't shoot."

"Take the safety off!" he yelled over his shoulder.

"Oh, right." Boom!—Boom! The gun roared twice, and a black figure spun around and dropped. She levered the bolt down, the empty shells spun out over her head, and she stamped two more in, closed the bolt, and flipped off the safety. Boom!—Boom!

Buzz reached the rocks as two of the Shadow Men were coming through the cleft, unslinging their rifles. Buzz slashed the right leg of the first man, deliberately missing the rifle he was holding across his chest to defend against the blows he anticipated. Then he cut deeply into the left side of the second man and, with a backhand stroke, sliced a gash through his neck. He then twisted around and executed a down stroke to sink his saber between the shoulder blades of the first man, who was trying vainly to rise.

With a high arc, Buzz brought his saber down on the head of a third Shadow Man. The blade stuck, and Buzz had to wrench it free with an up-and-down motion, leaving the lifeless body to drop to the ground. Now exposed was a fourth Shadow Man, who, terrified by what he had just witnessed, dropped his rifle, threw up his hands, and screamed, "Mercy, mercy!"

Kim could see the plane diving on the rebels climbing up the back side of the butte, firing its guns, and dropping something that burst into flames upon impact. She continued to fire on the attackers who had gained the top, cutting through them with each blast of buckshot. She could smell the heated oil from the barrel of her gun.

Suddenly, to her consternation, she became aware of the fact that no Shadow Men were charging her position; there were only limp forms strewn before her.

The plane dipped its wings several times, which Kim took to mean all clear. *Thank God*, she thought first, then, *Buzz. Is he all right?*

She jumped to her feet, and ran to him. With a sigh of relief, she saw him at the edge of the cliff, his rifle pointed menacingly at a kneeling rebel with hands raised in surrender. He motioned her to him.

She ran, throwing her arms around him tightly. He put his arm around her, kissed her with gentle warmth and tenderness, and then nodded at the plain below. Kim saw the remaining Shadow Men fleeing on horseback, and noticed that there were many horses with empty saddles.

"They're leaving!" she exclaimed.

"They won't get far," Buzz replied tiredly. He pointed with his saber to a column of riders led by a man on a black horse.

To Kim's surprise, the leader of the arriving troop leapt to stand atop his saddle, where all could see him. He waved his saber to the right, then to the left. The column fanned out to form a line of attack. He then circled the blade over his head, sliced it downward to the front, yelled "Charge!" and dropped back down into his saddle to lead the attack.

"That Boris," Buzz laughed. "He's always one for theatrics—the big ham!"

The charging line caught the rebels off guard. The riderless horses, closely following the fleeing marauders, got in the way as the Shadow Men attempted to turn to meet the charge from the rescue party.

The first volley fired was by Boris's troops and inflicted many casualties. The two groups of riders met with such a clash of shooting, screaming, and whinnying that Kim jumped back with a start. The battle was nearly over before it began.

Buzz and Kim descended the trail, their captive clearing his fallen comrades out of the way. Both were astounded and appalled at the waste of life.

Seeing the small party, with Buzz and Kim riding close together and their dejected captive slinking in front of them, Boris wheeled his horse around and rode to meet them, reining his horse just ten feet from the trio.

Buzz's torn shirt was stained with dried blood from shoulder to waist, and he was covered with dusty sweat. He carried his saber limply in his right hand, and clasped Kim's hand firmly in his left. Kim's once-white blouse was now a dingy, dirty gray with spatterings of blood. Her face was streaked with sweat and blood, which had made little rivulets through the black smudges left by the exploding rifle. Her hair was all astray, one lock covering her left eye, which was swollen partly shut by the lump on her forehead. A bandolier was slung across her chest, and the Greener double barrel was clutched in her left hand.

"Are you two all right?" Boris asked.

"Boris, we're engaged," Buzz replied, looking as though he had just discovered the cure for all the world's ills. "I'd like you to meet my fiancée, Kimberly Smith."

Boris noticed that Kim's chest swelled with pride and her eyes sparkled when Buzz introduced her as his affianced.

Yeah, Boris thought, *that's true love.* Aloud, he remarked only, "Damn! If this is the kind of engagement party you two throw, I don't know if I could survive the wedding."

The End

~ About Martin Krewson ~

In his long and varied career, Martin Krewson has done everything from sculpting life-size wax figures to working as a barker for the Royal American Carnival; and from construction, excavation, and running heavy machinery to flying small airplanes.

He also worked as a photographer for the Defense Department for seventeen years. He worked in front of and behind the cameras in films, and also served as historical consultant, gun wrangler, and certified pyro-technician for several indie movies.

He's prospected for gold, searched for lost Spanish treasure, was CEO of a gold mining operation, and was on the rescue squad in Central City, CO. He now owns and operates Odin Arms, Ltd., a nationally known gunsmithing operation.

CPSIA information can be obtained at www.ICGtesting.com
Printed in the USA
LVOW130815270313

326227LV00001B/3/P